Flannery O'Connor's country—

THE AMERICAN SOUTH

No other writer captures the southern rhythm, the throb of humor, hysteria and passion, so well as she in these short stories and two full-length novels.

Wise Blood evokes a terrifying world as it reveals a weird relationship between a sluttish young girl, a conniving widow, and a young man who deliberately blinds himself.

A Good Man Is Hard to Find is a collection of tales about healing preachers, Godless spectators, Civil War veterans, and a never-to-be-forgotten Bible salesman who steals a girl's wooden leg.

The Violent Bear It Away tells of a strangely decadent family—three generations of men obsessed by guilt and driven to violence.

"She understands her country and its people so well that in her hands they become all humanity."
— *New York Herald Tribune*

MENTOR Books of Special Interest

THREE

Wise Blood
A Good Man Is Hard to Find
The Violent Bear It Away

FLANNERY O'CONNOR

A SIGNET BOOK from
NEW AMERICAN LIBRARY
TIMES MIRROR

Published as a SIGNET BOOK
by arrangement with Farrar, Straus and Giroux, Inc.,
and Harcourt Brace Jovanovich, Inc.,
who have authorized this softcover edition.
Hardcover editions of Wise Blood *and* The Violent Bear It
Away *are available from Farrar, Straus and Giroux, Inc.;*
a hardcover edition of A Good Man Is Hard to Find
is available from Harcourt Brace Jovanovich, Inc.

 SIGNET TRADEMARK REG. U.S. PAT. OFF. AND FOREIGN COUNTRIES
REGISTERED TRADEMARK—MARCA REGISTRADA
HECHO EN CHICAGO, U.S.A.

SIGNET, SIGNET CLASSICS, MENTOR, PLUME, MERIDIAN AND NAL
BOOKS *are published by The New American Library, Inc.,*
1633 Broadway, New York, New York 10019

14   15   16   17   18   19   20   21

PRINTED IN THE UNITED STATES OF AMERICA

Contents

Contents

WISE BLOOD

for Regina

Wise Blood has reached the age of ten and is still alive. My critical powers are just sufficient to determine this, and I am gratified to be able to say it. The book was written with zest and, if possible, it should be read that way. It is a comic novel about a Christian *malgré lui,* and as such, very serious, for all comic novels that are any good must be about matters of life and death. *Wise Blood* was written by an author congenitally innocent of theory, but one with certain preoccupations. That belief in Christ is to some a matter of life and death has been a stumbling block for readers who would prefer to think it a matter of no great consequence. For them Hazel Motes' integrity lies in his trying with such vigor to get rid of the ragged figure who moves from tree to tree in the back of his mind. For the author Hazel's integrity lies in his not being able to. Does one's integrity ever lie in what he is not able to do? I think that usually it does, for free will does not mean one will, but many wills conflicting in one man. Freedom cannot be conceived simply. It is a mystery and one which a novel, even a comic novel, can only be asked to deepen.

1962

CHAPTER 1

Hazel Motes sat at a forward angle on the green plush train seat, looking one minute at the window as if he might want to jump out of it, and the next down the aisle at the other end of the car. The train was racing through tree tops that fell away at intervals and showed the sun standing, very red, on the edge of the farthest woods. Nearer, the plowed fields curved and faded and the few hogs nosing in the furrows looked like large spotted stones. Mrs. Wally Bee Hitchcock, who was facing Motes in the section, said that she thought the early evening like this was the prettiest time of day and she asked him if he didn't think so too. She was a fat woman with pink collars and cuffs and pear-shaped legs that slanted off the train seat and didn't reach the floor.

He looked at her a second and, without answering, leaned forward and stared down the length of the car again. She turned to see what was back there but all she saw was a child peering around one of the sections and, farther up at the end of the car, the porter opening the closet where the sheets were kept.

"I guess you're going home," she said, turning back to him again. He didn't look, to her, much over twenty, but he had a stiff black broad-brimmed hat on his lap, a hat that an elderly country preacher would wear. His suit was a glaring blue and the price tag was still stapled on the sleeve of it.

He didn't answer her or move his eyes from whatever he was looking at. The sack at his feet was an army duffel bag and she decided that he had been in the army and had been released and that now he was going home. She wanted to get close enough to see what the suit had cost him but she found herself squinting instead at his eyes, trying almost to look into them. They were the color of pecan shells and set in deep sockets. The outline of a skull under his skin was plain and insistent.

She felt irked and wrenched her attention loose and squinted at the price tag. The suit had cost him $11.98. She felt that that placed him and looked at his face again

9

as if she were fortified against it now. He had a nose like a shrike's bill and a long vertical crease on either side of his mouth; his hair looked as if it had been permanently flattened under the heavy hat, but his eyes were what held her attention longest. Their settings were so deep that they seemed, to her, almost like passages leading somewhere and she leaned halfway across the space that separated the two seats, trying to see into them. He turned toward the window suddenly and then almost as quickly turned back again to where his stare had been fixed.

What he was looking at was the porter. When he had first got on the train, the porter had been standing between the two cars—a thick-figured man with a round yellow bald head. Haze had stopped and the porter's eyes had turned toward him and away, indicating which car he was to go into. When he didn't go, the porter said, "To the left," irritably, "to the left," and Haze had moved on.

"Well," Mrs. Hitchcock said, "there's no place like home."

He gave her a glance and saw the flat of her face, reddish under a cap of fox-colored hair. She had got on two stops back. He had never seen her before that. "I got to go see the porter," he said. He got up and went toward the end of the car where the porter had begun making up a berth. He stopped beside him and leaned on a seat arm, but the porter didn't look at him. He was pulling a wall of the section farther out.

"How long does it take you to make one up?"

"Seven minutes," the porter said, not looking at him.

Haze sat down on the seat arm. He said, "I'm from Eastrod."

"That isn't on this line," the porter said. "You on the wrong train."

"Going to the city," Haze said. "I said I was raised in Eastrod."

The porter didn't say anything.

"Eastrod," Haze said, louder.

The porter jerked the shade down. "You want your berth made up now, or what you standing there for?" he asked.

"Eastrod," Haze said. "Near Melsy."

The porter wrenched one side of the seat flat. "I'm from Chicago," he said. He wrenched the other side down. When he bent over, the back of his neck came out in three bulges.

"Yeah, I bet you are," Haze said with a leer.

"Your feet in the middle of the aisle. Somebody going to want to get by you," the porter said, turning suddenly and brushing past.

Haze got up and hung there a few seconds. He looked as if he were held by a rope caught in the middle of his back and attached to the train ceiling. He watched the porter move in a fine controlled lurch down the aisle and disappear at the other end of the car. He knew him to be a Parrum nigger from Eastrod. He went back to his section and folded into a slouched position and settled one foot on a pipe that ran under the window. Eastrod filled his head and then went out beyond and filled the space that stretched from the train across the empty darkening fields. He saw the two houses and the rust-colored road and the few Negro shacks and the one barn and the stall with the red and white CCC snuff ad peeling across the side of it.

"Are you going home?" Mrs. Hitchcock asked.

He looked at her sourly and gripped the black hat by the brim. "No, I ain't," he said in a sharp high nasal Tennessee voice.

Mrs. Hitchcock said neither was she. She told him she had been a Miss Weatherman before she married and that she was going to Florida to visit her married daughter, Sarah Lucile. She said it seemed like she had never had time to take a trip that far off. The way things happened, one thing after another, it seemed like time went by so fast you couldn't tell if you were young or old.

He thought he could tell her she was old if she asked him. He stopped listening to her after a while. The porter passed back up the aisle and didn't look at him. Mrs. Hitchcock lost her train of talk. "I guess you're on your way to visit somebody?" she asked.

"Going to Taulkinham," he said and ground himself into the seat and looked at the window. "Don't know nobody there, but I'm going to do some things.

"I'm going to do some things I never have done before," he said and gave her a sidelong glance and curled his mouth slightly.

She said she knew an Albert Sparks from Taulkinham. She said he was her sister-in-law's brother-in-law and that he . . .

"I ain't from Taulkinham," he said. "I said I'm going there, that's all." Mrs. Hitchcock began to talk again but he cut her short and said, "That porter was raised in the same place where I was raised but he says he's from Chicago."

Mrs. Hitchcock said she knew a man who lived in Chi . . .

"You might as well go one place as another," he said. "That's all I know."

Mrs. Hitchcock said well that time flies. She said she hadn't seen her sister's children in five years and she didn't know if she'd know them if she saw them. There were three of them, Roy, Bubber, and John Wesley. John Wesley was six years old and he had written her a letter, dear Mammadoll. They called her Mammadoll and her husband Papadoll . . .

"I reckon you think you been redeemed," he said.

Mrs. Hitchcock snatched at her collar.

"I reckon you think you been redeemed," he repeated.

She blushed. After a second she said yes, life was an inspiration and then she said she was hungry and asked him if he didn't want to go into the diner. He put on the fierce black hat and followed her out of the car.

The dining car was full and people were waiting to get in it. He and Mrs. Hitchcock stood in line for a half-hour, rocking in the narrow passageway and every few minutes flattening themselves against the side to let a trickle of people through. Mrs. Hitchcock talked to the woman on the side of her. Hazel Motes looked at the wall. Mrs. Hitchcock told the woman about her sister's husband who was with the City Water Works in Toolafalls, Alabama, and the lady told about a cousin who had cancer of the throat. Finally they got almost up to the entrance of the diner and could see inside it. There was a steward beckoning people to places and handing out menus. He was a white man with greased black hair and a greased black look to his suit. He moved like a crow, darting from table to table. He motioned for two people and the line moved up so that Haze and Mrs. Hitchcock and the lady she was talking to were ready to go next. In a minute two more people left. The steward beckoned and Mrs. Hitchcock and the woman walked in and Haze followed them. The man stopped him and said, "Only two," and pushed him back to the doorway.

Haze's face turned an ugly red. He tried to get behind the next person and then he tried to get through the line to go back to the car he had come from but there were too many people bunched in the opening. He had to stand there while everyone around looked at him. No one left for a while. Finally a woman at the far end of the car got up and the steward jerked his hand. Haze hesitated and saw the hand jerk again. He lurched up the aisle, falling against two tables on the way and getting his hand wet in somebody's coffee. The steward placed him with three youngish women dressed like parrots.

Their hands were resting on the table, red-speared at

the tips. He sat down and wiped his hand on the tablecloth. He didn't take off his hat. The women had finished eating and were smoking cigarettes. They stopped talking when he sat down. He pointed to the first thing on the menu and the steward, standing over him, said, "Write it down, sonny," and winked at one of the women; she made a noise in her nose. He wrote it down and the steward went away with it. He sat and looked in front of him, glum and intense, at the neck of the woman across from him. At intervals her hand holding the cigarette would pass the spot on her neck; it would go out of his sight and then it would pass again, going back down to the table; in a second a straight line of smoke would blow in his face. After it had blown at him three or four times, he looked at her. She had a bold game-hen expression and small eyes pointed directly on him.

"If you've been redeemed," he said, "I wouldn't want to be." Then he turned his head to the window. He saw his pale reflection with the dark empty space outside coming through it. A boxcar roared past, chopping the empty space in two, and one of the women laughed.

"Do you think I believe in Jesus?" he said, leaning toward her and speaking almost as if he were breathless. "Well I wouldn't even if He existed. Even if He was on this train."

"Who said you had to?" she asked in a poisonous Eastern voice.

He drew back.

The waiter brought his dinner. He began eating slowly at first, then faster as the women concentrated on watching the muscles that stood out on his jaw when he chewed. He was eating something spotted with eggs and livers. He finished that and drank his coffee and then pulled his money out. The steward saw him but he wouldn't come total the bill. Every time he passed the table, he would wink at the women and stare at Haze. Mrs. Hitchcock and the lady had already finished and gone. Finally the man came and added up the bill. Haze shoved the money at him and then pushed past him out of the car.

For a while he stood between two train cars where there was fresh air of a sort and made a cigarette. Then the porter passed between the two cars. "Hey you, Parrum," he called.

The porter didn't stop.

Haze followed him into the car. All the berths were made up. The man in the station in Melsy had sold him a berth because he said he would have to sit up all night in the coaches; he had sold him an upper one. Haze went to it and pulled his sack down and went into the men's room and got ready for the night. He was too full and he wanted to hurry and get in the berth and lie down. He thought he would lie there and look out the window and watch how the country went by a train at night. A sign said to get the porter to let you into the uppers. He stuck his sack up into his berth and then went to look for the porter. He didn't find him at one end of the car and he started back to the other. Going around the corner he ran into something heavy and pink; it gasped and muttered, "Clumsy!" It was Mrs. Hitchcock in a pink wrapper, with her hair in knots around her head. She looked at him with her eyes squinted nearly shut. The knobs framed her face like dark toadstools. She tried to get past him and he tried to let her but they were both moving the same way each time. Her face became purplish except for little white marks over it that didn't heat up. She drew herself stiff and stopped and said, "What is the matter with you?" He slipped past her and dashed down the aisle and ran into the porter so that the porter fell down.

"You got to let me into the berth, Parrum," he said.

The porter picked himself up and went lurching down the aisle and after a minute he came lurching back again, stone-faced, with the ladder. Haze stood watching him while he put the ladder up; then he started up it. Halfway up, he turned and said, "I remember you. Your father was a nigger named Cash Parrum. You can't go back there neither, nor anybody else, not if they wanted to."

"I'm from Chicago," the porter said in an irritated voice. "My name is not Parrum."

"Cash is dead," Haze said. "He got the cholera from a pig."

The porter's mouth jerked down and he said, "My father was a railroad man."

Haze laughed. The porter jerked the ladder off suddenly with a wrench of his arm that sent the boy clutching at the blanket into the berth. He lay on his stomach for a few minutes and didn't move. After a while he turned and found the light and looked around him. There was no window. He was closed up in the thing except for a little space over the curtain. The top of the berth was low and curved over. He lay down and noticed that the curved top looked as if it were not quite closed; it looked as if it were closing. He lay there for a while, not moving. There was something in his throat like a sponge with an egg taste; he didn't want to turn over for fear it would move. He wanted the light off. He reached up without turning and felt for the button and snapped it and the darkness sank down on him and then faded a little with light from the aisle that came in through the foot of space not closed. He wanted it all dark, he didn't want it diluted. He heard the porter's footsteps coming down the aisle, soft into the rug, coming steadily down, brushing against the green curtains and fading up the other way out of hearing. Then after a while when he was almost asleep, he thought he heard them again coming back. His curtains stirred and the footsteps faded.

In his half-sleep he thought where he was lying was like a coffin. The first coffin he had seen with someone in it was his grandfather's. They had left it propped open with a stick of kindling the night it had sat in the house with the old man in it, and Haze had watched from a distance, thinking: he ain't going to let them shut it on him; when the time comes, his elbow is going to shoot into the crack. His grandfather had been a circuit preacher, a waspish old man who had ridden over three counties with Jesus hidden in his head like a stinger. When it was time to bury him, they shut the top of his box down and he didn't make a move.

Haze had had two younger brothers; one died in infancy and was put in a small box. The other fell in front of a mowing machine when he was seven. His box was about half the size of an ordinary one, and when they shut it, Haze ran and opened it up again. They said it was because he was heartbroken to part with his brother, but it was not; it was because he had thought, what if he had been in it and they had shut it on him.

He was asleep now and he dreamed he was at his father's burying again. He saw him humped over on his hands and knees in his coffin, being carried that way to the graveyard. "If I keep my can in the air," he heard the old man say, "nobody can shut nothing on me," but when they got his box to the hole, they let it drop down with a thud and his father flattened out like anybody else. The train jolted and stirred him half awake again and he thought, there must have been twenty-five people in Eastrod then, three Motes. Now there were no more Motes, no more Ashfields, no more Blasengames, Feys, Jacksons . . . or Parrums—even niggers wouldn't have it. Turning in the road, he saw in the dark the store boarded and the barn leaning and the smaller house half carted away, the porch gone and no floor in the hall.

It had not been that way when he was eighteen years old and had left it. Then there had been ten people there and he had not noticed that it had got smaller from his father's time. He had left it when he was eighteen years old because the army had called him. He had thought at first he would shoot his foot and not go. He was going to be a preacher like his grandfather and a preacher can always do without a foot. A preacher's power is in his neck and tongue and arm. His grandfather had traveled three counties in a Ford automobile. Every fourth Saturday he had driven into Eastrod as if he were just in time to save them all from Hell, and he was shouting before he had the car door open. People gathered around his Ford because he seemed to dare them to. He would climb up on the nose of it and preach from there and sometimes he would climb onto the top of it and shout down at them. They were like stones! he would shout. But Jesus had died to redeem them! Jesus was so soul-hungry that He had died, one death for all, but He would have died every soul's death for one! Did they understand that? Did they understand that for each stone soul, He would have died ten million deaths, had His arms and legs stretched on the cross and nailed ten million times for one of them? (The old man would point to his grandson, Haze. He had a particular disrespect for him because his own face was repeated almost exactly in the child's and seemed to mock him.) Did they know that even for that boy there, for that mean sinful unthinking boy standing there with his dirty hands clenching and unclenching at his sides, Jesus would die ten million deaths before He would let him lose his soul? He would chase him over the waters of sin! Did they doubt Jesus could walk on the waters of sin? That boy had been redeemed and Jesus wasn't going to leave him ever. Jesus would never let him forget he was redeemed. What did the sinner think there was to be gained? Jesus would have him in the end!

The boy didn't need to hear it. There was already a deep black wordless conviction in him that the way to avoid Jesus was to avoid sin. He knew by the time he was twelve years old that he was going to be a preacher. Later he saw Jesus move from tree to tree in the back of his mind, a wild ragged figure motioning him to turn around and come off into the dark where he was not sure of his footing, where he might be walking on the water and not know it and then suddenly know it and drown. Where he wanted to stay was in Eastrod with his two eyes open, and his hands always handling the familiar thing, his feet on the known track, and his tongue not too loose. When he was eighteen and the army called him, he saw the war as a trick to lead him into temptation, and he would have shot his foot except that he trusted himself to get back in a few months, uncorrupted. He had a strong confidence in his power to resist evil; it was something he had inherited, like his face, from his grandfather. He thought that if the government wasn't through with him in four months, he would leave anyway. He had thought, then when he was eighteen years old, that he would give them exactly four months of his time. He was gone four years; he didn't get back, even for a visit.

The only things from Eastrod he took into the army with him were a black Bible and a pair of silver-rimmed spectacles that had belonged to his mother. He had gone to a country school where he had learned to read and write but that it was wiser not to; the Bible was the only book he read. He didn't read it often but when he did he wore his mother's glasses. They tired his eyes so that after a short time he was always obliged to stop. He meant to tell anyone in the army who invited him to sin that he was from Eastrod, Tennessee, and that he meant to get back there and stay back there, that he was going to be a preacher of the gospel and that he wasn't going to have his soul damned by the government or by any foreign place it sent him to.

After a few weeks in the camp, when he had some friends —they were not actually friends but he had to live with them—he was offered the chance he had been waiting for; the invitation. He took his mother's glasses out of his pocket and put them on. Then he told them he wouldn't go with them for a million dollars and a feather bed to lie on; he said he was from Eastrod, Tennessee, and that he was not going to have his soul damned by the government or any foreign place they . . . but his voice cracked and he didn't finish. He only stared at them, trying to steel his face. His friends told him that nobody was interested in his goddam soul unless it was the priest and he managed to answer that no priest taking orders from no pope was going to tamper with his soul. They told him he didn't have any soul and left for their brothel.

He took a long time to believe them because he wanted to believe them. All he wanted was to believe them and get rid of it once and for all, and he saw the opportunity here to get rid of it without corruption, to be converted to nothing instead of to evil. The army sent him halfway around the world and forgot him. He was wounded and they remembered him long enough to take the shrapnel out of his chest—they said they took it out but they never showed it to him and he felt it still in there, rusted, and poisoning him—and then they sent him to another desert and forgot him again. He had all the time he could want to study his soul in and assure himself that it was not there. When he was thoroughly convinced, he saw that this was something that he had always known. The misery he had was a longing for home; it had nothing to do with Jesus. When the army finally let him go, he was pleased to think that he was still uncorrupted. All he wanted was to get back to Eastrod, Tennessee. The black Bible and his mother's glasses were still in the bottom of his duffel bag. He didn't read any book now but he kept the Bible because it had come from home. He kept the glasses in case his vision should ever become dim.

When the army had released him two days before in a city about three hundred miles north of where he wanted to be, he had gone immediately to the railroad station there and bought a ticket to Melsy, the nearest railroad stop to Eastrod. Then since he had to wait four hours for the train, he went into a dark dry-goods store near the station. It was a thin cardboard-smelling store that got darker as it got deeper. He went deep into it and was sold a blue suit and a dark hat. He had his army suit put in a paper sack and he stuffed it into a trashbox on the corner. Once outside in the light, the new suit turned glare-blue and the lines of the hat seemed to stiffen fiercely.

He was in Melsy at five o'clock in the afternoon and he caught a ride on a cotton-seed truck that took him more than half the distance to Eastrod. He walked the rest of the way and got there at nine o'clock at night, when it had just got dark. The house was as dark as the night and open to it and though he saw that the fence around it had partly fallen and that weeds were growing through the porch floor, he didn't realize all at once that it was only a shell, that there was nothing here but the skeleton of a house. He twisted an envelope and struck a match to it and went through all the empty rooms, upstairs and down. When the envelope burnt out, he lit another one and went through them all again. That night he slept on the floor in the kitchen, and a board fell on his head out of the roof and cut his face.

There was nothing left in the house but the chifforobe in the kitchen. His mother had always slept in the kitchen and had her walnut chifforobe in there. She had given thirty dollars for it and hadn't bought herself anything else big again. Whoever had got everything else, had left that. He opened all the drawers. There were two lengths of wrapping cord in the top one and nothing in the others. He was surprised nobody had come and stolen a chifforobe like that. He took the wrapping cord and tied it around the legs and through the floor boards and left a piece of paper in each of the drawers: THIS SHIFFER-ROBE BE-LONGS TO HAZEL MOTES. DO NOT STEAL IT OR YOU WILL BE HUNTED DOWN AND KILLED.

He thought about the chifforobe in his half-sleep and decided his mother would rest easier in her grave, knowing it was guarded. If she came looking any time at night, she would see. He wondered if she walked at night and came there ever. She would come with that look on her face, unrested and looking; the same look he had seen through the crack of her coffin. He had seen her face through the crack when they were shutting the top on her. He was sixteen then. He had seen the shadow that came down over her face and pulled her mouth down as if she wasn't any more satisfied dead than alive, as if she were going to spring up and shove the lid back and fly out and satisfy herself: but they shut it. She might have been going to fly out of there, she might have been going to spring. He saw her in his sleep, terrible, like a huge bat, dart from the closing, fly out of there, but it was falling dark on top of her, closing down all the time. From inside he saw it closing, coming closer closer down and cutting off the light and the room. He opened his eyes and saw it closing and he sprang up between the crack and wedged his head and shoulders through it and hung there, dizzy, with the dim light of the train slowly showing the rug below. He hung there over the top of the berth curtain and saw the porter at the other end of the car, a white shape in the darkness, standing there watching him and not moving.

"I'm sick!" he called. "I can't be closed up in this thing. Get me out!"

The porter stood watching him and didn't move.

"Jesus," Haze said, "Jesus."

The porter didn't move. "Jesus been a long time gone," he said in a sour triumphant voice.

CHAPTER 2

He didn't get to the city until six the next evening. That morning he had got off the train at a junction stop to get some air and while he had been looking the other way, the train had slid off. He had run after it but his hat had blown away and he had had to run in the other direction to save the hat. Fortunately, he had carried his duffel bag out with him lest someone should steal something out of it. He had to wait six hours at the junction stop until the right train came.

When he got to Taulkinham, as soon as he stepped off the train, he began to see signs and lights. PEANUTS, WESTERN UNION, AJAX, TAXI, HOTEL, CANDY. Most of them were electric and moved up and down or blinked frantically. He walked very slowly, carrying his duffel bag by the neck. His head turned to one side and then the other, first toward one sign and then another. He walked the length of the station and then he walked back as if he might be going to get on the train again. His face was stern and determined under the heavy hat. No one observing him would have known that he had no place to go. He walked up and down the crowded waiting room two or three times, but he did not want to sit on the benches there. He wanted a private place to go to.

Finally he pushed open a door at one end of the station where a plain black and white sign said, MEN'S TOILET. WHITE. He went into a narrow room lined on one side with wash-basins and on the other with a row of wooden stalls. The walls of this room had once been a bright cheerful yellow but now they were more nearly green and were decorated with handwriting and with various detailed drawings of the parts of the body of both men and women. Some of the stalls had doors on them and on one of the doors, written with what must have been a crayon, was the large word, WELCOME, followed by three exclamation points and something that looked like a snake. Haze entered this one.

He had been sitting in the narrow box for some time, studying the inscriptions on the sides and door, before he noticed one that was to the left over the toilet paper. It was written in a drunken-looking hand. It said,

> Mrs. Leora Watts!
> 60 Buckley Road
> The friendliest bed in town!
> Brother.

After a while he took a pencil out of his pocket and wrote down the address on the back of an envelope.

Outside he got in a yellow taxi and told the driver where he wanted to go. The driver was a small man with a big leather cap on his head and the tip of a cigar coming out from the center of his mouth. They had driven a few blocks before Haze noticed him squinting at him through the rear-view mirror. "You ain't no friend of hers, are you?" the driver asked.

"I never saw her before," Haze said.

"Where'd you hear about her? She don't usually have no preachers for company." He did not disturb the position of the cigar when he spoke; he was able to speak on either side of it.

"I ain't any preacher," Haze said, frowning. "I only seen her name in the toilet."

"You look like a preacher," the driver said. "That hat looks like a preacher's hat."

"It ain't," Haze said, and leaned forward and gripped the back of the front seat. "It's just a hat."

They stopped in front of a small one-story house between a filling station and a vacant lot. Haze got out and paid his fare through the window.

"It ain't only the hat," the driver said. "It's a look in your face somewheres."

"Listen," Haze said, tilting the hat over one eye, "I'm not a preacher."

"I understand," the driver said. "It ain't anybody perfect on this green earth of God's, preachers nor nobody else. And you can tell people better how terrible sin is if you know from your own personal experience."

Haze put his head in at the window, knocking the hat accidentally straight again. He seemed to have knocked his face straight too for it became completely expressionless. "Listen," he said, "get this: I don't believe in anything."

The driver took the stump of cigar out of his mouth. "Not in nothing at all?" he asked, leaving his mouth open after the question.

"I don't have to say it but once to nobody," Haze said.

The driver closed his mouth and after a second he returned the piece of cigar to it. "That's the trouble with you preachers," he said. "You've all got too good to believe in anything," and he drove off with a look of disgust and righteousness.

Haze turned and looked at the house he was going into. It was little more than a shack but there was a warm glow in one front window. He went up on the front porch and put his eye to a convenient crack in the shade, and found himself looking directly at a large white knee. After some time he moved away from the crack and tried the front door. It was not locked and he went into a small dark hall with a door on either side of it. The door to the left was cracked and let out a narrow shaft of light. He moved into the light and looked through the crack.

Mrs. Watts was sitting alone in a white iron bed, cutting her toenails with a large pair of scissors. She was a big woman with very yellow hair and white skin that glistened with a greasy preparation. She had on a pink nightgown that would better have fit a smaller figure.

Haze made a noise with the doorknob and she looked up and observed him standing behind the crack. She had a bold steady penetrating stare. After a minute, she turned it away from him and began cutting her toenails again.

He went in and stood looking around him. There was nothing much in the room but the bed and a bureau and a rocking chair full of dirty clothes. He went to the bureau and fingered a nail file and then an empty jelly glass while he looked into the yellowish mirror and watched Mrs. Watts, slightly distorted, grinning at him. His senses were stirred to the limit. He turned quickly and went to her bed and sat down on the far corner of it. He drew a long draught of air through one side of his nose and began to run his hand carefully along the sheet.

The pink tip of Mrs. Watts's tongue appeared and moistened her lower lip. She seemed just as glad to see him as if he had been an old friend but she didn't say anything.

He picked up her foot, which was heavy but not cold, and moved it about an inch to one side, and kept his hand on it.

Mrs. Watts's mouth split in a wide full grin that showed her teeth. They were small and pointed and speckled with green and there was a wide space between each one. She reached out and gripped Haze's arm just above the elbow. "You huntin' something?" she drawled.

If she had not had him so firmly by the arm, he might have leaped out the window. Involuntarily his lips formed the words, "Yes, mam," but no sound came through them.

"Something on your mind?" Mrs. Watts asked, pulling his rigid figure a little closer.

"Listen," he said, keeping his voice tightly under control, "I come for the usual business."

Mrs. Watts's mouth became more round, as if she were perplexed at this waste of words. "Make yourself at home," she said simply.

They stared at each other for almost a minute and neither moved. Then he said in a voice that was higher than his usual voice, "What I mean to have you know is: I'm no goddam preacher."

Mrs. Watts eyed him steadily with only a slight smirk. Then she put her other hand under his face and tickled it in a motherly way. "That's okay, son," she said. "Momma don't mind if you ain't a preacher."

CHAPTER 3

His second night in Taulkinham, Hazel Motes walked along down town close to the store fronts but not looking in them. The black sky was underpinned with long silver streaks that looked like scaffolding and depth on depth behind it were thousands of stars that all seemed to be moving very slowly as if they were about some vast construction work that involved the whole order of the universe and would take all time to complete. No one was paying any attention to the sky. The stores in Taulkinham stayed open on Thursday nights so that people could have an extra opportunity to see what was for sale. Haze's shadow was now behind him and now before him and now and then broken up by other people's shadows, but when it was by itself, stretching behind him, it was a thin nervous shadow walking backwards. His neck was thrust forward as if he were trying to smell something that was always being drawn away. The glary light from the store windows made his blue suit look purple.

After a while he stopped where a lean-faced man had a card table set up in front of a department store and was demonstrating a potato peeler. The man had on a small canvas hat and a shirt patterned with bunches of upside-down pheasants and quail and bronze turkeys. He was pitching his voice under the street noises so that it reached every ear distinctly as if in a private conversation. A few people gathered around. There were two buckets on the card table, one empty and the other full of potatoes. Between the two buckets there was a pyramid of green cardboard boxes and, on top of the stack, one peeler was open for demonstration. The man stood in front of this altar, pointing over it at various people. "How about you?" he said, pointing at a damp-haired pimpled boy. "You ain't gonna let one of these go by?" He stuck a brown potato in one side of the open machine. The machine was a square tin box with a red handle, and as he turned the handle, the potato went into the box and then in a second, backed out the other side, white. "You ain't gonna let one of these go by!" he said.

The boy guffawed and looked at the other people gathered around. He had yellow hair and a fox-shaped face.

24

"What's yer name?" the peeler man asked.

"Name Enoch Emery," the boy said and snuffled.

"Boy with a pretty name like that ought to have one of these," the man said, rolling his eyes, trying to warm up the others. Nobody laughed but the boy. Then a man standing across from Hazel Motes laughed, not a pleasant laugh but one that had a sharp edge. He was a tall cadaverous man with a black suit and a black hat on. He had on dark glasses and his cheeks were streaked with lines that looked as if they had been painted on and had faded. They gave him the expression of a grinning mandrill. As soon as he laughed, he began to move forward in a deliberate way, jiggling a tin cup in one hand and tapping a white cane in front of him with the other. Just behind him there came a child, handing out leaflets. She had on a black dress and a black knitted cap pulled down low on her forehead; there was a fringe of brown hair sticking out from it on either side; she had a long face and a short sharp nose. The man selling peelers was irritated when he saw the people looking at this pair instead of him. "How about you, you there," he said, pointing at Haze. "You'll never be able to get a bargain like this in any store."

Haze was looking at the blind man and the child. "Hey!" Enoch Emery said, reaching across a woman and punching his arm. "He's talking to you! He's talking to you!" Enoch had to punch him again before he looked at the peeler man.

"Whyn't you take one of these home to yer wife?" the peeler man was saying.

"Don't have one," Haze muttered, looking back at the blind man again.

"Well, you got a dear old mother, ain't you?"

"No."

"Well pshaw," the man said, with his hand cupped to the people, "he needs one theseyer just to keep him company."

Enoch Emery thought that was so funny that he doubled over and slapped his knee, but Hazel Motes didn't look as if he had heard it yet. "I'm going to give away a half a dozen peeled potatoes to the first person purchasing one theseyer machines," the man said. "Who's gonna step up first? Only a dollar and a half for a machine'd cost you three dollars in any store!" Enoch Emery began fumbling in his pockets. "You'll thank the day you ever stopped here," the man said, "you'll never forget it. Ever' one of you people purchasing one theseyer machines'll never forget it!"

The blind man was moving forward slowly, saying in a kind of garbled mutter, "Help a blind preacher. If you won't repent, give up a nickel. I can use it as good as you. Help a blind unemployed preacher. Wouldn't you rather have me beg than preach? Come on and give a nickel if you won't repent."

There were not many people gathered around but the ones who were began to move off. When the machine-seller saw this, he leaned, glaring over the card table. "Hey you!" he yelled at the blind man. "What you think you doing? Who you think you are, running people off from here?" The blind man didn't pay any attention to him. He kept on rattling the cup and the child kept on handing out the pamphlets. He passed Enoch Emery and came on toward Haze, hitting the white cane out at an angle from his leg. Haze leaned forward and saw that the lines on his face were not painted on; they were scars.

"What the hell you think you doing?" the man selling peelers yelled. "I got these people together, how you think you can horn in?"

The child held one of the pamphlets out to Haze and he grabbed it. The words on the outside of it said, "Jesus Calls You."

"I'd like to know who the hell you think you are!" the man with the peelers was yelling. The child went back to where he was and handed him a tract. He looked at it for an instant with his lip curled and then he charged around the card table, upsetting the bucket of potatoes. "These damn Jesus fanatics!" he yelled, glaring around, trying to find the blind man. New people gathered, hoping to see a disturbance. "These goddam Communist foreigners!" the peeler man screamed. "I got this crowd together!" He stopped, realizing there was a crowd.

"Listen folks," he said, "one at a time, there's plenty to go around, just don't push, a half a dozen peeled potatoes to the first person stepping up to buy." He got back behind the card table quietly and started holding up the peeler boxes. "Step on up, plenty to go around," he said, "no need to crowd."

Haze didn't open his tract. He looked at the outside of it and then he tore it across. He put the two pieces together and tore them across again. He kept re-stacking the pieces and tearing them again until he had a little handful of confetti. He turned his hand over and let the shredded leaflet sprinkle to the ground. Then he looked up and saw the blind man's child not three feet away, watching him. Her mouth was open and her eyes glittered on him like two chips of green bottle glass. She had a white gunny sack hung over her shoulder. Haze scowled and began rubbing his sticky hands on his pants.

"I seen you," she said. Then she moved quickly over to where the blind man was standing now, beside the card table, and turned her head and looked at Haze from there. Most of the people had moved off.

The peeler man leaned over the card table and said, "Hey!" to the blind man. "I reckon that showed you. Trying to horn in."

"Lookerhere," Enoch Emery said, "I ain't got but a dollar sixteen cent but I . . ."

"Yah," the man said, "I reckon that'll show you you can't muscle in on me. Sold eight peelers, sold . . ."

"Give me one of them," the blind man's child said, pointing to the peelers.

"Hanh," he said.

She was untying a handkerchief. She untied two fifty-cent pieces out of the knotted corner of it. "Give me one of them," she said, holding out the money.

The man eyed it with his mouth hiked to one side. "A buck fifty, sister," he said.

She pulled her hand in quickly and all at once glared at Hazel Motes as if he had made a noise at her. The blind man was moving on. She stood a second glaring at Haze, and then she turned and followed the blind man. Haze started.

"Listen," Enoch Emery said, "I ain't got but a dollar sixteen cent and I want me one of them . . ."

"You can keep it," the man said, taking the bucket off the card table. "This ain't no cut-rate joint."

Haze could see the blind man moving down the street some distance away. He stood staring after him, jerking his hands in and out of his pockets as if he were trying to move forward and backward at the same time. Then suddenly he thrust two dollars at the man selling peelers and snatched a box off the card table and started running down the street. In a second Enoch Emery was panting at his elbow. "My, I reckon you got a heap of money," Enoch Emery said.

Haze saw the child catch up with the blind man and take him by the elbow. They were about a block ahead of him. He slowed down some and saw Enoch Emery there. Enoch had on a yellowish white suit and a pinkish white shirt and his tie was the color of green peas. He was smiling. He looked like a friendly hound dog with light mange. "How long you been here?" he inquired.

"Two days," Haze muttered.

"I been here two months," Enoch said. "I work for the city. Where you work?"

"Not working," Haze said.

"That's too bad," Enoch said. "I work for the city." He skipped a step to get in line with Haze, then he said, "I'm eighteen year old and I ain't been here but two months and I already work for the city."

"That's fine," Haze said. He pulled his hat down farther on the side Enoch Emery was on and walked very fast. The blind man up ahead began to make mock bows to the right and left.

"I didn't ketch your name good," Enoch said.

Haze said his name.

"You look like you might be follerin' them hicks," Enoch remarked. "You go in for a lot of Jesus business?"

"No," Haze said.

"No, me neither, not much," Enoch agreed. "I went to thisyer Rodemill Boys' Bible Academy for four weeks. Thisyer woman that traded me from my daddy she sent me. She was a Welfare woman. Jesus, four weeks and I thought I was going to be sanctified crazy."

Haze walked to the end of the block and Enoch stayed at his elbow, panting and talking. When Haze started across the street, Enoch yelled, "Don't you see theter light! That means you got to wait!" A cop blew a whistle and a car blasted its horn and stopped short. Haze went on across, keeping his eyes on the blind man in the middle of the block. The policeman kept on blowing his whistle. He crossed the street to where Haze was and stopped him. He had a thin face and oval-shaped yellow eyes.

"You know what that little thing hanging up there is for?" he asked, pointing to the traffic light over the intersection.

"I didn't see it," Haze said.

The policeman looked at him without saying anything. A few people stopped. He rolled his eyes at them. "Maybe you thought the red ones was for white folks and the green ones for niggers," he said.

"Yeah I thought that," Haze said. "Take your hand off me."

The policeman took his hand off and put it on his hip. He backed one step away and said, "You tell all your friends about these lights. Red is to stop, green is to go—men and women, white folks and niggers, all go on the same light. You tell all your friends so when they come to town, they'll know." The people laughed.

"I'll look after him," Enoch Emery said, pushing in

by the policeman. "He ain't been here but only two days. I'll look after him."

"How long you been here?" the cop asked.

"I was born and raised here," Enoch said. "This is my ol' home town. I'll take care of him for you. Hey wait!" he yelled at Haze. "Wait on me!" He pushed out of the crowd and caught up with him. "I reckon I saved you that time," he said.

"I'm obliged," Haze said.

"It wasn't nothing," Enoch said. "Whyn't we go in Walgreen's and get us a soda? Ain't no night clubs open this early."

"I don't like drug stores," Haze said. "Good-by."

"That's all right," Enoch said. "I reckon I'll go along and keep you company for a while." He looked up ahead at the blind man and the child and said, "I sho wouldn't want to get messed up with no hicks this time of night, particularly the Jesus kind. I done had enough of them myself. Thisyer Welfare woman that traded me from my daddy didn't do nothing but pray. Me and daddy we moved around with a sawmill where we worked and it set up outside Boonville one summer and here come thisyer woman." He caught hold of Haze's coat. "Only objection I got to Taulkinham is there's too many people on the streets," he said confidentially. "Look like all they want to do is knock you down—well here she come and I reckon she took a fancy to me. I was twelve year old and I could sing some hymns good I learnt off a nigger. So here she comes taking a fancy to me and traded me off my daddy and took me to Boonville to live with her. She had a brick house but it was Jesus all day long." A little man lost in a pair of faded overalls jostled him. "Whyn't you look wher you going?" Enoch growled.

The little man stopped and raised his arm in a vicious gesture and a nasty-dog look came on his face. "Who you tellin' what?" he snarled.

"You see," Enoch said, jumping to catch up with Haze, "all they want to do is knock you down. I ain't never been to such a unfriendly place before. Even with that woman. I stayed with her for two months in that house of hers," he went on, "and then come fall she sent me to the Rodemill Boys' Bible Academy and I thought that sho was going to be some relief. This woman was hard to get along with— she wasn't old, I reckon she was forty year old—but she sho was ugly. She had theseyer brown glasses and her hair was so thin it looked like ham gravy trickling over her skull. I thought it was going to be some certain relief to get to theter Academy. I had run away oncet on her and she got me back and come to find out she had papers on me and she could send me to the penitentiary if I didn't stay with her so I sho was glad to get to theter Academy. You ever been to a academy?"

Haze didn't seem to hear the question.

"Well, it won't no relief," Enoch said. "Good Jesus, it won't no relief. I run away from there after four weeks and durn if she didn't get me back and brought me to that house of hers again. I got out though." He waited a minute. "You want to know how?"

After a second he said, "I scared hell out of that woman, that's how. I studied on it and studied on it. I even prayed. I said, 'Jesus, show me the way to get out of here without killing thisyer woman and getting sent to the penitentiary,' and durn if He didn't. I got up one morning at just daylight and I went in her room without my pants on and pulled the sheet off her and giver a heart attact. Then I went back to my daddy and we ain't seen hide of her since.

"Your jaw just crawls," he observed, watching the side of Haze's face. "You don't never laugh. I wouldn't be surprised if you wasn't a real wealthy man."

Haze turned down a side street. The blind man and the girl were on the corner a block ahead. "Well, I reckon we going to ketch up with them after all," Enoch said. "You know many people here?"

"No," Haze said.

"You ain't gonna know none neither. This is one more hard place to make friends in. I been here two months and I don't know nobody. Look like all they want to do is knock you down. I reckon you got a right heap of money," he said. "I ain't got none. Had, I'd sho know what to do with it." The blind man and his child stopped on the corner and turned up the left side of the street. "We ketchin' up," he said. "I bet we'll be at some meeting singing hymns with her and her daddy if we don't watch out."

Up in the next block there was a large building with columns and a dome. The blind man and the girl were going toward it. There was a car parked in every space around the building and on the other side of the street and up and down the streets near it. "That ain't no picture show," Enoch said. The blind man and the girl turned up the steps to the building. The steps went all the way across the front, and on either side there were stone lions sitting on pedestals. "Ain't no church," Enoch said. Haze stopped at the steps. He looked as if he were trying to settle his face into an expression. He pulled the black hat forward at a sharp angle and started toward the two, who had sat down in the corner by one of the lions. He came up to where the blind man was without saying anything and stood leaning forward in front of him as if he were trying to see through the black glasses. The child stared at him.

The blind man's mouth thinned slightly. "I can smell the sin on your breath," he said.

Haze drew back.

"What'd you follow me for?"

"I never followed you," Haze said.

"She said you were following," the blind man said, jerking his thumb in the direction of the child.

"I ain't followed you," Haze said. He felt the peeler box in his hand and looked at the girl. Her black knitted cap made a straight line across her forehead. She grinned suddenly and then quickly drew her expression back together as if she smelled something bad. "I ain't followed you nowhere," Haze said. "I followed her." He stuck the peeler out at her.

At first she looked as if she were going to grab it, but she didn't. "I don't want that thing," she said. "What you think I want with that thing? Take it. It ain't mine. I don't want it!"

"You take it," the blind man said. "You put it in your sack and shut up before I hit you."

Haze thrust the peeler at her again.

"I won't have it," she muttered.

"You take it like I told you," the blind man said. "He never followed you."

She took it and shoved it in the sack where the tracts were. "It ain't mine," she said. "I got it but it ain't mine."

"I followed her to say I ain't beholden for none of her fast eye like she gave me back there," Haze said, looking at the blind man.

"What you mean?" she shouted. "I never looked at you with no fast eye. I only watched you tearing up that tract. He tore it up in little pieces," she said, pushing the blind man's shoulder. "He tore it up and sprinkled it all over the ground like salt and wiped his hands on his pants."

"He followed me," the blind man said. "Nobody would follow you. I can hear the urge for Jesus in his voice."

"Jesus," Haze muttered. "My Jesus." He sat down by the girl's leg and set his hand on the step next to her foot. She had on sneakers and black cotton stockings.

"Listen at him cursing," she said in a low tone. "He never followed you, Papa."

The blind man gave his edgy laugh. "Listen boy," he said, "you can't run away from Jesus. Jesus is a fact."

"I know a whole heap about Jesus," Enoch said. "I attended thisyer Rodemill Boys' Bible Academy that a woman sent me to. If it's anything you want to know about Jesus, just ast me." He had got up on the lion's back and he was sitting there sideways, cross-legged.

"I come a long way," Haze said, "since I would believe anything. I come halfway around the world."

"Me too," Enoch Emery said.

"You ain't come so far that you could keep from following me," the blind man said. He reached out suddenly and his hands covered Haze's face. For a second Haze didn't move or make any sound. Then he knocked the hands off.

"Quit it," he said in a faint voice. "You don't know anything about me."

"My daddy looks just like Jesus," Enoch remarked from the lion's back. "His hair hangs to his shoulders. Only difference is he's got a scar acrost his chin. I ain't never seen who my mother is."

"Some preacher has left his mark on you," the blind man said with a kind of snicker. "Did you follow for me to take it off or give you another one?"

"Listen here, there's nothing for your pain but Jesus," the child said suddenly. She tapped Haze on the shoulder. He sat there with his black hat tilted forward over his face. "Listen," she said in a louder voice, "this here man and woman killed this little baby. It was her own child but it was ugly and she never give it any love. This child had Jesus and this woman didn't have nothing but good looks and a man she was living in sin with. She sent the child away and it come back and she sent it away again and it come back again and ever' time she sent it away, it come back to where her and this man was living in sin. They strangled it with a silk stocking and hung it up in the chimney. It didn't give her any peace after that, though. Everything she looked at was that child. Jesus made it beautiful to haunt her. She couldn't lie with that man without she saw it, staring through the chimney at her, shining through the brick in the middle of the night."

"My Jesus," Haze muttered.

"She didn't have nothing but good looks," she said in the loud fast voice. "That ain't enough. No sirree."

"I hear them scraping their feet inside there," the blind man said. "Get out the tracts, they're fixing to come out."

"It ain't enough," she repeated.

"What we gonna do?" Enoch asked. "What's inside theter building?"

"A program letting out," the blind man said. "My congregation."

The child took the tracts out of the gunny sack and gave him two bunches of them, tied with a string. "You and the other boy go over on that side and give out," he said to her. "Me and the one that followed me'll stay over here."

"He don't have no business touching them," she said. "He don't want to do anything but shred them up."

"Go like I told you," the blind man said.

She stood there a second, scowling. Then she said, "You come on if you're coming," to Enoch Emery and Enoch jumped off the lion and followed her over to the other side.

Haze ducked down a step but the blind man's hand shot out and clamped him around the arm. He said in a fast whisper, "Repent! Go to the head of the stairs and renounce your sins and distribute these tracts to the people!" and he thrust a stack of pamphlets into Haze's hand.

Haze jerked his arm away but he only pulled the blind man nearer. "Listen," he said, "I'm as clean as you are."

"Fornication and blasphemy and what else?" the blind man said.

"They ain't nothing but words," Haze said. "If I was in sin I was in it before I ever committed any. There's no change come in me." He was trying to pry the fingers off from around his arm but the blind man kept wrapping them tighter. "I don't believe in sin," Haze said, "take your hand off me."

"Jesus loves you," the blind man said in a flat mocking voice, "Jesus loves you, Jesus loves you . . ."

"Nothing matters but that Jesus don't exist," Haze said, pulling his arm free.

"Go to the head of the stairs and distribute these tracts and . . ."

"I'll take them up there and throw them over into the bushes!" Haze shouted. "You be watching and see can you see."

"I can see more than you!" the blind man yelled, laughing. "You got eyes and see not, ears and hear not, but you'll have to see some time."

"You be watching if you can see!" Haze said, and started running up the steps. A crowd of people were already coming out the auditorium doors and some were halfway down the steps. He pushed through them with his elbows out like sharp wings and when he got to the top, a new surge of them pushed him back almost to where he had started up. He fought through them again until somebody shouted, "Make room for this idiot!" and people got out of his way. He rushed to the top and pushed his way over to the side and stood there, glaring and panting.

"I never followed him," he said aloud. "I wouldn't follow a blind fool like that. My Jesus." He stood against the building, holding the stack of leaflets by the string. A fat man stopped near him to light a cigar and Haze pushed his shoulder. "Look down yonder," he said. "See that blind man down there? He's giving out tracts and begging. Jesus. You ought to see him and he's got this here ugly child dressed up in woman's clothes, giving them out too. My Jesus."

"There's always fanatics," the fat man said, moving on.

"My Jesus," Haze said. He leaned forward near an old woman with blue hair and a collar of red wooden beads. "You better get on the other side, lady," he said. "There's a fool down there giving out tracts." The crowd behind the old woman pushed her on, but she looked at him for an instant with two bright flea eyes. He started toward her through the people but she was already too far away and he pushed back to where he had been standing against the wall. "Sweet Jesus Christ Crucified," he said, "I want to tell you people something. Maybe you think you're not clean because you don't believe. Well you are clean, let me tell you that. Every one of you people are clean and let me tell you why if you think it's because of Jesus Christ Crucified you're wrong. I don't say he wasn't crucified but I say it wasn't for you. Listenhere, I'm a preacher myself and I preach the truth." The crowd was moving fast. It was like a large spread raveling and the separate threads disappeared down the dark streets. "Don't I know what exists and what don't?" he cried. "Don't I have eyes in my head? Am I a blind man? Listenhere," he called, "I'm going to preach a new church—the church of truth without Jesus Christ Crucified. It won't cost you nothing to join my church. It's not started yet but it's going to be." The few people who were left glanced at him once or twice. There were tracts scattered below over the sidewalk and out on the street. The blind man was sitting on the bottom step. Enoch Emery was on the other side, standing on the lion's head, trying to balance himself, and the child was standing near him, watching Haze. "I don't need Jesus," Haze said. "What do I need with Jesus? I got Leora Watts."

He went down the stairs quietly to where the blind man was and stopped. He stood there a second and the blind man laughed. Haze moved away, and started across the street. He was on the other side before the voice pierced after him. He turned and saw the blind man standing in the middle of the street, shouting, "Hawks, Hawks, my name is Asa Hawks when you try to follow me again!" A car had to swerve to the side to keep from hitting him. "Repent!" he shouted and laughed and ran forward a little way, pretending he was going to come after Haze and grab him.

Haze drew his head down nearer his hunched shoulders and went on quickly. He didn't look back until he heard other footsteps coming behind him.

"Now that we got shut of them," Enoch Emery panted, "whyn't we go somewher and have us some fun?"

"Listen," Haze said roughly, "I got business of my own. I seen all of you I want." He began walking very fast.

Enoch kept skipping steps to keep up. "I been here two months," he said, "and I don't know nobody. People ain't friendly here. I got me a room and there ain't never nobody in it but me. My daddy said I had to come. I wouldn't never have come but he made me. I think I seen you sommers before. You ain't from Stockwell, are you?"

"No."

"Melsy?"

"No."

"Sawmill set up there once," Enoch said. "Look like you had a kind of familer face."

They walked on without saying anything until they got on the main street again. It was almost deserted. "Goodby," Haze said.

"I'm going thisaway too," Enoch said in a sullen voice. On the left there was a movie house where the electric bill was being changed. "We hadn't got tied up with them hicks we could have gone to a show," he muttered. He strode along at Haze's elbow, talking in a half mumble, half whine. Once he caught at his sleeve to slow him down and Haze jerked it away. "My daddy made me come," he said in a cracked voice. Haze looked at him and saw he was crying, his face seamed and wet and a purple-pink color. "I ain't but eighteen year old," he cried, "an' he made me come and I don't know nobody, nobody here'll have nothing to do with nobody else. They ain't friendly. He done gone off with a woman and made me come but she ain't going to stay for long, he'll beat hell out of her before she gets herself stuck to a chair. You the first familer face I seen in two months. I seen you sommers before. I know I seen you sommers before."

Haze looked straight ahead with his face set and Enoch kept up the half mumble, half blubber. They passed a church and a hotel and an antique shop and turned up Mrs. Watts's street.

"If you want you a woman you don't have to be follering nothing looked like that kid you give a peeler to," Enoch said. "I heard about where there's a house where we could have us some fun. I could pay you back next week."

"Look," Haze said, "I'm going where I'm going—two doors from here. I got a woman. I got a woman, see? And that's where I'm going—to visit her. I don't need to go with you."

"I could pay you back next week," Enoch said. "I work at the city zoo. I guard a gate and I get paid ever' week."

"Get away from me," Haze said.

"People ain't friendly here. You ain't from here but you ain't friendly neither."

Haze didn't answer him. He went on with his neck drawn close to his shoulder blades as if he were cold.

"You don't know nobody neither," Enoch said. "You ain't got no woman nor nothing to do. I knew when I first seen you you didn't have nobody nor nothing but Jesus. I seen you and I knew it."

"This is where I'm going in at," Haze said, and he turned up the walk without looking back at Enoch.

Enoch stopped. "Yeah," he cried, "oh yeah," and he ran his sleeve under his nose to stop the snivel. "Yeah," he cried, "go on where you goin' but lookerhere." He slapped at his pocket and ran up and caught Haze's sleeve and rattled the peeler box at him. "She give me this. She give it to me and there ain't nothing you can do about it. She told me where they lived and ast me to visit them and bring you—not you bring me, me bring you—and it was you follerin' them." His eyes glinted through his tears and his face stretched in an evil crooked grin. "You act like you think you got wiser blood than anybody else," he said, "but you ain't! I'm the one has it. Not you. *Me*."

Haze didn't say anything. He stood there for an instant, small in the middle of the steps, and then he raised his arm and hurled the stack of tracts he had been carrying. It hit Enoch in the chest and knocked his mouth open. He stood looking, with his mouth hanging open, at where it had hit his front, and then he turned and tore off down the street; and Haze went into the house.

Since the night before was the first time he had slept with any woman, he had not been very successful with Mrs.

Watts. When he finished, he was like something washed ashore on her, and she had made obscene comments about him, which he remembered off and on during the day. He was uneasy in the thought of going to her again. He didn't know what she would say when he opened the door and she saw him there.

When he opened the door and she saw him there, she said, "Ha ha."

The black hat sat on his head squarely. He came in with it on and when it knocked the electric light bulb that hung down from the middle of the ceiling, he took it off. Mrs. Watts was in bed, applying a grease to her face. She rested her chin on her hand and watched him. He began to move around the room, examining this and that. His throat got dryer and his heart began to grip him like a little ape clutching the bars of its cage. He sat down on the edge of her bed, with his hat in his hand.

Mrs. Watts's grin was as curved and sharp as the blade of a sickle. It was plain that she was so well-adjusted that she didn't have to think any more. Her eyes took everything in whole, like quicksand. "That Jesus-seeing hat!" she said. She sat up and pulled her nightgown from under her and took it off. She reached for his hat and put it on her head and sat with her hands on her hips, walling her eyes in a comical way. Haze stared for a minute, then he made three quick noises that were laughs. He jumped for the electric light cord and took off his clothes in the dark.

Once when he was small, his father took him to a carnival that stopped in Melsy. There was one tent that cost more money a little off to one side. A dried-up man with a horn voice was barking it. He didn't say what was inside. He said it was so SINsational that it would cost any man that wanted to see it thirty-five cents, and it was so EXclusive, only fifteen could get in at a time. His father sent him to a tent where two monkeys danced, and then he made for it, moving close to the walls of things like he moved. Haze left the monkeys and followed him, but he didn't have thirty-five cents. He asked the barker what was inside.

"Beat it," the man said. "There ain't no pop and there ain't no monkeys."

"I already seen them," he said.

"That's fine," the man said, "beat it."

"I got fifteen cents," he said. "Whyn't you lemme in and I could see half of it?" It's something about a privy, he was thinking. It's some men in a privy. Then he thought, maybe it's a man and a woman in a privy. She wouldn't want me in there. "I got fifteen cents," he said.

"It's more than half over," the man said, fanning with his straw hat. "You run along."

"That'll be fifteen cents worth then," Haze said.

"Scram," the man said.

"Is it a nigger?" Haze asked. "Are they doing something to a nigger?"

The man leaned off his platform and his dried-up face drew into a glare. "Where'd you get that idear?" he said.

"I don't know," Haze said.

"How old are you?" the man asked.

"Twelve," Haze said. He was ten.

"Gimme that fifteen cents," the man said, "and get in there."

He slid the money on the platform and scrambled to get in before it was over. He went through the flap of the tent and inside there was another tent and he went through that. All he could see were the backs of the men. He climbed up on a bench and looked over their heads. They were looking down into a lowered place where something white was lying, squirming a little, in a box lined with black cloth. For a second he thought it was a skinned animal and then he saw it was a woman. She was fat and she had a face like an ordinary woman except there was a mole on the corner of her lip, that moved when she grinned, and one on her side.

"Had one of themther built into ever' casket," his father, up toward the front, said, "be a heap ready to go sooner."

Haze recognized the voice without looking. He slid down off the bench and scrambled out of the tent. He crawled out under the side of the outside one because he didn't want to pass the barker. He got in the back of a truck and sat down in the far corner of it. The carnival was making a tin roar outside.

His mother was standing by the washpot in the yard, looking at him, when he got home. She wore black all the time and her dresses were longer than other women's. She was standing there straight, looking at him. He moved behind a tree and got out of her view, but in a few minutes, he could feel her watching him through the tree. He saw the lowered place and the casket again and a thin woman in the casket who was too long for it. Her head stuck up at one end and her knees were raised to make her fit. She had a cross-shaped face and hair pulled close to her head. He stood flat against the tree, waiting. She left the washpot and came toward him with a stick. She said, "What you seen?

"What you seen?" she said.

"What you seen," she said, using the same tone of voice all the time. She hit him across the legs with the stick, but he was like part of the tree. "Jesus died to redeem you," she said.

"I never ast him," he muttered.

She didn't hit him again but she stood looking at him, shut-mouthed, and he forgot the guilt of the tent for the nameless unplaced guilt that was in him. In a minute she threw the stick away from her and went back to the washpot, still shut-mouthed.

The next day he took his shoes in secret out into the woods. He didn't wear them except for revivals and in the winter. He took them out of the box and filled the bottoms of them with stones and small rocks and then he put them on. He laced them up tight and walked in them through the woods for what he knew to be a mile, until he came to a creek, and then he sat down and took them off and eased his feet in the wet sand. He thought, that ought to satisfy Him. Nothing happened. If a stone had fallen he would have taken it as a sign. After a while he drew his feet out of the sand and let them dry, and then he put the shoes on again with the rocks still in them and he walked a half-mile back before he took them off.

CHAPTER 4

He got out of Mrs. Watts's bed early in the morning before any light came in the room. When he woke up, her arm was flung across him. He leaned up and lifted it off and eased it down by her side, but he didn't look at her. There was only one thought in his mind: he was going to buy a car. The thought was full grown in his head when he woke up, and he didn't think of anything else. He had never thought before of buying a car; he had never even wanted one before. He had driven one only a little in his life and he didn't have any license. He had only fifty dollars but he thought he could buy a car for that. He got stealthily out the bed, without disturbing Mrs. Watts, and put his clothes on silently. By six-thirty, he was down town, looking for used-car lots.

Used-car lots were scattered among the blocks of old buildings that separated the business section from the railroad yards. He wandered around in a few of them before they were open. He could tell from the outside of the lot if it would have a fifty-dollar car in it. When they began to be open for business, he went through them quickly, paying no attention to anyone who tried to show him the stock. His black hat sat on his head with a careful, placed expression and his face had a fragile look as if it might have been broken and stuck together again, or like a gun no one knows is loaded.

It was a wet glary day. The sky was like a piece of thin polished silver with a dark sour-looking sun in one corner of it. By ten o'clock he had canvassed all the better lots and was nearing the railroad yards. Even here, the lots were full of cars that cost more than fifty dollars. Finally he came to one between two deserted warehouses. A sign over the entrance said: SLADE'S FOR THE LATEST.

There was a gravel road going down the middle of the lot and over to one side near the front, a tin shack with the word, OFFICE, painted on the door. The rest of the lot was full of old cars and broken machinery. A white boy was sitting on a gasoline can in front of the office. He had the look of being there to keep people out. He wore a black raincoat and his face was partly hidden under a leather cap. There was a cigarette hanging out of one corner of his mouth and the ash on it was about an inch long.

Haze started off toward the back of the lot where he saw a particular car. "Hey!" the boy yelled. "You don't just walk in here like that. I'll show you what I got to show," but Haze didn't pay any attention to him. He went on toward the back of the lot where he saw the car. The boy came huffing behind him, cursing. The car he saw was on the last row of cars. It was a high rat-colored machine with large thin wheels and bulging headlights. When he got up to it, he saw that one door was tied on with a rope and that it had an oval window in the back. This was the car he was going to buy.

"Lemme see Slade," he said.

"What you want to see him for?" the boy asked in a testy voice. He had a wide mouth and when he talked he used one side only of it.

"I want to see him about this car," Haze said.

"I'm him," the boy said. His face under the cap was like a thin picked eagle's. He sat down on the running board of a car across the gravel road and kept on cursing.

Haze walked around the car. Then he looked through the window at the inside of it. Inside it was a dull greenish dust-color. The back seat was missing but it had a two-by-four stretched across the seat frame to sit on. There were dark green fringed window shades on the two side-back windows. He looked through the two front windows and he saw the boy sitting on the running board of the car across the gravel road. He had one trouser leg hitched up and he was scratching his ankle that stuck up out of a pulp of yellow sock. He cursed far down in his throat as if he were trying to get up phlegm. The two window glasses made him a yellow color and distorted his shape. Haze moved quickly from the far side of the car and came around in front. "How much is it?" he asked.

"Jesus on the cross," the boy said. "Christ nailed."

"How much is it?" Haze growled, paling a little.

"How much do you think it's worth?" the boy said. "Give us a estimit."

"It ain't worth what it would take to cart it off. I wouldn't have it."

The boy gave all his attention to his ankle where there was a scab. Haze looked up and saw a man coming from between two cars over on the boy's side. As he came closer, he saw that the man looked exactly like the boy except that he was two heads taller and he had on a sweat-stained brown felt hat. He was coming up behind the boy, between a row of cars. When he got just behind him, he stopped and waited a second. Then he said in a sort of controlled roar, "Get your butt off that running board!"

The boy snarled and disappeared, scrambling between two cars.

The man stood looking at Haze. "What you want?" he asked.

"This car here," Haze said.

"Seventy-fi' dollars," the man said.

On either side of the lot there were two old buildings, reddish with black empty windows, and behind there was another without any windows. "I'm obliged," Haze said, and he started back toward the office.

When he got to the entrance, he glanced back and saw the man about four feet behind him. "We might argue it some," he said.

Haze followed him back to where the car was.

"You won't find a car like that ever' day," the man said. He sat down on the running board that the boy had been sitting on. Haze didn't see the boy but he was there, sitting up on the hood of a car two cars over. He was sitting huddled up as if he were freezing but his face had a sour composed look. "All new tires," the man said.

"They were new when it was built," Haze said.

"They was better cars built a few years ago," the man said. "They don't make no more good cars."

"What you want for it?" Haze asked again.

The man stared off, thinking. After a while he said, "I might could let you have it for sixty-fi'."

Haze leaned against the car and started to roll a cigarette but he couldn't get it rolled. He kept spilling the tobacco and then the papers.

"Well, what you want to pay for it?" the man asked. "I wouldn't trade me a Chrysler for a Essex like that. That car yonder ain't been built by a bunch of niggers.

"All the niggers are living in Detroit now, putting cars together," he said, making conversation. "I was up there a while myself and I seen. I come home."

"I wouldn't pay over thirty dollars for it," Haze said.

"They got one nigger up there," the man said, "is almost as light as you or me." He took off his hat and ran his finger around the sweat band inside it. He had a little bit of carrot-colored hair.

"We'll drive it around," the man said, "or would you like to get under and look up it?"

"No," Haze said.

The man gave him a half look. "You pay when you leave," he said easily. "You don't find what you looking for in one there's others for the same price obliged to have it." Two cars over the boy began to curse again. It was like a hacking cough. Haze turned suddenly and kicked his foot into the front tire. "I done tole you them tires won't bust," the man said.

"How much?" Haze said.

"I might could make it fifty dollar," the man offered.

Before Haze bought the car, the man put some gas in it and drove him around a few blocks to prove it would run. The boy sat hunched up in the back on the two-by-four, cursing. "Something's wrong with him howcome he curses so much," the man said. "Just don't listen at him." The car rode with a high growling noise. The man put on the brakes to show how well they worked and the boy was thrown off the two-by-four at their heads. "Goddam you," the man roared, "quit jumping at us thataway. Keep your butt on the board." The boy didn't say anything. He didn't even curse. Haze looked back and he was sitting huddled up in the black raincoat with the black leather cap pulled down almost to his eyes. The only thing different was that the ash had been knocked off his cigarette.

He bought the car for forty dollars and then he paid the man extra for five gallons of gasoline. The man had the boy go in the office and bring out a five-gallon can of gas to fill up the tank with. The boy came cursing and lugging the yellow gas can, bent over almost double. "Give it here," Haze said, "I'll do it myself." He was in a terrible hurry to get away in the car. The boy jerked the can away from him and straightened up. It was only half full but he held it over the tank until five gallons would have spilled out slowly. All the time he kept saying, "Sweet Jesus, sweet Jesus, sweet Jesus."

"Why don't he shut up?" Haze said suddenly. "What's he keep talking like that for?"

"I don't never know what ails him," the man said and shrugged.

When the car was ready the man and the boy stood by to watch him drive it off. He didn't want anybody watching him because he hadn't driven a car in four or five years. The man and the boy didn't say anything while he tried to start it. They only stood there, looking in at him. "I wanted this car mostly to be a house for me," he said to the man. "I ain't got any place to be."

"You ain't took the brake off yet," the man said.

He took off the brake and the car shot backward because

the man had left it in reverse. In a second he got it going forward and he drove off crookedly, past the man and the boy still standing there watching. He kept going forward, thinking nothing and sweating. For a long time he stayed on the street he was on. He had a hard time holding the car in the road. He went past railroad yards for about a half-mile and then warehouses. When he tried to slow the car down, it stopped altogether and then he had to start it again. He went past long blocks of gray houses and then blocks of better, yellow houses. It began to drizzle rain and he turned on the windshield wipers; they made a great clatter like two idiots clapping in church. He went past blocks of white houses, each sitting with an ugly dog face on a square of grass. Finally he went over a viaduct and found the highway.

He began going very fast.

The highway was ragged with filling stations and trailer camps and roadhouses. After a while there were stretches where red gulleys dropped off on either side of the road and behind them there were patches of field buttoned together with 666 posts. The sky leaked over all of it and then it began to leak into the car. The head of a string of pigs appeared snout-up over the ditch and he had to screech to a stop and watch the rear of the last pig disappear shaking into the ditch on the other side. He started the car again and went on. He had the feeling that everything he saw was a broken-off piece of some giant blank thing that he had forgotten had happened to him. A black pick-up truck turned off a side road in front of him. On the back of it an iron bed and a chair and table were tied, and on top of them, a crate of barred-rock chickens. The truck went very slowly, with a rumbling sound, and in the middle of the road. Haze started pounding his horn and he had hit it three times before he realized it didn't make any sound. The crate was stuffed so full of wet barred-rock chickens that the ones facing him had their heads outside the bars. The truck didn't go any faster and he was forced to drive slowly. The fields stretched sodden on either side until they hit the scrub pines.

The road turned and went down hill and a high embankment appeared on one side with pines standing on it, facing a gray boulder that jutted out of the opposite gulley wall. White letters on the boulder said, WOE TO THE BLASPHEMER AND WHOREMONGER! WILL HELL SWALLOW YOU UP? The pick-up truck slowed even more as if it were reading the sign and Haze pounded his empty horn. He beat on it and beat on it but it didn't make any sound.

The pick-up truck went on, bumping the glum barred-rock chickens over the edge of the next hill. Haze's car was stopped and his eyes were turned toward the two words at the bottom of the sign. They said in smaller letters, "Jesus Saves."

He sat looking at the sign and he didn't hear the horn. An oil truck as long as a railroad car was behind him. In a second a red square face was at his car window. It watched the back of his neck and hat for a minute and then a hand came in and sat on his shoulder. "What you doing parked in the middle of the road?" the truck driver asked.

Haze turned his fragile placid-looking face toward him. "Take your hand off me," he said. "I'm reading the sign."

The driver's expression and his hand stayed exactly the way they were, as if he didn't hear very well.

"There's no person a whoremonger, who wasn't something worse first," Haze said. "That's not the sin, nor blasphemy. The sin came before them."

The truck driver's face remained exactly the same.

"Jesus is a trick on niggers," Haze said.

The driver put both his hands on the window and gripped it. He looked as if he intended to pick up the car. "Will you get your goddam outhouse off the middle of the road?" he said.

"I don't have to run from anything because I don't believe in anything," Haze said. He and the driver looked at each other for about a minute. Haze's look was the more distant; another plan was forming in his mind. "Which direction is the zoo in?" he asked.

"Back around the other way," the driver said. "Did you exscape from there?"

"I got to see a boy that works in it," Haze said. He started the car up and left the driver standing there, in front of the letters painted on the boulder.

CHAPTER 5

That morning Enoch Emery knew when he woke up that today the person he could show it to was going to come. He knew by his blood. He had wise blood like his daddy.

At two o'clock that afternoon, he greeted the second-shift gate guard. "You ain't but only fifteen minutes late," he said irritably. "But I stayed. I could of went on but I stayed." He wore a green uniform with yellow piping on the neck and sleeves and a yellow stripe down the outside of each leg. The second-shift guard, a boy with a jutting shale-textured face and a toothpick in his mouth, wore the same. The gate they were standing by was made of iron bars and the concrete arch that held it was fashioned to look like two trees; branches curved to form the top of it where twisted letters said, CITY FOREST PARK. The second-shift guard leaned against one of the trunks and began prodding between his teeth with the pick.

"Ever' day," Enoch complained; "look like ever' day I lose fifteen good minutes standing here waiting for you."

Every day when he got off duty, he went into the park, and every day when he went in, he did the same things. He went first to the swimming pool. He was afraid of the water but he liked to sit up on the bank above it if there were any women in the pool, and watch them. There was one woman who came every Monday who wore a bathing suit that was split on each hip. At first he thought she didn't know it, and instead of watching openly on the bank, he had crawled into some bushes, snickering to himself, and had watched from there. There had been no one else in the pool—the crowds didn't come until four o'clock—to tell her about the splits and she had splashed around in the water and then lain up on the edge of the pool asleep for almost an hour, all the time without suspecting there was somebody in the bushes looking at her. Then on another day when he stayed a little later, he saw three women, all with their suits split, the pool full of people, and nobody paying them any mind. That was how the city was—always surprising him. He visited a whore when he felt like it but he was always being shocked by the looseness he saw in the open. He crawled into the bushes out of

46

a sense of propriety. Very often the women would pull the suit straps down off their shoulders and lie stretched out.

The park was the heart of the city. He had come to the city and—with a knowing in his blood—he had established himself at the heart of it. Every day he looked at the heart of it; every day; and he was so stunned and awed and overwhelmed that just to think about it made him sweat. There was something, in the center of the park, that he had discovered. It was a mystery, although it was right there in a glass case for everybody to see and there was a typewritten card over it telling all about it. But there was something the card couldn't say and what it couldn't say was inside him, a terrible knowledge without any words to it, a terrible knowledge like a big nerve growing inside him. He could not show the mystery to just anybody; but he had to show it to somebody. Who he had to show it to was a special person. This person could not be from the city but he didn't know why. He knew he would know him when he saw him and he knew that he would have to see him soon or the nerve inside him would grow so big that he would be forced to steal a car or rob a bank or jump out of a dark alley onto a woman. His blood all morning had been saying the person would come today.

He left the second-shift guard and approached the pool from a discreet footpath that led behind the ladies' end of the bath house to a small clearing where the entire pool could be seen at once. There was nobody in it—the water was bottle-green and motionless—but he saw, coming up the other side and heading for the bath house, the woman with the two little boys. She came every other day or so and brought the two children. She would go in the water with them and swim down the pool and then she would lie up on the side in the sun. She had a stained white bathing suit that fit her like a sack, and Enoch had watched her with pleasure on several occasions. He moved from the clearing up a slope to some abelia bushes. There was a nice tunnel under them and he crawled into it until he came to a slightly wider place where he was accustomed to sit. He settled himself and adjusted the abelia so that he could see through it properly. His face was always very red in the bushes. Anyone who parted the abelia sprigs at just that place, would think he saw a devil and would fall down the slope and into the pool. The woman and the two little boys entered the bath house.

Enoch never went immediately to the dark secret center of the park. That was the peak of the afternoon. The other things he did built up to it. When he left the bushes, he would go to the FROSTY BOTTLE, a hotdog stand in the shape of an Orange Crush with frost painted in blue around the top of it. Here he would have a chocolate malted milkshake and would make some suggestive remarks to the waitress, whom he believed to be secretly in love with him. After that he would go to see the animals. They were in a long set of steel cages like Alcatraz Penitentiary in the movies. The cages were electrically heated in the winter and air-conditioned in the summer and there were six men hired to wait on the animals and feed them T-bone steaks. The animals didn't do anything but lie around. Enoch watched them every day, full of awe and hate. Then he went *there*.

The two little boys ran out of the bath house and dived into the water, and simultaneously a grating noise issued from the driveway on the other side of the pool. Enoch's head pierced out of the bushes. He saw a high rat-colored car passing, which sounded as if its motor were dragging out the back. The car passed and he could hear it rattle around the turn in the drive and on away. He listened carefully, trying to hear if it would stop. The noise receded and then gradually grew louder. The car passed again. Enoch saw this time that there was only one person in it, a man. The sound of it died away again and then grew louder. The car came around a third time and stopped almost directly opposite Enoch across the pool. The man in the car looked out the window and down the grass slope to the water where the two little boys were splashing and screaming. Enoch's head was as far out of the bushes as it would come and he was squinting. The door by the man was tied on with a rope. The man got out the other door and walked in front of the car and came halfway down the slope to the pool. He stood there a minute as if he were looking for somebody and then he sat down stiffly on the grass. He had on a blue suit and a black hat. He sat with his knees drawn up. "Well, I'll be dog," Enoch said. "Well, I'll be dog."

He began crawling out of the bushes immediately, his heart moving so fast it was like one of those motorcycles at fairs that the fellow drives around the walls of a pit. He even remembered the man's name—Mr. Hazel Motes. In a second he appeared on all fours at the end of the abelia and looked across the pool. The blue figure was still sitting there in the same position. He had the look of being held there, as if by an invisible hand, as if, if the hand lifted up, the figure would spring across the pool in one leap without the expression on his face changing once.

The woman came out of the bath house and went to the diving board. She spread her arms out and began to bounce, making a big flapping sound with the board. Then suddenly she swirled backward and disappeared below the water. Mr. Hazel Motes's head turned very slowly, following her down the pool.

Enoch got up and went down the path behind the bath house. He came stealthily out on the other side and started walking toward Haze. He stayed on the top of the slope, moving softly in the grass just off the sidewalk, and making no noise. When he was directly behind him, he sat down on the edge of the sidewalk. If his arms had been ten feet long, he could have put his hands on Haze's shoulders. He studied him quietly.

The woman was climbing out of the pool, chinning herself up on the side. First her face appeared, long and cadaverous, with a bandage-like bathing cap coming down almost to her eyes, and sharp teeth protruding from her mouth. Then she rose on her hands until a large foot and leg came up from behind her and another on the other side and she was out, squatting there, panting. She stood up loosely and shook herself, and stamped in the water dripping off her. She was facing them and she grinned. Enoch could see part of Hazel Motes's face watching the woman. It didn't grin in return but it kept on watching her as she padded over to a spot of sun almost directly under where they were sitting. Enoch had to move a little closer to see.

The woman sat down in the spot of sun and took off her bathing cap. Her hair was short and matted and all colors, from deep rust to a greenish yellow. She shook her head and then she looked up at Hazel Motes again, grinning through her pointed teeth. She stretched herself out in the spot of sun, raising her knees and settling her backbone down against the concrete. The two little boys, at the other end of the water, were knocking each other's heads against the side of the pool. She settled herself until she was flat against the concrete and then she reached up and pulled the bathing suit straps off her shoulders.

"King Jesus!" Enoch whispered and before he could get his eyes off the woman, Hazel Motes had sprung up and was almost to his car. The woman was sitting straight up with the suit half off her in front, and Enoch was looking both ways at once.

He wrenched his attention loose from the woman and

darted after Hazel Motes. "Wait on me!" he shouted and waved his arms in front of the car which was already rattling and starting to go. Hazel Motes cut off the motor. His face behind the windshield was sour and frog-like; it looked as if it had a shout closed up in it; it looked like one of those closet doors in gangster pictures where someone is tied to a chair behind it with a towel in his mouth.

"Well," Enoch said, "I declare if it ain't Hazel Motes. How are you, Hazel?"

"The guard said I'd find you at the swimming pool," Hazel Motes said. "He said you hid in the bushes and watched the swimming."

Enoch blushed. "I allus have admired swimming," he said. Then he stuck his head farther through the window. "You were looking for me?" he exclaimed.

"That blind man," Haze said, "that blind man named Hawks—did his child tell you where they lived?"

Enoch didn't seem to hear. "You came out here special to see me?" he said.

"Asa Hawks. His child gave you the peeler. Did she tell you where they lived?"

Enoch eased his head out of the car. He opened the door and climbed in beside Haze. For a minute he only looked at him, wetting his lips. Then he whispered, "I got to show you something."

"I'm looking for those people," Haze said. "I got to see that man. Did she tell you where they lived?"

"I got to show you this thing," Enoch said. "I got to show it to you, here, this afternoon. I got to." He gripped Hazel Motes's arm and Haze shook him off.

"Did she tell you where they live?" he said again.

Enoch kept wetting his lips. They were pale except for his fever blister, which was purple. "Cert'nly," he said. "Ain't she invited me to come to see her and bring my mouth organ? I got to show you this thing, then I'll tell you."

"What thing?" Haze muttered.

"This thing I got to show you," Enoch said. "Drive straight on ahead and I'll tell you where to stop."

"I don't want to see anything of yours," Haze Motes said. "I want that address."

Enoch didn't look at Hazel Motes. He looked out the window. "I won't be able to remember it unless you come," he said. In a minute the car started. Enoch's blood was beating fast. He knew he had to go to the FROSTY BOTTLE and the zoo before there, and he foresaw a terrible struggle with Hazel Motes. He would have to get him there, even if he had to hit him over the head with a rock and carry him on his back up to it.

Enoch's brain was divided into two parts. The part in communication with his blood did the figuring but it never said anything in words. The other part was stocked up with all kinds of words and phrases. While the first part was figuring how to get Hazel Motes through the FROSTY BOTTLE and the zoo, the second inquired, "Where'd you get thisyer fine car? You ought to paint you some signs on the outside it, like 'Step-in, baby'—I seen one with that on it, then I seen another, said . . ."

Hazel Motes's face might have been cut out of the side of a rock.

"My daddy once owned a yeller Ford automobile he won on a ticket," Enoch murmured. "It had a roll-top and two aerials and a squirrel tail all come with it. He swapped it off. Stop here! Stop here!" he yelled—they were passing the FROSTY BOTTLE.

"Where is it?" Hazel Motes said as soon as they were inside. They were in a dark room with a counter across the back of it and brown stools like toad stools in front of the counter. On the wall facing the door there was a large advertisement for ice cream, showing a cow dressed up like a housewife.

"It ain't here," Enoch said. "We have to stop here on the way and get something to eat. What you want?"

"Nothing," Haze said. He stood stiffly in the middle of the room with his hands in his pockets.

"Well, sit down," Enoch said. "I have to have a little drink."

Something stirred behind the counter and a woman with bobbed hair like a man's got up from a chair where she had been reading the newspaper, and came forward. She looked sourly at Enoch. She had on a once-white uniform clotted with brown stains. "What you want?" she said in a loud voice, leaning close to his ear. She had a man's face and big muscled arms.

"I want a chocolate malted milkshake, baby girl," Enoch said softly. "I want a lot of ice cream in it."

She turned fiercely from him and glared at Haze.

"He says he don't want nothing but to sit down and look at you for a while," Enoch said. "He ain't hungry but for just to see you."

Haze looked woodenly at the woman and she turned her back on him and began mixing the milkshake. He sat down on the last stool in the row and started cracking his knuckles.

Enoch watched him carefully. "I reckon you done changed some," he said after a few minutes.

Haze got up. "Give me those people's address. Right now," he said.

It came to Enoch in an instant—the police. His face was suddenly suffused with secret knowledge. "I reckon you ain't as uppity as you was last night," he said. "I reckon maybe," he said, "you ain't got so much cause now as you had then." Stole theter automobile, he thought.

Hazel Motes sat back down.

"Howcome you jumped up so fast down yonder by the pool?" Enoch asked. The woman turned around to him with the malted milk in her hand. "Of course," he said evilly, "I wouldn't have had no truck with a ugly dish like that neither."

The woman thumped the malted milk on the counter in front of him. "Fifteen cents," she roared.

"You're worth more than that, baby girl," Enoch said. He snickered and began gassing his malted milk through the straw.

The woman strode over to where Haze was. "What you come in here with a son of a bitch like that for?" she shouted. "A nice quiet boy like you to come in here with a son of a bitch. You ought to mind the company you keep." Her name was Maude and she drank whisky all day from a fruit jar under the counter. "Jesus," she said, wiping her hand under her nose. She sat down in a straight chair in front of Haze but facing Enoch, and folded her arms across her chest. "Ever' day," she said to Haze, looking at Enoch, "ever' day that son of a bitch comes in here."

Enoch was thinking about the animals. They had to go next to see the animals. He hated them; just thinking about them made his face turn a chocolate purple color as if the malted milk were rising in his head.

"You're a nice boy," she said. "I can see, you got a clean nose, well keep it clean, don't go messin' with a son a bitch like that yonder. I always know a clean boy when I see one." She was shouting at Enoch, but Enoch watched Hazel Motes. It was as if something inside Hazel Motes was winding up, although he didn't move on the outside. He only looked pressed down in that blue suit, as if inside it, the thing winding was getting tighter and tighter. Enoch's blood told him to hurry. He raced the milkshake up the straw.

"Yes sir," she said, "there ain't anything sweeter than a clean boy. God for my witness. And I know a clean one when I see him and I know a son a bitch when I see him and there's a heap of difference and that pus-marked bastard zlurping through that straw is a goddamned son a bitch and you a clean boy had better mind how you keep him company. I know a clean boy when I see one."

Enoch screeched in the bottom of his glass. He fished fifteen cents from his pocket and laid it on the counter and got up. But Hazel Motes was already up; he was leaning over the counter toward the woman. She didn't see him right away because she was looking at Enoch. He leaned on his hands over the counter until his face was just a foot from hers. She turned around and stared at him.

"Come on," Enoch started, "we don't have no time to be sassing around with her. I got to show you this right away, I got . . ."

"I AM clean," Haze said.

It was not until he said it again that Enoch caught the words.

"I AM clean," he said again, without any expression on his face or in his voice, just looking at the woman as if he were looking at a wall. "If Jesus existed, I wouldn't be clean," he said.

She stared at him, startled and then outraged. "What do you think I care!" she yelled. "Why should I give a goddam what you are!"

"Come on," Enoch whined, "come on or I won't tell you where them people live." He caught Haze's arm and pulled him back from the counter and toward the door.

"You bastard!" the woman screamed, "what do you think I care about any of you filthy boys?"

Hazel Motes pushed the door open quickly and went out. He got back in his car and Enoch climbed in behind him. "Okay," Enoch said, "drive straight on ahead down this road."

"What you want for telling me?" Haze said. "I'm not staying here. I have to go. I can't stay here any longer."

Enoch shuddered. He began wetting his lips. "I got to show it to you," he said hoarsely. "I can't show it to nobody but you. I had a sign it was you when I seen you drive up at the pool. I knew all morning somebody was going to come and then when I saw you at the pool, I had thisyer sign."

"I don't care about your signs," Haze said.

"I go to see it ever' day," Enoch said. "I go ever' day but I ain't ever been able to take nobody else with me. I had to wait on the sign. I'll tell you them people's address just as soon as you see it. You got to see it," he said. "When you see it, something's going to happen."

"Nothing's going to happen," Haze said.

He started the car again and Enoch sat forward on the seat. "Them animals," he muttered. "We got to walk by them first. It won't take long for that. It won't take a minute." He saw the animals waiting evil-eyed for him, ready to throw him off time. He thought, what if the police were screaming out here now with sirens and squad cars and they got Hazel Motes just before he showed it to him.

"I got to see those people," Haze said.

"Stop here! Stop here!" Enoch yelled.

There was a long shining row of steel cages over to the left and behind the bars, black shapes were sitting or pacing. "Get out," Enoch said. "This won't take one second."

Haze got out. Then he stopped. "I got to see those people," he said.

"Okay, okay, come on," Enoch whined.

"I don't believe you know the address."

"I do! I do!" Enoch cried. "It begins with a three, now come on!" He pulled Haze toward the cages. Two black bears sat in the first one, facing each other like two matrons having tea, their faces polite and self-absorbed. "They don't do nothing but sit there all day and stink," Enoch said. "A man comes and washes them cages out ever' morning with a hose and it stinks just as much as if he'd left it." He went past two more cages of bears, not looking at them, and then he stopped at the next cage where there were two yellow-eyed wolves nosing around the edges of the concrete. "Hyenas," he said. "I ain't got no use for hyenas." He leaned closer and spit into the cage, hitting one of the wolves on the leg. It shuttled to the side, giving him a slanted evil look. For a second he forgot Hazel Motes. Then he looked back quickly to make sure he was still there. He was right behind him. He was not looking at the animals. Thinking about them police, Enoch thought. He said, "Come on, we don't have time to look at all theseyer monkeys that come next." Usually he stopped at every cage and made an obscene comment aloud to himself, but today the animals were only a form he had to get through. He hurried past the cages of monkeys, looking back two or three times to make sure Hazel Motes was behind him. At the last of the monkey cages, he stopped as if he couldn't help himself.

"Look at that ape," he said, glaring. The animal had its back to him, gray except for a small pink seat. "If I had a ass like that," he said prudishly, "I'd sit on it. I wouldn't be exposing it to all these people come to this park. Come on, we don't have to look at theseyer birds that come next." He ran past the cages of birds and then he was at the end of the zoo. "Now we don't need the car," he said, going on ahead, "we'll go right down that hill yonder through them trees." Haze had stopped at the last cage for birds. "Oh Jesus," Enoch groaned. He stood and waved his arms wildly and shouted, "Come on!" but Haze didn't move from where he was looking into the cage.

Enoch ran back to him and grabbed him by the arm but Haze pushed him off and kept on looking in the cage. It was empty. Enoch stared. "It's empty!" he shouted. "What you have to look in that ole empty cage for? You come on!" He stood there, sweating and purple. "It's empty!" he shouted. And then he saw it wasn't empty. Over in one corner on the floor of the cage, there was an eye. The eye was in the middle of something that looked like a piece of mop sitting on an old rag. He squinted close to the wire and saw that the piece of mop was an owl with one eye open. It was looking directly at Hazel Motes. "That ain't nothing but a ole hoot owl," he moaned. "You seen them things before."

"I AM clean," Haze said to the eye. He said it just the way he said it to the woman in the FROSTY BOTTLE. The eye shut softly and the owl turned its face to the wall.

He's done murdered somebody, Enoch thought. "Oh sweet Jesus, come on!" he wailed. "I got to show you this right now." He pulled him away but a few feet from the cage, Haze stopped again, looking at something in the distance. Enoch's eyesight was very poor. He squinted and made out a figure far down the road behind them. There were two smaller figures jumping on either side of it.

Hazel Motes turned back to him suddenly and said, "Where's this thing? Let's see it right now and get it over with. Come on."

"Ain't that where I been trying to take you?" Enoch said. He felt the perspiration drying on him and stinging and his skin was pin-pointed, even in his scalp. "We got to cross this road and go down this hill. We got to go on foot," he said.

"Why?" Haze muttered.

"I don't know," Enoch said. He knew something was going to happen to him. His blood stopped beating. All the time it had been beating like drum noises and now it had stopped. They started down the hill. It was a steep hill, full of trees painted white from the ground up four feet. They looked as if they had on ankle-socks. He gripped

Hazel Motes's arm. "It gets damp as you go down," he said, looking around vaguely. Hazel Motes shook him off. In a second, Enoch gripped his arm again and stopped him. He pointed down through the trees. "Muvseevum," he said. The strange word made him shiver. That was the first time he had ever said it aloud. A piece of gray building was showing where he pointed. It grew larger as they went down the hill, then as they came to the end of the wood and stepped out on the gravel driveway, it seemed to shrink suddenly. It was round and soot-colored. There were columns at the front of it and in between each column there was an eyeless stone woman holding a pot on her head. A concrete band was over the columns and the letters, M V S E V M, were cut into it. Enoch was afraid to pronounce the word again.

"We got to go up the steps and through the front door," he whispered. There were ten steps up to the porch. The door was wide and black. Enoch pushed it in cautiously and inserted his head in the crack. In a minute he brought it out again and said, "All right, go on in and walk easy. I don't want to wake up theter ole guard. He ain't very friendly with me." They went into a dark hall. It was heavy with the odor of linoleum and creosote and another odor behind these two. The third one was an undersmell and Enoch couldn't name it as anything he had ever smelled before. There was nothing in the hall but two urns and an old man asleep in a straight chair against the wall. He had on the same kind of uniform as Enoch and he looked like a dried-up spider stuck there. Enoch looked at Hazel Motes to see if he was smelling the undersmell. He looked as if he were. Enoch's blood began to beat again, urging him forward. He gripped Haze's arm and tiptoed through the hall to another black door at the end of it. He cracked it a little and inserted his head in the crack. Then in a second he drew it out and crooked his finger in a gesture for Haze to follow him. They went into another hall, like the last one, but running crosswise. "It's in that first door yonder," Enoch said in a small voice. They went into a dark room full of glass cases. The glass cases covered the walls and there were three coffin-like ones in the middle of the floor. The ones on the walls were full of birds tilted on varnished sticks and looking down with dried piquant expressions.

"Come on," Enoch whispered. He went past the two cases in the middle of the floor and toward the third one. He went to the farthest end of it and stopped. He stood

looking down with his neck thrust forward and his hands
clutched together; Hazel Motes moved up beside him.

The two of them stood there, Enoch rigid and Hazel
Motes bent slightly forward. There were three bowls and
a row of blunt weapons and a man in the case. It was the
man Enoch was looking at. He was about three feet long.
He was naked and a dried yellow color and his eyes were
drawn almost shut as if a giant block of steel were falling
down on top of him.

"See theter notice," Enoch said in a church whisper, pointing
to a typewritten card at the man's foot, "it says he was
once as tall as you or me. Some A-rabs did it to him in
six months." He turned his head cautiously to see Hazel
Motes.

All he could tell was that Hazel Motes's eyes were on
the shrunken man. He was bent forward so that his face
was reflected on the glass top of the case. The reflection
was pale and the eyes were like two clean bullet holes.
Enoch waited, rigid. He heard footsteps in the hall. Oh
Jesus Jesus, he prayed, let him hurry up and do whatever
he's going to do! The woman with the two little boys came
in the door. She had one by each hand, and she was grinning.
Hazel Motes had not raised his eyes once from the shrunken
man. The woman came toward them. She stopped on the
other side of the case and looked down into it and the
reflection of her face appeared grinning on the glass,
over Hazel Motes's.

She snickered and put two fingers in front of her teeth.
The little boys' faces were like pans set on either side
to catch the grins that overflowed from her. When Haze
saw her face on the glass, his neck jerked back and he
made a noise. It might have come from the man inside
the case. In a second Enoch knew it had. "Wait!" he screamed,
and tore out of the room after Hazel Motes.

He overtook him halfway up the hill. He caught him
by the arm and swung him around and then he stood there,
suddenly weak and light as a balloon, and stared. Hazel
Motes grabbed him by the shoulders and shook him. "What
is that address!" he shouted. "Give me that address!"

Even if Enoch had been sure what the address was,
he couldn't have thought of it then. He could not even
stand up. As soon as Hazel Motes let him go, he fell
backward and landed against one of the white-socked trees.
He rolled over and lay stretched out on the ground, with
an exalted look on his face. He thought he was floating.
A long way off he saw the blue figure spring and pick

up a rock, and he saw the wild face turn, and the rock hurtle toward him; he shut his eyes tight and the rock hit him on the forehead.

When he came to again, Hazel Motes was gone. He lay there a minute. He put his fingers to his forehead and then held them in front of his eyes. They were streaked with red. He turned his head and saw a drop of blood on the ground and as he looked at it, he thought it widened like a little spring. He sat straight up, frozen-skinned, and put his finger in it, and very faintly he could hear his blood beating, his secret blood, in the center of the city.

Then he knew that whatever was expected of him was only just beginning.

CHAPTER 6

That evening Haze drove his car around the streets until he found the blind man and the child again. They were standing on a corner, waiting for the light to change. He drove the Essex at some distance behind them for about four blocks up the main street and then turned it after them down a side street. He followed them on into a dark section past the railroad yards and watched them go up on the porch of a box-like two-story house. When the blind man opened the door a shaft of light fell on him and Haze craned his neck to see him better. The child turned her head, slowly, as if it worked on a screw, and watched his car pass. His face was so close to the glass that it looked like a paper face pasted there. He noted the number of the house and a sign on it that said, ROOMS FOR RENT.

Then he drove back down town and parked the Essex in front of a movie house where he could catch the drain of people coming out from the picture show. The lights around the marquee were so bright that the moon, moving overhead with a small procession of clouds behind it, looked pale and insignificant. Haze got out of the Essex and climbed up on the nose of it.

A thin little man with a long upper lip was at the glass ticket box, buying tickets for three portly women who were behind him. "Gotta get these girls some refreshments too," he said to the woman in the ticket box. "Can't have 'em starve right before my eyes."

"Ain't he a card?" one of the women hollered. "He keeps me in stitches!"

Three boys in red satin lumberjackets came out of the foyer. Haze raised his arms. "Where has the blood you think you been redeemed by touched you?" he cried.

The women all turned around at once and stared at him.

"A wise guy," the little thin man said, and glared as if someone were about to insult him.

The three boys moved up, pushing each other's shoulders.

Haze waited a second and then he cried again. "Where has the blood you think you been redeemed by touched you?"

"Rabble rouser," the little man said. "One thing I can't stand it's a rabble rouser."

"What church you belong to, you boy there?" Haze asked, pointing at the tallest boy in the red satin lumberjacket.

The boy giggled.

"You then," he said impatiently, pointing at the next one. "What church you belong to?"

"Church of Christ," the boy said in a falsetto to hide the truth.

"Church of Christ!" Haze repeated. "Well, I preach the Church Without Christ. I'm member and preacher to that church where the blind don't see and the lame don't walk and what's dead stays that way. Ask me about that church and I'll tell you it's the church that the blood of Jesus don't foul with redemption."

"He's a preacher," one of the women said. "Let's go."

"Listen, you people, I'm going to take the truth with me wherever I go," Haze called. "I'm going to preach it to whoever'll listen at whatever place. I'm going to preach there was no Fall because there was nothing to fall from and no Redemption because there was no Fall and no Judgment because there wasn't the first two. Nothing matters but that Jesus was a liar."

The little man herded his girls into the picture show quickly and the three boys left but more people came out and he began over and said the same thing again. They left and some more came and he said it a third time. Then they left and no one else came out; there was no one there but the woman in the glass box. She had been glaring at him all the time but he had not noticed her. She wore glasses with rhinestones in the bows and she had white hair stacked in sausages around her head. She stuck her mouth to a hole in the glass and shouted, "Listen, if you don't have a church to do it in, you don't have to do it in front of this show."

"My church is the Church Without Christ, lady," he said. "If there's no Christ, there's no reason to have a set place to do it in."

"Listen," she said, "if you don't get from in front of this show, I'll call the police."

"There's plenty of shows," he said and got down and got back in the Essex and drove off. That night he preached in front of three other picture shows before he went to Mrs. Watts.

In the morning he drove back to the house where the blind man and the child had gone in the night before. It was yellow clapboard, the second one in a block of them, all alike. He went up to the front door and rang the bell.

After a few minutes a woman with a mop opened it. He said he wanted to rent a room.

"What you do?" she asked. She was a tall bony woman, resembling the mop she carried upside-down.

He said he was a preacher.

The woman looked at him thoroughly and then she looked behind him at his car. "What church?" she asked.

He said the Church Without Christ.

"Protestant?" she asked suspiciously, "or something foreign?"

He said no mam, it was Protestant.

After a minute she said, "Well, you can look at it," and he followed her into a white plastered hall and up some steps at the side of it. She opened a door into a back room that was a little larger than his car, with a cot and a chest of drawers and a table and straight chair in it. There were two nails on the wall to hang clothes on. "Three dollars a week in advance," she said. There was one window and another door opposite the door they had come in by. Haze opened the extra door, expecting it to be a closet. It opened out onto a drop of about thirty feet and looked down into a narrow bare back yard where the garbage was collected. There was a plank nailed across the door frame at knee level to keep anyone from falling out. "A man named Hawks lives here, don't he?" Haze asked quickly.

"Downstairs in the front room," she said, "him and his child." She was looking down into the drop too. "It used to be a fire-escape there," she said, "but I don't know what happened to it."

He paid her three dollars and took possession of the room, and as soon as she was out of the way, he went down the stairs and knocked on the Hawkses' door.

The blind man's child opened it a crack and stood looking at him. She seemed at once to have to balance her face so that her expression would be the same on both sides. "It's that boy, Papa," she said in a low tone. "The one that keeps following me." She held the door close to her head so he couldn't see in past her. The blind man came to the door but he didn't open it any wider. His look was not the same as it had been two nights before; it was sour and unfriendly, and he didn't speak, he only stood there.

Haze had got what he had to say in mind before he left his room. "I live here," he said. "I thought if your girl wanted to give me so much eye, I might return her some of it." He wasn't looking at the girl; he was staring at the black glasses and the curious scars that started somewhere behind them and ran down the blind man's cheeks.

"What I give you the other night," she said, "was a

looker indignation for what I seen you do. It was you give me the eye. You should have seen him, Papa," she said, "looked me up and down."

"I've started my own church," Haze said. "The Church Without Christ. I preach on the street."

"You can't let me alone, can you?" Hawks said. His voice was flat, nothing like it had been the other time. "I didn't ask you to come here and I ain't asking you to hang around," he said.

Haze had expected a secret welcome. He waited, trying to think of something to say. "What kind of a preacher are you?" he heard himself murmur, "not to see if you can save my soul?" The blind man pushed the door shut in his face. Haze stood there a second facing the blank door, and then he ran his sleeve across his mouth and went out.

Inside, Hawks took off his dark glasses and, from a hole in the window shade, watched him get in his car and drive off. The eye he put to the hole was slightly rounder and smaller than his other one, but it was obvious he could see out of both of them. The child watched from a lower crack. "Howcome you don't like him, Papa?" she asked, "—because he's after me?"

"If he was after you, that would be enough to make me welcome him," he said.

"I like his eyes," she observed. "They don't look like they see what he's looking at but they keep on looking."

Their room was the same size as Haze's but there were two cots and an oil cooking stove and a wash basin in it and a trunk that they used for a table. Hawks sat down on one of the cots and put a cigarette in his mouth. "Goddam Jesus-hog," he muttered.

"Well, look what you used to be," she said. "Look what you tried to do. You got over it and so will he."

"I don't want him hanging around," he said. "He makes me nervous."

"Listen here," she said, sitting down on the cot with him, "you help me to get him and then you go away and do what you please and I can live with him."

"He don't even know you exist," Hawks said.

"Even if he don't," she said, "that's all right. That's howcome I can get him easy. I want him and you ought to help and then you could go on off like you want to."

He lay down on the cot and finished the cigarette; his face was thoughtful and evil. Once while he was lying there, he laughed and then his expression constricted again. "Well, that might be fine," he said after a while. "That might be the oil on Aaron's beard."

"Listen here," she said, "it would be the nuts! I'm just crazy about him. I never seen a boy that I liked the looks of any better. Don't run him off. Tell him how you blinded yourself for Jesus and show him that clipping you got."

"Yeah, the clipping," he said.

Haze had gone out in his car to think and he had decided that he would seduce Hawks's child. He thought that when the blind preacher saw his daughter ruined, he would realize that he was in earnest when he said he preached The Church Without Christ. Besides this reason, there was another: he didn't want to go back to Mrs. Watts. The night before, after he was asleep, she had got up and cut the top of his hat out in an obscene shape. He felt that he should have a woman, not for the sake of the pleasure in her, but to prove that he didn't believe in sin since he practiced what was called it; but he had had enough of her. He wanted someone he could teach something to and he took it for granted that the blind man's child, since she was so homely, would also be innocent.

Before he went back to his room, he went to a dry-goods store to buy a new hat. He wanted one that was completely opposite to the old one. This time he was sold a white panama with a red and green and yellow band around it. The man said they were really the thing and particularly if he was going to Florida.

"I ain't going to Florida," he said. "This hat is opposite from the one I used to have is all."

"You can use it anywheres," the man said; "it's new."

"I know that," Haze said. He went outside and took the red and green and yellow band off it and thumped out the crease in the top and turned down the brim. When he put it on, it looked just as fierce as the other one had.

He didn't go back to the Hawkses' door until late in the afternoon, when he thought they would be eating their supper. It opened almost at once and the child's head appeared in the crack. He pushed the door out of her hand and went in without looking at her directly. Hawks was sitting at the trunk. The remains of his supper were in front of him but he wasn't eating. He had barely got the black glasses on in time.

"If Jesus cured blind men, howcome you don't get Him to cure you?" Haze asked. He had prepared this sentence in his room.

"He blinded Paul," Hawks said.

Haze sat down on the edge of one of the cots. He looked around him and then back at Hawks. He crossed and uncrossed his knees and then he crossed them again. "Where'd you get them scars?" he asked.

The fake blind man leaned forward and smiled. "You still have a chance to save yourself if you repent," he said. "I can't save you but you can save yourself."

"That's what I've already done," Haze said. "Without the repenting. I preach how I done it every night on the . . ."

"Look at this," Hawks said. He took a yellow newspaper clipping from his pocket and handed it to him, and his mouth twisted out of the smile. "This is how I got the scars," he muttered. The child made a sign to him from the door to smile and not look sour. As he waited for Haze to finish reading, the smile slowly returned.

The headline on the clipping said, EVANGELIST PROMISES TO BLIND SELF. The rest of it said that Asa Hawks, an evangelist of the Free Church of Christ, had promised to blind himself to justify his belief that Christ Jesus had redeemed him. It said he would do it at a revival on Saturday night at eight o'clock, the fourth of October. The date on it was more than ten years before. Over the headline was a picture of Hawks, a scarless, straight-mouthed man of about thirty, with one eye a little smaller and rounder than the other. The mouth had a look that might have been either holy or calculating, but there was a wildness in the eyes that suggested terror.

Haze sat staring at the clipping after he had read it. He read it three times. He took his hat off and put it on again and got up and stood looking around the room as if he were trying to remember where the door was.

"He did it with lime," the child said, "and there was hundreds converted. Anybody that blinded himself for justification ought to be able to save you—or even somebody of his blood," she added, inspired.

"Nobody with a good car needs to be justified," Haze murmured. He scowled at her and hurried out the door, but as soon as it was shut behind him, he remembered something. He turned around and opened it and handed her a piece of paper, folded up several times into a small pellet shape; then he hurried out to his car.

Hawks took the note away from her and opened it up. It said, BABE, I NEVER SAW ANYBODY THAT LOOKED AS GOOD AS YOU BEFORE IS WHY I CAME HERE. She read it over her arm, coloring pleasantly.

"Now you got the written proof for it, Papa," she said.

"That bastard got away with my clipping," Hawks muttered.

"Well you got another clipping, ain't you?" she asked, with a little smirk.

"Shut your mouth," he said and flung himself down on

the cot. The other clipping was one that said, EVANGE-
LIST'S NERVE FAILS.

"I can get it for you," she offered, standing close to
the door so that she could run if she disturbed him too
much, but he had turned toward the wall as if he were
going to sleep.

Ten years ago at a revival he had intended to blind himself
and two hundred people or more were there, waiting for
him to do it. He had preached for an hour on the blindness
of Paul, working himself up until he saw himself struck
blind by a Divine flash of lightning and, with courage
enough then, he had thrust his hands into the bucket of
wet lime and streaked them down his face; but he hadn't
been able to let any of it get into his eyes. He had been
possessed of as many devils as were necessary to do it,
but at that instant, they disappeared, and he saw himself
standing there as he was. He fancied Jesus, Who had expelled
them, was standing there too, beckoning to him; and he
had fled out of the tent into the alley and disappeared.

"Okay, Pa," she said, "I'll go out for a while and leave
you in peace."

Haze had driven his car immediately to the nearest garage
where a man with black bangs and a short expressionless
face had come out to wait on him. He told the man he
wanted the horn made to blow and the leaks taken out
of the gas tank, the starter made to work smoother and
the windshield wipers tightened.

The man lifted the hood and glanced inside and then
shut it again. Then he walked around the car, stopping
to lean on it here and there, and thumping it in one place
and another. Haze asked him how long it would take to
put it in the best order.

"It can't be done," the man said.

"This is a good car," Haze said. "I knew when I first
saw it that it was the car for me, and since I've had it,
I've had a place to be that I can always get away in."

"Was you going some place in this?" the man asked.

"To another garage," Haze said, and he got in the Essex
and drove off. At the other garage he went to, there was
a man who said he could put the car in the best shape overnight, because it was such a good car to begin with, so
well put together and with such good materials in it, and
because, he added, he was the best mechanic in town, working
in the best-equipped shop. Haze left it with him, certain
that it was in honest hands.

CHAPTER 7

The next afternoon when he got his car back, he drove it out into the country to see how well it worked on the open road. The sky was just a little lighter blue than his suit, clear and even, with only one cloud in it, a large blinding white one with curls and a beard. He had gone about a mile out of town when he heard a throat cleared behind him. He slowed down and turned his head and saw Hawks's child getting up off the floor onto the two-by-four that stretched across the seat frame. "I been here all the time," she said, "and you never known it." She had a bunch of dandelions in her hair and a wide red mouth on her pale face.

"What do you want to hide in my car for?" he said angrily. "I got business before me. I don't have time for foolishness." Then he checked his ugly tone and stretched his mouth a little, remembering that he was going to seduce her. "Yeah sure," he said, "glad to see you."

She swung one thin black-stockinged leg over the back of the front seat and then let the rest of herself over. "Did you mean 'good to look at' in that note, or only 'good'?" she asked.

"The both," he said stiffly.

"My name is Sabbath," she said. "Sabbath Lily Hawks. My mother named me that just after I was born because I was born on the Sabbath and then she turned over in her bed and died and I never seen her."

"Unh," Haze said. His jaw tightened and he entrenched himself behind it and drove on. He had not wanted any company. His sense of pleasure in the car and in the afternoon was gone.

"Him and her wasn't married," she continued, "and that makes me a bastard, but I can't help it. It was what he done to me and not what I done to myself."

"A bastard?" he murmured. He couldn't see how a preacher who had blinded himself for Jesus could have a bastard. He turned his head and looked at her with interest for the first time.

She nodded and the corners of her mouth turned up. "A real bastard," she said, catching his elbow, "and do

66

you know what? A bastard shall not enter the kingdom of heaven!" she said.

Haze was driving his car toward the ditch while he stared at her. "How could you be . . . ," he started and saw the red embankment in front of him and pulled the car back on the road.

"Do you read the papers?" she asked.

"No," he said.

"Well, there's this woman in it named Mary Brittle that tells you what to do when you don't know. I wrote her a letter and ast her what I was to do."

"How could you be a bastard when he blinded him . . . ," he started again.

"I says, 'Dear Mary, I am a bastard and a bastard shall not enter the kingdom of heaven as we all know, but I have this personality that makes boys follow me. Do you think I should neck or not? I shall not enter the kingdom of heaven anyway so I don't see what difference it makes.' "

"Listen here," Haze said, "if he blinded himself how . . ."

"Then she answered my letter in the paper. She said, 'Dear Sabbath, Light necking is acceptable, but I think your real problem is one of adjustment to the modern world. Perhaps you ought to re-examine your religious values to see if they meet your needs in Life. A religious experience can be a beautiful addition to living if you put it in the proper prespective and do not let it warf you. Read some books on Ethical Culture.' "

"You couldn't be a bastard," Haze said, getting very pale. "You must be mixed up. Your daddy blinded himself."

"Then I wrote her another letter," she said, scratching his ankle with the toe of her sneaker, and smiling. "I says, 'Dear Mary, What I really want to know is should I go the whole hog or not? That's my real problem. I'm adjusted okay to the modern world.' "

"Your daddy blinded himself," Haze repeated.

"He wasn't always as good as he is now," she said. "She never answered my second letter."

"You mean in his youth he didn't believe but he came to?" he asked. "Is that what you mean or ain't it?" and he kicked her foot roughly away from his.

"That's right," she said. Then she drew herself up a little. "Quit that feeling my leg with yours," she said.

The blinding white cloud was a little ahead of them, moving to the left. "Why don't you turn down that dirt road?" she asked. The highway forked off onto a clay road and he turned onto it. It was hilly and shady and the country showed to advantage on either side. One side was dense honeysuckle and the other was open and slanted down to a telescoped view of the city. The white cloud was directly in front of them.

"How did he come to believe?" Haze asked. "What changed him into a preacher for Jesus?"

"I do like a dirt road," she said, "particularly when it's hilly like this one here. Why don't we get out and sit under a tree where we could get better acquainted?"

After a few hundred feet Haze stopped the car and they got out. "Was he a very evil-seeming man before he came to believe," he asked, "or just part way evil-seeming?"

"All the way evil," she said, going under the barbed wire fence on the side of the road. Once under it she sat down and began to take off her shoes and stockings. "How I like to walk in a field is barefooted," she said with gusto.

"Listenhere," Haze muttered, "I got to be going back to town. I don't have time to walk in any field," but he went under the fence and on the other side he said, "I suppose before he came to believe he didn't believe at all."

"Let's us go over that hill yonder and sit under the trees," she said.

They climbed the hill and went down the other side of it, she a little ahead of Haze. He saw that sitting under a tree with her might help him to seduce her, but he was in no hurry to get on with it, considering her innocence. He felt it was too hard a job to be done in an afternoon. She sat down under a large pine and patted the ground close beside her for him to sit on, but he sat about five feet away from her on a rock. He rested his chin on his knees and looked straight ahead.

"I can save you," she said. "I got a church in my heart where Jesus is King."

He leaned in her direction, glaring. "I believe in a new kind of jesus," he said, "one that can't waste his blood redeeming people with it, because he's all man and ain't got any God in him. My church is the Church Without Christ!"

She moved up closer to him. "Can a bastard be saved in it?" she asked.

"There's no such thing as a bastard in the Church Without Christ," he said. "Everything is all one. A bastard wouldn't be any different from anybody else."

"That's good," she said.

He looked at her irritably, for something in his mind was already contradicting him and saying that a bastard couldn't, that there was only one truth—that Jesus was a liar—and that her case was hopeless. She pulled open her collar and lay down on the ground full length. "Ain't my feet white, though?" she asked raising them slightly.

Haze didn't look at her feet. The thing in his mind said that the truth didn't contradict itself and that a bastard couldn't be saved in the Church Without Christ. He decided he would forget it, that it was not important.

"There was this child once," she said, turning over on her stomach, "that nobody cared if it lived or died. Its kin sent it around from one to another of them and finally to its grandmother who was a very evil woman and she couldn't stand to have it around because the least good thing made her break out in these welps. She would get all itching and swoll. Even her eyes would itch her and swell up and there wasn't nothing she could do but run up and down the road, shaking her hands and cursing and it was twicet as bad when this child was there so she kept the child locked up in a chicken crate. It seen its granny in hell-fire, swoll and burning, and it told her everything it seen and she got so swoll until finally she went to the well and wrapped the well rope around her neck and let down the bucket and broke her neck.

"Would you guess me to be fifteen years old?" she asked.

"There wouldn't be any sense to the word, bastard, in the Church Without Christ," Haze said.

"Why don't you lie down and rest yourself?" she inquired.

Haze moved a few feet away and lay down. He put his hat over his face and folded his arms across his chest. She lifted herself up on her hands and knees and crawled over to him and gazed at the top of his hat. Then she lifted if off like a lid and peered into his eyes. They stared straight upward. "It don't make any difference to me," she said softly, "how much you like me."

He trained his eyes into her neck. Gradually she lowered her head until the tips of their noses almost touched but still he didn't look at her. "I see you," she said in a playful voice.

"Git away!" he said, jumping violently.

She scrambled up and ran around behind the tree. Haze put his hat back on and stood up, shaken. He wanted to get back in the Essex. He realized suddenly that it was parked on a country road, unlocked, and that the first person passing would drive off in it.

"I see you," a voice said from behind the tree.

He walked off quickly in the opposite direction toward the car. The jubilant expression on the face that looked from around the tree, flattened.

He got in his car and went through the motions of starting it but it only made a noise like water lost somewhere in the pipes. A panic took him and he began to pound the starter. There were two instruments on the dashboard with needles that pointed dizzily in first one direction and then another, but they worked on a private system, independent of the whole car. He couldn't tell if it was out of gas or not. Sabbath Hawks came running up to the fence. She got down on the ground and rolled under the barbed wire and then stood at the window of the car, looking in at him. He turned his head at her fiercely and said, "What did you do to my car?" Then he got out and started walking down the road, without waiting for her to answer. After a second, she followed him, keeping her distance.

Where the highway had forked off onto the dirt road, there had been a store with a gas pump in front of it. It was about a half-mile back; Haze kept up a steady fast pace until he reached it. It had a deserted look, but after a few minutes a man appeared from out of the woods behind it, and Haze told him what he wanted. While the man got out his pick-up truck to drive them back to the Essex, Sabbath Hawks arrived and went over to a cage about six feet high that was at the side of the shack. Haze had not noticed it until she came up. He saw that there was something alive in it, and went near enough to read a sign that said, TWO DEADLY ENEMIES. HAVE A LOOK FREE.

There was a black bear about four feet long and very thin, resting on the floor of the cage; his back was spotted with bird lime that had been shot down on him by a small chicken hawk that was sitting on a perch in the upper part of the same apartment. Most of the hawk's tail was gone; the bear had only one eye.

"Come on here if you don't want to get left," Haze said roughly, grabbing her by the arm. The man had his truck ready and the three of them drove back in it to the Essex. On the way Haze told him about the Church Without Christ; he explained its principles and said there was no such thing as a bastard in it. The man didn't comment. When they got out at the Essex, he put a can of gas in the tank and Haze got in and tried to start it but nothing happened. The man opened up the hood and studied the inside for a while. He was a one-armed man with two sandy-colored teeth and eyes that were slate-blue and thoughtful. He had not spoken more than two words yet. He looked for a long time under the hood while Haze stood by, but he didn't touch anything. After a while he shut it and blew his nose.

"What's wrong in there?" Haze asked in an agitated voice. "It's a good car, ain't it?"

The man didn't answer him. He sat down on the ground and eased under the Essex. He wore hightop shoes and gray socks. He stayed under the car a long time. Haze got down on his hands and knees and looked under to see what he was doing but he wasn't doing anything. He was just lying there, looking up, as if he were contemplating; his good arm was folded on his chest. After a while, he eased himself out and wiped his face and neck with a piece of flannel rag he had in his pocket.

"Listenhere," Haze said, "that's a good car. You just give me a push, that's all. That car'll get me anywhere I want to go."

The man didn't say anything but he got back in the truck and Haze and Sabbath Hawks got in the Essex and he pushed them. After a few hundred yards the Essex began to belch and gasp and jiggle. Haze stuck his head out the window and motioned for the truck to come alongside. "Ha!" he said. "I told you, didn't I? This car'll get me anywhere I want to go. It may stop here and there but it won't stop permanent. What do I owe you?"

"Nothing," the man said, "not a thing."

"But the gas," Haze said, "how much for the gas?"

"Nothing," the man said with the same level look. "Not a thing."

"All right, I thank you," Haze said and drove on. "I don't need no favors from him," he said.

"It's a grand auto," Sabbath Hawks said. "It goes as smooth as honey."

"It ain't been built by a bunch of foreigners or niggers or one-arm men," Haze said. "It was built by people with their eyes open that knew where they were at."

When they came to the end of the dirt road and were facing the paved one, the pick-up truck pulled alongside again and while the two cars paused side by side, Haze and the slate-eyed man looked at each other out of their two windows. "I told you this car would get me anywhere I wanted to go," Haze said sourly.

"Some things," the man said, " 'll get some folks somewheres," and he turned the truck up the highway.

Haze drove on. The blinding white cloud had turned into a bird with long thin wings and was disappearing in the opposite direction.

CHAPTER 8

Enoch Emery knew now that his life would never be the same again, because the thing that was going to happen to him had started to happen. He had always known that something was going to happen but he hadn't known what. If he had been much given to thought, he might have thought that now was the time for him to justify his daddy's blood, but he didn't think in broad sweeps like that, he thought what he would do next. Sometimes he didn't think, he only wondered; then before long he would find himself doing this or that, like a bird finds itself building a nest when it hasn't actually been planning to.

What was going to happen to him had started to happen when he showed what was in the glass case to Haze Motes. That was a mystery beyond his understanding, but he knew that what was going to be expected of him was something awful. His blood was more sensitive than any other part of him; it wrote doom all through him, except possibly in his brain, and the result was that his tongue, which edged out every few minutes to test his fever blister, knew more than he did.

The first thing that he found himself doing that was not normal was saving his pay. He was saving all of it, except what his landlady came to collect every week and what he had to use to buy something to eat with. Then to his surprise, he found he wasn't eating very much and he was saving that money too. He had a fondness for super-markets; it was his custom to spend an hour or so in one every afternoon after he left the city park, browsing around among the canned goods and reading the cereal stories. Lately he had been compelled to pick up a few things here and there that would not be bulky in his pockets, and he wondered if this could be the reason he was saving so much money on food. It could have been, but he had the suspicion that saving the money was connected with some larger thing. He had always been given to stealing but he had never saved before.

At the same time, he began cleaning up his room. It was a little green room, or it had once been green, in the

72

attic of an elderly rooming house. There was a mummified look and feel to this residence, but Enoch had never thought before of brightening the part (corresponding to the head) that he lived in. Then he simply found himself doing it.

First, he removed the rug from the floor and hung it out the window. This was a mistake because when he went to pull it back in, there were only a few long strings left with a carpet tack caught in one of them. He imagined that it must have been a very old rug and he decided to handle the rest of the furniture with more care. He washed the bed frame with soap and water and found that under the second layer of dirt, it was pure gold, and this affected him so strongly that he washed the chair. It was a low round chair that bulged around the legs so that it seemed to be in the act of squatting. The gold began to appear with the first touch of water but it disappeared with the second and with a little more, the chair sat down as if this were the end of long years of inner struggle. Enoch didn't know if it was for him or against him. He had a nasty impulse to kick it to pieces, but he let it stay there, exactly in the position it had sat down in, because for the time anyway, he was not a foolhardy boy who took chances on the meanings of things. For the time, he knew that what he didn't know was what mattered.

The only other piece of furniture in the room was a washstand. This was built in three parts and stood on bird legs six inches high. The legs had clawed feet that were each one gripped around a small cannon ball. The lowest part was a tabernacle-like cabinet which was meant to contain a slop-jar. Enoch didn't own a slop-jar but he had a certain reverence for the purpose of things and since he didn't have the right thing to put in it, he left it empty. Directly over this place for the treasure, there was a gray marble slab and coming up from behind it was a wooden trellis-work of hearts, scrolls and flowers, extending into a hunched eagle wing on either side, and containing in the middle, just at the level of Enoch's face when he stood in front of it, a small oval mirror. The wooden frame continued again over the mirror and ended in a crowned, horned head-piece, showing that the artist had not lost faith in his work.

As far as Enoch was concerned, this piece had always been the center of the room and the one that most connected him with what he didn't know. More than once after a big supper, he had dreamed of unlocking the cabinet and getting in it and then proceeding to certain rites and mysteries that he had a very vague idea about in the morning. In his cleaning up, his mind was on the washstand from the first, but as was usual with him, he began with the least important thing and worked around and in toward the center where the meaning was. So before he tackled the washstand, he took care of the pictures in the room.

These were three, one belonging to his landlady (who was almost totally blind but moved about by an acute sense of smell) and two of his own. Hers was a brown portrait of a moose standing in a small lake. The look of superiority on this animal's face was so insufferable to Enoch that, if he hadn't been afraid of him, he would have done something about it a long time ago. As it was, he couldn't do anything in his room but what the smug face was watching, not shocked because nothing better could be expected and not amused because nothing was funny. If he had looked all over for one, he couldn't have found a roommate that irritated him more. He kept up a constant stream of inner comment, uncomplimentary to the moose, though when he said anything aloud, he was more guarded. The moose was in a heavy brown frame with leaf designs on it and this added to his weight and his self-satisfied look. Enoch knew the time had come when something had to be done; he didn't know what was going to happen in his room, but when it happened, he didn't want to have the feeling that the moose was running it. The answer came to him fully prepared: he realized with a sudden intuition that taking the frame off him would be equal to taking the clothes off him (although he didn't have on any) and he was right because when he had done it, the animal looked so reduced that Enoch could only snicker and look at him out the corner of his eye.

After this success he turned his attention to the other two pictures. They were over calendars and had been sent him by the Hilltop Funeral Home and the American Rubber Tire Company. One showed a small boy in a pair of blue Doctor Denton sleepers, kneeling at his bed, saying, "And bless daddy," while the moon looked in at the window. This was Enoch's favorite painting and it hung directly over his bed. The other pictured a lady wearing a rubber tire and it hung directly across from the moose on the opposite wall. He left it where it was, pretty certain that the moose only pretended not to see it. Immediately after he finished with the pictures, he went out and bought chintz curtains, a bottle of gilt, and a paint brush with all the money he had saved.

This was a disappointment to him because he had hoped that the money would be for some new clothes for him, and here he saw it going into a set of drapes. He didn't know what the gilt was for until he got home with it; when he got home with it, he sat down in front of the slop-jar cabinet in the washstand, unlocked it, and painted the inside of it with the gilt. Then he realized that the cabinet was to be used FOR something.

Enoch never nagged his blood to tell him a thing until it was ready. He wasn't the kind of a boy who grabs at any possibility and runs off, proposing this or that preposterous thing. In a large matter like this, he was always willing to wait for a certainty, and he waited for this one, certain at least that he would know in a few days. Then for about a week his blood was in secret conference with itself every day, only stopping now and then to shout some order at him.

On the following Monday, he was certain when he woke up that today was the day he was going to know on. His blood was rushing around like a woman who cleans up the house after the company has come, and he was surly and rebellious. When he realized that today was the day, he decided not to get up. He didn't want to justify his daddy's blood, he didn't want to be always having to do something that something else wanted him to do, that he didn't know what it was and that was always dangerous.

Naturally, his blood was not going to put up with any attitude like this. He was at the zoo by nine-thirty, only a half-hour later than he was supposed to be. All morning his mind was not on the gate he was supposed to guard but was chasing around after his blood, like a boy with a mop and a bucket, beating something here and sloshing down something there, without a second's rest. As soon as the second-shift guard came, Enoch headed toward town.

Town was the last place he wanted to be because anything could happen there. All the time his mind had been chasing around it had been thinking how as soon as he got off duty he was going to sneak off home and go to bed.

By the time he got into the center of the business district he was exhausted and he had to lean against Walgreen's window and cool off. Sweat crept down his back and provoked him to itch so that in just a few minutes he appeared to be working his way across the glass by his muscles, against a background of alarm clocks, toilet waters, candies, sanitary pads, fountain pens, and pocket flashlights, displayed in all colors to twice his height. He appeared to be working his way to a rumbling noise which came from the center of a small alcove that formed the entrance to the drug store. Here was a yellow and blue, glass and steel machine, belching popcorn into a cauldron of butter and salt. Enoch approached, already with his purse out, sorting his money. His purse was a long gray leather pouch, tied at the top with a drawstring. It was one he had stolen from his daddy and he treasured it because it was the only thing he owned now that his daddy had touched (besides himself). He sorted out two nickels and handed them to a pasty boy in a white apron who was there to serve the machine. The boy felt around in its vitals and filled a white paper bag with the corn, not taking his eye off Enoch's purse the while. On any other day Enoch would have tried to make friends with him but today he was too preoccupied even to see him. He took the bag and began stuffing the pouch back where it had come from. The youth's eye followed to the very edge of the pocket. "That thang looks like a hawg bladder," he observed enviously.

"I got to go now," Enoch murmured and hurried into the drug store. Inside, he walked abstractedly to the back of the store, and then up to the front again by the other aisle as if he wanted any person who might be looking for him to see he was there. He paused in front of the soda fountain to see if he would sit down and have something to eat. The fountain counter was pink and green marble linoleum and behind it there was a red-headed waitress in a lime-colored uniform and a pink apron. She had green eyes set in pink and they resembled a picture behind her of a Lime-Cherry Surprise, a special that day for ten cents. She confronted Enoch while he studied the information over her head. After a minute she laid her chest on the counter and surrounded it by her folded arms, to wait. Enoch couldn't decide which of several concoctions was the one for him to have until she ended it by moving one arm under the counter and bringing out a Lime-Cherry Surprise. "It's okay," she said, "I fixed it this morning after breakfast."

"Something's going to happen to me today," Enoch said.

"I told you it was okay," she said. "I fixed it today."

"I seen it this morning when I woke up," he said, with the look of a visionary.

"God," she said, and jerked it from under his face. She turned around and began slapping things together; in a second she slammed another—exactly like it, but fresh—in front of him.

"I got to go now," Enoch said, and hurried out. An eye caught at his pocket as he passed the popcorn machine but he didn't stop. I don't want to do it, he was saying to himself. Whatever it is, I don't want to do it. I'm going home. It'll be something I don't want to do. It'll be something

I ain't got no business doing. And he thought of how he had had to spend all his money on drapes and gilt when he could have bought him a shirt and a phosphorescent tie. It'll be something against the law, he said. It's always something against the law. I ain't going to do it, he said, and stopped. He had stopped in front of a movie house where there was a large illustration of a monster stuffing a young woman into an incinerator.

I ain't going in no picture show like that, he said, giving it a nervous look. I'm going home. I ain't going to wait around in no picture show. I ain't got the money to buy a ticket, he said, taking out his purse again. I ain't even going to count thisyer change.

It ain't but forty-three cent here, he said, that ain't enough. A sign said the price of a ticket for adults was forty-five cents, balcony, thirty-five. I ain't going to sit in no balcony, he said, buying a thirty-five cent ticket.

I ain't going in, he said.

Two doors flew open and he found himself moving down a long red foyer and then up a darker tunnel and then up a higher, still darker tunnel. In a few minutes he was up in a high part of the maw, feeling around, like Jonah, for a seat. I ain't going to look at it, he said furiously. He didn't like any picture shows but colored musical ones.

The first picture was about a scientist named The Eye who performed operations by remote control. You would wake up in the morning and find a slit in your chest or head or stomach and something you couldn't do without would be gone. Enoch pulled his hat down very low and drew his knees up in front of his face; only his eyes looked at the screen. That picture lasted an hour.

The second picture was about life at Devil's Island Penitentiary. After a while, Enoch had to grip the two arms of his seat to keep himself from falling over the rail in front of him.

The third picture was called, "Lonnie Comes Home Again." It was about a baboon named Lonnie who rescued attractive children from a burning orphanage. Enoch kept hoping Lonnie would get burned up but he didn't appear to get even hot. In the end a nice-looking girl gave him a medal. It was more than Enoch could stand. He made a dive for the aisle, fell down the two higher tunnels, and raced out the red foyer and into the street. He collapsed as soon as the air hit him.

When he recovered himself, he was sitting against the wall of the picture show building and he was not thinking any more about escaping his duty. It was night and he had the feeling that the knowledge he couldn't avoid was almost on him. His resignation was perfect. He leaned against the wall for about twenty minutes and then he got up and began to walk down the street as if he were led by a silent melody or by one of those whistles that only dogs hear. At the end of two blocks he stopped, his attention directed across the street. There, facing him under a street light, was a high rat-colored car and up on the nose of it, a dark figure with a fierce white hat on. The figure's arms were working up and down and he had thin, gesticulating hands, almost as pale as the hat. "Hazel Motes!" Enoch breathed, and his heart began to slam from side to side like a wild bell clapper.

There were a few people standing on the sidewalk near the car. Enoch didn't know that Hazel Motes had started the Church Without Christ and was preaching it every night on the street; he hadn't seen him since that day at the park when he had showed him the shriveled man in the glass case.

"If you had been redeemed," Hazel Motes was shouting, "you would care about redemption but you don't. Look inside yourselves and see if you hadn't rather it wasn't if it was. There's no peace for the redeemed," he shouted, "and I preach peace, I preach the Church Without Christ, the church peaceful and satisfied!"

Two or three people who had stopped near the car started walking off the other way. "Leave!" Hazel Motes cried. "Go ahead and leave! The truth don't matter to you. Listen," he said, pointing his finger at the rest of them, "the truth don't matter to you. If Jesus had redeemed you, what difference would it make to you? You wouldn't do nothing about it. Your faces wouldn't move, neither this way nor that, and if it was three crosses there and Him hung on the middle one, that one wouldn't mean no more to you and me than the other two. Listen here. What you need is something to take the place of Jesus, something that would speak plain. The Church Without Christ don't have a Jesus but it needs one! It needs a new jesus! It needs one that's all man, without blood to waste, and it needs one that don't look like any other man so you'll look at him. Give me such a jesus, you people. Give me such a new jesus and you'll see how far the Church Without Christ can go!"

One of the people watching walked off so there were only two left. Enoch was standing in the middle of the street, paralyzed.

"Show me where this new jesus is," Hazel Motes cried, "and I'll set him up in the Church Without Christ and then you'll see the truth. Then you'll know once and for all that you haven't been redeemed. Give me this new jesus, somebody, so we'll all be saved by the sight of him!"

Enoch began shouting without a sound. He shouted that way for a full minute while Hazel Motes went on.

"Look at me!" Hazel Motes cried, with a tare in his throat, "and you look at a peaceful man! Peaceful because my blood has set me free. Take counsel from your blood and come into the Church Without Christ and maybe somebody will bring us a new jesus and we'll all be saved by the sight of him!"

An unintelligible sound spluttered out of Enoch. He tried to bellow, but his blood held him back. He whispered, "Listenhere, I got him! I mean I can get him! You know! Him! Him I shown you to. You seen him yourself!"

His blood reminded him that the last time he had seen Haze Motes was when Haze Motes had hit him over the head with a rock. And he didn't even know yet how he would steal it out of the glass case. The only thing he knew was that he had a place in his room prepared to keep it in until Haze was ready to take it. His blood suggested he just let it come as a surprise to Haze Motes. He began to back away. He backed across the street and over a piece of sidewalk and out into the other street and a taxi had to stop short to keep from hitting him. The driver put his head out the window and asked him how he got around so well when God had made him by putting two backs together instead of a back and a front.

Enoch was too preoccupied to think about it. "I got to go now," he murmured, and hurried off.

CHAPTER 9

Hawks kept his door bolted and whenever Haze knocked on it, which he did two or three times a day, the ex-evangelist sent his child out to him and bolted the door again behind her. It infuriated him to have Haze lurking in the house, thinking up some excuse to get in and look at his face; and he was often drunk and didn't want to be discovered that way.

Haze couldn't understand why the preacher didn't welcome him and act like a preacher should when he sees what he believes is a lost soul. He kept trying to get into the room again; the window he could have reached was kept locked and the shade pulled down. He wanted to see, if he could, *behind* the black glasses.

Every time he went to the door, the girl came out and the bolt shut inside; then he couldn't get rid of her. She followed him out to his car and climbed in and spoiled his rides or she followed him up to his room and sat. He abandoned the notion of seducing her and tried to protect himself. He hadn't been in the house a week before she appeared in his room one night after he had gone to bed. She was holding a candle burning in a jelly glass and wore, hanging onto her thin shoulders, a woman's nightgown that dragged on the floor behind her. Haze didn't wake up until she was almost up to his bed, and when he did, he sprang from under his cover into the middle of the room.

"What you want?" he said.

She didn't say anything and her grin widened in the candle light. He stood glowering at her for an instant and then he picked up the straight chair and raised it as if he were going to bring it down on her. She lingered only a fraction of a second. His door didn't bolt so he propped the chair under the knob before he went back to bed.

"Listen," she said when she got back to their room, "nothing works. He would have hit me with a chair."

"I'm leaving out of here in a couple of days," Hawks said, "you better make it work if you want to eat after I'm gone." He was drunk but he meant it.

Nothing was working the way Haze had expected it to. He had spent every evening preaching, but the membership of the Church Without Christ was still only one person: himself. He had wanted to have a large following quickly to impress the blind man with his powers, but no one had followed him. There had been a sort of follower but that had been a mistake. That had been a boy about sixteen years old who had wanted someone to go to a whorehouse with him because he had never been to one before. He knew where the place was but he didn't want to go without a person of experience, and when he heard Haze, he hung around until he stopped preaching and then asked him to go. But it was all a mistake because after they had gone and got out again and Haze had asked him to be a member of the Church Without Christ, or more than that, a disciple, an apostle, the boy said he was sorry but he couldn't be a member of that church because he was a Lapsed Catholic. He said that what they had just done was a mortal sin, and that should they die unrepentant of it they would suffer eternal punishment and never see God. Haze had not enjoyed the whorehouse anywhere near as much as the boy had and he had wasted half his evening. He shouted that there was no such thing as sin or judgment, but the boy only shook his head and asked him if he would like to go again the next night.

If Haze had believed in praying, he would have prayed for a disciple, but as it was all he could do was worry about it a lot. Then two nights after the boy, the disciple appeared.

That night he preached outside of four different picture shows and every time he looked up, he saw the same big face smiling at him. The man was plumpish, and he had curly blond hair that was cut with showy sideburns. He wore a black suit with a silver stripe in it and a wide-brimmed white hat pushed onto the back of his head, and he had on tight-fitting black pointed shoes and no socks. He looked like an ex-preacher turned cowboy, or an ex-cowboy turned mortician. He was not handsome but under his smile, there was an honest look that fitted into his face like a set of false teeth.

Every time Haze looked at him, the man winked.

At the last picture show he preached in front of, there were three people listening to him besides the man. "Do you people care anything about the truth?" he asked. "The only way to the truth is through blasphemy, but do you care? Are you going to pay any attention to what I've been saying or are you just going to walk off like everybody else?"

There were two men and a woman with a cat-faced baby sprawled over her shoulder. She had been looking at Haze as if he were in a booth at the fair. "Well, come on," she said, "he's finished. We got to be going." She turned away and the two men fell in behind her.

"Go ahead and go," Haze said, "but remember that the truth don't lurk around every street corner."

The man who had been following reached up quickly and pulled Haze's pantsleg and gave him a wink. "Come on back heah, you folks," he said. "I want to tell you all about *me*."

The woman turned around again and he smiled at her as if he had been struck all along with her good looks. She had a square red face and her hair was freshly set. "I wisht I had my gittarr here," the man said, " 'cause I just somehow can say sweet things to music bettern plain. And when you talk about Jesus you need a little music, don't you, friends?" He looked at the two men as if he were appealing to the good judgment that was impressed on their faces. They had on brown felt hats and black town suits, and they looked like older and younger brother. "Listen, friends," the disciple said confidentially, "two months ago before I met the Prophet here, you wouldn't know me for the same man. I didn't have a friend in the world. Do you know what it's like not to have a friend in the world?"

"It ain't no worsen havinum that would put a knife in your back when you wasn't looking," the older man said, barely parting his lips.

"Friend, you said a mouthful when you said that," the man said. "If we had time, I would have you repeat that just so ever'body could hear it like I did." The picture show was over and more people were coming up. "Friends," the man said, "I know you're all interested in the Prophet here," pointing to Haze on the nose of the car, "and if you'll just give me time I'm going to tell you what him and his idears've done for me. Don't crowd because I'm willing to stay here all night and tell you if it takes that long."

Haze stood where he was, motionless, with his head slightly forward, as if he weren't sure what he was hearing.

"Friends," the man said, "lemme innerduce myself. My name is Onnie Jay Holy and I'm telling it to you so you can check up and see I don't tell you any lie. I'm a preacher and I don't mind who knows it but I wouldn't have you believe nothing you can't feel in your own hearts. You people coming up on the edge push right on up in here where you can hear good," he said. "I'm not selling a thing, I'm giving something away!" A considerable number of people had stopped.

"Friends," he said, "two months ago you wouldn't know me for the same man. I didn't have a friend in the world. Do you know what it's like not to have a friend in the world?"

A loud voice said, "It ain't no worsen havinum that would put . . ."

"Why, friends," Onnie Jay Holy said, "not to have a friend in the world is just about the most miserable and lonesome thing that can happen to a man or woman! And that's the way it was with me. I was ready to hang myself or to despair completely. Not even my own dear old mother loved me, and it wasn't because I wasn't sweet inside, it was because I never known how to make the natural sweetness inside me show. Every person that comes onto this earth," he said, stretching out his arms, "is born sweet and full of love. A little child loves ever'body, friends, and its nature is sweetness—until something happens. Something happens, friends, I don't need to tell people like you that can think for theirselves. As that little child gets bigger, its sweetness don't show so much, cares and troubles come to perplext it, and all its sweetness is driven inside it. Then it gets miserable and lonesome and sick, friends. It says, 'Where is all my sweetness gone? where are all the friends that loved me?' and all the time, that little beat-up rose of its sweetness is inside, not a petal dropped, and on the outside is just a mean lonesomeness. It may want to take its own life or yours or mine, or to despair completely, friends." He said it in a sad nasal voice but he was smiling all the time so that they could tell he had been through what he was talking about and come out on top. "That was the way it was with me, friends. I know what of I speak," he said, and folded his hands in front of him. "But all the time that I was ready to hang myself or to despair completely, I was sweet inside, like ever'body else, and I only needed something to bring it out. I only needed a little help, friends.

"Then I met this Prophet here," he said, pointing at Haze on the nose of the car. "That was two months ago, folks, that I heard how he was out to help me, how he was preaching the Church of Christ Without Christ, the church that was going to get a new jesus to help me bring my sweet nature into the open where ever'body could enjoy it. That was two months ago, friends, and now you wouldn't know me for the same man. I love ever'one of you people and I want you to listen to him and me and join our church, the Holy Church of Christ Without Christ, the new church with the new jesus, and then you'll all be helped like me!"

Haze leaned forward. "This man is not true," he said. "I never saw him before tonight. I wasn't preaching this church two months ago and the name of it ain't the Holy Church of Christ Without Christ!"

The man ignored this and so did the people. There were ten or twelve gathered around. "Friends," Onnie Jay Holy said, "I'm mighty glad you're seeing me now instead of two months ago because then I couldn't have testified to this new church and this Prophet here. If I had my gittarr with me I could say all this better but I'll just have to do the best I can by myself." He had a winning smile and it was evident that he didn't think he was any better than anybody else even though he was.

"Now I just want to give you folks a few reasons why you can trust this church," he said. "In the first place, friends, you can rely on it that it's nothing foreign connected with it. You don't have to believe nothing you don't understand and approve of. If you don't understand it, it ain't true, and that's all there is to it. No jokers in the deck, friends."

Haze leaned forward. "Blasphemy is the way to the truth," he said, "and there's no other way whether you understand it or not!"

"Now, friends," Onnie Jay said, "I want to tell you a second reason why you can absolutely trust this church—it's based on the Bible. Yes sir! It's based on your own personal interpitation of the Bible, friends. You can sit at home and interpit your own Bible however you feel in your heart it ought to be interpited. That's right," he said, "just the way Jesus would have done it. Gee, I wisht I had my gittarr here," he complained.

"This man is a liar," Haze said. "I never saw him before tonight. I never . . ."

"That ought to be enough reasons, friends," Onnie Jay Holy said, "but I'm going to tell you one more, just to show I can. This church is up-to-date! When you're in this church you can know that there's nothing or nobody ahead of you, nobody knows nothing you don't know, all the cards are on the table, friends, and that's a fack!"

Haze's face under the white hat began to take on a look of fierceness. Just as he was about to open his mouth again, Onnie Jay Holy pointed in astonishment to the baby in the blue bonnet who was sprawled limp over the woman's shoulder. "Why yonder is a little babe," he said, "a little bundle of helpless sweetness. Why, I know you people aren't

going to let that little thing grow up and have all his sweetness
pushed inside him when it could be on the outside to win
friends and make him loved. That's why I want ever' one
of you people to join the Holy Church of Christ Without
Christ. It'll cost you each a dollar but what is a dollar?
A few dimes! Not too much to pay to unlock that little
rose of sweetness inside you!"

"Listen!" Haze shouted. "It don't cost you any money
to know the truth! You can't know it for money!"

"You hear what the Prophet says, friends," Onnie Jay
Holy said, "a dollar is not too much to pay. No amount
of money is too much to learn the truth! Now I want each
of you people that are going to take advantage of this
church to sign on this little pad I have in my pocket here
and give me your dollar personally and let me shake your
hand!"

Haze slid down from the nose of his car and got in it
and slammed his foot on the starter.

"Hey wait! Wait!" Onnie Jay Holy shouted, "I ain't
got any of these friends' names yet!"

The Essex had a tendency to develop a tic by nightfall.
It would go forward about six inches and then back about
four; it did that now a succession of times rapidly; otherwise
Haze would have shot off in it and been gone. He had to
grip the steering wheel with both hands to keep from being
thrown either out the windshield or into the back. It
stopped this after a few seconds and slid about twenty feet
and then began it again.

Onnie Jay Holy's face showed a great strain; he put his
hand to the side of it as if the only way he could keep his
smile on was to hold it. "I got to go now, friends," he said
quickly, "but I'll be at this same spot tomorrow night. I
got to go catch the Prophet now," and he ran off just as
the Essex began to slide again. He wouldn't have caught
it, except that it stopped before it had gone ten feet farther.
He jumped on the running board and got the door open and
plumped in, panting, beside Haze. "Friend," he said, "we
just lost ten dollars. What you in such a hurry for?" His
face showed that he was in some kind of genuine pain
even though he looked at Haze with a smile that revealed
all his upper teeth and the tops of his lowers.

Haze turned his head and looked at him long enough to
see the smile before it was thrown forward at the windshield.
After that the Essex began running smoothly. Onnie Jay
took out a lavender handkerchief and held it in front of
his mouth for some time. When he removed it, the smile
was back on his face. "Friend," he said, "you and me have

to get together on this thing. I said when I first heard you open your mouth, 'Why, yonder is a great man with great idears.' "

Haze didn't turn his head.

Onnie Jay took in a long breath. "Why, do you know who you put me in mind of when I first saw you?" he asked. After a minute of waiting, he said in a soft voice, "Jesus Christ and Abraham Lincoln, friend."

Haze's face was suddenly swamped with outrage. All the expression on it was obliterated. "You ain't true," he said in a barely audible voice.

"Friend, how can you say that?" Onnie Jay said. "Why I was on the radio for three years with a program that give real religious experiences to the whole family. Didn't you ever listen to it—called Soulsease, a quarter hour of Mood, Melody, and Mentality? I'm a real preacher, friend."

Haze stopped the Essex. "You get out," he said.

"Why friend!" Onnie Jay said. "You ought not to say such a thing! That's the absolute truth that I'm a preacher and a radio star."

"Get out," Haze said, reaching across and opening the door for him.

"I never thought you would treat a friend thisaway," Onnie Jay said. "All I wanted to ast you about was this new jesus."

"Get out," Haze said, and began to push him toward the door. He pushed him to the edge of the seat and gave him a shove and Onnie Jay fell out the door and into the road.

"I never thought a friend would treat me thisaway," he complained. Haze kicked his leg off the running board and shut the door again. He put his foot on the starter but nothing happened except a noise somewhere underneath him that sounded like a person gargling without water. Onnie Jay got up off the pavement and stood at the window. "If you would just tell me where this new jesus is you was mentioning," he began.

Haze put his foot on the starter a succession of times but nothing happened.

"Pull out the choke," Onnie Jay advised, getting up on the running board.

"There's no choke on it," Haze snarled.

"Maybe it's flooded," Onnie Jay said. "While we're waiting, you and me can talk about the Holy Church of Christ Without Christ."

"My church is the Church Without Christ," Haze said. "I've seen all of you I want to."

"It don't make any difference how many Christs you

add to the name if you don't add none to the meaning, friend," Onnie Jay said in a hurt tone. "You ought to listen to me because I'm not just an amateur. I'm an artist-type. If you want to get anywheres in religion, you got to keep it sweet. You got good idears but what you need is an artist-type to work with you."

Haze rammed his foot on the gas and then on the starter and then on the starter and then on the gas. Nothing happened. The street was practically deserted. "Me and you could get behind it and push it over to the curb," Onnie Jay suggested.

"I ain't asked for your help," Haze said.

"You know, friend, I certainly would like to see this new jesus," Onnie Jay said. "I never heard a idear before that had more in it than that one. All it would need is a little promotion."

Haze tried to start the car by forcing his weight forward on the steering wheel, but that didn't work. He got out and got behind it and began to push it over to the curb. Onnie Jay got behind it with him and added his weight. "I kind of have had that idear about a new jesus myself," he remarked. "I seen how a new one would be more up-to-date.

"Where you keeping him, friend?" he asked. "Is he somebody you see ever' day? I certainly would like to meet him and hear some of his idears."

They pushed the car into a parking space. There was no way to lock it and Haze was afraid that if he left it out all night so far away from where he lived someone would be able to steal it. There was nothing for him to do but sleep in it. He got in the back and began to pull down the fringed shades. Onnie Jay had his head in the front, however. "You needn't to be afraid that if I seen this new jesus I would cut you out of anything," he said. "Why friend, it would just mean a lot to me for the good of my spirit."

Haze moved the two-by-four off the seat frame to make more room to fix up his pallet. He kept a pillow and an army blanket back there and he had a sterno stove and a coffee pot up on the shelf under the back oval window. "Friend, I would even be glad to pay you a little something to see him," Onnie Jay suggested.

"Listen here," Haze said, "you get away from here. I've seen all of you I want to. There's no such thing as any new jesus. That ain't anything but a way to say something."

The smile more or less slithered off Onnie Jay's face. "What you mean by that?" he asked.

"That there's no such thing or person," Haze said. "It

wasn't nothing but a way to say a thing." He put his hand
on the door handle and began to close it in spite of Onnie
Jay's head. "No such thing exists!" he shouted.

"That's the trouble with you innerleckchuls," Onnie Jay
muttered, "you don't never have nothing to show for what
you're saying."

"Get your head out my car door, Holy," Haze said.

"My name is Hoover Shoats," the man with his head
in the door growled. "I known when I first seen you that
you wasn't nothing but a crackpot."

Haze opened the door enough to be able to slam it.
Hoover Shoats got his head out the way but not his thumb.
A howl arose that would have rended almost any heart.
Haze opened the door and released the thumb and then
slammed the door again. He pulled down the front shades
and lay down in the back of the car on the army blanket.
Outside he could hear Hoover Shoats jumping around on
the pavement and howling. When the howls died down,
Haze heard a few steps up to the car and then an impassioned,
breathless voice say through the tin, "You watch out,
friend. I'm going to run you out of business. I can get my
own new jesus and I can get Prophets for peanuts, you hear?
Do you hear me, friend?" the hoarse voice said.

Haze didn't answer.

"Yeah and I'll be out there doing my own preaching tomorrow night. What you need is a little competition," the
voice said. "Do you hear me, friend?"

Haze got up and leaned over the front seat and banged
his hand down on the horn of the Essex. It made a sound
like a goat's laugh cut off with a buzz saw. Hoover Shoats
jumped back as if a charge of electricity had gone through
him. "All right, friend," he said, standing about fifteen
feet away, trembling, "you just wait, you ain't heard the
last of me yet," and he turned and went off down the quiet
street.

Haze stayed in his car about an hour and had a bad
experience in it: he dreamed he was not dead but only
buried. He was not waiting on the Judgment because there
was no Judgment, he was waiting on nothing. Various eyes
looked through the back oval window at his situation, some
with considerable reverence, like the boy from the zoo,
and some only to see what they could see. There were three
women with paper sacks who looked at him critically
as if he were something—a piece of fish—they might buy,
but they passed on after a minute. A man in a canvas hat
looked in and put his thumb to his nose and wiggled his
fingers. Then a woman with two little boys on either side

of her stopped and looked in, grinning. After a second, she pushed the boys out of view and indicated that she would climb in and keep him company for a while, but she couldn't get through the glass and finally she went off. All this time Haze was bent on getting out but since there was no use to try, he didn't make any move one way or the other. He kept expecting Hawks to appear at the oval window with a wrench, but the blind man didn't come.

Finally he shook off the dream and woke up. He thought it should be morning but it was only midnight. He pulled himself over into the front of the car and eased his foot on the starter and the Essex rolled off quietly as if nothing were the matter with it. He drove back to the house and let himself in but instead of going upstairs to his room, he stood in the hall, looking at the blind man's door. He went over to it and put his ear to the keyhole and heard the sound of snoring; he turned the knob gently but the door didn't move.

For the first time, the idea of picking the lock occurred to him. He felt in his pockets for an instrument and came on a small piece of wire that he sometimes used for a toothpick. There was only a dim light in the hall but it was enough for him to work by and he knelt down at the keyhole and inserted the wire into it carefully, trying not to make a noise.

After a while when he had tried the wire five or six different ways, there was a slight click in the lock. He stood up, trembling, and opened the door. His breath came short and his heart was palpitating as if he had run all the way here from a great distance. He stood just inside the room until his eyes got accustomed to the darkness and then he moved slowly over to the iron bed and stood there. Hawks was lying across it. His head was hanging over the edge. Haze squatted down by him and struck a match close to his face and he opened his eyes. The two sets of eyes looked at each other as long as the match lasted; Haze's expression seemed to open onto a deeper blankness and reflect something and then close again.

"Now you can get out," Hawks said in a short thick voice, "now you can leave me alone," and he made a jab at the face over him without touching it. It moved back, expressionless under the white hat, and was gone in a second.

CHAPTER 10

The next night, Haze parked the Essex in front of the Odeon Theater and climbed up on it and began to preach. "Let me tell you what I and this church stand for!" he called from the nose of the car. "Stop one minute to listen to the truth because you may never hear it again." He stood there with his neck thrust forward, moving one arm upward in a vague arc. Two women and a boy stopped.

"I preach there are all kinds of truth, your truth and somebody else's, but behind all of them, there's only one truth and that is that there's no truth," he called. "No truth behind all truths is what I and this church preach! Where you come from is gone, where you thought you were going to never was there, and where you are is no good unless you can get away from it. Where is there a place for you to be? No place.

"Nothing outside you can give you any place," he said. "You needn't to look at the sky because it's not going to open up and show no place behind it. You needn't to search for any hole in the ground to look through into somewhere else. You can't go neither forwards nor backwards into your daddy's time nor your children's if you have them. In yourself right now is all the place you've got. If there was any Fall, look there, if there was any Redemption, look there, and if you expect any Judgment, look there, because they all three will have to be in your time and your body and where in your time and your body can they be?

"Where in your time and your body has Jesus redeemed you?" he cried. "Show me where because I don't see the place. If there was a place where Jesus had redeemed you that would be the place for you to be, but which of you can find it?"

Another trickle of people came out of the Odeon and two stopped to look at him. "Who is that that says it's your conscience?" he cried, looking around with a constricted face as if he could smell the particular person who thought that. "Your conscience is a trick," he said, "it don't exist though you may think it does, and if you think it does, you had best get it out in the open and hunt it down and kill it, because it's no more than your face in the mirror is or your shadow behind you."

He was preaching with such concentration that he didn't notice a high rat-colored car that had been driven around the block three times already, while the two men in it hunted a place to park. He didn't see it when it pulled in two cars over from him in a space that another car had just pulled out of, and he didn't see Hoover Shoats and a man in a glare-blue suit and white hat get out of it, but after a few seconds, his head turned that way and he saw the man in the glare-blue suit and white hat up on the nose of it. He was so struck with how gaunt and thin he looked in the illusion that he stopped preaching. He had never pictured himself that way before. The man he saw was hollow-chested and carried his neck thrust forward and his arms down by his side; he stood there as if he were waiting for some signal he was afraid he might not catch.

Hoover Shoats was walking about on the sidewalk, striking a few chords on his guitar. "Friends," he called, "I want to innerduce you to the True Prophet here and I want you all to listen to his words because I think they're going to make you happy like they've made me!" If Haze had noticed Hoover he might have been impressed by how happy he looked, but his attention was fixed on the man on the nose of the car. He slid down from his own car and moved up closer, never taking his eyes from the bleak figure. Hoover Shoats raised his hand with two fingers pointed and the man suddenly cried out in a high nasal singsong voice. "The unredeemed are redeeming theirselves and the new jesus is at hand! Watch for this miracle! Help yourself to salvation in the Holy Church of Christ Without Christ!" He called it over again in exactly the same tone of voice, but faster. Then he began to cough. He had a loud consumptive cough that started somewhere deep in him and finished with a long wheeze. He expectorated a white fluid at the end of it.

Haze was standing next to a fat woman who after a minute turned her head and stared at him and then turned it again and stared at the True Prophet. Finally she touched his elbow with hers and grinned at him. "Him and you twins?" she asked.

"If you don't hunt it down and kill it, it'll hunt you down and kill you," Haze answered.

"Huh? Who?" she said.

He turned away and she stared at him as he got back

in his car and drove off. Then she touched the elbow of a man on the other side of her. "He's nuts," she said. "I never seen no twins that hunted each other down."

When he got back to his room, Sabbath Hawks was in his bed. She was pushed over into one corner of it, sitting with one arm drawn around her knees and one hand holding onto the sheet as if she meant to hang on by it. Her face was sullen and apprehensive. Haze sat down on the bed but he barely glanced at her. "I don't care if you hit me with the table," she said. "I'm not going. There's no place for me to go. He's run off on me and it was you run him off. I was watching last night and I seen you come in and hold that match to his face. I thought anybody would have seen what he was before that without having to strike no match. He's just a crook. He ain't even a big crook, just a little one, and when he gets tired of that, he begs on the street."

Haze leaned down and began untying his shoes. They were old army shoes that he had painted black to get the government off. He untied them and eased his feet out and sat there looking down, while she watched him cautiously.

"Are you going to hit me or not?" she asked. "If you are, go ahead and do it right now because I'm not going. I ain't got any place to go." He didn't look as if he were going to hit anything; he looked as if he were going to sit there until he died. "Listen," she said, with a quick change of tone, "from the minute I set eyes on you I said to myself, that's what I got to have, just give me some of him! I said look at those pee-can eyes and go crazy, girl! That innocent look don't hide a thing, he's just pure filthy right down to the guts, like me. The only difference is I like being that way and he don't. Yes sir!" she said. "I like being that way, and I can teach you how to like it. Don't you want to learn how to like it?"

He turned his head slightly and just over his shoulder he saw a pinched homely little face with bright green eyes and a grin. "Yeah," he said with no change in his stony expression, "I want to." He stood up and took off his coat and his trousers and his drawers and put them on the straight chair. Then he turned off the light and sat down on the cot again and pulled off his socks. His feet were big and white and damp to the floor and he sat there, looking at the two white shapes they made.

"Come on! Make haste," she said, knocking his back with her knee.

He unbuttoned his shirt and took it off and wiped his

face with it and dropped it on the floor. Then he slid his legs under the cover by her and sat there as if he were waiting to remember one more thing.

She was breathing very quickly. "Take off your hat, king of the beasts," she said gruffly and her hand came up behind his head and snatched the hat off and sent it flying across the room in the dark.

CHAPTER 11

The next morning toward noon a person in a long black raincoat, with a lightish hat pulled down low on his face and the brim of it turned down to meet the turned-up collar of the raincoat, was moving rapidly along certain back streets, close to the walls of the buildings. He was carrying something about the size of a baby, wrapped up in newspapers, and he carried a dark umbrella too, as the sky was an unpredictable surly gray like the back of an old goat. He had on a pair of dark glasses and a black beard which a keen observer would have said was not a natural growth but was pinned onto his hat on either side with safety pins. As he walked along, the umbrella kept slipping from under his arm and getting tangled in his feet, as if it meant to keep him from going anywhere.

He had not gone half a block before large putty-colored drops began to splatter on the pavement and there was an ugly growl in the sky behind him. He began to run, clutching the bundle in one arm and the umbrella in the other. In a second, the storm overtook him and he ducked between two show-windows into the blue and white tiled entrance of a drug store. He lowered his dark glasses a little. The pale eyes that looked over the rims belonged to Enoch Emery. Enoch was on his way to Hazel Motes's room.

He had never been to Hazel Motes's place before but the instinct that was guiding him was very sure of itself. What was in the bundle was what he had shown Hazel at the museum. He had stolen it the day before.

He had darkened his face and hands with brown shoe polish so that if he were seen in the act, he would be taken for a colored person; then he had sneaked into the museum while the guard was asleep and had broken the glass case with a wrench he'd borrowed from his landlady; then, shaking and sweating, he had lifted the shriveled man out and thrust him in a paper sack, and had crept out again past the guard, who was still asleep. He realized as soon as he got out of the museum that since no one had seen him to think he was a colored boy, he would be suspected immediately and would have to disguise himself. That was why he had on the black beard and dark glasses.

When he'd got back to his room, he had taken the new jesus out of the sack and, hardly daring to look at him, had laid him in the gilted cabinet; then he had sat down on the edge of his bed to wait. He was waiting for something to happen, he didn't know what. He knew something was going to happen and his entire system was waiting on it. He thought it was going to be one of the supreme moments in his life but apart from that, he didn't have the vaguest notion what it might be. He pictured himself, after it was over, as an entirely new man, with an even better personality than he had now. He sat there for about fifteen minutes and nothing happened.

He sat there for about five more.

Then he realized that he had to make the first move. He got up and tiptoed to the cabinet and squatted down at the door of it; in a second he opened it a crack and looked in. After a while, very slowly, he broadened the crack and inserted his head into the tabernacle.

Some time passed.

From directly behind him, only the soles of his shoes and the seat of his trousers were visible. The room was absolutely silent; there was no sound even from the street; the Universe might have been shut off; not a flea jumped. Then without any warning, a loud liquid noise burst from the cabinet and there was the thump of bone cracked once against a piece of wood. Enoch staggered backward, clutching his head and his face. He sat on the floor for a few minutes with a shocked expression on his whole figure. At the first instant, he had thought it was the shriveled man who had sneezed, but after a second, he perceived the condition of his own nose. He wiped it off with his sleeve and then he sat there on the floor for some time longer. His expression had showed that a deep unpleasant knowledge was breaking on him slowly. After a while he had kicked the ark door shut in the new jesus' face, and then he had got up and begun to eat a candy bar very rapidly. He had eaten it as if he had something against it.

The next morning he had not got up until ten o'clock—it was his day off—and he had not set out until nearly noon to look for Hazel Motes. He remembered the address Sabbath Hawks had given him and that was where his instinct was leading him. He was very sullen and disgruntled at having to spend his day off in such a way as this, and in bad weather, but he wanted to get rid of the new jesus so that if the police had to catch anybody for the robbery, they could catch Hazel Motes instead of him. He couldn't understand at all why he had let himself risk his skin for a dead shriveled-up part-nigger dwarf that had never done anything but get himself embalmed and then lain stinking in a museum the rest of his life. It was far beyond his understanding. He was very sullen. So far as he was now concerned, one jesus was as bad as another.

He had borrowed his landlady's umbrella and he discovered as he stood in the entrance of the drug store, trying to open it, that it was at least as old as she was. When he finally got it hoisted, he pushed his dark glasses back on his eyes and re-entered the downpour.

The umbrella was one his landlady had stopped using fifteen years before (which was the only reason she had lent it to him) and as soon as the rain touched the top of it, it came down with a shriek and stabbed him in the back of the neck. He ran a few feet with it over his head and then backed into another store entrance and removed it. Then to get it up again, he had to place the tip of it on the ground and ram it open with his foot. He ran out again, holding his hand up near the spokes to keep them open and this allowed the handle, which was carved to represent the head of a fox terrier, to jab him every few seconds in the stomach. He proceeded for another quarter of a block this way before the back half of the silk stood up off the spokes and allowed the storm to sweep down his collar. Then he ducked under the marquee of a movie house. It was Saturday and there were a lot of children standing more or less in a line in front of the ticket box.

Enoch was not very fond of children but children always seemed to like to look at him. The line turned and twenty or thirty eyes began to observe him with a steady interest. The umbrella had assumed an ugly position, half up and half down, and the half that was up was about to come down and spill more water under his collar. When this happened the children laughed and jumped up and down. Enoch glared at them and turned his back and lowered his dark glasses. He found himself facing a life-size four-color picture of a gorilla. Over the gorilla's head, written in red letters was, "GONGA! Giant Jungle Monarch and a Great Star! HERE IN PERSON! ! !" At the level of the gorilla's knee, there was more that said, "Gonga will appear in person in front of this theater at 12 A.M. *TODAY!* A free pass to the first ten brave enough to step up and shake his hand!"

Enoch was usually thinking of something else at the moment that Fate began drawing back her leg to kick him. When he was four years old, his father had brought him home a tin box from the penitentiary. It was orange and had a picture of some peanut brittle on the outside of it and green letters that said, A NUTTY SURPRISE! When Enoch had opened it, a coiled piece of steel had sprung out at him and broken off the ends of his two front teeth. His life was full of so many happenings like that that it would seem he should have been more sensitive to his times of danger. He stood there and read the poster twice through carefully. To his mind, an opportunity to insult a successful ape came from the hand of Providence. He suddenly regained all his reverence for the new jesus. He saw that he was going to be rewarded after all and have the supreme moment he had expected.

He turned around and asked the nearest child what time it was. The child said it was twelve-ten and that Gonga was already ten minutes late. Another child said that maybe the rain had delayed him. Another said, no not the rain, his director was taking a plane from Hollywood. Enoch gritted his teeth. The first child said that if he wanted to shake the star's hand, he would have to get in line like the rest of them and wait his turn. Enoch got in line. A child asked him how old he was. Another observed that he had funny-looking teeth. He ignored all this as best he could and began to straighten out the umbrella.

In a few minutes a black truck turned around the corner and came slowly up the street in the heavy rain. Enoch pushed the umbrella under his arm and began to squint through his dark glasses. As the truck approached, a phonograph inside it began to play "Tarara Boom Di Aye," but the music was almost drowned out by the rain. There was a large illustration of a blonde on the outside of the truck, advertising some picture other than the gorilla's.

The children held their line carefully as the truck stopped in front of the movie house. The back door of it was constructed like a paddy wagon, with a grate, but the ape was not at it. Two men in raincoats got out of the cab part, cursing, and ran around to the back and opened the door. One of them stuck his head in and said, "Okay, make it snappy, willya?" The other jerked his thumb at the children and said, "Get back willya, willya get back?"

A voice on the record inside the truck said, "Here's Gonga, folks, Roaring Gonga and a Great Star! Give Gonga a big hand, folks!" The voice was barely a mumble in the rain.

The man who was waiting by the door of the truck stuck his head in again. "Okay willya get out?" he said.

There was a faint thump somewhere inside the van. After a second a dark furry arm emerged just enough for the rain to touch it and then drew back inside.

"Goddam," the man who was under the marquee said; he took off his raincoat and threw it to the man by the door, who threw it into the wagon. After two or three minutes more, the gorilla appeared at the door, with the raincoat buttoned up to his chin and the collar turned up. There was an iron chain hanging from around his neck; the man grabbed it and pulled him down and the two of them bounded under the marquee together. A motherly-looking woman was in the glass ticket box, getting the passes ready for the first ten children brave enough to step up and shake hands.

The gorilla ignored the children entirely and followed the man over to the other side of the entrance where there was a small platform raised about a foot off the ground. He stepped up on it and turned facing the children and began to growl. His growls were not so much loud as poisonous; they appeared to issue from a black heart. Enoch was terrified and if he had not been surrounded by the children, he would have run away.

"Who'll step up first?" the man said. "Come on come on, who'll step up first? A free pass to the first kid stepping up."

There was no movement from the group of children. The man glared at them. "What's the matter with you kids?" he barked. "You yellow? He won't hurt you as long as I got him by this chain." He tightened his grip on the chain and jangled it at them to show he was holding it securely.

After a minute a little girl separated herself from the group. She had long wood-shaving curls and a fierce triangular face. She moved up to within four feet of the star.

"Okay okay," the man said, rattling the chain, "make it snappy."

The ape reached out and gave her hand a quick shake. By this time there was another little girl ready and then two boys. The line re-formed and began to move up.

The gorilla kept his hand extended and turned his head away with a bored look at the rain. Enoch had got over his fear and was trying frantically to think of an obscene remark that would be suitable to insult him with. Usually he didn't have any trouble with this kind of composition but nothing came to him now. His brain, both parts, was completely empty. He couldn't think even of the insulting phrases he used every day.

There were only two children in front of him by now. The first one shook hands and stepped aside. Enoch's heart was beating violently. The child in front of him finished and stepped aside and left him facing the ape, who took his hand with an automatic motion.

It was the first hand that had been extended to Enoch since he had come to the city. It was warm and soft.

For a second he only stood there, clasping it. Then he began to stammer. "My name is Enoch Emery," he mumbled. "I attended the Rodemill Boys' Bible Academy. I work at the city zoo. I seen two of your pictures. I'm only eighteen year old but I already work for the city. My daddy made me com . . ." and his voice cracked.

The star leaned slightly forward and a change came in his eyes: an ugly pair of human ones moved closer and squinted at Enoch from behind the celluloid pair. "You go to hell," a surly voice inside the ape-suit said, low but distinctly, and the hand was jerked away.

Enoch's humiliation was so sharp and painful that he turned around three times before he realized which direction he wanted to go in. Then he ran off into the rain as fast as he could.

By the time he reached Sabbath Hawks's house, he was soaked through and so was his bundle. He held it in a fierce grip but all he wanted was to get rid of it and never see it again. Haze's landlady was out on the porch, looking distrustfully into the storm. He found out from her where Haze's room was and went up to it. The door was ajar and he stuck his head in the crack. Haze was lying on his cot, with a washrag over his eyes; the exposed part of his face was ashen and set in a grimace, as if he were in some permanent pain. Sabbath Hawks was sitting at the table by the window, studying herself in a pocket mirror. Enoch scratched on the wall and she looked up. She put the mirror down and tiptoed out into the hall and shut the door behind her.

"My man is sick today and sleeping," she said, "because he didn't sleep none last night. What you want?"

"This is for him, it ain't for you," Enoch said, handing her the wet bundle. "A friend of his give it to me to give to him. I don't know what's in it."

"I'll take care of it," she said. "You needn't to worry none."

Enoch had an urgent need to insult somebody immediately; it was the only thing that could give his feelings even a temporary relief. "I never known he would have nothing to do with you," he remarked, giving her one of his special looks.

"He couldn't leave off following me," she said. "Sometimes it's thataway with them. You don't know what's in this package?"

"Lay-overs to catch meddlers," he said. "You just give it to him and he'll know what it is and you can tell him I'm glad to get shut of it." He started down the stairs and halfway he turned and gave her another special look. "I see why he has to put theter washrag over his eyes," he said.

"You keep your beeswax in your ears," she said. "Nobody asked you." When she heard the front door slam behind him, she turned the bundle over and began to examine it. There was no telling from the outside what was in it; it was too hard to be clothes and too soft to be a machine. She tore a hole in the paper at one end and saw what looked like five dried peas in a row but the hall was too dark for her to see clearly what they were. She decided to take the package to the bathroom, where there was a good light, and open it up before she gave it to Haze. If he was so sick as he said he was, he wouldn't want to be bothered with any bundle.

Early that morning he had claimed to have a terrible pain in his chest. He had begun to cough during the night—a hard hollow cough that sounded as if he were making it up as he went along. She was certain he was only trying to drive her off by letting her think he had a catching disease.

He's not really sick, she said to herself going down the hall, he just ain't used to me yet. She went in and sat down on the edge of a large green claw-footed tub and ripped the string off the package. "But he'll get used to me," she muttered. She pulled off the wet paper and let it fall on the floor; then she sat with a stunned look, staring at what was in her lap.

Two days out of the glass case had not improved the new jesus' condition. One side of his face had been partly mashed in and on the other side, his eyelid had split and a pale dust was seeping out of it. For a while her face had an empty look, as if she didn't know what she thought about him or didn't think anything. She might have sat there for ten minutes, without a thought, held by whatever it was that was familiar about him. She had never known anyone who looked like him before, but there was something in him of everyone she had ever known, as if they had all been rolled into one person and killed and shrunk and dried.

She held him up and began to examine him and after a minute her hands grew accustomed to the feel of his skin. Some of his hair had come undone and she brushed it back where it belonged, holding him in the crook of her arm and looking down into his squinched face. His mouth had been knocked a little to one side so that there was just a trace of a grin covering his terrified look. She began to rock him a little in her arm and a slight reflection of the same grin appeared on her own face. "Well I declare," she murmured, "you're right cute, ain't you?"

His head fitted exactly into the hollow of her shoulder. "Who's your momma and daddy?" she asked.

An answer came into her mind at once and she let out a short little bark and sat grinning, with a pleased expression in her eyes. "Well, let's go give him a jolt," she said after a while.

Haze had already been jolted awake when the front door slammed behind Enoch Emery. He had sat up and seeing she was not in the room, he had jumped up and begun to put on his clothes. He had one thought in mind and it had come to him, like his decision to buy a car, out of his sleep and without any indication of it beforehand: he was going to move immediately to some other city and preach the Church Without Christ where they had never heard of it. He would get another room there and another woman and make a new start with nothing on his mind. The entire possibility of this came from the advantage of having a car—of having something that moved fast, in privacy, to the place you wanted to be. He looked out the window at the Essex. It sat high and square in the pouring rain. He didn't notice the rain, only the car; if asked he would not have been able to say that it was raining. He was charged with energy and he left the window and finished putting on his clothes. Earlier that morning, when he had waked up for the first time, he had felt as if he were about to be caught by a complete consumption in his chest; it had seemed to be growing hollow all night and yawning underneath him, and he had kept hearing his coughs as if they came from a distance. After a while he had been sucked down into a strengthless sleep, but he had waked up with this plan, and with the energy to carry it out right away.

He snatched his duffel bag from under the table and began plunging his extra belongings into it. He didn't have much and a quarter of what he had was already in. His hand managed the packing so that it never touched the Bible that had sat like a rock in the bottom of the bag for the last few years, but as he rooted out a place for his second shoes, his fingers clutched around a small oblong object and he pulled it out. It was the case with his mother's glasses in it. He had forgotten that he had a pair of glasses. He put them on and the wall that he was facing moved up closer and wavered. There was a small white-framed mirror hung on the back of the door and he made his way to it and looked at himself. His blurred face was dark with excitement and the lines in it were deep and crooked. The little silver-rimmed glasses gave him a look of deflected sharpness, as if they were hiding some dishonest plan that would show in his naked eyes. His fingers began to snap nervously and he forgot what he had been going to do. He saw his mother's face in his, looking at the face in the mirror. He moved back quickly and raised his hand to take off the glasses but the door opened and two more faces floated into his line of vision; one of them said, "Call me Momma now."

The smaller dark one, just under the other, only squinted as if it were trying to identify an old friend who was going to kill it.

Haze stood motionless with one hand still on the bow of the glasses and the other arrested in the air at the level of his chest; his head was thrust forward as if he had to use his whole face to see with. He was about four feet from them but they seemed just under his eyes.

"Ask your daddy yonder where he was running off to—sick as he is?" Sabbath said. "Ask him isn't he going to take you and me with him?"

The hand that had been arrested in the air moved forward and plucked at the squinting face but without touching it; it reached again, slowly, and plucked at nothing and then it lunged and snatched the shriveled body and threw it against the wall. The head popped and the trash inside sprayed out in a little cloud of dust.

"You've broken him!" Sabbath shouted, "and he was mine!"

Haze snatched the skin off the floor. He opened the outside door where the landlady thought there had once been a fire-escape, and flung out what he had in his hand. The rain blew in his face and he jumped back and stood, with a cautious look, as if he were bracing himself for a blow.

"You didn't have to throw him out," she yelled. "I might have fixed him!"

He moved up closer and hung out the door, staring into the gray blur around him. The rain fell on his hat with loud splatters as if it were falling on tin.

"I knew when I first seen you you were mean and evil," a furious voice behind him said. "I seen you wouldn't let nobody have nothing. I seen you were mean enough to slam a baby against a wall. I seen you wouldn't never have no fun or let anybody else because you didn't want nothing but Jesus!"

He turned and raised his arm in a vicious gesture, almost

losing his balance in the door. Drops of rain water were splattered over the front of the glasses and on his red face and here and there they hung sparkling from the brim of his hat. "I don't want nothing but the truth!" he shouted, "and what you see is the truth and I've seen it!"

"Preacher talk," she said. "Where were you going to run off to?"

"I've seen the only truth there is!" he shouted.

"Where were you going to run off to?"

"To some other city," he said in a loud hoarse voice, "to preach the truth. The Church Without Christ! And I got a car to get there in, I got . . ." but he was stopped by a cough. It was not much of a cough—it sounded like a little yell for help at the bottom of a canyon—but the color and the expression drained out of his face until it was as straight and blank as the rain falling down behind him.

"And when were you going?" she asked.

"After I get some more sleep," he said, and pulled off the glasses and threw them out the door.

"You ain't going to get none," she said.

CHAPTER 12

In spite of himself, Enoch couldn't get over the expectation that the new jesus was going to do something for him in return for his services. This was the virtue of Hope, which was made up, in Enoch, of two parts suspicion and one part lust. It operated on him all the rest of the day after he left Sabbath Hawks. He had only a vague idea how he wanted to be rewarded, but he was not a boy without ambition: he wanted to become something. He wanted to better his condition until it was the best. He wanted to be THE young man of the future, like the ones in the insurance ads. He wanted, some day, to see a line of people waiting to shake his hand.

All afternoon, he fidgeted and fooled in his room, biting his nails and shredding what was left of the silk off the landlady's umbrella. Finally he denuded it entirely and broke off the spokes. What was left was a black stick with a sharp steel point at one end and a dog's head at the other. It might have been an instrument for some specialized kind of torture that had gone out of fashion. Enoch walked up and down his room with it under his arm and realized that it would distinguish him on the sidewalk.

About seven o'clock in the evening, he put on his coat and took the stick and headed for a little restaurant two blocks away. He had the sense that he was setting off to get some honor, but he was very nervous, as if he were afraid he might have to snatch it instead of receive it.

He never set out for anything without eating first. The restaurant was called the Paris Diner; it was a tunnel about six feet wide, located between a shoe shine parlor and a dry-cleaning establishment. Enoch slid in and climbed up on the far stool at the counter and said he would have a bowl of split-pea soup and a chocolate malted milkshake.

The waitress was a tall woman with a big yellow dental plate and the same color hair done up in a black hairnet. One hand never left her hip; she filled orders with the other one. Although Enoch came in every night, she had never learned to like him.

Instead of filling his order, she began to fry bacon; there

was only one other customer in the place and he had finished his meal and was reading a newspaper; there was no one to eat the bacon but her. Enoch reached over the counter and prodded her hip with his stick. "Listenhere," he said, "I got to go. I'm in a hurry."

"Go then," she said. Her jaw began to work and she stared into the skillet with a fixed attention.

"Lemme just have a piece of theter cake yonder," he said, pointing to a half of pink and yellow cake on a round glass stand. "I think I got something to do. I got to be going. Set it up there next to him," he said, indicating the customer reading the newspaper. He slid over the stools and began reading the outside sheet of the man's paper.

The man lowered the paper and looked at him. Enoch smiled. The man raised the paper again. "Could I borrow some part of your paper that you ain't studying?" Enoch asked. The man lowered it again and stared at him; he had muddy unflinching eyes. He leafed deliberately through the paper and shook out the sheet with the comic strips and handed it to Enoch. It was Enoch's favorite part. He read it every evening like an office. While he ate the cake that the waitress had torpedoed down the counter at him, he read and felt himself surge with kindness and courage and strength.

When he finished one side, he turned the sheet over and began to scan the advertisements for movies that filled the other side. His eye went over three columns without stopping; then it came to a box that advertised Gonga, Giant Jungle Monarch, and listed the theaters he would visit on his tour and the hours he would be at each one. In thirty minutes he would arrive at the Victory on 57th Street and that would be his last appearance in the city.

If anyone had watched Enoch read this, he would have seen a certain transformation in his countenance. It still shone with the inspiration he had absorbed from the comic strips, but something else had come over it: a look of awakening.

The waitress happened to turn around to see if he hadn't gone. "What's the matter with you?" she said. "Did you swallow a seed?"

"I know what I want," Enoch murmured.

"I know what I want too," she said with a dark look.

Enoch felt for his stick and laid his change on the counter. "I got to be going."

"Don't let me keep you," she said.

"You may not see me again," he said, "—the way I am."

"Any way I don't see you will be all right with me," she said.

Enoch left. It was a pleasant damp evening. The puddles on the sidewalk shone and the store windows were steamy and bright with junk. He disappeared down a side street and made his way rapidly along the darker passages of the city, pausing only once or twice at the end of an alley to dart a glance in each direction before he ran on. The Victory was a small theater, suited to the needs of the family, in one of the closer subdivisions; he passed through a succession of lighted areas and then on through more alleys and back streets until he came to the business section that surrounded it. Then he slowed up. He saw it about a block away, glittering in its darker setting. He didn't cross the street to the side it was on but kept on the far side, moving forward with his squint fixed on the glary spot. He stopped when he was directly across from it and hid himself in a narrow stair cavity that divided a building.

The truck that carried Gonga was parked across the street and the star was standing under the marquee, shaking hands with an elderly woman. She moved aside and a gentleman in a polo shirt stepped up and shook hands vigorously, like a sportsman. He was followed by a boy of about three who wore a tall Western hat that nearly covered his face; he had to be pushed ahead by the line. Enoch watched for some time, his face working with envy. The small boy was followed by a lady in shorts, she by an old man who tried to draw extra attention to himself by dancing up instead of walking in a dignified way. Enoch suddenly darted across the street and slipped noiselessly into the open back door of the truck.

The handshaking went on until the feature picture was ready to begin. Then the star got back in the van and the people filed into the theater. The driver and the man who was master of ceremonies climbed in the cab part and the truck rumbled off. It crossed the city rapidly and continued on the highway, going very fast.

There came from the van certain thumping noises, not those of the normal gorilla, but they were drowned out by the drone of the motor and the steady sound of wheels against the road. The night was pale and quiet, with nothing to stir it but an occasional complaint from a hoot owl and the distant muted jarring of a freight train. The truck sped on until it slowed for a crossing, and as the van rattled over the tracks, a figure slipped from the door and almost fell, and then limped hurriedly off toward the woods.

Once in the darkness of a pine thicket, he laid down a pointed stick he had been clutching and something bulky and loose that he had been carrying under his arm, and began to undress. He folded each garment neatly after he had taken it off and then stacked it on top of the last thing he had removed. When all his clothes were in the pile, he took up the stick and began making a hole in the ground with it.

The darkness of the pine grove was broken by paler moonlit spots that moved over him now and again and showed him to be Enoch. His natural appearance was marred by a gash that ran from the corner of his lip to his collarbone and by a lump under his eye that gave him a dulled insensitive look. Nothing could have been more deceptive for he was burning with the intensest kind of happiness.

He dug rapidly until he had made a trench about a foot long and a foot deep. Then he placed the stack of clothes in it and stood aside to rest a second. Burying his clothes was not a symbol to him of burying his former self; he only knew he wouldn't need them any more. As soon as he got his breath, he pushed the displaced dirt over the hole and stamped it down with his foot. He discovered while he did this that he still had his shoes on, and when he finished, he removed them and threw them from him. Then he picked up the loose bulky object and shook it vigorously.

In the uncertain light, one of his lean white legs could be seen to disappear and then the other, one arm and then the other: a black heavier shaggier figure replaced his. For an instant, it had two heads, one light and one dark, but after a second, it pulled the dark back head over the other and corrected this. It busied itself with certain hidden fastenings and what appeared to be minor adjustments of its hide.

For a time after this, it stood very still and didn't do anything. Then it began to growl and beat its chest; it jumped up and down and flung its arms and thrust its head forward. The growls were thin and uncertain at first but they grew louder after a second. They became low and poisonous, louder again, low and poisonous again; they stopped altogether. The figure extended its hand, clutched nothing, and shook its arm vigorously; it withdrew the arm, extended it again, clutched nothing, and shook. It repeated this four or five times. Then it picked up the pointed stick and placed it at a cocky angle under its arm and left the woods for the highway. No gorilla in existence, whether in the jungles of Africa or California, or in New York City in the finest apartment in the world, was happier at that moment than this one, whose god had finally rewarded it.

A man and woman sitting close together on a rock just off the highway were looking across an open stretch of valley at a view of the city in the distance and they didn't see the shaggy figure approaching. The smokestacks and square tops of buildings made a black uneven wall against the lighter sky and here and there a steeple cut a sharp wedge out of a cloud. The young man turned his neck just in time to see the gorilla standing a few feet away, hideous and black, with its hand extended. He eased his arm from around the woman and disappeared silently into the woods. She, as soon as she turned her eyes, fled screaming down the highway. The gorilla stood as though surprised and presently its arm fell to its side. It sat down on the rock where they had been sitting and stared over the valley at the uneven skyline of the city.

CHAPTER 13

On his second night out, working with his hired Prophet
and the Holy Church of Christ Without Christ, Hoover
Shoats made fifteen dollars and thirty-five cents clear.
The Prophet got three dollars an evening for his services
and the use of his car. His name was Solace Layfield; he
had consumption and a wife and six children and being
a Prophet was as much work as he wanted to do. It
never occurred to him that it might be a dangerous job.
The second night out, he failed to observe a high rat-colored
car parked about a half-block away and a white face inside
it, watching him with the kind of intensity that means something is going to happen no matter what is done to keep
it from happening.

The face watched him for almost an hour while he
performed on the nose of his car every time Hoover Shoats
raised his hand with two fingers pointed. When the last
showing of the movie was over and there were no more
people to attract, Hoover paid him and the two of them
got in his car and drove off. They drove about ten blocks
to where Hoover lived; the car stopped and Hoover jumped
out, calling, "See you tomorrow night, friend"; then he
went inside a dark doorway and Solace Layfield drove
on. A half-block behind him the other rat-colored car was
following steadily. The driver was Hazel Motes.

Both cars increased their speed and in a few minutes
they were heading rapidly toward the outskirts of town.
The first car cut off onto a lonesome road where the trees
were hung over with moss and the only light came like
stiff antennae from the two cars. Haze gradually shortened
the distance between them and then, grinding his motor
suddenly, he shot ahead and rammed the back end of
the other car. Both cars came to a stop.

Haze backed the Essex a little way down the road, while
the other Prophet got out of his car and stood squinting
in the glare from Haze's lights. After a second, he came
up to the window of the Essex and looked in. There was
no sound but from crickets and tree frogs. "What you want?"

he said in a nervous voice. Haze didn't answer, he only looked at him, and in a second the man's jaw slackened and he seemed to perceive the resemblance in their clothes and possibly in their faces. "What you want?" he said in a higher voice. "I ain't done nothing to you."

Haze ground the motor of the Essex again and shot forward. This time he rammed the other car at such an angle that it rolled to the side of the road and over into the ditch.

The man got up off the ground where he had been thrown and ran back to the window of the Essex. He stood about four feet away, looking in.

"What you keep a thing like that on the road for?" Haze said.

"It ain't nothing wrong with that car," the man said. "Howcome you knockt it in the ditch?"

"Take off that hat," Haze said.

"Listenere," the man said, beginning to cough, "what you want? Quit just looking at me. Say what you want."

"You ain't true," Haze said. "What do you get up on top of a car and say you don't believe in what you do believe in for?"

"Whatsit to you?" the man wheezed. "Whatsit to you what I do?"

"What do you do it for?" Haze said. "That's what I asked you."

"A man has to look out for hisself," the other Prophet said.

"You ain't true," Haze said. "You believe in Jesus."

"Whatsit to you?" the man said. "What you knockt my car off the road for?"

"Take off that hat and that suit," Haze said.

"Listenere," the man said, "I ain't trying to mock you. He bought me thisyer suit. I thrown my othern away."

Haze reached out and brushed the man's white hat off. "And take off that suit," he said.

The man began to sidle off, out into the middle of the road.

"Take off that suit," Haze shouted and started the car forward after him. Solace began to lope down the road, taking off his coat as he went. "Take it all off," Haze yelled, with his face close to the windshield.

The Prophet began to run in earnest. He tore off his shirt and unbuckled his belt and ran out of the trousers. He began grabbing for his feet as if he would take off his shoes too, but before he could get at them, the Essex knocked him flat and ran over him. Haze drove about twenty feet and stopped the car and then began to back it. He backed it over the body and then stopped and got out. The Essex stood half over the other Prophet as if it were pleased to guard what it had finally brought down. The man didn't look so much like Haze, lying on the ground on his face without his hat or suit on. A lot of blood was coming out of him and forming a puddle around his head. He was motionless all but for one finger that moved up and down in front of his face as if he were marking time with it. Haze poked his toe in his side and he wheezed for a second and then was quiet. "Two things I can't stand," Haze said, "—a man that ain't true and one that mocks what is. You shouldn't ever have tampered with me if you didn't want what you got."

The man was trying to say something but he was only wheezing. Haze squatted down by his face to listen. "Give my mother a lot of trouble," he said through a kind of bubbling in his throat. "Never giver no rest. Stole theter car. Never told the truth to my daddy or give Henry what, never give him . . ."

"You shut up," Haze said, leaning his head closer to hear the confession.

"Told where his still was and got five dollars for it," the man gasped.

"You shut up now," Haze said.

"Jesus . . ." the man said.

"Shut up like I told you to now," Haze said.

"Jesus hep me," the man wheezed.

Haze gave him a hard slap on the back and he was quiet. He leaned down to hear if he was going to say anything else but he wasn't breathing any more. Haze turned around and examined the front of the Essex to see if there had been any damage done to it. The bumper had a few splurts of blood on it but that was all. Before he turned around and drove back to town, he wiped them off with a rag.

Early the next morning he got out of the back of the car and drove to a filling station to get the Essex filled up and checked for his trip. He hadn't gone back to his room but had spent the night parked in an alley, not sleeping but thinking about the life he was going to begin, preaching the Church Without Christ in the new city.

At the filling station a sleepy-looking white boy came out to wait on him and he said he wanted the tank filled up, the oil and water checked, and the tires tested for air, that he was going on a long trip. The boy asked him where he was going and he told him to another city. The boy asked him if he was going that far in this car here and he said yes he was. He tapped the boy on the front of his shirt. He said nobody with a good car needed to worry about anything, and he asked the boy if he understood that. The boy said yes he did, that that was his opinion too. Haze introduced himself and said that he was a preacher for the Church Without Christ and that he preached every night on the nose of this very car here. He explained that he was going to another city to preach. The boy filled up the gas tank and checked the water and oil and tested the tires, and while he was working, Haze followed him around, telling him what it was right to believe. He said it was not right to believe anything you couldn't see or hold in your hands or test with your teeth. He said he had only a few days ago believed in blasphemy as the way to salvation, but that you couldn't even believe in that because then you were believing in something to blaspheme. As for the Jesus who was reported to have been born at Bethlehem and crucified on Calvary for man's sins, Haze said, He was too foul a notion for a sane person to carry in his head, and he picked up the boy's water bucket and bammed it on the concrete pavement to emphasize what he was saying. He began to curse and blaspheme Jesus in a quiet intense way but with such conviction that the boy paused from his work to listen. When he had finished checking the Essex, he said that there was a leak in the gas tank and two in the radiator and that the rear tire would probably last twenty miles if he went slow.

"Listen," Haze said, "this car is just beginning its life. A lightning bolt couldn't stop it!"

"It ain't any use to put water in it," the boy said, "because it won't hold it."

"You put it in just the same," Haze said, and he stood there and watched while the boy put it in. Then he got a road map from him and drove off, leaving little bead-chains of water and oil and gas on the road.

He drove very fast out onto the highway, but once he had gone a few miles, he had the sense that he was not gaining ground. Shacks and filling stations and road camps and 666 signs passed him, and deserted barns with CCC snuff ads peeling across them, even a sign that said, "Jesus Died for YOU," which he saw and deliberately did not read. He had the sense that the road was really slipping back under him. He had known all along that there was no more country but he didn't know that there was not another city.

He had not gone five miles on the highway before he

heard a siren behind him. He looked around and saw a black patrol car coming up. It drove alongside him and the patrolman in it motioned for him to pull over to the edge of the road. The patrolman had a red pleasant face and eyes the color of clear fresh ice.

"I wasn't speeding," Haze said.

"No," the patrolman agreed, "you wasn't."

"I was on the right side of the road."

"Yes you was, that's right," the cop said.

"What you want with me?"

"I just don't like your face," the patrolman said. "Where's your license?"

"I don't like your face either," Haze said, "and I don't have a license."

"Well," the patrolman said in a kindly voice, "I don't reckon *you* need one."

"Well I ain't got one if I do," Haze said.

"Listen," the patrolman said, taking another tone, "would you mind driving your car up to the top of the next hill? I want you to see the view from up there, puttiest view you ever did see."

Haze shrugged but he started the car up. He didn't mind fighting the patrolman if that was what he wanted. He drove to the top of the hill, with the patrol car following close behind him. "Now you turn it facing the embankment," the patrolman called. "You'll be able to see better thataway." Haze turned it facing the embankment. "Now maybe you better had get out," the cop said. "I think you could see better if you was out."

Haze got out and glanced at the view. The embankment dropped down for about thirty feet, sheer washed-out red clay, into a partly burnt pasture where there was one scrub cow lying near a puddle. Over in the middle distance there was a one-room shack with a buzzard standing hunch-shouldered on the roof.

The patrolman got behind the Essex and pushed it over the embankment and the cow stumbled up and galloped across the field and into the woods; the buzzard flapped off to a tree at the edge of the clearing. The car landed on its top, with the three wheels that stayed on, spinning. The motor bounced out and rolled some distance away and various odd pieces scattered this way and that.

"Them that don't have a car, don't need a license," the patrolman said, dusting his hands on his pants.

Haze stood for a few minutes, looking over at the scene. His face seemed to reflect the entire distance across the clearing and on beyond, the entire distance that extended from his eyes to the blank gray sky that went on, depth after depth, into space. His knees bent under him and he sat down on the edge of the embankment with his feet hanging over.

The patrolman stood staring at him. "Could I give you a lift to where you was going?" he asked.

After a minute he came a little closer and said, "Where was you going?"

He leaned on down with his hands on his knees and said in an anxious voice, "Was you going anywheres?"

"No," Haze said.

The patrolman squatted down and put his hand on Haze's shoulder. "You hadn't planned to go anywheres?" he asked anxiously.

Haze shook his head. His face didn't change and he didn't turn it toward the patrolman. It seemed to be concentrated on space.

The patrolman got up and went back to his car and stood at the door of it, staring at the back of Haze's hat and shoulder. Then he said, "Well, I'll be seeing you," and got in and drove off.

After a while Haze got up and started walking back to town. It took him three hours to get inside the city again. He stopped at a supply store and bought a tin bucket and a sack of quicklime and then he went on to where he lived, carrying these. When he reached the house, he stopped outside on the sidewalk and opened the sack of lime and poured the bucket half full of it. Then he went to a water spigot by the front steps and filled up the rest of the bucket with water and started up the steps. His landlady was sitting on the porch, rocking a cat. "What you going to do with that, Mr. Motes?" she asked.

"Blind myself," he said and went on in the house.

The landlady sat there for a while longer. She was not a woman who felt more violence in one word than in another; she took every word at its face value but all the faces were the same. Still, instead of blinding herself, if she had felt that bad, she would have killed herself and she wondered why anybody wouldn't do that. She would simply have put her head in an oven or maybe have given herself too many painless sleeping pills and that would have been that. Perhaps Mr. Motes was only being ugly, for what possible reason could a person have for wanting to destroy their sight? A woman like her, who was so clear-sighted, could never stand to be blind. If she had to be blind she would rather be dead. It occurred to her suddenly that when she was dead she would be blind too.

She stared in front of her intensely, facing this for the first time. She recalled the phrase, "eternal death," that preachers used, but she cleared it out of her mind immediately, with no more change of expression than the cat. She was not religious or morbid, for which every day she thanked her stars. She would credit a person who had that streak with anything, though, and Mr. Motes had it or he wouldn't be a preacher. He might put lime in his eyes and she wouldn't doubt it a bit, because they were all, if the truth was only known, a little bit off in their heads. What possible reason could a sane person have for wanting to not enjoy himself any more?

She certainly couldn't say.

CHAPTER 14

But she kept it in mind because after he had done it, he continued to live in her house and every day the sight of him presented her with the question. She first told him he couldn't stay because he wouldn't wear dark glasses and she didn't like to look at the mess he had made in his eye sockets. At least she didn't think she did. If she didn't keep her mind going on something else when he was near her, she would find herself leaning forward, staring into his face as if she expected to see something she hadn't seen before. This irritated her with him and gave her the sense that he was cheating her in some secret way. He sat on her porch a good part of every afternoon, but sitting out there with him was like sitting by yourself; he didn't talk except when it suited him. You asked him a question in the morning and he might answer it in the afternoon, or he might never. He offered to pay her extra to let him keep his room because he knew his way in and out, and she decided to let him stay, at least until she found out how she was being cheated.

He got money from the government every month for something the war had done to his insides and so he was not obliged to work. The landlady had always been impressed with the ability to pay. When she found a stream of wealth, she followed it to its source and before long, it was not distinguishable from her own. She felt that the money she paid out in taxes returned to all the worthless pockets in the world, that the government not only sent it to foreign niggers and a-rabs, but wasted it at home on blind fools and on every idiot who could sign his name on a card. She felt justified in getting any of it back that she could. She felt justified in getting anything at all back that she could, money or anything else, as if she had once owned the earth and been dispossessed of it. She couldn't look at anything steadily without wanting it, and what provoked her most was the thought that there might be something valuable hidden near her, something she couldn't see.

To her, the blind man had the look of seeing something. His face had a peculiar pushing look, as if it were going forward after something it could just distinguish in the distance. Even when he was sitting motionless in a chair, his face had the look of straining toward something. But she knew he was totally blind. She had satisfied herself of that as soon as he took off the rag he used for a while as a bandage. She had got one long good look and it had been enough to tell her he had done what he'd said he was going to do. The other boarders, after he had taken off the rag, would pass him slowly in the hall, tiptoeing, and looking as long as they could, but now they didn't pay any attention to him; some of the new ones didn't know he had done it himself. The Hawks girl had spread it over the house as soon as it happened. She had watched him do it and then she had run to every room, yelling what he had done, and all the boarders had come running. That girl was a harpy if one ever lived, the landlady felt. She had hung around pestering him for a few days and then she had gone on off; she said she hadn't counted on no honest-to-Jesus blind man and she was homesick for her papa; he had deserted her, gone off on a banana boat. The landlady hoped he was at the bottom of the salt sea; he had been a month behind in his rent. In two weeks, of course, she was back, ready to start pestering him again. She had the disposition of a yellow jacket and you could hear her a block away, shouting and screaming at him, and him never opening his mouth.

The landlady conducted an orderly house and she told him so. She told him that when the girl lived with him, he would have to pay double; she said there were things she didn't mind and things she did. She left him to draw his own conclusions about what she meant by that, but she waited, with her arms folded, until he had drawn them. He didn't say anything, he only counted out three more dollars and handed them to her. "That girl, Mr. Motes," she said, "is only after your money."

"If that was what she wanted she could have it," he said. "I'd pay her to stay away."

The thought that her tax money would go to support such trash was more than the landlady could bear. "Don't do that," she said quickly. "She's got no right to it." The next day she called the Welfare people and made arrangements to have the girl sent to a detention home; she was eligible.

She was curious to know how much he got every month from the government and with that set of eyes removed, she felt at liberty to find out. She steamed open the government envelope as soon as she found it in the mailbox the next time; in a few days she felt obliged to raise his rent. He had made arrangements with her to give him his meals and as the price of food went up, she was obliged to raise his board also; but she didn't get rid of the feeling that she was being cheated. Why had he destroyed his eyes and saved himself unless he had some plan, unless he saw something that he couldn't get without being blind to everything else? She meant to find out everything she could about him.

"Where were your people from, Mr. Motes?" she asked him one afternoon when they were sitting on the porch. "I don't suppose they're alive?"

She supposed she might suppose what she pleased; he didn't disturb his doing nothing to answer her. "None of my people's alive either," she said. "All Mr. Flood's people's alive but him." She was a Mrs. Flood. "They all come here when they want a hand-out," she said, "but Mr. Flood had money. He died in the crack-up of an airplane."

After a while he said, "My people are all dead."

"Mr. Flood," she said, "died in the crack-up of an airplane."

She began to enjoy sitting on the porch with him, but she could never tell if he knew she was there or not. Even when he answered her, she couldn't tell if he knew it was she. She herself. Mrs. Flood, the landlady. Not just anybody. They would sit, he only sit, and she sit rocking, for half an afternoon and not two words seemed to pass between them, though she might talk at length. If she didn't talk and keep her mind going, she would find herself sitting forward in her chair, looking at him with her mouth not closed. Anyone who saw her from the sidewalk would think she was being courted by a corpse.

She observed his habits carefully. He didn't eat much or seem to mind anything she gave him. If she had been blind, she would have sat by the radio all day, eating cake and ice cream, and soaking her feet. He ate anything and never knew the difference. He kept getting thinner and his cough deepened and he developed a limp. During the first cold months, he took the virus, but he walked out every day in spite of that. He walked about half of each day. He got up early in the morning and walked in his room—she could hear him below in hers, up and down, up and down—and then he went out and walked before breakfast and after breakfast, he went out again and walked until midday. He knew the four or five blocks around the house and he didn't go any farther than those. He could have kept on one for all she saw. He could have stayed in his room, in one spot, moving his feet up and down. He could have been dead and get all he got out of life but the exercise. He might as well be one of them monks, she thought, he might as well be in a monkery. She didn't understand it. She didn't like the thought that something was being put over her head. She liked the clear light of day. She liked to see things.

She could not make up her mind what would be inside his head and what out. She thought of her own head as a switchbox where she controlled from; but with him, she could only imagine the outside in, the whole black world in his head and his head bigger than the world, his head big enough to include the sky and planets and whatever was or had been or would be. How would he know if time was going backwards or forwards or if he was going with it? She imagined it was like you were walking in a tunnel and all you could see was a pin point of light. She had to imagine the pin point of light; she couldn't think of it at all without that. She saw it as some kind of a star, like the star on Christmas cards. She saw him going backwards to Bethlehem and she had to laugh.

She thought it would be a good thing if he had something to do with his hands, something to bring him out of himself and get him in connection with the real world again. She was certain he was out of connection with it; she was not certain at times that he even knew she existed. She suggested he get himself a guitar and learn to strum it; she had a picture of them sitting on the porch in the evening and him strumming it. She had bought two rubber plants to make where they sat more private from the street, and she thought that the sound of him strumming it from behind the rubber plant would take away the dead look he had. She suggested it but he never answered the suggestion.

After he paid his room and board every month, he had a good third of the government check left but that she could see, he never spent any money. He didn't use tobacco or drink whisky; there was nothing for him to do with all that money but lose it, since there was only himself. She thought of benefits that might accrue to his widow should he leave one. She had seen money drop out of his pocket and him not bother to reach down and feel for it. One day when she was cleaning his room, she found four dollar bills and some change in his trash can. He came in about that time from one of his walks. "Mr. Motes," she said, "here's a dollar bill and some change in this waste basket. You know where your waste basket is. How did you make that mistake?"

"It was left over," he said. "I didn't need it."

She dropped onto his straight chair. "Do you throw it away every month?" she asked after a time.

"Only when it's left over," he said.

"The poor and needy," she muttered. "The poor and needy. Don't you ever think about the poor and needy? If you don't want that money somebody else might."

"You can have it," he said.

"Mr. Motes," she said coldly, "I'm not charity yet!" She realized now that he was a mad man and that he ought to be under the control of a sensible person.

The landlady was past her middle years and her plate was too large but she had long race-horse legs and a nose that had been called Grecian by one boarder. She wore her hair clustered like grapes on her brow and over each ear and in the middle behind, but none of these advantages were any use to her in attracting his attention. She saw that the only way was to be interested in what he was interested in. "Mr. Motes," she said one afternoon when they were sitting on the porch, "why don't you preach any more? Being blind wouldn't be a hinderance. People would like to go see a blind preacher. It would be something different." She was used to going on without an answer. "You could get you one of those seeing dogs," she said, "and he and you could get up a good crowd. People'll always go to see a dog.

"For myself," she continued, "I don't have that streak. I believe that what's right today is wrong tomorrow and that the time to enjoy yourself is now so long as you let others do the same. I'm as good, Mr. Motes," she said, "not believing in Jesus as a many a one that does."

"You're better," he said, leaning forward suddenly. "If you believed in Jesus, you wouldn't be so good."

He had never paid her a compliment before! "Why Mr. Motes," she said, "I expect you're a fine preacher! You certainly ought to start it again. It would give you something to do. As it is, you don't have anything to do but walk. Why don't you start preaching again?"

"I can't preach any more," he muttered.

"Why?"

"I don't have time," he said, and got up and walked off the porch as if she had reminded him of some urgent business. He walked as if his feet hurt him but he had to go on.

Some time later she discovered why he limped. She was cleaning his room and happened to knock over his extra pair of shoes. She picked them up and looked into them as if she thought she might find something hidden there. The bottoms of them were lined with gravel and broken glass and pieces of small stone. She spilled this out and sifted it through her fingers, looking for a glitter that might mean something valuable, but she saw that what she had in her hand was trash that anybody could pick up in the alley. She stood for some time, holding the shoes, and finally she put them back under the cot. In a few days she examined them again and they were lined with fresh rocks. Who's he doing this for? she asked herself. What's he getting out of doing it? Every now and then she would have an intimation of something hidden near her but out of her reach. "Mr. Motes," she said that day, when he was in her kitchen eating his dinner, "what do you walk on rocks for?"

"To pay," he said in a harsh voice.

"Pay for what?"

"It don't make any difference for what," he said. "I'm paying."

"But what have you got to show that you're paying for?" she persisted.

"Mind your business," he said rudely. "You can't see."

The landlady continued to chew very slowly. "Do you think, Mr. Motes," she said hoarsely, "that when you're dead, you're blind?"

"I hope so," he said after a minute.

"Why?" she asked, staring at him.

After a while he said, "If there's no bottom in your eyes, they hold more."

The landlady stared for a long time, seeing nothing at all.

She began to fasten all her attention on him, to the neglect of other things. She began to follow him in his walks, meeting him accidentally and accompanying him. He didn't seem to know she was there, except occasionally when he would slap at his face as if her voice bothered him, like the singing of a mosquito. He had a deep wheezing cough and she began to badger him about his health. "There's no one," she would say, "to look after you but me, Mr. Motes. No one that has your interest at heart but me. Nobody would care if I didn't." She began to make him tasty dishes and carry them to his room. He would eat what she brought, immediately, with a wry face, and hand back the plate without thanking her, as if all his attention were directed elsewhere and this was an interruption he had to suffer. One morning he told her abruptly that he was going to get his food somewhere else, and named the place, a diner around the corner, run by a foreigner. "And you'll rue the day!" she said. "You'll pick up an infection. No sane person eats there. A dark and filthy place. Encrusted! It's you that can't see, Mr. Motes."

"Crazy fool," she muttered when he had walked off. "Wait till winter comes. Where will you eat when winter comes, when the first wind blows the virus into you?"

She didn't have to wait long. He caught influenza before winter and for a while he was too weak to walk out and she had the satisfaction of bringing his meals to his room. She came earlier than usual one morning and found him asleep, breathing heavily. The old shirt he wore to sleep in was open down the front and showed three strands of barbed wire, wrapped around his chest. She retreated backwards to the door and then she dropped the tray. "Mr. Motes," she said in a thick voice, "what do you do these things for? It's not natural."

He pulled himself up.

"What's that wire around you for? It's not natural," she repeated.

After a second he began to button the shirt. "It's natural," he said.

"Well, it's not normal. It's like one of them gory stories, it's something that people have quit doing—like boiling in oil or being a saint or walling up cats," she said. "There's no reason for it. People have quit doing it."

"They ain't quit doing it as long as I'm doing it," he said.

"People have quit doing it," she repeated. "What do you do it for?"

"I'm not clean," he said.

She stood staring at him, unmindful of the broken dishes at her feet. "I know it," she said after a minute, "you got blood on that night shirt and on the bed. You ought to get you a washwoman . . ."

"That's not the kind of clean," he said.

"There's only one kind of clean, Mr. Motes," she muttered. She looked down and observed the dishes he had made her break and the mess she would have to get up and she left for the hall closet and returned in a minute with the dust pan and broom. "It's easier to bleed than sweat, Mr. Motes," she said in the voice of High Sarcasm. "You must believe in Jesus or you wouldn't do these foolish things. You must have been lying to me when you named your fine church. I wouldn't be surprised if you weren't some kind of a agent of the pope or got some connection with something funny."

"I ain't treatin' with you," he said and lay back down, coughing.

"You got nobody to take care of you but me," she reminded him.

Her first plan had been to marry him and then have him committed to the state institution for the insane, but gradually her plan had become to marry him and keep him. Watching his face had become a habit with her; she wanted to penetrate the darkness behind it and see for herself what was there. She had the sense that she had tarried long enough and that she must get him now while he was weak, or not at all. He was so weak from the influenza that he tottered when he walked; winter had already begun and the wind slashed at the house from every angle, making a sound like sharp knives swirling in the air.

"Nobody in their right mind would like to be out on a day like this," she said, putting her head suddenly into his room in the middle of the morning on one of the coldest days of the year. "Do you hear that wind, Mr. Motes? It's fortunate for you that you have this warm place to be and someone to take care of you." She made her voice more than usually soft. "Every blind and sick man is not so fortunate," she said, "as to have somebody that cares about him." She came in and sat down on the straight chair that was just at the door. She sat on the edge of it, leaning forward with her legs apart and her hands braced on her knees. "Let me tell you, Mr. Motes," she said, "few men are as fortunate as you but I can't keep climbing these stairs. It wears me out. I've been thinking what we could do about it."

He had been lying motionless on the bed but he sat up suddenly as if he were listening, almost as if he had been alarmed by the tone of her voice. "I know you wouldn't want to give up your room here," she said, and waited for the effect of this. He turned his face toward her; she could tell she had his attention. "I know you like it here and wouldn't want to leave and you're a sick man and need somebody to take care of you as well as being blind," she said and found herself breathless and her heart beginning to flutter. He reached to the foot of the bed and felt for his clothes that were rolled up there. He began to put them on hurriedly over his night shirt. "I been thinking how we could arrange it so you would have a home and somebody to take care of you and I wouldn't have to climb these stairs, what you dressing for today, Mr. Motes? You don't want to go out in this weather.

"I been thinking," she went on, watching him as he

went on with what he was doing, "and I see there's only one thing for you and me to do. Get married. I wouldn't do it under any ordinary condition but I would do it for a blind man and a sick one. If we don't help each other, Mr. Motes, there's nobody to help us," she said. "Nobody. The world is a empty place."

The suit that had been glare-blue when it was bought was a softer shade now. The panama hat was wheat-colored. He kept it on the floor by his shoes when he was not wearing it. He reached for it and put it on and then he began to put on his shoes that were still lined with rocks.

"Nobody ought to be without a place of their own to be," she said, "and I'm willing to give you a home here with me, a place where you can always stay, Mr. Motes, and never worry yourself about."

His cane was on the floor near where his shoes had been. He felt for it and then stood up and began to walk slowly toward her. "I got a place for you in my heart, Mr. Motes," she said and felt it shaking like a bird cage; she didn't know whether he was coming toward her to embrace her or not. He passed her, expressionless, out the door and into the hall. "Mr. Motes!" she said, turning sharply in the chair, "I can't allow you to stay here under no other circumstances. I can't climb these stairs. I don't want a thing," she said, "but to help you. You don't have anybody to look after you but me. Nobody to care if you live or die but me! No other place to be but mine!"

He was feeling for the first step with his cane.

"Or were you planning to find you another rooming house?" she asked in a voice getting higher. "Maybe you were planning to go to some other city!"

"That's not where I'm going," he said. "There's no other house nor no other city."

"There's nothing, Mr. Motes," she said, "and time goes forward, it don't go backward and unless you take what's offered you, you'll find yourself out in the cold pitch black and just how far do you think you'll get?"

He felt for each step with his cane before he put his foot on it. When he reached the bottom, she called down to him. "You needn't to return to a place you don't value, Mr. Motes. The door won't be open to you. You can come back and get your belongings and then go on to wherever you think you're going." She stood at the top of the stairs for a long time. "He'll be back," she muttered. "Let the wind cut into him a little."

That night a driving icy rain came up and lying in her

bed, awake at midnight, Mrs. Flood, the landlady, began
to weep. She wanted to run out into the rain and cold
and hunt him and find him huddled in some half-sheltered
place and bring him back and say, Mr. Motes, Mr. Motes,
you can stay here forever, or the two of us will go where
you're going, the two of us will go. She had had a hard life,
without pain and without pleasure, and she thought that
now that she was coming to the last part of it, she deserved
a friend. If she was going to be blind when she was dead,
who better to guide her than a blind man? Who better
to lead the blind than the blind, who knew what it was
like?

As soon as it was daylight, she went out in the rain
and searched the five or six blocks he knew and went from
door to door, asking for him, but no one had seen him.
She came back and called the police and described him
and asked for him to be picked up and brought back to
her to pay his rent. She waited all day for them to bring
him in the squad car, or for him to come back of his own
accord, but he didn't come. The rain and wind continued
and she thought he was probably drowned in some alley
by now. She paced up and down in her room, walking faster
and faster, thinking of his eyes without any bottom in
them and of the blindness of death.

Two days later, two young policemen cruising in a
squad car found him lying in a drainage ditch near an
abandoned construction project. The driver drew the squad
car up to the edge of the ditch and looked into it for some
time. "Ain't we been looking for a blind one?" he asked.

The other consulted a pad. "Blind and got on a blue
suit and ain't paid his rent," he said.

"Yonder he is," the first one said, and pointed into
the ditch. The other moved up closer and looked out of
the window too.

"His suit ain't blue," he said.

"Yes it is blue," the first one said. "Quit pushing up
so close to me. Get out and I'll show you it's blue." They
got out and walked around the car and squatted down
on the edge of the ditch. They both had on tall new boots
and new policemen's clothes; they both had yellow hair
with sideburns, and they were both fat, but one was much
fatter than the other.

"It might have uster been blue," the fatter one admitted.

"You reckon he's daid?" the first one asked.

"Ast him," the other said.

"No, he ain't daid. He's moving."

"Maybe he's just unconscious," the fatter one said,

taking out his new billy. They watched him for a few seconds. His hand was moving along the edge of the ditch as if it were hunting something to grip. He asked them in a hoarse whisper where he was and if it was day or night.

"It's day," the thinner one said, looking at the sky. "We got to take you back to pay your rent."

"I want to go on where I'm going," the blind man said.

"You got to pay your rent first," the policeman said. "Ever' bit of it!"

The other, perceiving that he was conscious, hit him over the head with his new billy. "We don't want to have no trouble with him," he said. "You take his feet."

He died in the squad car but they didn't notice and took him on to the landlady's. She had them put him on her bed and when she had pushed them out the door, she locked it behind them and drew up a straight chair and sat down close to his face where she could talk to him. "Well, Mr. Motes," she said, "I see you've come home!"

His face was stern and tranquil. "I knew you'd come back," she said. "And I've been waiting for you. And you needn't to pay any more rent but have it free here, any way you like, upstairs or down. Just however you want it and with me to wait on you, or if you want to go on somewhere, we'll both go."

She had never observed his face more composed and she grabbed his hand and held it to her heart. It was resistless and dry. The outline of a skull was plain under his skin and the deep burned eye sockets seemed to lead into the dark tunnel where he had disappeared. She leaned closer and closer to his face, looking deep into them, trying to see how she had been cheated or what had cheated her, but she couldn't see anything. She shut her eyes and saw the pin point of light but so far away that she could not hold it steady in her mind. She felt as if she were blocked at the entrance of something. She sat staring with her eyes shut, into his eyes, and felt as if she had finally got to the beginning of something she couldn't begin, and she saw him moving farther and farther away, farther and farther into the darkness until he was the pin point of light.

A GOOD MAN IS HARD TO FIND

for Sally and Robert Fitzgerald

THE DRAGON IS BY THE SIDE OF THE ROAD, WATCHING
THOSE WHO PASS. BEWARE LEST HE DEVOUR YOU. WE
GO TO THE FATHER OF SOULS, BUT IT IS NECESSARY TO
PASS BY THE DRAGON.

St. Cyril of Jerusalem

A GOOD MAN IS HARD TO FIND

The grandmother didn't want to go to Florida. She wanted to visit some of her connections in east Tennessee and she was seizing at every chance to change Bailey's mind. Bailey was the son she lived with, her only boy. He was sitting on the edge of his chair at the table, bent over the orange sports section of the *Journal*. "Now look here, Bailey," she said, "see here, read this," and she stood with one hand on her thin hip and the other rattling the newspaper at his bald head. "Here this fellow that calls himself The Misfit is aloose from the Federal Pen and headed toward Florida and you read here what it says he did to these people. Just you read it. I wouldn't take my children in any direction with a criminal like that aloose in it. I couldn't answer to my conscience if I did."

Bailey didn't look up from his reading so she wheeled around then and faced the children's mother, a young woman in slacks, whose face was as broad and innocent as a cabbage and was tied around with a green head-kerchief that had two points on the top like a rabbit's ears. She was sitting on the sofa, feeding the baby his apricots out of a jar. "The children have been to Florida before," the old lady said. "You all ought to take them somewhere else for a change so they would see different parts of the world and be broad. They never have been to east Tennessee."

The children's mother didn't seem to hear her but the eight-year-old boy, John Wesley, a stocky child with glasses, said, "If you don't want to go to Florida, why dontcha stay at home?" He and the little girl, June Star, were reading the funny papers on the floor.

"She wouldn't stay at home to be queen for a day," June Star said without raising her yellow head.

"Yes and what would you do if this fellow, the Misfit, caught you?" the grandmother asked.

"I'd smack his face," John Wesley said.

"She wouldn't stay at home for a million bucks," June Star said. "Afraid she'd miss something. She has to go everywhere we go."

129

"All right, Miss," the grandmother said. "Just remember that the next time you want me to curl your hair."

June Star said her hair was naturally curly.

The next morning the grandmother was the first one in the car, ready to go. She had her big black valise that looked like the head of a hippopotamus in one corner, and underneath it she was hiding a basket with Pitty Sing, the cat, in it. She didn't intend for the cat to be left alone in the house for three days because he would miss her too much and she was afraid he might brush against one of the gas burners and accidentally asphyxiate himself. Her son, Bailey, didn't like to arrive at a motel with a cat.

She sat in the middle of the back seat with John Wesley and June Star on either side of her. Bailey and the children's mother and the baby sat in front and they left Atlanta at eight forty-five with the mileage on the car at 55890. The grandmother wrote this down because she thought it would be interesting to say how many miles they had been when they got back. It took them twenty minutes to reach the outskirts of the city.

The old lady settled herself comfortably, removing her white cotton gloves and putting them up with her purse on the shelf in front of the back window. The children's mother still had on slacks and still had her head tied up in a green kerchief, but the grandmother had on a navy blue straw sailor hat with a bunch of white violets on the brim and a navy blue dress with a small white dot in the print. Her collars and cuffs were white organdy trimmed with lace and at her neckline she had pinned a purple spray of cloth violets containing a sachet. In case of an accident, anyone seeing her dead on the highway would know at once that she was a lady.

She said she thought it was going to be a good day for driving, neither too hot nor too cold, and she cautioned Bailey that the speed limit was fifty-five miles an hour and that the patrolmen hid themselves behind billboards and small clumps of trees and sped out after you before you had a chance to slow down. She pointed out interesting details of the scenery: Stone Mountain; the blue granite that in some places came up to both sides of the highway; the brilliant red clay banks slightly streaked with purple; and the various crops that made rows of green lace-work on the ground. The trees were full of silver-white sunlight and the meanest of them sparkled. The children were reading comic magazines and their mother had gone back to sleep.

"Let's go through Georgia fast so we won't have to look at it much," John Wesley said.

"If I were a little boy," said the grandmother, "I wouldn't talk about my native state that way. Tennessee has the mountains and Georgia has the hills."

"Tennessee is just a hillbilly dumping ground," John Wesley said, "and Georgia is a lousy state too."

"You said it," June Star said.

"In my time," said the grandmother, folding her thin veined fingers, "children were more respectful of their native states and their parents and everything else. People did right then. Oh look at the cute little pickaninny!" she said and pointed to a Negro child standing in the door of a shack. "Wouldn't that make a picture, now?" she asked and they all turned and looked at the little Negro out of the back window. He waved.

"He didn't have any britches on," June Star said.

"He probably didn't have any," the grandmother explained. "Little niggers in the country don't have things like we do. If I could paint, I'd paint that picture," she said.

The children exchanged comic books.

The grandmother offered to hold the baby and the children's mother passed him over the front seat to her. She set him on her knee and bounced him and told him about the things they were passing. She rolled her eyes and screwed up her mouth and stuck her leathery thin face into his smooth bland one. Occasionally he gave her a faraway smile. They passed a large cotton field with five or six graves fenced in the middle of it, like a small island. "Look at the graveyard!" the grandmother said, pointing it out. "That was the old family burying ground. That belonged to the plantation."

"Where's the plantation?" John Wesley asked.

"Gone With the Wind," said the grandmother. "Ha. Ha."

When the children finished all the comic books they had brought, they opened the lunch and ate it. The grandmother ate a peanut butter sandwich and an olive and would not let the children throw the box and the paper napkins out the window. When there was nothing else to do they played a game by choosing a cloud and making the other two guess what shape it suggested. John Wesley took one the shape of a cow and June Star guessed a cow and John Wesley said, no, an automobile, and June Star said he didn't play fair, and they began to slap each other over the grandmother.

The grandmother said she would tell them a story if

they would keep quiet. When she told a story, she rolled her eyes and waved her head and was very dramatic. She said once when she was a maiden lady she had been courted by a Mr. Edgar Atkins Teagarden from Jasper, Georgia. She said he was a very good-looking man and a gentleman and that he brought her a watermelon every Saturday afternoon with his initials cut in it, E. A. T. Well, one Saturday, she said, Mr. Teagarden brought the watermelon and there was nobody at home and he left it on the front porch and returned in his buggy to Jasper, but she never got the watermelon, she said, because a nigger boy ate it when he saw the initials, E. A. T.! This story tickled John Wesley's funny bone and he giggled and giggled but June Star didn't think it was any good. She said she wouldn't marry a man that just brought her a watermelon on Saturday. The grandmother said she would have done well to marry Mr. Teagarden because he was a gentleman and had bought Coca-Cola stock when it first came out and that he had died only a few years ago, a very wealthy man.

They stopped at The Tower for barbecued sandwiches. The Tower was a part stucco and part wood filling station and dance hall set in a clearing outside of Timothy. A fat man named Red Sammy Butts ran it and there were signs stuck here and there on the building and for miles up and down the highway saying, TRY RED SAMMY'S FAMOUS BARBECUE. NONE LIKE FAMOUS RED SAMMY'S! RED SAM! THE FAT BOY WITH THE HAPPY LAUGH. A VETERAN! RED SAMMY'S YOUR MAN!

Red Sammy was lying on the bare ground outside The Tower with his head under a truck while a gray monkey about a foot high, chained to a small chinaberry tree, chattered nearby. The monkey sprang back into the tree and got on the highest limb as soon as he saw the children jump out of the car and run toward him.

Inside, The Tower was a long dark room with a counter at one end and tables at the other and dancing space in the middle. They all sat down at a board table next to the nickelodeon and Red Sam's wife, a tall burnt-brown woman with hair and eyes lighter than her skin, came and took their order. The children's mother put a dime in the machine and played "The Tennessee Waltz," and the grandmother said that tune always made her want to dance. She asked Bailey if he would like to dance but he only glared at her. He didn't have a naturally sunny disposition like she did and trips made him nervous. The grandmother's brown eyes were very bright. She swayed her head from side to side and pretended she was dancing in her chair. June Star said play something she could tap to so the children's mother put in another dime and played a fast number and June Star stepped out onto the dance floor and did her tap routine.

"Ain't she cute?" Red Sam's wife said, leaning over the counter. "Would you like to come be my little girl?"

"No I certainly wouldn't," June Star said. "I wouldn't live in a broken-down place like this for a million bucks!" and she ran back to the table.

"Ain't she cute?" the woman repeated, stretching her mouth politely.

"Aren't you ashamed?" hissed the grandmother.

Red Sam came in and told his wife to quit lounging on the counter and hurry up with these people's order. His khaki trousers reached just to his hip bones and his stomach hung over them like a sack of meal swaying under his shirt. He came over and sat down at a table nearby and let out a combination sigh and yodel. "You can't win," he said. "You can't win," and he wiped his sweating red face off with a gray handkerchief. "These days you don't know who to trust," he said. "Ain't that the truth?"

"People are certainly not nice like they used to be," said the grandmother.

"Two fellers come in here last week," Red Sammy said, "driving a Chrysler. It was a old beat-up car but it was a good one and these boys looked all right to me. Said they worked at the mill and you know I let them fellers charge the gas they bought? Now why did I do that?"

"Because you're a good man!" the grandmother said at once.

"Yes'm, I suppose so," Red Sam said as if he were struck with this answer.

His wife brought the orders, carrying the five plates all at once without a tray, two in each hand and one balanced on her arm. "It isn't a soul in this green world of God's that you can trust," she said. "And I don't count nobody out of that, not nobody," she repeated, looking at Red Sammy.

"Did you read about that criminal, The Misfit, that's escaped?" asked the grandmother.

"I wouldn't be a bit surprised if he didn't attact this place right here," said the woman. "If he hears about it being here, I wouldn't be none surprised to see him. If he hears it's two cent in the cash register, I wouldn't be a tall surprised if he ..."

"That'll do," Red Sam said. "Go bring these people their Co'-Colas," and the woman went off to get the rest of the order.

"A good man is hard to find," Red Sammy said. "Everything is getting terrible. I remember the day you could go off and leave your screen door unlatched. Not no more."

He and the grandmother discussed better times. The old lady said that in her opinion Europe was entirely to blame for the way things were now. She said the way Europe acted you would think we were made of money and Red Sam said it was no use talking about it, she was exactly right. The children ran outside into the white sunlight and looked at the monkey in the lacy chinaberry tree. He was busy catching fleas on himself and biting each one carefully between his teeth as if it were a delicacy.

They drove off again into the hot afternoon. The grandmother took cat naps and woke up every few minutes with her own snoring. Outside of Toombsboro she woke up and recalled an old plantation that she had visited in this neighborhood once when she was a young lady. She said the house had six white columns across the front and that there was an avenue of oaks leading up to it and two little wooden trellis arbors on either side in front where you sat down with your suitor after a stroll in the garden. She recalled exactly which road to turn off to get to it. She knew that Bailey would not be willing to lose any time looking at an old house, but the more she talked about it, the more she wanted to see it once again and find out if the little twin arbors were still standing. "There was a secret panel in this house," she said craftily, not telling the truth but wishing that she were, "and the story went that all the family silver was hidden in it when Sherman came through but it was never found . . ."

"Hey!" John Wesley said. "Let's go see it! We'll find it! We'll poke all the woodwork and find it! Who lives there? Where do you turn off at? Hey Pop, can't we turn off there?"

"We never have seen a house with a secret panel!" June Star shrieked. "Let's go to the house with the secret panel! Hey Pop, can't we go see the house with the secret panel!"

"It's not far from here, I know," the grandmother said. "It wouldn't take over twenty minutes."

Bailey was looking straight ahead. His jaw was as rigid as a horseshoe. "No," he said.

The children began to yell and scream that they wanted to see the house with the secret panel. John Wesley kicked the back of the front seat and June Star hung over her mother's shoulder and whined desperately into her ear that they never had any fun even on their vacation, that they could never do what THEY wanted to do. The baby began to scream and John Wesley kicked the back of the seat so hard that his father could feel the blows in his kidney.

"All right!" he shouted and drew the car to a stop at the side of the road. "Will you all shut up? Will you all just shut up for one second? If you don't shut up, we won't go anywhere."

"It would be very educational for them," the grandmother murmured.

"All right," Bailey said, "but get this: this is the only time we're going to stop for anything like this. This is the one and only time."

"The dirt road that you have to turn down is about a mile back," the grandmother directed. "I marked it when we passed."

"A dirt road," Bailey groaned.

After they had turned around and were headed toward the dirt road, the grandmother recalled other points about the house, the beautiful glass over the front doorway and the candle-lamp in the hall. John Wesley said that the secret panel was probably in the fireplace.

"You can't go inside this house," Bailey said. "You don't know who lives there."

"While you all talk to the people in front, I'll run around behind and get in a window," John Wesley suggested.

"We'll all stay in the car," his mother said.

They turned onto the dirt road and the car raced roughly along in a swirl of pink dust. The grandmother recalled the times when there were no paved roads and thirty miles was a day's journey. The dirt road was hilly and there were sudden washes in it and sharp curves on dangerous embankments. All at once they would be on a hill, looking down over the blue tops of trees for miles around, then the next minute, they would be in a red depression with the dust-coated trees looking down on them.

"This place had better turn up in a minute," Bailey said, "or I'm going to turn around."

The road looked as if no one had traveled on it in months.

"It's not much farther," the grandmother said and just as she said it, a horrible thought came to her. The thought was so embarrassing that she turned red in the face and her eyes dilated and her feet jumped up, upsetting her valise in the corner. The instant the valise moved, the

newspaper top she had over the basket under it rose with
a snarl and Pitty Sing, the cat, sprang onto Bailey's shoulder.

The children were thrown to the floor and their mother,
clutching the baby, was thrown out the door onto the ground;
the old lady was thrown into the front seat. The car turned
over once and landed right-side-up in a gulch off the side
of the road. Bailey remained in the driver's seat with the
cat—gray-striped with a broad white face and an orange
nose—clinging to his neck like a caterpillar.

As soon as the children saw they could move their arms
and legs, they scrambled out of the car, shouting, "We've
had an ACCIDENT!" The grandmother was curled up
under the dashboard, hoping she was injured so that Bailey's
wrath would not come down on her all at once. The horrible
thought she had had before the accident was that the house
she had remembered so vividly was not in Georgia but
in Tennessee.

Bailey removed the cat from his neck with both hands
and flung it out the window against the side of a pine
tree. Then he got out of the car and started looking for
the children's mother. She was sitting against the side
of the red gutted ditch, holding the screaming baby, but
she only had a cut down her face and a broken shoulder.
"We've had an ACCIDENT!" the children screamed in
a frenzy of delight.

"But nobody's killed," June Star said with disappointment
as the grandmother limped out of the car, her hat still
pinned to her head but the broken front brim standing up
at a jaunty angle and the violet spray hanging off the side.
They all sat down in the ditch, except the children, to
recover from the shock. They were all shaking.

"Maybe a car will come along," said the children's mother
hoarsely.

"I believe I have injured an organ," said the grandmother,
pressing her side, but no one answered her. Bailey's teeth
were clattering. He had on a yellow sport shirt with bright
blue parrots designed in it and his face was as yellow as
the shirt. The grandmother decided that she would not
mention that the house was in Tennessee.

The road was about ten feet above and they could see
only the tops of the trees on the other side of it. Behind
the ditch they were sitting in there were more woods,
tall and dark and deep. In a few minutes they saw a car
some distance away on top of a hill, coming slowly as
if the occupants were watching them. The grandmother
stood up and waved both arms dramatically to attract

their attention. The car continued to come on slowly, disappeared around a bend and appeared again, moving even slower, on top of the hill they had gone over. It was a big black battered hearse-like automobile. There were three men in it.

It came to a stop just over them and for some minutes, the driver looked down with a steady expressionless gaze to where they were sitting, and didn't speak. Then he turned his head and muttered something to the other two and they got out. One was a fat boy in black trousers and a red sweat shirt with a silver stallion embossed on the front of it. He moved around on the right side of them and stood staring, his mouth partly open in a kind of loose grin. The other had on khaki pants and a blue striped coat and a gray hat pulled down very low, hiding most of his face. He came around slowly on the left side. Neither spoke.

The driver got out of the car and stood by the side of it, looking down at them. He was an older man than the other two. His hair was just beginning to gray and he wore silver-rimmed spectacles that gave him a scholarly look. He had a long creased face and didn't have on any shirt or undershirt. He had on blue jeans that were too tight for him and was holding a black hat and a gun. The two boys also had guns.

"We've had an ACCIDENT!" the children screamed.

The grandmother had the peculiar feeling that the bespectacled man was someone she knew. His face was as familiar to her as if she had known him all her life but she could not recall who he was. He moved away from the car and began to come down the embankment, placing his feet carefully so that he wouldn't slip. He had on tan and white shoes and no socks, and his ankles were red and thin. "Good afternoon," he said. "I see you all had you a little spill."

"We turned over twice!" said the grandmother.

"Oncet," he corrected. "We seen it happen. Try their car and see will it run, Hiram," he said quietly to the boy with the gray hat.

"What you got that gun for?" John Wesley asked. "Whatcha gonna do with that gun?"

"Lady," the man said to the children's mother, "would you mind calling them children to sit down by you? Children make me nervous. I want all you all to sit down right together there where you're at."

"What are you telling US what to do for?" June Star asked.

Behind them the line of woods gaped like a dark open mouth. "Come here," said their mother.

"Look here now," Bailey began suddenly, "we're in a predicament! We're in . . ."

The grandmother shrieked. She scrambled to her feet and stood staring. "You're The Misfit!" she said. "I recognized you at once!"

"Yes'm," the man said, smiling slightly as if he were pleased in spite of himself to be known, "but it would have been better for all of you, lady, if you hadn't of reckernized me."

Bailey turned his head sharply and said something to his mother that shocked even the children. The old lady began to cry and The Misfit reddened.

"Lady," he said, "don't you get upset. Sometimes a man says things he don't mean. I don't reckon he meant to talk to you thataway."

"You wouldn't shoot a lady, would you?" the grandmother said and removed a clean handkerchief from her cuff and began to slap at her eyes with it.

The Misfit pointed the toe of his shoe into the ground and made a little hole and then covered it up again. "I would hate to have to," he said.

"Listen," the grandmother almost screamed, "I know you're a good man. You don't look a bit like you have common blood. I know you must come from nice people!"

"Yes mam," he said, "finest people in the world." When he smiled he showed a row of strong white teeth. "God never made a finer woman than my mother and my daddy's heart was pure gold," he said. The boy with the red sweat shirt had come around behind them and was standing with his gun at his hip. The Misfit squatted down on the ground. "Watch them children, Bobby Lee," he said. "You know they make me nervous." He looked at the six of them huddled together in front of him and he seemed to be embarrassed as if he couldn't think of anything to say. "Ain't a cloud in the sky," he remarked, looking up at it. "Don't see no sun but don't see no cloud neither."

"Yes, it's a beautiful day," said the grandmother. "Listen," she said, "you shouldn't call yourself The Misfit because I know you're a good man at heart. I can just look at you and tell."

"Hush!" Bailey yelled. "Hush! Everybody shut up and let me handle this!" He was squatting in the position of a runner about to sprint forward but he didn't move.

"I pre-chate that, lady," The Misfit said and drew a little circle in the ground with the butt of his gun.

"It'll take a half a hour to fix this here car," Hiram called, looking over the raised hood of it.

"Well, first you and Bobby Lee get him and that little boy to step over yonder with you," The Misfit said, pointing to Bailey and John Wesley. "The boys want to ast you something," he said to Bailey. "Would you mind stepping back in them woods there with them?"

"Listen," Bailey began, "we're in a terrible predicament! Nobody realizes what this is," and his voice cracked. His eyes were as blue and intense as the parrots in his shirt and he remained perfectly still.

The grandmother reached up to adjust her hat brim as if she were going to the woods with him but it came off in her hand. She stood staring at it and after a second she let it fall on the ground. Hiram pulled Bailey up by the arm as if he were assisting an old man. John Wesley caught hold of his father's hand and Bobby Lee followed. They went off toward the woods and just as they reached the dark edge, Bailey turned and supporting himself against a gray naked pine trunk, he shouted, "I'll be back in a minute, Mamma, wait on me!"

"Come back this instant!" his mother shrilled but they all disappeared into the woods.

"Bailey Boy!" the grandmother called in a tragic voice but she found she was looking at The Misfit squatting on the ground in front of her. "I just know you're a good man," she said desperately. "You're not a bit common!"

"Nome, I ain't a good man," The Misfit said after a second as if he had considered her statement carefully, "but I ain't the worst in the world neither. My daddy said I was a different breed of dog from my brothers and sisters. 'You know,' Daddy said, 'it's some that can live their whole life out without asking about it and it's others has to know why it is, and this boy is one of the latters. He's going to be into everything!' " He put on his black hat and looked up suddenly and then away deep into the woods as if he were embarrassed again. "I'm sorry I don't have on a shirt before you ladies," he said, hunching his shoulders slightly. "We buried our clothes that we had on when we escaped and we're just making do until we can get better. We borrowed these from some folks we met," he explained.

"That's perfectly all right," the grandmother said. "Maybe Bailey has an extra shirt in his suitcase."

"I'll look and see terrectly," The Misfit said.

"Where are they taking him?" the children's mother screamed.

"Daddy was a card himself," The Misfit said. "You couldn't

put anything over on him. He never got in trouble with the Authorities though. Just had the knack of handling them."

"You could be honest too if you'd only try," said the grandmother. "Think how wonderful it would be to settle down and live a comfortable life and not have to think about somebody chasing you all the time."

The Misfit kept scratching in the ground with the butt of his gun as if he were thinking about it. "Yes'm, somebody is always after you," he murmured.

The grandmother noticed how thin his shoulder blades were just behind his hat because she was standing up looking down on him. "Do you ever pray?" she asked.

He shook his head. All she saw was the black hat wiggle between his shoulder blades. "Nome," he said.

There was a pistol shot from the woods, followed closely by another. Then silence. The old lady's head jerked around. She could hear the wind move through the tree tops like a long satisfied insuck of breath. "Bailey Boy!" she called.

"I was a gospel singer for a while," The Misfit said. "I been most everything. Been in the arm service, both land and sea, at home and abroad, been twict married, been an undertaker, been with the railroads, plowed Mother Earth, been in a tornado, seen a man burnt alive oncet," and he looked up at the children's mother and the little girl who were sitting close together, their faces white and their eyes glassy; "I even seen a woman flogged," he said.

"Pray, pray," the grandmother began, "pray, pray . . ."

"I never was a bad boy that I remember of," The Misfit said in an almost dreamy voice, "but somewheres along the line I done something wrong and got sent to the penitentiary. I was buried alive," and he looked up and held her attention to him by a steady stare.

"That's when you should have started to pray," she said. "What did you do to get sent to the penitentiary that first time?"

"Turn to the right, it was a wall," The Misfit said, looking up again at the cloudless sky. "Turn to the left, it was a wall. Look up it was a ceiling, look down it was a floor. I forget what I done, lady. I set there and set there, trying to remember what it was I done and I ain't recalled it to this day. Oncet in a while, I would think it was coming to me, but it never come."

"Maybe they put you in by mistake," the old lady said vaguely.

"Nome," he said. "It wasn't no mistake. They had the papers on me."

"You must have stolen something," she said.

The Misfit sneered slightly. "Nobody had nothing I wanted," he said. "It was a head-doctor at the penitentiary said what I had done was kill my daddy but I known that for a lie. My daddy died in nineteen ought nineteen of the epidemic flu and I never had a thing to do with it. He was buried in the Mount Hopewell Baptist churchyard and you can go there and see for yourself."

"If you would pray," the old lady said, "Jesus would help you."

"That's right," The Misfit said.

"Well then, why don't you pray?" she asked trembling with delight suddenly.

"I don't want no hep," he said. "I'm doing all right by myself."

Bobby Lee and Hiram came ambling back from the woods. Bobby Lee was dragging a yellow shirt with bright blue parrots in it.

"Thow me that shirt, Bobby Lee," The Misfit said. The shirt came flying at him and landed on his shoulder and he put it on. The grandmother couldn't name what the shirt reminded her of. "No, lady," The Misfit said while he was buttoning it up, "I found out the crime don't matter. You can do one thing or you can do another, kill a man or take a tire off his car, because sooner or later you're going to forget what it was you done and just be punished for it."

The children's mother had begun to make heaving noises as if she couldn't get her breath. "Lady," he asked, "would you and that little girl like to step off yonder with Bobby Lee and Hiram and join your husband?"

"Yes, thank you," the mother said faintly. Her left arm dangled helplessly and she was holding the baby, who had gone to sleep, in the other. "Hep that lady up, Hiram," The Misfit said as she struggled to climb out of the ditch, "and Bobby Lee, you hold onto that little girl's hand."

"I don't want to hold hands with him," June Star said. "He reminds me of a pig."

The fat boy blushed and laughed and caught her by the arm and pulled her off into the woods after Hiram and her mother.

Alone with The Misfit, the grandmother found that she had lost her voice. There was not a cloud in the sky nor any sun. There was nothing around her but woods. She wanted to tell him that he must pray. She opened and closed her mouth several times before anything came out. Finally she found herself saying, "Jesus, Jesus," meaning,

Jesus will help you, but the way she was saying it, it sounded as if she might be cursing.

"Yes'm," The Misfit said as if he agreed. "Jesus thown everything off balance. It was the same case with Him as with me except He hadn't committed any crime and they could prove I had committed one because they had the papers on me. Of course," he said, "they never shown me my papers. That's why I sign myself now. I said long ago, you get you a signature and sign everything you do and keep a copy of it. Then you'll know what you done and you can hold up the crime to the punishment and see do they match and in the end you'll have something to prove you ain't been treated right. I call myself The Misfit," he said, "because I can't make what all I done wrong fit what all I gone through in punishment."

There was a piercing scream from the woods, followed closely by a pistol report. "Does it seem right to you, lady, that one is punished a heap and another ain't punished at all?"

"Jesus!" the old lady cried. "You've got good blood! I know you wouldn't shoot a lady! I know you come from nice people! Pray! Jesus, you ought not to shoot a lady. I'll give you all the money I've got!"

"Lady," The Misfit said, looking beyond her far into the woods, "there never was a body that give the undertaker a tip."

There were two more pistol reports and the grandmother raised her head like a parched old turkey hen crying for water and called, "Bailey Boy, Bailey Boy!" as if her heart would break.

"Jesus was the only One that ever raised the dead," The Misfit continued, "and He shouldn't have done it. He thown everything off balance. If He did what He said, then it's nothing for you to do but thow away everything and follow Him, and if He didn't, then it's nothing for you to do but enjoy the few minutes you got left the best way you can—by killing somebody or burning down his house or doing some other meanness to him. No pleasure but meanness," he said and his voice had become almost a snarl.

"Maybe He didn't raise the dead," the old lady mumbled, not knowing what she was saying and feeling so dizzy that she sank down in the ditch with her legs twisted under her.

"I wasn't there so I can't say He didn't," The Misfit said. "I wisht I had of been there," he said, hitting the ground with his fist. "It ain't right I wasn't there because

if I had of been there I would of known. Listen lady,"
he said in a high voice, "if I had of been there I would
of known and I wouldn't be like I am now." His voice
seemed about to crack and the grandmother's head cleared
for an instant. She saw the man's face twisted close to
her own as if he were going to cry and she murmured, "Why
you're one of my babies. You're one of my own children!"
She reached out and touched him on the shoulder. The
Misfit sprang back as if a snake had bitten him and shot
her three times through the chest. Then he put his gun
down on the ground and took off his glasses and began
to clean them.

Hiram and Bobby Lee returned from the woods and
stood over the ditch, looking down at the grandmother
who half sat and half lay in a puddle of blood with her
legs crossed under her like a child's and her face smiling
up at the cloudless sky.

Without his glasses, The Misfit's eyes were red-rimmed
and pale and defenseless-looking. "Take her off and thow
her where you thown the others," he said, picking up the
cat that was rubbing itself against his leg.

"She was a talker, wasn't she?" Bobby Lee said, sliding
down the ditch with a yodel.

"She would of been a good woman," The Misfit said,
"if it had been somebody there to shoot her every minute
of her life."

"Some fun!" Bobby Lee said.

"Shut up, Bobby Lee," The Misfit said. "It's no real
pleasure in life."

THE RIVER

The child stood glum and limp in the middle of the dark living room while his father pulled him into a plaid coat. His right arm was hung in the sleeve but the father buttoned the coat anyway and pushed him forward toward a pale spotted hand that stuck through the half-open door.

"He ain't fixed right," a loud voice said from the hall.

"Well then for Christ's sake fix him," the father muttered. "It's six o'clock in the morning." He was in his bathrobe and barefooted. When he got the child to the door and tried to shut it, he found her looming in it, a speckled skeleton in a long pea-green coat and felt helmet.

"And his and my carfare," she said. "It'll be twict we have to ride the car."

He went in the bedroom again to get the money and when he came back, she and the boy were both standing in the middle of the room. She was taking stock. "I couldn't smell those dead cigarette butts long if I was ever to come sit with you," she said, shaking him down in his coat.

"Here's the change," the father said. He went to the door and opened it wide and waited.

After she had counted the money she slipped it somewhere inside her coat and walked over to a watercolor hanging near the phonograph. "I know what time it is," she said, peering closely at the black lines crossing into broken planes of violent color. "I ought to. My shift goes on at 10 P.M. and don't get off till 5 and it takes me one hour to ride the Vine Street car."

"Oh, I see," he said. "Well, we'll expect him back tonight, about eight or nine?"

"Maybe later," she said. "We're going to the river to a healing. This particular preacher don't get around this way often. I wouldn't have paid for that," she said, nodding at the painting, "I would have drew it myself."

"All right, Mrs. Connin, we'll see you then," he said drumming on the door.

A toneless voice called from the bedroom, "Bring me an icepack."

144

"Too bad his mamma's sick," Mrs. Connin said. "What's her trouble?"

"We don't know," he muttered.

"We'll ask the preacher to pray for her. He's healed a lot of folks. The Reverend Bevel Summers. Maybe she ought to see him sometime."

"Maybe so," he said. "We'll see you tonight," and he disappeared into the bedroom and left them to go.

The little boy stared at her silently, his nose and eyes running. He was four or five. He had a long face and bulging chin and half-shut eyes set far apart. He seemed mute and patient, like an old sheep waiting to be let out.

"You'll like this preacher," she said. "The Reverend Bevel Summers. You ought to hear him sing."

The bedroom door opened suddenly and the father stuck his head out and said, "Good-by, old man. Have a good time."

"Good-by," the little boy said and jumped as if he had been shot.

Mrs. Connin gave the watercolor another look. Then they went out into the hall and rang for the elevator. "I wouldn't have drew it," she said.

Outside the gray morning was blocked off on either side by the unlit empty buildings. "It's going to fair up later," she said, "but this is the last time we'll be able to have any preaching at the river this year. Wipe your nose, Sugar Boy."

He began rubbing his sleeve across it but she stopped him. "That ain't nice," she said. "Where's your handkerchief?"

He put his hands in his pockets and pretended to look for it while she waited. "Some people don't care how they send one off," she murmured to her reflection in the coffee shop window. "You pervide." She took a red and blue flowered handkerchief out of her pocket and stooped down and began to work on his nose. "Now blow," she said and he blew. "You can borry it. Put it in your pocket."

He folded it up and put it in his pocket carefully and they walked on to the corner and leaned against the side of a closed drugstore to wait for the car. Mrs. Connin turned up her coat collar so that it met her hat in the back. Her eyelids began to droop and she looked as if she might go to sleep against the wall. The little boy put a slight pressure on her hand.

"What's your name?" she asked in a drowsy voice. "I

don't know but only your last name. I should have found out your first name."

His name was Harry Ashfield and he had never thought at any time before of changing it. "Bevel," he said.

Mrs. Connin raised herself from the wall. "Why ain't that a coincident!" she said. "I told you that's the name of this preacher!"

"Bevel," he repeated.

She stood looking down at him as if he had become a marvel to her. "I'll have to see you meet him today," she said. "He's no ordinary preacher. He's a healer. He couldn't do nothing for Mr. Connin though. Mr. Connin didn't have the faith but he said he would try anything once. He had this griping in his gut."

The trolley appeared as a yellow spot at the end of the deserted street.

"He's gone to the government hospital now," she said, "and they taken one-third of his stomach. I tell him he better thank Jesus for what he's got left but he says he ain't thanking nobody. Well I declare," she murmured, "Bevel!"

They walked out to the tracks to wait. "Will he heal me?" Bevel asked.

"What you got?"

"I'm hungry," he decided finally.

"Didn't you have your breakfast?"

"I didn't have time to be hungry yet then," he said.

"Well when we get home we'll both have us something," she said. "I'm ready myself."

They got in the car and sat down a few seats behind the driver and Mrs. Connin took Bevel on her knees. "Now you be a good boy," she said, "and let me get some sleep. Just don't get off my lap." She lay her head back and as he watched, gradually her eyes closed and her mouth fell open to show a few long scattered teeth, some gold and some darker than her face; she began to whistle and blow like a musical skeleton. There was no one in the car but themselves and the driver and when he saw she was asleep, he took out the flowered handkerchief and unfolded it and examined it carefully. Then he folded it up again and unzipped a place in the innerlining of his coat and hid it in there and shortly he went to sleep himself.

Her house was a half-mile from the end of the car line, set back a little from the road. It was tan paper brick with a porch across the front of it and a tin top. On the porch there were three little boys of different sizes with identical speckled faces and one tall girl who had her hair up in

so many aluminum curlers that it glared like the roof.
The three boys followed them inside and closed in on Bevel.
They looked at him silently, not smiling.

"That's Bevel," Mrs. Connin said, taking off her coat.
"It's a coincident he's named the same as the preacher.
These boys are J. C., Spivey, and Sinclair, and that's Sarah
Mildred on the porch. Take off that coat and hang it
on the bed post, Bevel."

The three boys watched him while he unbuttoned the
coat and took it off. Then they watched him hang it on
the bed post and then they stood, watching the coat. They
turned abruptly and went out the door and had a conference
on the porch.

Bevel stood looking around him at the room. It was part
kitchen and part bedroom. The entire house was two rooms
and two porches. Close to his foot the tail of a light-colored
dog moved up and down between two floor boards as
he scratched his back on the underside of the house. Bevel
jumped on it but the hound was experienced and had already
withdrawn when his feet hit the spot.

The walls were filled with pictures and calendars. There
were two round photographs of an old man and woman
with collapsed mouths and another picture of a man whose
eyebrows dashed out of two bushes of hair and clashed
in a heap on the bridge of his nose; the rest of his face stuck
out like a bare cliff to fall from. "That's Mr. Connin,"
Mrs. Connin said, standing back from the stove for a
second to admire the face with him, "but it don't favor
him any more." Bevel turned from Mr. Connin to a colored
picture over the bed of a man wearing a white sheet.
He had long hair and a gold circle around his head and
he was sawing on a board while some children stood watching
him. He was going to ask who that was when the three
boys came in again and motioned for him to follow them.
He thought of crawling under the bed and hanging onto
one of the legs but the three boys only stood there, speckled
and silent, waiting, and after a second he followed them
at a little distance out on the porch and around the corner
of the house. They started off through a field of rough yellow
weeds to the hog pen, a five-foot boarded square full
of shoats, which they intended to ease him over into. When
they reached it, they turned and waited silently, leaning against
the side.

He was coming very slowly, deliberately bumping his
feet together as if he had trouble walking. Once he had
been beaten up in the park by some strange boys when
his sitter forgot him, but he hadn't known anything was

going to happen that time until it was over. He began to smell a strong odor of garbage and to hear the noises of a wild animal. He stopped a few feet from the pen and waited, pale but dogged.

The three boys didn't move. Something seemed to have happened to them. They stared over his head as if they saw something coming behind him but he was afraid to turn his own head and look. Their speckles were pale and their eyes were still and gray as glass. Only their ears twitched slightly. Nothing happened. Finally, the one in the middle said, "She'd kill us," and turned, dejected and hacked, and climbed up on the pen and hung over, staring in.

Bevel sat down on the ground, dazed with relief, and grinned up at them.

The one sitting on the pen glanced at him severely. "Hey you," he said after a second, "if you can't climb up and see these pigs you can lift that bottom board off and look in thataway." He appeared to offer this as a kindness.

Bevel had never seen a real pig but he had seen a pig in a book and knew they were small fat pink animals with curly tails and round grinning faces and bow ties. He leaned forward and pulled eagerly at the board.

"Pull harder," the littlest boy said. "It's nice and rotten. Just life out thet nail."

He eased a long reddish nail out of the soft wood.

"Now you can lift up the board and put your face to the . . ." a quiet voice began.

He had already done it and another face, gray, wet and sour, was pushing into his, knocking him down and back as it scraped out under the plank. Something snorted over him and charged back again, rolling him over and pushing him up from behind and then sending him forward, screaming through the yellow field, while it bounded behind.

The three Connins watched from where they were. The one sitting on the pen held the loose board back with his gangling foot. Their stern faces didn't brighten any but they seemed to become less taut, as if some great need had been partly satisfied. "Maw ain't going to like him lettin' out thet hawg," the smallest one said.

Mrs. Connin was on the back porch and caught Bevel up as he reached the steps. The hog ran under the house and subsided, panting, but the child screamed for five minutes. When she had finally calmed him down, she gave him his breakfast and let him sit on her lap while he ate it. The shoat climbed the two steps onto the back porch and stood outside the screen door, looking in with his head lowered sullenly. He was long-legged and humpbacked and part of one of his ears had been bitten off.

"Git away!" Mrs. Connin shouted. "That one yonder favors Mr. Paradise that has the gas station," she said. "You'll see him today at the healing. He's got the cancer over his ear. He always comes to show he ain't been healed."

The shoat stood squinting a few seconds longer and then moved off slowly. "I don't want to see him," Bevel said.

They walked to the river, Mrs. Connin in front with him and the three boys strung out behind and Sarah Mildred, the tall girl, at the end to holler if one of them ran out on the road. They looked like the skeleton of an old boat with two pointed ends, sailing slowly on the edge of the highway. The white Sunday sun followed at a little distance, climbing fast through a scum of gray cloud as if it meant to overtake them. Bevel walked on the outside edge, holding Mrs. Connin's hand and looking down into the orange and purple gulley that dropped off from the concrete.

It occurred to him that he was lucky this time that they had found Mrs. Connin who would take you away for the day instead of an ordinary sitter who only sat where you lived or went to the park. You found out more when you left where you lived. He had found out already this morning that he had been made by a carpenter named Jesus Christ. Before he had thought it had been a doctor named Sladewall, a fat man with a yellow mustache who gave him shots and thought his name was Herbert, but this must have been a joke. They joked a lot where he lived. If he had thought about it before, he would have thought Jesus Christ was a word like "oh" or "damn" or "God," or maybe somebody who had cheated them out of something sometime. When he had asked Mrs. Connin who the man in the sheet in the picture over her bed was, she had looked at him a while with her mouth open. Then she had said, "That's Jesus," and she had kept on looking at him.

In a few minutes she had got up and got a book out of the other room. "See here," she said, turning over the cover, "this belonged to my great grandmamma. I wouldn't part with it for nothing on earth." She ran her finger under some brown writing on a spotted page. "Emma Stevens Oakley, 1832," she said. "Ain't that something to have? And every word of it the gospel truth." She turned the next page and read him the name: "The Life of Jesus Christ for Readers Under Twelve." Then she read him the book.

It was a small book, pale brown on the outside with gold

edges and a smell like old putty. It was full of pictures, one of the carpenter driving a crowd of pigs out of a man. They were real pigs, gray and sour-looking, and Mrs. Connin said Jesus had driven them all out of this one man. When she finished reading, she let him sit on the floor and look at the pictures again.

Just before they left for the healing, he had managed to get the book inside his innerlining without her seeing him. Now it made his coat hang down a little farther on one side than the other. His mind was dreamy and serene as they walked along and when they turned off the highway onto a long red clay road winding between banks of honeysuckle, he began to make wild leaps and pull forward on her hand as if he wanted to dash off and snatch the sun which was rolling away ahead of them now.

They walked on the dirt road for a while and then they crossed a field stippled with purple weeds and entered the shadows of a wood where the ground was covered with thick pine needles. He had never been in woods before and he walked carefully, looking from side to side as if he were entering a strange country. They moved along a bridle path that twisted downhill through crackling red leaves, and once, catching at a branch to keep himself from slipping, he looked into two frozen green-gold eyes enclosed in the darkness of a tree hole. At the bottom of the hill, the woods opened suddenly onto a pasture dotted here and there with black and white cows and sloping down, tier after tier, to a broad orange stream where the reflection of the sun was set like a diamond.

There were people standing on the near bank in a group, singing. Long tables were set up behind them and a few cars and trucks were parked in a road that came up by the river. They crossed the pasture, hurrying, because Mrs. Connin, using her hand for a shed over her eyes, saw the preacher already standing out in the water. She dropped her basket on one of the tables and pushed the three boys in front of her into the knot of people so that they wouldn't linger by the food. She kept Bevel by the hand and eased her way up to the front.

The preacher was standing about ten feet out in the stream where the water came up to his knees. He was a tall youth in khaki trousers that he had rolled up higher than the water. He had on a blue shirt and a red scarf around his neck but no hat and his light-colored hair was cut in sideburns that curved into the hollows of his cheeks. His face was all bone and red light reflected from the river. He looked as if he might have been nineteen years old.

He was singing in a high twangy voice, above the singing on the bank, and he kept his hands behind him and his head tilted back.

He ended the hymn on a high note and stood silent, looking down at the water and shifting his feet in it. Then he looked up at the people on the bank. They stood close together, waiting; their faces were solemn but expectant and every eye was on him. He shifted his feet again.

"Maybe I know why you come," he said in the twangy voice, "maybe I don't.

"If you ain't come for Jesus, you ain't come for me. If you just come to see can you leave your pain in the river, you ain't come for Jesus. You can't leave your pain in the river," he said. "I never told nobody that." He stopped and looked down at his knees.

"I seen you cure a woman oncet!" a sudden high voice shouted from the hump of people. "Seen that woman git up and walk out straight where she had limped in!"

The preacher lifted one foot and then the other. He seemed almost but not quite to smile. "You might as well go home if that's what you come for," he said.

Then he lifted his head and arms and shouted, "Listen to what I got to say, you people! There ain't but one river and that's the River of Life, made out of Jesus' Blood. That's the river you have to lay your pain in, in the River of Faith, in the River of Life, in the River of Love, in the rich red river of Jesus' Blood, you people!"

His voice grew soft and musical. "All the rivers come from that one River and go back to it like it was the ocean sea and if you believe, you can lay your pain in that River and get rid of it because that's the River that was made to carry sin. It's a River full of pain itself, pain itself, moving toward the Kingdom of Christ, to be washed away, slow, you people, slow as this here old red water river round my feet.

"Listen," he sang, "I read in Mark about an unclean man, I read in Luke about a blind man, I read in John about a dead man! Oh you people hear! The same blood that makes this River red, made that leper clean, made that blind man stare, made that dead man leap! You people with trouble," he cried, "lay it in that River of Blood, lay it in that River of Pain, and watch it move away toward the Kingdom of Christ."

While he preached, Bevel's eyes followed drowsily the slow circles of two silent birds revolving high in the air. Across the river there was a low red and gold grove of sassafras with hills of dark blue trees behind it and an occasional pine jutting over the skyline. Behind, in the distance, the city rose like a cluster of warts on the side of the mountain. The birds revolved downward and dropped lightly in the top of the highest pine and sat hunch-shouldered as if they were supporting the sky.

"If it's this River of Life you want to lay your pain in, then come up," the preacher said, "and lay your sorrow here. But don't be thinking this is the last of it because this old red river don't end here. This old red suffering stream goes on, you people, slow to the Kingdom of Christ. This old red river is good to Baptize in, good to lay your faith in, good to lay your pain in, but it ain't this muddy water here that saves you. I been all up and down this river this week," he said. "Tuesday I was in Fortune Lake, next day in Ideal, Friday me and my wife drove to Lulawillow to see a sick man there. Them people didn't see no healing," he said and his face burned redder for a second. "I never said they would."

While he was talking a fluttering figure had begun to move forward with a kind of butterfly movement—an old woman with flapping arms whose head wobbled as if it might fall off any second. She managed to lower herself at the edge of the bank and let her arms churn in the water. Then she bent farther and pushed her face down in it and raised herself up finally, streaming wet; and still flapping, she turned a time or two in a blind circle until someone reached out and pulled her back into the group.

"She's been that way for thirteen years," a rough voice shouted. "Pass the hat and give this kid his money. That's what he's here for." The shout, directed out to the boy in the river, came from a huge old man who sat like a humped stone on the bumper of a long ancient gray automobile. He had on a gray hat that was turned down over one ear and up over the other to expose a purple bulge on his left temple. He sat bent forward with his hands hanging between his knees and his small eyes half closed.

Bevel stared at him once and then moved into the folds of Mrs. Connin's coat and hid himself.

The boy in the river glanced at the old man quickly and raised his fist. "Believe Jesus or the devil!" he cried. "Testify to one or the other!"

"I know from my own self-experience," a woman's mysterious voice called from the knot of people, "I know from it that this preacher can heal. My eyes have been opened! I testify to Jesus!"

The preacher lifted his arms quickly and began to repeat all that he had said before about the River and the Kingdom

of Christ and the old man sat on the bumper, fixing him
with a narrow squint. From time to time Bevel stared at him
again from around Mrs. Connin.

A man in overalls and a brown coat leaned forward and
dipped his hand in the water quickly and shook it and leaned
back, and a woman held a baby over the edge of the bank
and splashed its feet with water. One man moved a little
distance away and sat down on the bank and took off
his shoes and waded out into the stream; he stood there
for a few minutes with his face tilted as far back as it
would go, then he waded back and put on his shoes. All
this time, the preacher sang and did not appear to watch
what went on.

As soon as he stopped singing, Mrs. Connin lifted Bevel
up and said, "Listen here, preacher, I got a boy from town
today that I'm keeping. His mamma's sick and he wants
you to pray for her. And this is a coincident—his name is
Bevel! Bevel," she said, turning to look at the people behind
her, "same as his. Ain't that a coincident, though?"

There were some murmurs and Bevel turned and grinned
over her shoulder at the faces looking at him. "Bevel,"
he said in a loud jaunty voice.

"Listen," Mrs. Connin said, "have you ever been Baptized,
Bevel?"

He only grinned.

"I suspect he ain't ever been Baptized," Mrs. Connin
said, raising her eyebrows at the preacher.

"Swang him over here," the preacher said and took
a stride forward and caught him.

He held him in the crook of his arm and looked at the
grinning face. Bevel rolled his eyes in a comical way and
thrust his face forward, close to the preacher's. "My name
is Bevvvuuuuul," he said in a loud deep voice and let
the tip of his tongue slide across his mouth.

The preacher didn't smile. His bony face was rigid and
his narrow gray eyes reflected the almost colorless sky.
There was a loud laugh from the old man sitting on the
car bumper and Bevel grasped the back of the preacher's
collar and held it tightly. The grin had already disappeared
from his face. He had the sudden feeling that this was
not a joke. Where he lived everything was a joke. From
the preacher's face, he knew immediately that nothing the
preacher said or did was a joke. "My mother named me
that," he said quickly.

"Have you ever been Baptized?" the preacher asked.

"What's that?" he murmured.

"If I Baptize you," the preacher said, "you'll be able

to go to the Kingdom of Christ. You'll be washed in the river of suffering, son, and you'll go by the deep river of life. Do you want that?"

"Yes," the child said, and thought, I won't go back to the apartment then, I'll go under the river.

"You won't be the same again," the preacher said. "You'll count." Then he turned his face to the people and began to preach and Bevel looked over his shoulder at the pieces of the white sun scattered in the river. Suddenly the preacher said, "All right, I'm going to Baptize you now," and without more warning, he tightened his hold and swung him upside down and plunged his head into the water. He held him under while he said the words of Baptism and then he jerked him up again and looked sternly at the gasping child. Bevel's eyes were dark and dilated. "You count now," the preacher said. "You didn't even count before."

The little boy was too shocked to cry. He spit out the muddy water and rubbed his wet sleeve into his eyes and over his face.

"Don't forget his mamma," Mrs. Connin called. "He wants you to pray for his mamma. She's sick."

"Lord," the preacher said, "we pray for somebody in affliction who isn't here to testify. Is your mother sick in the hospital?" he asked. "Is she in pain?"

The child stared at him. "She hasn't got up yet," he said in a high dazed voice. "She has a hangover." The air was so quiet he could hear the broken pieces of the sun knocking the water.

The preacher looked angry and startled. The red drained out of his face and the sky appeared to darken in his eyes. There was a loud guffaw from the bank and Mr. Paradise shouted, "Haw! Cure the afflicted woman with the hangover!" and began to beat his knee with his fist.

"He's had a long day," Mrs. Connin said, standing with him in the door of the apartment and looking sharply into the room where the party was going on. "I reckon it's past his regular bedtime." One of Bevel's eyes was closed and the other half closed; his nose was running and he kept his mouth open and breathed through it. The damp plain coat dragged down on one side.

That would be her, Mrs. Connin decided, in the black britches—long black satin britches and barefoot sandals and red toenails. She was lying on half the sofa, with her knees crossed in the air and her head propped on the arm. She didn't get up.

"Hello Harry," she said. "Did you have a big day?"

She had a long pale face, smooth and blank, and straight sweet-potato-colored hair, pulled back.

The father went off to get the money. There were two other couples. One of the men, blond with little violet-blue eyes, leaned out of his chair and said, "Well Harry, old man, have a big day?"

"His name ain't Harry. It's Bevel," Mrs. Connin said.

"His name is Harry," *she* said from the sofa. "Whoever heard of anybody named Bevel?"

The little boy had seemed to be going to sleep on his feet, his head drooping farther and farther forward; he pulled it back suddenly and opened one eye; the other was stuck.

"He told me this morning his name was Bevel," Mrs. Connin said in a shocked voice. "The same as our preacher. We been all day at a preaching and healing at the river. He said his name was Bevel, the same as the preacher's. That's what he told me."

"Bevel!" his mother said. "My God! what a name."

"This preacher is name Bevel and there's no better preacher around," Mrs. Connin said. "And furthermore," she added in a defiant tone, "he Baptized this child this morning!"

His mother sat straight up. "Well the nerve!" she muttered.

"Furthermore," Mrs. Connin said, "he's a healer and he prayed for you to be healed."

"Healed!" she almost shouted. "Healed of what for Christ's sake?"

"Of your affliction," Mrs. Connin said icily.

The father had returned with the money and was standing near Mrs. Connin waiting to give it to her. His eyes were lined with red threads. "Go on, go on," he said, "I want to hear more about her affliction. The exact nature of it has escaped . . ." He waved the bill and his voice trailed off. "Healing by prayer is mighty inexpensive," he murmured.

Mrs. Connin stood a second, staring into the room, with a skeleton's appearance of seeing everything. Then, without taking the money, she turned and shut the door behind her. The father swung around, smiling vaguely, and shrugged. The rest of them were looking at Harry. The little boy began to shamble toward the bedroom.

"Come here, Harry," his mother said. He automatically shifted his direction toward her without opening his eyes any farther. "Tell me what happened today," she said when he reached her. She began to pull off his coat.

"I don't know," he muttered.

"Yes you do know," she said, feeling the coat heavier

on one side. She unzipped the innerlining and caught the book and a dirty handkerchief as they fell out. "Where did you get these?"

"I don't know," he said and grabbed for them. "They're mine. She gave them to me."

She threw the handkerchief down and held the book too high for him to reach and began to read it, her face after a second assuming an exaggerated comical expression. The others moved around and looked at it over her shoulder. "My God," somebody said.

One of the men peered at it sharply from behind a thick pair of glasses. "That's valuable," he said. "That's a collector's item," and he took it away from the rest of them and retired to another chair.

"Don't let George go off with that," his girl said.

"I tell you it's valuable," George said. "1832."

Bevel shifted his direction again toward the room where he slept. He shut the door behind him and moved slowly in the darkness to the bed and sat down and took off his shoes and got under the cover. After a minute a shaft of light let in the tall silhouette of his mother. She tiptoed lightly across the room and sat down on the edge of his bed. "What did that dolt of a preacher say about me?" she whispered. "What lies have you been telling today, honey?"

He shut his eye and heard her voice from a long way away, as if he were under the river and she on top of it. She shook his shoulder. "Harry," she said, leaning down and putting her mouth to his ear, "tell me what he said." She pulled him into a sitting position and he felt as if he had been drawn up from under the river. "Tell me," she whispered and her bitter breath covered his face.

He saw the pale oval close to him in the dark. "He said I'm not the same now," he muttered. "I count."

After a second, she lowered him by his shirt front onto the pillow. She hung over him an instant and brushed her lips against his forehead. Then she got up and moved away, swaying her hips lightly through the shaft of light.

He didn't wake up early but the apartment was still dark and close when he did. For a while he lay there, picking his nose and eyes. Then he sat up in bed and looked out the window. The sun came in palely, stained gray by the glass. Across the street at the Empire Hotel, a colored cleaning woman was looking down from an upper window, resting her face on her folded arms. He got up and put on his shoes and went to the bathroom and then into the front

room. He ate two crackers spread with anchovy paste,
that he found on the coffee table, and drank some ginger
ale left in a bottle and looked around for his book but
it was not there.

The apartment was silent except for the faint humming
of the refrigerator. He went into the kitchen and found
some raisin bread heels and spread a half jar of peanut butter
between them and climbed up on the tall kitchen stool
and sat chewing the sandwich slowly, wiping his nose every
now and then on his shoulder. When he finished he found
some chocolate milk and drank that. He would rather have
had the ginger ale he saw but they left the bottle openers
where he couldn't reach them. He studied what was left
in the refrigerator for a while—some shriveled vegetables
that she had forgot were there and a lot of brown oranges
that she bought and didn't squeeze; there were three or
four kinds of cheese and something fishy in a paper bag;
the rest was a pork bone. He left the refrigerator door
open and wandered back into the dark living room and
sat down on the sofa.

He decided they would be out cold until one o'clock and
that they would all have to go to a restaurant for lunch.
He wasn't high enough for the table yet and the waiter
would bring a highchair and he was too big for a highchair.
He sat in the middle of the sofa, kicking it with his heels.
Then he got up and wandered around the room, looking
into the ashtrays at the butts as if this might be a habit.
In his own room he had picture books and blocks but they
were for the most part torn up; he found the way to get
new ones was to tear up the ones he had. There was very
little to do at any time but eat; however, he was not a
fat boy.

He decided he would empty a few of the ashtrays on
the floor. If he only emptied a few, she would think they
had fallen. He emptied two, rubbing the ashes carefully
into the rug with his finger. Then he lay on the floor for
a while, studying his feet which he held up in the air.
His shoes were still damp and he began to think about the
river.

Very slowly, his expression changed as if he were gradually
seeing appear what he didn't know he'd been looking for.
Then all of a sudden he knew what he wanted to do.

He got up and tiptoed into their bedroom and stood
in the dim light there, looking for her pocketbook. His
glance passed her long pale arm hanging off the edge of
the bed down to the floor, and across the white mound his
father made, and past the crowded bureau, until it rested

on the pocketbook hung on the back of a chair. He took a car-token out of it and half a package of Life Savers. Then he left the apartment and caught the car at the corner. He hadn't taken a suitcase because there was nothing from there he wanted to keep.

He got off the car at the end of the line and started down the road he and Mrs. Connin had taken the day before. He knew there wouldn't be anybody at her house because the three boys and the girl went to school and Mrs. Connin had told him she went out to clean. He passed her yard and walked on the way they had gone to the river. The paper brick houses were far apart and after a while the dirt place to walk on ended and he had to walk on the edge of the highway. The sun was pale yellow and high and hot.

He passed a shack with an orange gas pump in front of it but he didn't see the old man looking out at nothing in particular from the doorway. Mr. Paradise was having an orange drink. He finished it slowly, squinting over the bottle at the small plaid-coated figure disappearing down the road. Then he set the empty bottle on a bench and, still squinting, wiped his sleeve over his mouth. He went in the shack and picked out a peppermint stick, a foot long and two inches thick, from the candy shelf, and stuck it in his hip pocket. Then he got in his car and drove slowly down the highway after the boy.

By the time Bevel came to the field speckled with purple weeds, he was dusty and sweating and he crossed it at a trot to get into the woods as fast as he could. Once inside, he wandered from tree to tree, trying to find the path they had taken yesterday. Finally he found a line worn in the pine needles and followed it until he saw the steep trail twisting down through the trees.

Mr. Paradise had left his automobile back some way on the road and had walked to the place where he was accustomed to sit almost every day, holding an unbaited fishline in the water while he stared at the river passing in front of him. Anyone looking at him from a distance would have seen an old boulder half hidden in the bushes.

Bevel didn't see him at all. He only saw the river, shimmering reddish yellow, and bounded into it with his shoes and his coat on and took a gulp. He swallowed some and spit the rest out and then he stood there in water up to his chest and looked around him. The sky was a clear pale blue, all in one piece—except for the hole the sun made—and fringed around the bottom with treetops. His coat floated to the surface and surrounded him like a strange gay lily pad and he stood grinning in the sun. He intended not to fool with preachers any more but to Baptize himself and to keep on going this time until he found the Kingdom of Christ in the river. He didn't mean to waste any more time. He put his head under the water at once and pushed forward.

In a second he began to gasp and sputter and his head reappeared on the surface; he started under again and the same thing happened. The river wouldn't have him. He tried again and came up, choking. This was the way it had been when the preacher held him under—he had had to fight with something that pushed him back in the face. He stopped and thought suddenly: it's another joke, it's just another joke! He thought how far he had come for nothing and he began to hit and splash and kick the filthy river. His feet were already treading on nothing. He gave one low cry of pain and indignation. Then he heard a shout and turned his head and saw something like a giant pig bounding after him, shaking a red and white club and shouting. He plunged under once and this time, the waiting current caught him like a long gentle hand and pulled him swiftly forward and down. For an instant he was overcome with surprise; then since he was moving quickly and knew that he was getting somewhere, all his fury and fear left him.

Mr. Paradise's head appeared from time to time on the surface of the water. Finally, far downstream, the old man rose like some ancient water monster and stood empty-handed, staring with his dull eyes as far down the river line as he could see.

THE LIFE YOU SAVE MAY BE YOUR OWN

The old woman and her daughter were sitting on their porch when Mr. Shiftlet came up their road for the first time. The old woman slid to the edge of her chair and leaned forward, shading her eyes from the piercing sunset with her hand. The daughter could not see far in front of her and continued to play with her fingers. Although the old woman lived in this desolate spot with only her daughter and she had never seen Mr. Shiftlet before, she could tell, even from a distance, that he was a tramp and no one to be afraid of. His left coat sleeve was folded up to show there was only half an arm in it and his gaunt figure listed slightly to the side as if the breeze were pushing him. He had on a black town suit and a brown felt hat that was turned up in the front and down in the back and he carried a tin tool box by a handle. He came on, at an amble, up her road, his face turned toward the sun which appeared to be balancing itself on the peak of a small mountain.

The old woman didn't change her position until he was almost into her yard; then she rose with one hand fisted on her hip. The daughter, a large girl in a short blue organdy dress, saw him all at once and jumped up and began to stamp and point and make excited speechless sounds.

Mr. Shiftlet stopped just inside the yard and set his box on the ground and tipped his hat at her as if she were not in the least afflicted; then he turned toward the old woman and swung the hat all the way off. He had long black slick hair that hung flat from a part in the middle to beyond the tips of his ears on either side. His face descended in forehead for more than half its length and ended suddenly with his features just balanced over a jutting steel-trap jaw. He seemed to be a young man but he had a look of composed dissatisfaction as if he understood life thoroughly.

"Good evening," the old woman said. She was about the size of a cedar fence post and she had a man's gray hat pulled down low over her head.

The tramp stood looking at her and didn't answer. He

turned his back and faced the sunset. He swung both his whole and his short arm up slowly so that they indicated an expanse of sky and his figure formed a crooked cross. The old woman watched him with her arms folded across her chest as if she were the owner of the sun, and the daughter watched, her head thrust forward and her fat helpless hands hanging at the wrists. She had long pink-gold hair and eyes as blue as a peacock's neck.

He held the pose for almost fifty seconds and then he picked up his box and came on to the porch and dropped down on the bottom step. "Lady," he said in a firm nasal voice, "I'd give a fortune to live where I could see me a sun do that every evening."

"Does it every evening," the old woman said and sat back down. The daughter sat down too and watched him with a cautious sly look as if he were a bird that had come up very close. He leaned to one side, rooting in his pants pocket, and in a second he brought out a package of chewing gum and offered her a piece. She took it and unpeeled it and began to chew without taking her eyes off him. He offered the old woman a piece but she only raised her upper lip to indicate she had no teeth.

Mr. Shiftlet's pale sharp glance had already passed over everything in the yard—the pump near the corner of the house and the big fig tree that three or four chickens were preparing to roost in—and had moved to a shed where he saw the square rusted back of an automobile. "You ladies drive?" he asked.

"That car ain't run in fifteen year," the old woman said. "The day my husband died, it quit running."

"Nothing is like it used to be, lady," he said. "The world is almost rotten."

"That's right," the old woman said. "You from around here?"

"Name Tom T. Shiftlet," he murmured, looking at the tires.

"I'm pleased to meet you," the old woman said. "Name Lucynell Crater and daughter Lucynell Crater. What you doing around here, Mr. Shiftlet?"

He judged the car to be about a 1928 or '29 Ford. "Lady," he said, and turned and gave her his full attention, "lemme tell you something. There's one of these doctors in Atlanta that's taken a knife and cut the human heart—the human heart," he repeated, leaning forward, "out of a man's chest and held it in his hand," and he held his hand out, palm up, as if it were slightly weighted with the human heart, "and studied it like it was a day-old chicken, and lady," he said, allowing a long significant pause in which his head slid forward and his clay-colored eyes brightened, "he don't know no more about it than you or me."

"That's right," the old woman said.

"Why, if he was to take that knife and cut into every corner of it, he still wouldn't know no more than you or me. What you want to bet?"

"Nothing," the old woman said wisely. "Where you come from, Mr. Shiftlet?"

He didn't answer. He reached into his pocket and brought out a sack of tobacco and a package of cigarette papers and rolled himself a cigarette, expertly with one hand, and attached it in a hanging position to his upper lip. Then he took a box of wooden matches from his pocket and struck one on his shoe. He held the burning match as if he were studying the mystery of flame while it traveled dangerously toward his skin. The daughter began to make loud noises and to point to his hand and shake her finger at him, but when the flame was just before touching him, he leaned down with his hand cupped over it as if he were going to set fire to his nose and lit the cigarette.

He flipped away the dead match and blew a stream of gray into the evening. A sly look came over his face. "Lady," he said, "nowadays, people'll do anything anyways. I can tell you my name is Tom T. Shiftlet and I come from Tarwater, Tennessee, but you never have seen me before: how you know I ain't lying? How you know my name ain't Aaron Sparks, lady, and I come from Singleberry, Georgia, or how you know it's not George Speeds and I come from Lucy, Alabama, or how you know I ain't Thompson Bright from Toolafalls, Mississippi?"

"I don't know nothing about you," the old woman muttered, irked.

"Lady," he said, "people don't care how they lie. Maybe the best I can tell you is, I'm a man; but listen lady," he said and paused and made his tone more ominous still, "what is a man?"

The old woman began to gum a seed. "What you carry in that tin box, Mr. Shiftlet?" she asked.

"Tools," he said, put back. "I'm a carpenter."

"Well, if you come out here to work, I'll be able to feed you and give you a place to sleep but I can't pay. I'll tell you that before you begin," she said.

There was no answer at once and no particular expression on his face. He leaned back against the two-by-four that helped support the porch roof. "Lady," he said slowly, "there's some men that some things mean more to them than money." The old woman rocked without comment and the daughter watched the trigger that moved up and down in his neck. He told the old woman then that all most people were interested in was money, but he asked what a man was made for. He asked her if a man was made for money, or what. He asked her what she thought she was made for but she didn't answer, she only sat rocking and wondered if a one-armed man could put a new roof on her garden house. He asked a lot of questions that she didn't answer. He told her that he was twenty-eight years old and had lived a varied life. He had been a gospel singer, a foreman on the railroad, an assistant in an undertaking parlor, and he come over the radio for three months with Uncle Roy and his Red Creek Wranglers. He said he had fought and bled in the Arm Service of his country and visited every foreign land and that everywhere he had seen people that didn't care if they did a thing one way or another. He said he hadn't been raised thataway.

A fat yellow moon appeared in the branches of the fig tree as if it were going to roost there with the chickens. He said that a man had to escape to the country to see the world whole and that he wished he lived in a desolate place like this where he could see the sun go down every evening like God made it to do.

"Are you married or are you single?" the old woman asked.

There was a long silence. "Lady," he asked finally, "where would you find you an innocent woman today? I wouldn't have any of this trash I could just pick up."

The daughter was leaning very far down, hanging her head almost between her knees, watching him through a triangular door she had made in her overturned hair; and she suddenly fell in a heap on the floor and began to whimper. Mr. Shiftlet straightened her out and helped her get back in the chair.

"Is she your baby girl?" he asked.

"My only," the old woman said, "and she's the sweetest girl in the world. I would give her up for nothing on earth. She's smart too. She can sweep the floor, cook, wash, feed the chickens, and hoe. I wouldn't give her up for a casket of jewels."

"No," he said kindly, "don't ever let any man take her away from you."

"Any man come after her," the old woman said, " 'll have to stay around the place."

Mr. Shiftlet's eye in the darkness was focused on a part of the automobile bumper that glittered in the distance.

"Lady," he said, jerking his short arm up as if he could point with it to her house and yard and pump, "there ain't a broken thing on this plantation that I couldn't fix for you, one-arm jackleg or not. I'm a man," he said with a sullen dignity, "even if I ain't a whole one. I got," he said, tapping his knuckles on the floor to emphasize the immensity of what he was going to say, "a moral intelligence!" and his face pierced out of the darkness into a shaft of doorlight and he stared at her as if he were astonished himself at this impossible truth.

The old woman was not impressed with the phrase. "I told you you could hang around and work for food," she said, "if you don't mind sleeping in that car yonder."

"Why listen, lady," he said with a grin of delight, "the monks of old slept in their coffins!"

"They wasn't as advanced as we are," the old woman said.

The next morning he began on the roof of the garden house while Lucynell, the daughter, sat on a rock and watched him work. He had not been around a week before the change he had made in the place was apparent. He had patched the front and back steps, built a new hog pen, restored a fence, and taught Lucynell, who was completely deaf and had never said a word in her life, to say the word "bird." The big rosy-faced girl followed him everywhere, saying "Burrttddt ddbirrrttdt," and clapping her hands. The old woman watched from a distance, secretly pleased. She was ravenous for a son-in-law.

Mr. Shiftlet slept on the hard narrow back seat of the car with his feet out the side window. He had his razor and a can of water on a crate that served him as a bedside table and he put up a piece of mirror against the back glass and kept his coat neatly on a hanger that he hung over one of the windows.

In the evenings he sat on the steps and talked while the old woman and Lucynell rocked violently in their chairs on either side of him. The old woman's three mountains were black against the dark blue sky and were visited off and on by various planets and by the moon after it had left the chickens. Mr. Shiftlet pointed out that the reason he had improved this plantation was because he had taken a personal interest in it. He said he was even going to make the automobile run.

He had raised the hood and studied the mechanism and he said he could tell that the car had been built in the days when cars were really built. You take now, he said, one man puts in one bolt and another man puts in another bolt and another man puts in another bolt so that it's a man for a bolt. That's why you have to pay so much for a car: you're paying all those men. Now if you didn't have to pay but one man, you could get you a cheaper car and one that had had a personal interest taken in it, and it would be a better car. The old woman agreed with him that this was so.

Mr. Shiftlet said that the trouble with the world was that nobody cared, or stopped and took any trouble. He said he never would have been able to teach Lucynell to say a word if he hadn't cared and stopped long enough.

"Teach her to say something else," the old woman said.

"What you want her to say next?" Mr. Shiftlet asked.

The old woman's smile was broad and toothless and suggestive. "Teach her to say 'sugarpie,' " she said.

Mr. Shiftlet already knew what was on her mind.

The next day he began to tinker with the automobile and that evening he told her that if she would buy a fan belt, he would be able to make the car run.

The old woman said she would give him the money. "You see that girl yonder?" she asked, pointing to Lucynell who was sitting on the floor a foot away, watching him, her eyes blue even in the dark. "If it was ever a man wanted to take her away, I would say, 'No man on earth is going to take that sweet girl of mine away from me!' but if he was to say, 'Lady, I don't want to take her away, I want her right here,' I would say, 'Mister, I don't blame you none. I wouldn't pass up a chance to live in a permanent place and get the sweetest girl in the world myself. You ain't no fool,' I would say."

"How old is she?" Mr. Shiftlet asked casually.

"Fifteen, sixteen," the old woman said. The girl was nearly thirty but because of her innocence it was impossible to guess.

"It would be a good idea to paint it too," Mr. Shiftlet remarked. "You don't want it to rust out."

"We'll see about that later," the old woman said.

The next day he walked into town and returned with the parts he needed and a can of gasoline. Late in the afternoon, terrible noises issued from the shed and the old woman rushed out of the house, thinking Lucynell was somewhere having a fit. Lucynell was sitting on a chicken crate, stamping her feet and screaming, "Burrddttt! bddurrddttttt!" but her fuss was drowned out by the car. With a volley of blasts it emerged from the shed, moving in a fierce and stately

way. Mr. Shiftlet was in the driver's seat, sitting very
erect. He had an expression of serious modesty on his
face as if he had just raised the dead.

That night, rocking on the porch, the old woman began
her business at once. "You want you an innocent woman,
don't you?" she asked sympathetically. "You don't want
none of this trash."

"No'm, I don't," Mr. Shiftlet said.

"One that can't talk," she continued, "can't sass you
back or use foul language. That's the kind for you to
have. Right there," and she pointed to Lucynell sitting
cross-legged in her chair, holding both feet in her hands.

"That's right," he admitted. "She wouldn't give me any
trouble."

"Saturday," the old woman said, "you and her and me
can drive into town and get married."

Mr. Shiftlet eased his position on the steps.

"I can't get married right now," he said. "Everything
you want to do takes money and I ain't got any."

"What you need with money?" she asked.

"It takes money," he said. "Some people'll do anything
anyhow these days, but the way I think, I wouldn't marry
no woman that I couldn't take on a trip like she was somebody. I mean take her to a hotel and treat her. I wouldn't
marry the Duchesser Windsor," he said firmly, "unless
I could take her to a hotel and giver something good to eat.

"I was raised thataway and there ain't a thing I can
do about it. My old mother taught me how to do."

"Lucynell don't even know what a hotel is," the old
woman muttered. "Listen here, Mr. Shiftlet," she said,
sliding forward in her chair, "you'd be getting a permanent
house and a deep well and the most innocent girl in the
world. You don't need no money. Lemme tell you something: there ain't any place in the world for a poor disabled
friendless drifting man."

The ugly words settled in Mr. Shiftlet's head like a
group of buzzards in the top of a tree. He didn't answer
at once. He rolled himself a cigarette and lit it and then
he said in an even voice, "Lady, a man is divided into
two parts, body and spirit."

The old woman clamped her gums together.

"A body and a spirit," he repeated. "The body, lady,
is like a house: it don't go anywhere; but the spirit, lady,
is like a automobile: always on the move, always . . ."

"Listen, Mr. Shiftlet," she said, "my well never goes
dry and my house is always warm in the winter and there's

no mortgage on a thing about this place. You can go to the courthouse and see for yourself. And yonder under that shed is a fine automobile." She laid the bait carefully. "You can have it painted by Saturday. I'll pay for the paint."

In the darkness, Mr. Shiftlet's smile stretched like a weary snake waking up by a fire. After a second he recalled himself and said, "I'm only saying a man's spirit means more to him than anything else. I would have to take my wife off for the week end without no regards at all for cost. I got to follow where my spirit says to go."

"I'll give you fifteen dollars for a week-end trip," the old woman said in a crabbed voice. "That's the best I can do."

"That wouldn't hardly pay for more than the gas and the hotel," he said. "It wouldn't feed her."

"Seventeen-fifty," the old woman said. "That's all I got so it isn't any use you trying to milk me. You can take a lunch."

Mr. Shiftlet was deeply hurt by the word "milk." He didn't doubt that she had more money sewed up in her mattress but he had already told her he was not interested in her money. "I'll make that do," he said and rose and walked off without treating with her further.

On Saturday the three of them drove into town in the car that the paint had barely dried on and Mr. Shiftlet and Lucynell were married in the Ordinary's office while the old woman witnessed. As they came out of the courthouse, Mr. Shiftlet began twisting his neck in his collar. He looked morose and bitter as if he had been insulted while someone held him. "That didn't satisfy me none," he said. "That was just something a woman in an office did, nothing but paper work and blood tests. What do they know about my blood? If they was to take my heart and cut it out," he said, "they wouldn't know a thing about me. It didn't satisfy me at all."

"It satisfied the law," the old woman said sharply.

"The law," Mr. Shiftlet said and spit. "It's the law that don't satisfy me."

He had painted the car dark green with a yellow band around it just under the windows. The three of them climbed in the front seat and the old woman said, "Don't Lucynell look pretty? Looks like a baby doll." Lucynell was dressed up in a white dress that her mother had uprooted from a trunk and there was a Panama hat on her head with a bunch of red wooden cherries on the brim. Every

now and then her placid expression was changed by a
sly isolated little thought like a shoot of green in the desert.
"You got a prize!" the old woman said.

Mr. Shiftlet didn't even look at her.

They drove back to the house to let the old woman off
and pick up the lunch. When they were ready to leave,
she stood staring in the window of the car, with her fingers
clenched around the glass. Tears began to seep sideways
out of her eyes and run along the dirty creases in her face.
"I ain't ever been parted with her for two days before,"
she said.

Mr. Shiftlet started the motor.

"And I wouldn't let no man have her but you because
I seen you would do right. Good-by, Sugarbaby," she said,
clutching at the sleeve of the white dress. Lucynell looked
straight at her and didn't seem to see her there at all.
Mr. Shiftlet eased the car forward so that she had to
move her hands.

The early afternoon was clear and open and surrounded
by pale blue sky. Although the car would go only thirty
miles an hour, Mr. Shiftlet imagined a terrific climb and
dip and swerve that went entirely to his head so that he
forgot his morning bitterness. He had always wanted an automobile but he had never been able to afford one before.
He drove very fast because he wanted to make Mobile by
nightfall.

Occasionally he stopped his thoughts long enough to
look at Lucynell in the seat beside him. She had eaten
the lunch as soon as they were out of the yard and now
she was pulling the cherries off the hat one by one and
throwing them out the window. He became depressed in
spite of the car. He had driven about a hundred miles
when he decided that she must be hungry again and at
the next small town they came to, he stopped in front
of an aluminum-painted eating place called The Hot Spot
and took her in and ordered her a plate of ham and grits.
The ride had made her sleepy and as soon as she got up
on the stool, she rested her head on the counter and shut
her eyes. There was no one in The Hot Spot but Mr.
Shiftlet and the boy behind the counter, a pale youth with
a greasy rag hung over his shoulder. Before he could dish
up the food, she was snoring gently.

"Give it to her when she wakes up," Mr. Shiftlet said.
"I'll pay for it now."

The boy bent over her and stared at the long pink-gold
hair and the half-shut sleeping eyes. Then he looked up

and stared at Mr. Shiftlet. "She looks like an angel of Gawd," he murmured.

"Hitch-hiker," Mr. Shiftlet explained. "I can't wait. I got to make Tuscaloosa."

The boy bent over again and very carefully touched his finger to a strand of the golden hair and Mr. Shiftlet left.

He was more depressed than ever as he drove on by himself. The late afternoon had grown hot and sultry and the country had flattened out. Deep in the sky a storm was preparing very slowly and without thunder as if it meant to drain every drop of air from the earth before it broke. There were times when Mr. Shiftlet preferred not to be alone. He felt too that a man with a car had a responsibility to others and he kept his eye out for a hitchhiker. Occasionally he saw a sign that warned: "Drive carefully. The life you save may be your own."

The narrow road dropped off on either side into dry fields and here and there a shack or a filling station stood in a clearing. The sun began to set directly in front of the automobile. It was a reddening ball that through his windshield was slightly flat on the bottom and top. He saw a boy in overalls and a gray hat standing on the edge of the road and he slowed the car down and stopped in front of him. The boy didn't have his hand raised to thumb the ride, he was only standing there, but he had a small cardboard suitcase and his hat was set on his head in a way to indicate that he had left somewhere for good. "Son," Mr. Shiftlet said, "I see you want a ride."

The boy didn't say he did or he didn't but he opened the door of the car and got in, and Mr. Shiftlet started driving again. The child held the suitcase on his lap and folded his arms on top of it. He turned his head and looked out the window away from Mr. Shiftlet. Mr. Shiftlet felt oppressed. "Son," he said after a minute, "I got the best old mother in the world so I reckon you only got the second best."

The boy gave him a quick dark glance and then turned his face back out the window.

"It's nothing so sweet," Mr. Shiftlet continued, "as a boy's mother. She taught him his first prayers at her knee, she give him love when no other would, she told him what was right and what wasn't, and she seen that he done the right thing. Son," he said, "I never rued a day in my life like the one I rued when I left that old mother of mine."

The boy shifted in his seat but he didn't look at Mr.

Shiftlet. He unfolded his arms and put one hand on the door handle.

"My mother was a angel of Gawd," Mr. Shiftlet said in a very strained voice. "He took her from heaven and giver to me and I left her." His eyes were instantly clouded over with a mist of tears. The car was barely moving.

The boy turned angrily in the seat. "You go to the devil!" he cried. "My old woman is a flea bag and yours is a stinking pole cat!" and with that he flung the door open and jumped out with his suitcase into the ditch.

Mr. Shiftlet was so shocked that for about a hundred feet he drove along slowly with the door still open. A cloud, the exact color of the boy's hat and shaped like a turnip, had descended over the sun, and another, worse looking, crouched behind the car. Mr. Shiftlet felt that the rottenness of the world was about to engulf him. He raised his arm and let it fall again to his breast. "Oh Lord!" he prayed. "Break forth and wash the slime from this earth!"

The turnip continued slowly to descend. After a few minutes there was a guffawing peal of thunder from behind and fantastic raindrops, like tin-can tops, crashed over the rear of Mr. Shiftlet's car. Very quickly he stepped on the gas and with his stump sticking out the window he raced the galloping shower into Mobile.

A STROKE OF GOOD FORTUNE

Ruby came in the front door of the apartment building and lowered the paper sack with the four cans of number three beans in it onto the hall table. She was too tired to take her arms from around it or to straighten up and she hung there collapsed from the hips, her head balanced like a big florid vegetable at the top of the sack. She gazed with stony unrecognition at the face that confronted her in the dark yellow-spotted mirror over the table. Against her right cheek was a gritty collard leaf that had been stuck there half the way home. She gave it a vicious swipe with her arm and straightened up, muttering, "Collards, collards," in a voice of sultry subdued wrath. Standing up straight, she was a short woman, shaped nearly like a funeral urn. She had mulberry-colored hair stacked in sausage rolls around her head but some of these had come loose with the heat and the long walk from the grocery store and pointed frantically in various directions. "Collard greens!" she said, spitting the word from her mouth this time as if it were a poisonous seed.

She and Bill Hill hadn't eaten collard greens for five years and she wasn't going to start cooking them now. She had bought these on account of Rufus but she wasn't going to buy them but once. You would have thought that after two years in the armed forces Rufus would have come back ready to eat like somebody from somewhere; but no. When she asked him what he would like to have *special*, he had not had the gumption to think of one civilized dish—he had said collard greens. She had expected Rufus to have turned out into somebody with some get in him. Well, he had about as much get as a floor mop.

Rufus was her baby brother who had just come back from the European Theater. He had come to live with her because Pitman where they were raised was not there any more. All the people who had lived at Pitman had had the good sense to leave it, either by dying or by moving to the city. She had married Bill B. Hill, a Florida man who sold Miracle Products, and had come to live in the city. If Pitman had still been there, Rufus would have

171

been in Pitman. If one chicken had been left to walk across the road in Pitman, Rufus would have been there too to keep him company. She didn't like to admit it about her own kin, least about her own brother, but there he was—good for absolutely nothing. "I seen it after five minutes of him," she had told Bill Hill and Bill Hill, with no expression whatsoever, had said, "It taken me three." It was mortifying to let that kind of a husband see you had that kind of a brother.

She supposed there was no help for it. Rufus was like the other children. She was the only one in her family who had been different, who had had any get. She took a stub of pencil from her pocketbook and wrote on the side of the sack: Bill you bring this upstairs. Then she braced herself at the bottom of the steps for the climb to the fourth floor.

The steps were thin black rent in the middle of the house, covered with a mole-colored carpet that looked as if it grew from the floor. They stuck straight up like steeple steps, it seemed to her. They reared up. The minute she stood at the bottom of them, they reared up and got steeper for her benefit. As she gazed up them, her mouth widened and turned down in a look of complete disgust. She was in no condition to go up anything. She was sick. Madam Zoleeda had told her but not before she knew it herself.

Madam Zoleeda was the palmist on Highway 87. She had said, "A long illness," but she had added, whispering, with a very I-already-know-but-I-won't-tell look, "It will bring you a stroke of good fortune!" and then had sat back grinning, a stout woman with green eyes that moved in their sockets as if they had been oiled. Ruby didn't need to be told. She had already figured out the good fortune. Moving. For two months she had had a distinct feeling that they were going to move. Bill Hill couldn't hold off much longer. He couldn't kill her. Where she wanted to be was in a subdivision—she started up the steps, leaning forward and holding onto the banisters—where you had your drugstores and grocery and a picture show right in your own neighborhood. As it was now, living downtown, she had to walk eight blocks to the main business streets and farther than that to get to a supermarket. She hadn't made any complaints for five years much but now with her health at stake as young as she was what did he think she was going to do, kill herself? She had her eye on a place in Meadowcrest Heights, a duplex bungalow with yellow awnings. She stopped on the fifth step to blow. As young as she was—thirty-four—you wouldn't think five steps would stew her. You better take it easy, baby, she told herself, you're too young to bust your gears.

Thirty-four wasn't old, wasn't any age at all. She remembered her mother at thirty-four—she had looked like a puckered-up old yellow apple, sour, she had always looked sour, she had always looked like she wasn't satisfied with anything. She compared herself at thirty-four with her mother at that age. Her mother's hair had been gray—hers wouldn't be gray now even if she hadn't touched it up. All those children were what did her mother in—eight of them: two born dead, one died the first year, one crushed under a mowing machine. Her mother had got deader with every one of them. And all of for what? Because she hadn't known any better. Pure ignorance. The purest of downright ignorance!

And there her two sisters were, both married four years with four children apiece. She didn't see how they stood it, always going to the doctor to be jabbed at with instruments. She remembered when her mother had had Rufus. She was the only one of the children who couldn't stand it and she walked all the way in to Melsy, in the hot sun ten miles, to the picture show to get clear of the screaming, and had sat through two westerns and a horror picture and a serial and then had walked all the way back and found it was just beginning, and she had had to listen all night. All that misery for Rufus! And him turned out now to have no more charge than a dish rag. She saw him waiting out nowhere before he was born, just waiting, waiting to make his mother, only thirty-four, into an old woman. She gripped the banister rail fiercely and heaved herself up another step, shaking her head. Lord, she was disappointed in him! After she had told all her friends her brother was back from the European Theater, here he comes—sounding like he'd never been out of a hog lot.

He looked old too. He looked older than she did and he was fourteen years younger. She was extremely young looking for her age. Not that thirty-four is any age and anyway she was married. She had to smile, thinking about that, because she had done so much better than her sisters—they had married from around. "This breathlessness," she muttered, stopping again. She decided she would have to sit down.

There were twenty-eight steps in each flight—twenty-eight.

She sat down and jumped quickly, feeling something under her. She caught her breath and then pulled the thing out: it was Hartley Gilfeet's pistol. Nine inches of treacherous tin! He was a six-year-old boy who lived on the fifth floor. If he had been hers, she'd have worn him out so hard so many times he wouldn't know how to leave his mess on a public stair. She could have fallen down those stairs as easy as not and ruined herself! But his stupid mother wasn't going to do anything to him even if she told her. All she did was scream at him and tell people how smart he was. "Little Mister Good Fortune!" she called him. "All his poor daddy left me!" His daddy had said on his death bed, "There's nothing but him I ever given you," and she had said, "Rodman, you given me a fortune!" and so she called him Little Mister Good Fortune. "I'd wear the seat of his good fortune out!" Ruby muttered.

The steps were going up and down like a seesaw with her in the middle of it. She did not want to get nauseated. Not that again. Now no. No. She was not. She sat tightly to the steps with her eyes shut until the dizziness stopped a little and the nausea subsided. No, I'm not going to no doctor, she said. No. No. She was not. They would have to carry her there knocked out before she would go. She had done all right doctoring herself all these years—no bad sick spells, no teeth out, no children, all that by herself. She would have had five children right now if she hadn't been careful.

She had wondered more than once if this breathlessness could be heart trouble. Once in a while, going up the steps, there'd be a pain in her chest along with it. That was what she wanted it to be—heart trouble. They couldn't very well remove your heart. They'd have to knock her in the head before they'd get her near a hospital, they'd have to—suppose she would die if they didn't?

She wouldn't.

Suppose she would?

She made herself stop this gory thinking. She was only thirty-four. There was nothing permanent wrong with her. She was fat and her color was good. She thought of herself again in comparison with her mother at thirty-four and she pinched her arm and smiled. Seeing that her mother or father neither had been much to look at, she had done very well. They had been the dried-up type, dried up and Pitman dried into them, them and Pitman shrunk down into something all dried and puckered up. And she had come out of that! A somebody as alive as her! She got up, gripping the banister rail but smiling to herself. She was warm and fat and beautiful and not too fat because Bill Hill liked her that way. She had gained some weight but he hadn't noticed except that he was maybe more happy lately and didn't know why. She felt the wholeness of herself, a whole thing climbing the stairs. She was up the first flight now and she looked back, pleased. As soon as Bill Hill fell down these steps once, maybe they would move. But they would move before that! Madam Zoleeda had known. She laughed aloud and moved on down the hall. Mr. Jerger's door grated and startled her. Oh Lord, she thought, *him*. He was a second-floor resident who was peculiar.

He peered at her coming down the hall. "Good morning!" he said, bowing the upper part of his body out the door. "Good morning to you!" He looked like a goat. He had little raisin eyes and a string beard and his jacket was a green that was almost black or a black that was almost green.

"Morning," she said. "Hower you?"

"Well!" he screamed. "Well indeed on this glorious day!" He was seventy-eight years old and his face looked as if it had mildew on it. In the mornings he studied and in the afternoons, he walked up and down the sidewalks, stopping children and asking them questions. Whenever he heard anyone in the hall, he opened his door and looked out.

"Yeah, it's a nice day," she said languidly.

"Do you know what great birthday this is?" he asked.

"Uh-uh," Ruby said. He always had a question like that. A history question that nobody knew; he would ask it and then make a speech on it. He used to teach in a high school.

"Guess," he urged her.

"Abraham Lincoln," she muttered.

"Hah! You are not trying," he said. "Try."

"George Washington," she said, starting up the stairs.

"Shame on you!" he cried. "And your husband from there! Florida! Florida! Florida's birthday," he shouted. "Come in here." He disappeared into his room, beckoning a long finger at her.

She came down the two steps and said, "I gotta be going," and stuck her head inside the door. The room was the size of a large closet and the walls were completely covered with picture postcards of local buildings; this gave an illusion of space. A single transparent bulb hung down on Mr. Jerger and a small table.

"Now examine this," he said. He was bending over a book, running his finger under the lines: " 'On Easter Sunday, April 3, 1516, he arrived on the tip of this continent.' Do you know who this *he* was?" he demanded.

"Yeah, Christopher Columbus," Ruby said.

"Ponce de Leon!" he screamed. "Ponce de Leon! You should know something about Florida," he said. "Your husband is from Florida."

"Yeah, he was born in Miami," Ruby said. "He's not from Tennessee."

"Florida is not a noble state," Mr. Jerger said, "but it is an important one."

"It's important alrighto," Ruby said.

"Do you know who Ponce de Leon was?"

"He was the founder of Florida," Ruby said brightly.

"He was a Spaniard," Mr. Jerger said. "Do you know what he was looking for?"

"Florida," Ruby said.

"Ponce de Leon was looking for the fountain of youth," Mr. Jerger said, closing his eyes.

"Oh," Ruby muttered.

"A certain spring," Mr. Jerger went on, "whose water gave perpetual youth to those who drank it. In other words," he said, "he was trying to be young always."

"Did he find it?" Ruby asked.

Mr. Jerger paused with his eyes still closed. After a minute he said, "Do you think he found it? Do you think he found it? Do you think nobody else would have got to it if he had found it? Do you think there would be one person living on this earth who hadn't drunk it?"

"I hadn't thought," Ruby said.

"Nobody thinks any more," Mr. Jerger complained.

"I got to be going."

"Yes, it's been found," Mr. Jerger said.

"Where at?" Ruby asked.

"I have drunk of it."

"Where'd you have to go to?" she asked. She leaned a little closer and got a whiff of him that was like putting her nose under a buzzard's wing.

"Into my heart," he said, placing his hand over it.

"Oh." Ruby moved back. "I gotta be going. I think my brother's home." She got over the door sill.

"Ask your husband if he knows what great birthday this is," Mr. Jerger said, looking at her coyly.

"Yeah, I will." She turned and waited until she heard his door click. She looked back to see that it was shut and then she blew out her breath and stood facing the dark remaining steep of steps. "God Almighty," she commented. They got darker and steeper as you went up.

By the time she had climbed five steps her breath was gone. She continued up a few more, blowing. Then she stopped. There was a pain in her stomach. It was a pain like a piece of something pushing something else. She had felt it before, a few days ago. It was the one that frightened her most. She had thought the word *cancer* once and dropped it instantly because no horror like that was coming to her because it couldn't. The word came back to her immediately with the pain but she slashed it in two with Madam Zoleeda. It will end in good fortune. She slashed it twice through and then again until there were only pieces of it that couldn't be recognized. She was going to stop on the next floor—God, if she ever got up there—and talk to Laverne Watts. Laverne Watts was a third-floor resident, the secretary to a chiropodist, and an especial friend of hers.

She got up there, gasping and feeling as if her knees were full of fizz, and knocked on Laverne's door with the butt of Hartley Gilfeet's gun. She leaned on the door frame to rest and suddenly the floor around her dropped on both sides. The walls turned black and she felt herself reeling, without breath, in the middle of the air, terrified at the drop that was coming. She saw the door open a great distance away and Laverne, about four inches high, standing in it.

Laverne, a tall straw-haired girl, let out a great guffaw and slapped her side as if she had just opened the door on the most comical sight she had yet seen. "That gun!" she yelled. "That gun! That look!" She staggered back to the sofa and fell on it, her legs rising higher than her hips and falling down again helplessly with a thud.

The floor came up to where Ruby could see it and remained, dipping a little. With a terrible stare of concentration, she stepped down to get on it. She scrutinized a chair across the room and then headed for it, putting her feet carefully one before the other.

"You should be in a wild-west show!" Laverne Watts said. "You're a howl!"

Ruby reached the chair and then edged herself onto it. "Shut up," she said hoarsely.

Laverne sat forward, pointing at her, and then fell back on the sofa, shaking again.

"Quit that!" Ruby yelled. "Quit that! I'm sick."

Laverne got up and took two or three long strides across the room. She leaned down in front of Ruby and looked into her face with one eye shut as if she were squinting through a keyhole. "You are sort of purple," she said.

"I'm damn sick," Ruby glowered.

Laverne stood looking at her and after a second she folded her arms and very pointedly stuck her stomach out and began to sway back and forth. "Well, what'd you come in here with that gun for? Where'd you get it?" she asked.

"Sat on it," Ruby muttered.

Laverne stood there, swaying with her stomach stuck out, and a very wise expression growing on her face. Ruby sat sprawled in the chair, looking at her feet. The room was getting still. She sat up and glared at her ankles. They were swollen! I'm not going to no doctor, she started, I'm not going to one. I'm not going. "Not going," she began to mumble, "to no doctor, not . . ."

"How long you think you can hold off?" Laverne murmured and began to giggle.

"Are my ankles swollen?" Ruby asked.

"They look like they've always looked to me," Laverne said, throwing herself down on the sofa again. "Kind of fat." She lifted her own ankles up on the end pillow and turned them slightly. "How do you like these shoes?" she asked. They were a grasshopper green with very high thin heels.

"I think they're swollen," Ruby said. "When I was coming up that last flight of stairs I had the awfulest feeling, all over me like . . ."

"You ought to go on to the doctor."

"I don't need to go to no doctor," Ruby muttered. "I can take care of myself. I haven't done bad at it all this time."

"Is Rufus at home?"

"I don't know. I kept myself away from doctors all my life. I kept—why?"

"Why what?"

"Why, is Rufus at home?"

"Rufus is cute," Laverne said. "I thought I'd ask him how he liked my shoes."

Ruby sat up with a fierce look, very pink and purple. "Why Rufus?" she growled. "He ain't but a baby." Laverne was thirty years old. "He don't care about women's shoes."

Laverne sat up and took off one of the shoes and peered inside it. "Nine B," she said. "I bet he'd like what's in it."

"That Rufus ain't but an enfant!" Ruby said. "He don't have time to be looking at your feet. He ain't got that kind of time."

"Oh, he's got plenty of time," Laverne said.

"Yeah," Ruby muttered and saw him again, waiting, with plenty of time, out nowhere before he was born, just waiting to make his mother that much deader.

"I believe your ankles are swollen," Laverne said.

"Yeah," Ruby said, twisting them. "Yeah. They feel tight sort of. I had the awfulest feeling when I got up those steps, like sort of out of breath all over, sort of tight all over, sort of—awful."

"You ought to go on to the doctor."

"No."

"You ever been to one?"

"They carried me once when I was ten," Ruby said, "but I got away. Three of them holding me didn't do any good."

"What was it that time?"

"What you looking at me that way for?" Ruby muttered.

"What way?"

"That way," Ruby said, "—swagging out that stomach of yours that way."

"I just asked you what it was that time?"

"It was a boil. A nigger woman up the road told me what to do and I did it and it went away." She sat slumped on the edge of the chair, staring in front of her as if she were remembering an easier time.

Laverne began to do a kind of comic dance up and down the room. She took two or three slow steps in one direction with her knees bent and then she came back and kicked her leg slowly and painfully in the other. She began to sing in a loud guttural voice, rolling her eyes, "Put them all together, they spell MOTHER! MOTHER!" and stretching out her arms as if she were on the stage.

Ruby's mouth opened wordlessly and her fierce expression vanished. For a half-second she was motionless; then she sprang from the chair. "Not me!" she shouted. "Not me!"

Laverne stopped and only watched her with the wise look.

"Not me!" Ruby shouted. "Oh no not me! Bill Hill takes care of that. Bill Hill takes care of that! Bill Hill's been taking care of that for five years! That ain't going to happen to me!"

"Well old Bill Hill just slipped up about four or five months ago, my friend," Laverne said. "Just slipped up . . ."

"I don't reckon you know anything about it, you ain't even married, you ain't even . . ."

"I bet it's not one, I bet it's two," Laverne said. "You better go on to the doctor and find out how many it is."

"It is not!" Ruby shrilled. She thought she was so smart! She didn't know a sick woman when she saw one, all she could do was look at her feet and shoe em to Rufus, shoe em to Rufus and he was an enfant and she was thirty-four years old. "Rufus is an enfant!" she wailed.

"That will make two!" Laverne said.

"You shut up talking like that!" Ruby shouted. "You shut up this minute. I ain't going to have any baby!"

"Ha ha," Laverne said.

"I don't know how you think you know so much," Ruby said, "single as you are. If I was so single I wouldn't go around telling married people what their business is."

"Not just your ankles," Laverne said, "you're swollen all over."

"I ain't going to stay here and be insulted," Ruby said and walked carefully to the door, keeping herself erect and not looking down at her stomach the way she wanted to.

"Well I hope *all* of you feel better tomorrow," Laverne said.

"I think my heart will be better tomorrow," Ruby said. "But I hope we will be moving soon. I can't climb these steps with this heart trouble and," she added with a dignified glare, "Rufus don't care nothing about your big feet."

"You better put that gun up," Laverne said, "before you shoot somebody."

Ruby slammed the door shut and looked down at herself quickly. She was big there but she had always had a kind of big stomach. She did not stick out there different from the way she did any place else. It was natural when you took on some weight to take it on in the middle and Bill Hill didn't mind her being fat, he was just more happy and didn't know why. She saw Bill Hill's long happy face, grinning at her from the eyes downward in a way he had as if his look got happier as it neared his teeth. He would never slip up. She rubbed her hand across her skirt and felt the tightness of it but hadn't she felt that before? She had. It was the skirt—she had on the tight one that she didn't wear often, she had . . . she didn't have on the tight skirt. She had on the loose one. But it wasn't very loose. But that didn't make any difference, she was just fat.

She put her fingers on her stomach and pushed down and then took them off quickly. She began walking toward the stairs, slowly, as if the floor were going to move under her. She began the steps. The pain came back at once. It came back with the first step. "No," she whimpered, "no." It was just a little feeling, just a little feeling like a piece of her inside rolling over but it made her breath tighten in her throat. Nothing in her was supposed to roll over. "Just one step," she whispered, "Just one step and it did it." It couldn't be cancer. Madam Zoleeda said it would end in good fortune. She began crying and saying, "Just one step and it did it," and going on up them absently as if she thought she were standing still. On the sixth one, she sat down suddenly, her hand slipping weakly down the banister spoke onto the floor.

"Noooo," she said and leaned her round red face between the two nearest poles. She looked down into the stairwell and gave a long hollow wail that widened and echoed as it went down. The stair cavern was dark green and mole-colored and the wail sounded at the very bottom like a voice answering her. She gasped and shut her eyes. No. No. It couldn't be any baby. She was not going to have something waiting in her to make her deader, she was not. Bill Hill couldn't have slipped up. He said it was guaranteed and it had worked all this time and it could not be that, it could not. She shuddered and held her hand tightly over her mouth. She felt her face drawn puckered: two born dead one died the first year and one run under like a dried yellow apple no she was only thirty-four years old, she was old. Madam Zoleeda said it would end in no drying up. Madam Zoleeda said oh but it will end in a stroke of good fortune! Moving. She had said it would end in a stroke of good moving.

She felt herself getting calmer. She felt herself, after a minute, getting almost calm and thought she got upset too easy; heck, it was gas. Madam Zoleeda hadn't been wrong about anything yet, she knew more than . . .

She jumped: there was a bang at the bottom of the stairwell and a rumble rattling up the steps, shaking them even up where she was. She looked through the banister poles and saw Hartley Gilfeet, with two pistols leveled, galloping up the stairs and heard a voice pierce down from the floor over her, "You Hartley, shut up that racket! You're shaking the house!" But he came on, thundering louder as he rounded the bend on the first floor and streaked up the hall. She saw Mr. Jerger's door fly open and him spring with clawed fingers and grasp a flying piece of shirt that whirled and shot off again with a high-pitched, "Leggo, you old goat teacher!" and came on nearer until the stairs rumbled directly under her and a charging chipmunk face crashed into her and rocketed through her head, smaller and smaller into a whirl of dark.

She sat on the step, clutching the banister spoke while the breath came back into her a thimbleful at a time and the stairs stopped seesawing. She opened her eyes and gazed down into the dark hold, down to the very bottom where

she had started up so long ago. "Good Fortune," she said
in a hollow voice that echoed along all the levels of the
cavern, "Baby."

"Good Fortune, Baby," the three echoes leered.

Then she recognized the feeling again, a little roll.
It was as if it were not in her stomach. It was as if it
were out nowhere in nothing, out nowhere, resting and
waiting, with plenty of time.

A TEMPLE OF THE
HOLY GHOST

All week end the two girls were calling each other Temple One and Temple Two, shaking with laughter and getting so red and hot that they were positively ugly, particularly Joanne who had spots on her face anyway. They came in the brown convent uniforms they had to wear at Mount St. Scholastica but as soon as they opened their suitcases, they took off the uniforms and put on red skirts and loud blouses. They put on lipstick and their Sunday shoes and walked around in the high heels all over the house, always passing the long mirror in the hall slowly to get a look at their legs. None of their ways were lost on the child. If only one of them had come, that one would have played with her, but since there were two of them, she was out of it and watched them suspiciously from a distance.

They were fourteen—two years older than she was—but neither of them was bright, which was why they had been sent to the convent. If they had gone to a regular school, they wouldn't have done anything but think about boys; at the convent the sisters, her mother said, would keep a grip on their necks. The child decided, after observing them for a few hours, that they were practically morons and she was glad to think that they were only second cousins and she couldn't have inherited any of their stupidity. Susan called herself Su-zan. She was very skinny but she had a pretty pointed face and red hair. Joanne had yellow hair that was naturally curly but she talked through her nose and when she laughed, she turned purple in patches. Neither one of them could say an intelligent thing and all their sentences began, "You know this boy I know well one time he . . ."

They were to stay all week end and her mother said she didn't see how she would entertain them since she didn't know any boys their age. At this, the child, struck suddenly with genius, shouted, "There's Cheat! Get Cheat to come! Ask Miss Kirby to get Cheat to come show them around!" and she nearly choked on the food she had in her mouth. She doubled over laughing and hit the table with her fist and looked at the two bewildered girls while water started in her eyes and rolled down her fat cheeks and the braces she had in her mouth glared like tin. She had never thought of anything so funny before.

Her mother laughed in a guarded way and Miss Kirby blushed and carried her fork delicately to her mouth with one pea on it. She was a long-faced blonde schoolteacher who boarded with them and Mr. Cheatam was her admirer, a rich old farmer who arrived every Saturday afternoon in a fifteen-year-old baby-blue Pontiac powdered with red clay dust and black inside with Negroes that he charged ten cents apiece to bring into town on Saturday afternoons. After he dumped them he came to see Miss Kirby, always bringing a little gift—a bag of boiled peanuts or a watermelon or a stalk of sugar cane and once a wholesale box of Baby Ruth candy bars. He was bald-headed except for a little fringe of rust-colored hair and his face was nearly the same color as the unpaved roads and washed like them with ruts and gulleys. He wore a pale green shirt with a thin black stripe in it and blue galluses and his trousers cut across a protruding stomach that he pressed tenderly from time to time with his big flat thumb. All his teeth were backed with gold and he would roll his eyes at Miss Kirby in an impish way and say, "Haw haw," sitting in their porch swing with his legs spread apart and his high-topped shoes pointing in opposite directions on the floor.

"I don't think Cheat is going to be in town this week end," Miss Kirby said, not in the least understanding that this was a joke, and the child was convulsed afresh, threw herself backward in her chair, fell out of it, rolled on the floor and lay there heaving. Her mother told her if she didn't stop this foolishness she would have to leave the table.

Yesterday her mother had arranged with Alonzo Myers to drive them the forty-five miles to Mayville, where the convent was, to get the girls for the week end and Sunday afternoon he was hired to drive them back again. He was an eighteen-year-old boy who weighed two hundred and fifty pounds and worked for the taxi company and he was all you could get to drive you anywhere. He smoked or rather chewed a short black cigar and he had a round sweaty chest that showed through the yellow nylon shirt he wore. When he drove all the windows of the car had to be open.

"Well there's Alonzo!" the child roared from the floor. "Get Alonzo to show em around! Get Alonzo!"

The two girls, who had seen Alonzo, began to scream their indignation.

Her mother thought this was funny too but she said, "That'll be about enough out of you," and changed the subject. She asked them why they called each other Temple One and Temple Two and this sent them off into gales of giggles. Finally they managed to explain. Sister Perpetua, the oldest nun at the Sisters of Mercy in Mayville, had given them a lecture on what to do if a young man should—here they laughed so hard they were not able to go on without going back to the beginning—on what to do if a young man should—they put their heads in their laps—on what to do if—they finally managed to shout it out—if he should "behave in an ungentlemanly manner with them in the back of an automobile." Sister Perpetua said they were to say, "Stop sir! I am a Temple of the Holy Ghost!" and that would put an end to it. The child sat up off the floor with a blank face. She didn't see anything so funny in this. What was really funny was the idea of Mr. Cheatam or Alonzo Myers beauing them around. That killed her.

Her mother didn't laugh at what they had said. "I think you girls are pretty silly," she said. "After all, that's what you are—Temples of the Holy Ghost."

The two of them looked up at her, politely concealing their giggles, but with astonished faces as if they were beginning to realize that she was made of the same stuff as Sister Perpetua.

Miss Kirby preserved her set expression and the child thought, it's all over her head anyhow. I am a Temple of the Holy Ghost, she said to herself, and was pleased with the phrase. It made her feel as if somebody had given her a present.

After dinner, her mother collapsed on the bed and said, "Those girls are going to drive me crazy if I don't get some entertainment for them. They're awful."

"I bet I know who you could get," the child started.

"Now listen. I don't want to hear any more about Mr. Cheatam," her mother said. "You embarrass Miss Kirby. He's her only friend. Oh my Lord," and she sat up and looked mournfully out the window, "that poor soul is so lonesome she'll even ride in that car that smells like the last circle in hell."

And she's a Temple of the Holy Ghost too, the child reflected. "I wasn't thinking of him," she said. "I was thinking of those two Wilkinses, Wendell and Cory, that visit old lady Buchell out on her farm. They're her grandsons. They work for her."

"Now that's an idea," her mother murmured and gave her an appreciative look. But then she slumped again.

"They're only farm boys. These girls would turn up their noses at them."

"Huh," the child said. "They wear pants. They're sixteen and they got a car. Somebody said they were both going to be Church of God preachers because you don't have to know nothing to be one."

"They would be perfectly safe with those boys all right," her mother said and in a minute she got up and called their grandmother on the telephone and after she had talked to the old woman a half an hour, it was arranged that Wendell and Cory would come to supper and afterwards take the girls to the fair.

Susan and Joanne were so pleased that they washed their hair and rolled it up on aluminum curlers. Hah, thought the child, sitting cross-legged on the bed to watch them undo the curlers, wait'll you get a load of Wendell and Cory! "You'll like these boys," she said. "Wendell is six feet tall ands got red hair. Cory is six feet six inches talls got black hair and wears a sport jacket and they gottem this car with a squirrel tail on the front."

"How does a child like you know so much about these men?" Susan asked and pushed her face up close to the mirror to watch the pupils in her eyes dilate.

The child lay back on the bed and began to count the narrow boards in the ceiling until she lost her place. I know them all right, she said to someone. We fought in the world war together. They were under me and I saved them five times from Japanese suicide divers and Wendell said I am going to marry that kid and the other said oh no you ain't I am and I said neither one of you is because I will court marshall you all before you can bat an eye. "I've seen them around is all," she said.

When they came the girls stared at them a second and then began to giggle and talk to each other about the convent. They sat in the swing together and Wendell and Cory sat on the banisters together. They sat like monkeys, their knees on a level with their shoulders and their arms hanging down between. They were short thin boys with red faces and high cheekbones and pale seed-like eyes. They had brought a harmonica and a guitar. One of them began to blow softly on the mouth organ, watching the girls over it, and the other started strumming the guitar and then began to sing, not watching them but keeping his head tilted upward as if he were only interested in hearing himself. He was singing a hillbilly song that sounded half like a love song and half like a hymn.

The child was standing on a barrel pushed into some

bushes at the side of the house, her face on a level with the porch floor. The sun was going down and the sky was turning a bruised violet color that seemed to be connected with the sweet mournful sound of the music. Wendell began to smile as he sang and to look at the girls. He looked at Susan with a dog-like loving look and sang,

> "I've found a friend in Jesus,
> He's everything to me,
> He's the lily of the valley,
> He's the One who's set me free!"

Then he turned the same look on Joanne and sang,

> "A wall of fire about me,
> I've nothing now to fear,
> He's the lily of the valley,
> And I'll always have Him near!"

The girls looked at each other and held their lips stiff so as not to giggle but Susan let out one anyway and clapped her hand on her mouth. The singer frowned and for a few seconds only strummed the guitar. Then he began "The Old Rugged Cross" and they listened politely but when he had finished they said, "Let us sing one!" and before he could start another, they began to sing with their convent-trained voices,

> *"Tantum ergo Sacramentum*
> *Veneremur Cernui:*
> *Et antiquum documentum*
> *Novo cedat ritui:"*

The child watched the boys' solemn faces turn with perplexed frowning stares at each other as if they were uncertain whether they were being made fun of.

> *"Praestet fides supplementum*
> *Sensuum defectui.*
> *Genitori, Genitoque*
> *Laus et jubilatio*
>
> *Salus, honor, virtus quoque . . ."*

The boys' faces were dark red in the gray-purple light. They looked fierce and startled.

"Sit et benedictio;
Procedenti ab utroque
Compar sit laudatio.
                    Amen."

The girls dragged out the Amen and then there was a silence.

"That must be Jew singing," Wendell said and began to tune the guitar.

The girls giggled idiotically but the child stamped her foot on the barrel. "You big dumb ox!" she shouted. "You big dumb Church of God ox!" she roared and fell off the barrel and scrambled up and shot around the corner of the house as they jumped from the banister to see who was shouting.

Her mother had arranged for them to have supper in the back yard and she had a table laid out there under some Japanese lanterns that she pulled out for garden parties. "I ain't eating with them," the child said and snatched her plate off the table and carried it to the kitchen and sat down with the thin blue-gummed cook and ate her supper.

"Howcome you be so ugly sometime?" the cook asked.

"Those stupid idiots," the child said.

The lanterns gilded the leaves of the trees orange on the level where they hung and above them was black-green and below them were different dim muted colors that made the girls sitting at the table look prettier than they were. From time to time, the child turned her head and glared out the kitchen window at the scene below.

"God could strike you deaf dumb and blind," the cook said, "and then you wouldn't be as smart as you is."

"I would still be smarter than some," the child said.

After supper they left for the fair. She wanted to go to the fair but not with them so even if they had asked her she wouldn't have gone. She went upstairs and paced the long bedroom with her hands locked together behind her back and her head thrust forward and an expression, fierce and dreamy both, on her face. She didn't turn on the electric light but let the darkness collect and make the room smaller and more private. At regular intervals a light crossed the open window and threw shadows on the wall. She stopped and stood looking out over the dark slopes, past where the pond glinted silver, past the wall of woods to the speckled sky where a long finger of light was revolving up and around and away, searching the air as if it were hunting for the lost sun. It was the beacon light from the fair.

She could hear the distant sound of the calliope and she saw in her head all the tents raised up in a kind of gold sawdust light and the diamond ring of the ferris wheel going around and around up in the air and down again and the screeking merry-go-round going around and around on the ground. A fair lasted five or six days and there was a special afternoon for school children and a special night for niggers. She had gone last year on the afternoon for school children and had seen the monkeys and the fat man and had ridden on the ferris wheel. Certain tents were closed then because they contained things that would be known only to grown people but she had looked with interest at the advertising on the closed tents, at the faded-looking pictures on the canvas of people in tights, with stiff stretched composed faces like the faces of the martyrs waiting to have their tongues cut out by the Roman soldier. She had imagined that what was inside these tents concerned medicine and she had made up her mind to be a doctor when she grew up.

She had since changed and decided to be an engineer but as she looked out the window and followed the revolving searchlight as it widened and shortened and wheeled in its arc, she felt that she would have to be much more than just a doctor or an engineer. She would have to be a saint because that was the occupation that included everything you could know; and yet she knew she would never be a saint. She did not steal or murder but she was a born liar and slothful and she sassed her mother and was deliberately ugly to almost everybody. She was eaten up also with the sin of Pride, the worst one. She made fun of the Baptist preacher who came to the school at commencement to give the devotional. She would pull down her mouth and hold her forehead as if she were in agony and groan, "Fawther, we thank Thee," exactly the way he did and she had been told many times not to do it. She could never be a saint, but she thought she could be a martyr if they killed her quick.

She could stand to be shot but not to be burned in oil. She didn't know if she could stand to be torn to pieces by lions or not. She began to prepare her martyrdom, seeing herself in a pair of tights in a great arena, lit by the early Christians hanging in cages of fire, making a gold dusty light that fell on her and the lions. The first lion charged forward and fell at her feet, converted. A whole series of lions did the same. The lions liked her so much she even slept with them and finally the Romans were obliged to burn her but to their astonishment she would not burn down and finding she was so hard to kill, they finally cut off her head very quickly with a sword and she went immediately to heaven. She rehearsed this several times, returning each time at the entrance of Paradise to the lions.

Finally she got up from the window and got ready for bed and got in without saying her prayers. There were two heavy double beds in the room. The girls were occupying the other one and she tried to think of something cold and clammy that she could hide in their bed but her thought was fruitless. She didn't have anything she could think of, like a chicken carcass or a piece of beef liver. The sound of the calliope coming through the window kept her awake and she remembered that she hadn't said her prayers and got up and knelt down and began them. She took a running start and went through to the other side of the Apostle's Creed and then hung by her chin on the side of the bed, empty-minded. Her prayers, when she remembered to say them, were usually perfunctory but sometimes when she had done something wrong or heard music or lost something, or sometimes for no reason at all, she would be moved to fervor and would think of Christ on the long journey to Calvary, crushed three times under the rough cross. Her mind would stay on this a while and then get empty and when something roused her, she would find that she was thinking of a different thing entirely, of some dog or some girl or something she was going to do some day. Tonight, remembering Wendell and Cory, she was filled with thanksgiving and almost weeping with delight, she said, "Lord, Lord, thank You that I'm not in the Church of God, thank You Lord, thank You!" and got back in bed and kept repeating it until she went to sleep.

The girls came in at a quarter to twelve and waked her up with their giggling. They turned on the small blue-shaded lamp to see to get undressed by and their skinny shadows climbed up the wall and broke and continued moving about softly on the ceiling. The child sat up to hear what all they had seen at the fair. Susan had a plastic pistol full of cheap candy and Joanne a pasteboard cat with red polka dots on it. "Did you see the monkeys dance?" the child asked. "Did you see that fat man and those midgets?"

"All kinds of freaks," Joanne said. And then she said to Susan, "I enjoyed it all but the you-know-what," and her face assumed a peculiar expression as if she had bit into something that she didn't know if she liked or not.

The other stood still and shook her head once and nodded slightly at the child. "Little pitchers," she said in a low voice but the child heard it and her heart began to beat very fast.

She got out of her bed and climbed onto the footboard of theirs. They turned off the light and got in but she didn't move. She sat there, looking hard at them until their faces were well defined in the dark. "I'm not as old as you all," she said, "but I'm about a million times smarter."

"There are some things," Susan said, "that a child of your age doesn't know," and they both began to giggle.

"Go back to your own bed," Joanne said.

The child didn't move. "One time," she said, her voice hollow-sounding in the dark, "I saw this rabbit have rabbits."

There was a silence. Then Susan said, "How?" in an indifferent tone and she knew that she had them. She said she wouldn't tell until they told about the you-know-what. Actually she had never seen a rabbit have rabbits but she forgot this as they began to tell what they had seen in the tent.

It had been a freak with a particular name but they couldn't remember the name. The tent where it was had been divided into two parts by a black curtain, one side for men and one for women. The freak went from one side to the other, talking first to the men and then to the women, but everyone could hear. The stage ran all the way across the front. The girls heard the freak say to the men, "I'm going to show you this and if you laugh, God may strike you the same way." The freak had a country voice, slow and nasal and neither high nor low, just flat. "God made me thisaway and if you laugh He may strike you the same way. This is the way He wanted me to be and I ain't disputing His way. I'm showing you because I got to make the best of it. I expect you to act like ladies and gentlemen. I never done it to myself nor had a thing to do with it but I'm making the best of it. I don't dispute hit." Then there was a long silence on the other side of the tent and finally the freak left the men and came over onto the women's side and said the same thing.

The child felt every muscle strained as if she were hearing the answer to a riddle that was more puzzling than the riddle itself. "You mean it had two heads?" she said.

"No," Susan said, "it was a man and woman both. It pulled up its dress and showed us. It had on a blue dress."

The child wanted to ask how it could be a man and woman both without two heads but she did not. She wanted to get back into her own bed and think it out and she began to climb down off the footboard.

"What about the rabbit?" Joanne asked.

The child stopped and only her face appeared over the footboard, abstracted, absent. "It spit them out of its mouth," she said, "six of them."

She lay in bed trying to picture the tent with the freak walking from side to side but she was too sleepy to figure it out. She was better able to see the faces of the country people watching, the men more solemn than they were in church, and the women stern and polite, with painted-looking eyes, standing as if they were waiting for the first note of the piano to begin the hymn. She could hear the freak saying, "God made me thisaway and I don't dispute hit," and the people saying, "Amen. Amen."

"God done this to me and I praise Him."

"Amen. Amen."

"He could strike you thisaway."

"Amen. Amen."

"But he has not."

"Amen."

"Raise yourself up. A temple of the Holy Ghost. You! You are God's temple, don't you know? Don't you know? God's Spirit has a dwelling in you, don't you know?"

"Amen. Amen."

"If anybody desecrates the temple of God, God will bring him to ruin and if you laugh, He may strike you thisaway. A temple of God is a holy thing. Amen. Amen."

"I am a temple of the Holy Ghost."

"Amen."

The people began to slap their hands without making a loud noise and with a regular beat between the Amens, more and more softly, as if they knew there was a child near, half asleep.

The next afternoon the girls put on their brown convent uniforms again and the child and her mother took them back to Mount St. Scholastica. "Oh glory, oh Pete!" they said. "Back to the salt mines." Alonzo Myers drove them and the child sat in front with him and her mother sat in back between the two girls, telling them such things as how pleased she was to have had them and how they must come back again and then about the good times she and their mothers had had when they were girls at the convent. The child didn't listen to any of this twaddle but kept as close to the locked door as she could get and held her head out the window. They had thought Alonzo would smell better on Sunday but he did not. With her hair blowing over her face she could look directly into the ivory sun which was framed in the middle of the blue afternoon but when she pulled it away from her eyes she had to squint.

Mount St. Scholastica was a red brick house set back in a garden in the center of town. There was a filling station on one side of it and a firehouse on the other. It had a high black grillework fence around it and narrow bricked walks between old trees and japonica bushes that were heavy with blooms. A big moon-faced nun came bustling to the door to let them in and embraced her mother and would have done the same to her but that she stuck out her hand and preserved a frigid frown, looking just past the sister's shoes at the wainscoting. They had a tendency to kiss even homely children, but the nun shook her hand vigorously and even cracked her knuckles a little and said they must come to the chapel, that benediction was just beginning. You put your foot in their door and they got you praying, the child thought as they hurried down the polished corridor.

You'd think she had to catch a train, she continued in the same ugly vein as they entered the chapel where the sisters were kneeling on one side and the girls, all in brown uniforms, on the other. The chapel smelled of incense. It was light green and gold, a series of springing arches that ended with the one over the altar where the priest was kneeling in front of the monstrance, bowed low. A small boy in a surplice was standing behind him, swinging the censer. The child knelt down between her mother and the nun and they were well into the *"Tantum Ergo"* before her ugly thoughts stopped and she began to realize that she was in the presence of God. Hep me not to be so mean, she began mechanically. Hep me not to give her so much sass. Hep me not to talk like I do. Her mind began to get quiet and then empty but when the priest raised the monstrance with the Host shining ivory-colored in the center of it, she was thinking of the tent at the fair that had the freak in it. The freak was saying, "I don't dispute hit. This is the way He wanted me to be."

As they were leaving the convent door, the big nun swooped down on her mischievously and nearly smothered her in the black habit, mashing the side of her face into the crucifix hitched onto her belt and then holding her off and looking at her with little periwinkle eyes.

On the way home she and her mother sat in the back and Alonzo drove by himself in the front. The child observed

three folds of fat in the back of his neck and noted that
his ears were pointed almost like a pig's. Her mother, making
conversation, asked him if he had gone to the fair.

"Gone," he said, "and never missed a thing and it
was good I gone when I did because they ain't going to
have it next week like they said they was."

"Why?" asked her mother.

"They shut it on down," he said. "Some of the preachers
from town gone out and inspected it and got the police
to shut it on down."

Her mother let the conversation drop and the child's
round face was lost in thought. She turned it toward the
window and looked out over a stretch of pasture land
that rose and fell with a gathering greenness until it touched
the dark woods. The sun was a huge red ball like an
elevated Host drenched in blood and when it sank out
of sight, it left a line in the sky like a red clay road hanging
over the trees.

Mr. Head awakened to discover that the room was full of moonlight. He sat up and stared at the floor boards—the color of silver—and then at the ticking on his pillow, which might have been brocade, and after a second, he saw half of the moon five feet away in his shaving mirror, paused as if it were waiting for his permission to enter. It rolled forward and cast a dignifying light on everything. The straight chair against the wall looked stiff and attentive as if it were awaiting an order and Mr. Head's trousers, hanging to the back of it, had an almost noble air, like the garment some great man had just flung to his servant; but the face on the moon was a grave one. It gazed across the room and out the window where it floated over the horse stall and appeared to contemplate itself with the look of a young man who sees his old age before him.

Mr. Head could have said to it that age was a choice blessing and that only with years does a man enter into that calm understanding of life that makes him a suitable guide for the young. This, at least, had been his own experience.

He sat up and grasped the iron posts at the foot of his bed and raised himself until he could see the face on the alarm clock which sat on an overturned bucket beside the chair. The hour was two in the morning. The alarm on the clock did not work but he was not dependent on any mechanical means to awaken him. Sixty years had not dulled his responses; his physical reactions, like his moral ones, were guided by his will and strong character, and these could be seen plainly in his features. He had a long tube-like face with a long rounded open jaw and a long depressed nose. His eyes were alert but quiet, and in the miraculous moonlight they had a look of composure and of ancient wisdom as if they belonged to one of the great guides of men. He might have been Vergil summoned in the middle of the night to go to Dante, or better, Raphael, awakened by a blast of God's light to fly to the side of Tobias. The only dark spot in the room was Nelson's pallet, underneath the shadow of the window.

Nelson was hunched over on his side, his knees under

195

his chin and his heels under his bottom. His new suit and hat were in the boxes that they had been sent in and these were on the floor at the foot of the pallet where he could get his hands on them as soon as he woke up. The slop jar, out of the shadow and made snow-white in the moonlight, appeared to stand guard over him like a small personal angel. Mr. Head lay back down, feeling entirely confident that he could carry out the moral mission of the coming day. He meant to be up before Nelson and to have the breakfast cooking by the time he awakened. The boy was always irked when Mr. Head was the first up. They would have to leave the house at four to get to the railroad junction by five-thirty. The train was to stop for them at five forty-five and they had to be there on time for this train was stopping merely to accommodate them.

This would be the boy's first trip to the city though he claimed it would be his second because he had been born there. Mr. Head had tried to point out to him that when he was born he didn't have the intelligence to determine his whereabouts but this had made no impression on the child at all and he continued to insist that this was to be his second trip. It would be Mr. Head's third trip. Nelson had said, "I will've already been there twict and I ain't but ten."

Mr. Head had contradicted him.

"If you ain't been there in fifteen years, how you know you'll be able to find your way about?" Nelson had asked. "How you know it hasn't changed some?"

"Have you ever," Mr. Head had asked, "seen me lost?"

Nelson certainly had not but he was a child who was never satisfied until he had given an impudent answer and he replied, "It's nowhere around here to get lost at."

"The day is going to come," Mr. Head prophesied, "when you'll find you ain't as smart as you think you are." He had been thinking about this trip for several months but it was for the most part in moral terms that he conceived it. It was to be a lesson that the boy would never forget. He was to find out from it that he had no cause for pride merely because he had been born in a city. He was to find out that the city is not a great place. Mr. Head meant him to see everything there is to see in a city so that he would be content to stay at home for the rest of his life. He fell asleep thinking how the boy would at last find out that he was not as smart as he thought he was.

He was awakened at three-thirty by the smell of fatback frying and he leaped off his cot. The pallet was empty and the clothes boxes had been thrown open. He put on his trousers and ran into the other room. The boy had a corn pone on cooking and had fried the meat. He was sitting in the half-dark at the table, drinking cold coffee out of a can. He had on his new suit and his new gray hat pulled low over his eyes. It was too big for him but they had ordered it a size large because they expected his head to grow. He didn't say anything but his entire figure suggested satisfaction at having arisen before Mr. Head.

Mr. Head went to the stove and brought the meat to the table in the skillet. "It's no hurry," he said. "You'll get there soon enough and it's no guarantee you'll like it when you do neither," and he sat down across from the boy whose hat teetered back slowly to reveal a fiercely expressionless face, very much the same shape as the old man's. They were grandfather and grandson but they looked enough alike to be brothers and brothers not too far apart in age, for Mr. Head had a youthful expression by daylight, while the boy's look was ancient, as if he knew everything already and would be pleased to forget it.

Mr. Head had once had a wife and daughter and when the wife died, the daughter ran away and returned after an interval with Nelson. Then one morning, without getting out of bed, she died and left Mr. Head with sole care of the year-old child. He had made the mistake of telling Nelson that he had been born in Atlanta. If he hadn't told him that, Nelson couldn't have insisted that this was going to be his second trip.

"You may not like it a bit," Mr. Head continued. "It'll be full of niggers."

The boy made a face as if he could handle a nigger.

"All right," Mr. Head said. "You ain't ever seen a nigger."

"You wasn't up very early," Nelson said.

"You ain't ever seen a nigger," Mr. Head repeated. "There hasn't been a nigger in this county since we run that one out twelve years ago and that was before you were born." He looked at the boy as if he were daring him to say he had ever seen a Negro.

"How you know I never saw a nigger when I lived there before?" Nelson asked. "I probably saw a lot of niggers."

"If you seen one you didn't know what he was," Mr. Head said, completely exasperated. "A six-month-old child don't know a nigger from anybody else."

"I reckon I'll know a nigger if I see one," the boy said and got up and straightened his slick sharply creased gray hat and went outside to the privy.

They reached the junction some time before the train was due to arrive and stood about two feet from the first set of tracks. Mr. Head carried a paper sack with some biscuits and a can of sardines in it for their lunch. A coarse-looking orange-colored sun coming up behind the east range of mountains was making the sky a dull red behind them, but in front of them it was still gray and they faced a gray transparent moon, hardly stronger than a thumbprint and completely without light. A small tin switch box and a black fuel tank were all there was to mark the place as a junction; the tracks were double and did not converge again until they were hidden behind the bends at either end of the clearing. Trains passing appeared to emerge from a tunnel of trees and, hit for a second by the cold sky, vanish terrified into the woods again. Mr. Head had had to make special arrangements with the ticket agent to have this train stop and he was secretly afraid it would not, in which case, he knew Nelson would say, "I never thought no train was going to stop for you." Under the useless morning moon the tracks looked white and fragile. Both the old man and the child stared ahead as if they were awaiting an apparition.

Then suddenly, before Mr. Head could make up his mind to turn back, there was a deep warning bleat and the train appeared, gliding very slowly, almost silently around the bend of trees about two hundred yards down the track, with one yellow front light shining. Mr. Head was still not certain it would stop and he felt it would make an even bigger idiot of him if it went by slowly. Both he and Nelson, however, were prepared to ignore the train if it passed them.

The engine charged by, filling their noses with the smell of hot metal and then the second coach came to a stop exactly where they were standing. A conductor with the face of an ancient bloated bulldog was on the step as if he expected them, though he did not look as if it mattered one way or the other to him if they got on or not. "To the right," he said.

Their entry took only a fraction of a second and the train was already speeding on as they entered the quiet car. Most of the travelers were still sleeping, some with their heads hanging off the chair arms, some stretched across two seats, and some sprawled out with their feet in the aisle. Mr. Head saw two unoccupied seats and pushed Nelson toward them. "Get in there by the winder," he said in his normal voice which was very loud at this hour of the morning. "Nobody cares if you sit there because it's nobody in it. Sit right there."

"I heard you," the boy muttered. "It's no use in you yelling," and he sat down and turned his head to the glass. There he saw a pale ghost-like face scowling at him beneath the brim of a pale ghost-like hat. His grandfather, looking quickly too, saw a different ghost, pale but grinning, under a black hat.

Mr. Head sat down and settled himself and took out his ticket and started reading aloud everything that was printed on it. People began to stir. Several woke up and stared at him. "Take off your hat," he said to Nelson and took off his own and put it on his knee. He had a small amount of white hair that had turned tobacco-colored over the years and this lay flat across the back of his head. The front of his head was bald and creased. Nelson took off his hat and put it on his knee and they waited for the conductor to come ask for their tickets.

The man across the aisle from them was spread out over two seats, his feet propped on the window and his head jutting into the aisle. He had on a light blue suit and a yellow shirt unbuttoned at the neck. His eyes had just opened and Mr. Head was ready to introduce himself when the conductor came up from behind and growled, "Tickets."

When the conductor had gone, Mr. Head gave Nelson the return half of his ticket and said, "Now put that in your pocket and don't lose it or you'll have to stay in the city."

"Maybe I will," Nelson said as if this were a reasonable suggestion.

Mr. Head ignored him. "First time this boy has ever been on a train," he explained to the man across the aisle, who was sitting up now on the edge of his seat with both feet on the floor.

Nelson jerked his hat on again and turned angrily to the window.

"He's never seen anything before," Mr. Head continued. "Ignorant as the day he was born, but I mean for him to get his fill once and for all."

The boy leaned forward, across his grandfather and toward the stranger. "I was born in the city," he said. "I was born there. This is my second trip." He said it in a high positive voice but the man across the aisle didn't look as if he understood. There were heavy purple circles under his eyes.

Mr. Head reached across the aisle and tapped him on

the arm. "The thing to do with a boy," he said sagely, "is to show him all it is to show. Don't hold nothing back."

"Yeah," the man said. He gazed down at his swollen feet and lifted the left one about ten inches from the floor. After a minute he put it down and lifted the other. All through the car people began to get up and move about and yawn and stretch. Separate voices could be heard here and there and then a general hum. Suddenly Mr. Head's serene expression changed. His mouth almost closed and a light, fierce and cautious both, came into his eyes. He was looking down the length of the car. Without turning, he caught Nelson by the arm and pulled him forward. "Look," he said.

A huge coffee-colored man was coming slowly forward. He had on a light suit and a yellow satin tie with a ruby pin in it. One of his hands rested on his stomach which rode majestically under his buttoned coat, and in the other he held the head of a black walking stick that he picked up and set down with a deliberate outward motion each time he took a step. He was proceeding very slowly, his large brown eyes gazing over the heads of the passengers. He had a small white mustache and white crinkly hair. Behind him there were two young women, both coffee-colored, one in a yellow dress and one in a green. Their progress was kept at the rate of his and they chatted in low throaty voices as they followed him.

Mr. Head's grip was tightening insistently on Nelson's arm. As the procession passed them, the light from a sapphire ring on the brown hand that picked up the cane reflected in Mr. Head's eye, but he did not look up nor did the tremendous man look at him. The group proceeded up the rest of the aisle and out of the car. Mr. Head's grip on Nelson's arm loosened. "What was that?" he asked.

"A man," the boy said and gave him an indignant look as if he were tired of having his intelligence insulted.

"What kind of a man?" Mr. Head persisted, his voice expressionless.

"A fat man," Nelson said. He was beginning to feel that he had better be cautious.

"You don't know what kind?" Mr. Head said in a final tone.

"An old man," the boy said and had a sudden foreboding that he was not going to enjoy the day.

"That was a nigger," Mr. Head said and sat back.

Nelson jumped up on the seat and stood looking backward to the end of the car but the Negro had gone.

"I'd of thought you'd know a nigger since you seen

so many when you was in the city on your first visit," Mr. Head continued. "That's his first nigger," he said to the man across the aisle.

The boy slid down into the seat. "You said they were black," he said in an angry voice. "You never said they were tan. How do you expect me to know anything when you don't tell me right?"

"You're just ignorant is all," Mr. Head said and he got up and moved over in the vacant seat by the man across the aisle.

Nelson turned backward again and looked where the Negro had disappeared. He felt that the Negro had deliberately walked down the aisle in order to make a fool of him and he hated him with a fierce raw fresh hate; and also, he understood now why his grandfather disliked them. He looked toward the window and the face there seemed to suggest that he might be inadequate to the day's exactions. He wondered if he would even recognize the city when they came to it.

After he had told several stories, Mr. Head realized that the man he was talking to was asleep and he got up and suggested to Nelson that they walk over the train and see the parts of it. He particularly wanted the boy to see the toilet so they went first to the men's room and examined the plumbing. Mr. Head demonstrated the ice-water cooler as if he had invented it and showed Nelson the bowl with the single spigot where the travelers brushed their teeth. They went through several cars and came to the diner.

This was the most elegant car in the train. It was painted a rich egg-yellow and had a wine-colored carpet on the floor. There were wide windows over the tables and great spaces of the rolling view were caught in miniature in the sides of the coffee pots and in the glasses. Three very black Negroes in white suits and aprons were running up and down the aisle, swinging trays and bowing and bending over the travelers eating breakfast. One of them rushed up to Mr. Head and Nelson and said, holding up two fingers, "Space for two!" but Mr. Head replied in a loud voice, "We eaten before we left!"

The waiter wore large brown spectacles that increased the size of his eye whites. "Stan' aside then please," he said with an airy wave of the arm as if he were brushing aside flies.

Neither Nelson nor Mr. Head moved a fraction of an inch. "Look," Mr. Head said.

The near corner of the diner, containing two tables, was set off from the rest by a saffron-colored curtain. One table was set but empty but at the other, facing them, his back to the drape, sat the tremendous Negro. He was speaking in a soft voice to the two women while he buttered a muffin. He had a heavy sad face and his neck bulged over his white collar on either side. "They rope them off," Mr. Head explained. Then he said, "Let's go see the kitchen," and they walked the length of the diner but the black waiter was coming fast behind them.

"Passengers are not allowed in the kitchen!" he said in a haughty voice. "Passengers are NOT allowed in the kitchen!"

Mr. Head stopped where he was and turned. "And there's good reason for that," he shouted into the Negro's chest, "because the cockroaches would run the passengers out!"

All the travelers laughed and Mr. Head and Nelson walked out, grinning. Mr. Head was known at home for his quick wit and Nelson felt a sudden keen pride in him. He realized the old man would be his only support in the strange place they were approaching. He would be entirely alone in the world if he were ever lost from his grandfather. A terrible excitement shook him and he wanted to take hold of Mr. Head's coat and hold on like a child.

As they went back to their seats they could see through the passing windows that the countryside was becoming speckled with small houses and shacks and that a highway ran alongside the train. Cars sped by on it, very small and fast. Nelson felt that there was less breath in the air than there had been thirty minutes ago. The man across the aisle had left and there was no one near for Mr. Head to hold a conversation with so he looked out the window, through his own reflection, and read aloud the names of the buildings they were passing. "The Dixie Chemical Corp!" he announced. "Southern Maid Flour! Dixie Doors! Southern Belle Cotton Products! Patty's Peanut Butter! Southern Mammy Cane Syrup!"

"Hush up!" Nelson hissed.

All over the car people were beginning to get up and take their luggage off the overhead racks. Women were putting on their coats and hats. The conductor stuck his head in the car and snarled, "Firstoppppppmry," and Nelson lunged out of his sitting position, trembling. Mr. Head pushed him down by the shoulder.

"Keep your seat," he said in dignified tones. "The first stop is on the edge of town. The second stop is at the main railroad station." He had come by this knowledge on his first trip when he had got off at the first stop and had had to pay a man fifteen cents to take him into the heart of

town. Nelson sat back down, very pale. For the first time
in his life, he understood that his grandfather was indispens-
able to him.

The train stopped and let off a few passengers and glided
on as if it had never ceased moving. Outside, behind rows
of brown rickety houses, a line of blue buildings stood
up, and beyond them a pale rose-gray sky faded away to
nothing. The train moved into the railroad yard. Looking
down, Nelson saw lines and lines of silver tracks multiplying
and criss-crossing. Then before he could start counting
them, the face in the window started out at him, gray but
distinct, and he looked the other way. The train was in
the station. Both he and Mr. Head jumped up and ran
to the door. Neither noticed that they had left the paper
sack with the lunch in it on the seat.

They walked stiffly through the small station and came
out of a heavy door into the squall of traffic. Crowds were
hurrying to work. Nelson didn't know where to look. Mr.
Head leaned against the side of the building and glared
in front of him.

Finally Nelson said, "Well, how do you see what all
it is to see?"

Mr. Head didn't answer. Then as if the sight of people
passing had given him the clue, he said, "You walk,"
and started off down the street. Nelson followed, steadying
his hat. So many sights and sounds were flooding in on
him that for the first block he hardly knew what he was
seeing. At the second corner, Mr. Head turned and looked
behind him at the station they had left, a putty-colored
terminal with a concrete dome on top. He thought that
if he could keep the dome always in sight, he would be
able to get back in the afternoon to catch the train again.

As they walked along, Nelson began to distinguish
details and take note of the store windows, jammed with
every kind of equipment—hardware, drygoods, chicken feed,
liquor. They passed one that Mr. Head called his particular
attention to where you walked in and sat on a chair with
your feet upon two rests and let a Negro polish your shoes.
They walked slowly and stopped and stood at the entrances
so he could see what went on in each place but they did
not go into any of them. Mr. Head was determined not
to go into any city store because on his first trip here,
he had got lost in a large one and had found his way out
only after many people had insulted him.

They came in the middle of the next block to a store
that had a weighing machine in front of it and they both
in turn stepped up on it and put in a penny and received

a ticket. Mr. Head's ticket said, "You weigh 120 pounds. You are upright and brave and all your friends admire you." He put the ticket in his pocket, surprised that the machine should have got his character correct but his weight wrong, for he had weighed on a grain scale not long before and knew he weighed 110. Nelson's ticket said, "You weigh 98 pounds. You have a great destiny ahead of you but beware of dark women." Nelson did not know any women and he weighed only 68 pounds but Mr. Head pointed out that the machine had probably printed the number upside down, meaning the 9 for a 6.

They walked on and at the end of five blocks the dome of the terminal sank out of sight and Mr. Head turned to the left. Nelson could have stood in front of every store window for an hour if there had not been another more interesting one next to it. Suddenly he said, "I was born here!" Mr. Head turned and looked at him with horror. There was a sweaty brightness about his face. "This is where I come from!" he said.

Mr. Head was appalled. He saw the moment had come for drastic action. "Lemme show you one thing you ain't seen yet," he said and took him to the corner where there was a sewer entrance. "Squat down," he said, "and stick you head in there," and he held the back of the boy's coat while he got down and put his head in the sewer. He drew it back quickly, hearing a gurgling in the depths under the sidewalk. Then Mr. Head explained the sewer system, how the entire city was underlined with it, how it contained all the drainage and was full of rats and how a man could slide into it and be sucked along down endless pitchblack tunnels. At any minute any man in the city might be sucked into the sewer and never heard from again. He described it so well that Nelson was for some seconds shaken. He connected the sewer passages with the entrance to hell and understood for the first time how the world was put together in its lower parts. He drew away from the curb.

Then he said, "Yes, but you can stay away from the holes," and his face took on that stubborn look that was so exasperating to his grandfather. "This is where I come from!" he said.

Mr. Head was dismayed but he only muttered, "You'll get your fill," and they walked on. At the end of two more blocks he turned to the left, feeling that he was circling the dome; and he was correct for in a half-hour they passed in front of the railroad station again. At first Nelson did not notice that he was seeing the same stores twice but when they passed the one where you put your feet on the rests while the Negro polished your shoes, he perceived that they were walking in a circle.

"We done been here!" he shouted. "I don't believe you know where you're at!"

"The direction just slipped my mind for a minute," Mr. Head said and they turned down a different street. He still did not intend to let the dome get too far away and after two blocks in their new direction, he turned to the left. This street contained two and three-story wooden dwellings. Anyone passing on the sidewalk could see into the rooms and Mr. Head, glancing through one window, saw a woman lying on an iron bed, looking out, with a sheet pulled over her. Her knowing expression shook him. A fierce-looking boy on a bicycle came driving down out of nowhere and he had to jump to the side to keep from being hit. "It's nothing to them if they knock you down," he said. "You better keep closer to me."

They walked on for some time on streets like this before he remembered to turn again. The houses they were passing now were all unpainted and the wood in them looked rotten; the street between was narrower. Nelson saw a colored man. Then another. Then another. "Niggers live in these houses," he observed.

"Well come on and we'll go somewheres else," Mr. Head said. "We didn't come to look at niggers," and they turned down another street but they continued to see Negroes everywhere. Nelson's skin began to prickle and they stepped along at a faster pace in order to leave the neighborhood as soon as possible. There were colored men in their undershirts standing in the doors and colored women rocking on the sagging porches. Colored children played in the gutters and stopped what they were doing to look at them. Before long they began to pass rows of stores with colored customers in them but they didn't pause at the entrances of these. Black eyes in black faces were watching them from every direction. "Yes," Mr. Head said, "this is where you were born—right here with all these niggers."

Nelson scowled. "I think you done got us lost," he said.

Mr. Head swung around sharply and looked for the dome. It was nowhere in sight. "I ain't got us lost either," he said. "You're just tired of walking."

"I ain't tired, I'm hungry," Nelson said. "Give me a biscuit."

They discovered then that they had lost the lunch.

"You were the one holding the sack," Nelson said. "I would have kepaholt of it."

"If you want to direct this trip, I'll go on by myself

and leave you right here," Mr. Head said and was pleased to see the boy turn white. However, he realized they were lost and drifting farther every minute from the station. He was hungry himself and beginning to be thirsty and since they had been in the colored neighborhood, they had both begun to sweat. Nelson had on his shoes and he was unaccustomed to them. The concrete sidewalks were very hard. They both wanted to find a place to sit down but this was impossible and they kept on walking, the boy muttering under his breath, "First you lost the sack and then you lost the way," and Mr. Head growling from time to time, "Anybody wants to be from this nigger heaven can be from it!"

By now the sun was well forward in the sky. The odor of dinners cooking drifted out to them. The Negroes were all at their doors to see them pass. "Whyn't you ast one of these niggers the way?" Nelson said. "You got us lost."

"This is where you were born," Mr. Head said. "You can ast one yourself if you want to."

Nelson was afraid of the colored men and he didn't want to be laughed at by the colored children. Up ahead he saw a large colored woman leaning in a doorway that opened onto the sidewalk. Her hair stood straight out from her head for about four inches all around and she was resting on bare brown feet that turned pink at the sides. She had on a pink dress that showed her exact shape. As they came abreast of her, she lazily lifted one hand to her head and her fingers disappeared into her hair.

Nelson stopped. He felt his breath drawn up by the woman's dark eyes. "How do you get back to town?" he said in a voice that did not sound like his own.

After a minute she said, "You in town now," in a rich low tone that made Nelson feel as if a cool spray had been turned on him.

"How do you get back to the train?" he said in the same reed-like voice.

"You can catch you a car," she said.

He understood she was making fun of him but he was too paralyzed even to scowl. He stood drinking in every detail of her. His eyes traveled up from her great knees to her forehead and then made a triangular path from the glistening sweat on her neck down and across her tremendous bosom and over her bare arm back to where her fingers lay hidden in her hair. He suddenly wanted her to reach down and pick him up and draw him against her and then he wanted to feel her breath on his face. He wanted to look down and down into her eyes while she held him tighter and tighter. He had never had such a feeling before. He felt as if he were reeling down through a pitchblack tunnel.

"You can go a block down yonder and catch you a car take you to the railroad station, Sugarpie," she said.

Nelson would have collapsed at her feet if Mr. Head had not pulled him roughly away. "You act like you don't have any sense!" the old man growled.

They hurried down the street and Nelson did not look back at the woman. He pushed his hat sharply forward over his face which was already burning with shame. The sneering ghost he had seen in the train window and all the foreboding feelings he had on the way returned to him and he remembered that his ticket from the scale had said to beware of dark women and that his grandfather's had said he was upright and brave. He took hold of the old man's hand, a sign of dependence that he seldom showed.

They headed down the street toward the car tracks where a long yellow rattling trolley was coming. Mr. Head had never boarded a streetcar and he let that one pass. Nelson was silent. From time to time his mouth trembled slightly but his grandfather, occupied with his own problems, paid him no attention. They stood on the corner and neither looked at the Negroes who were passing, going about their business just as if they had been white, except that most of them stopped and eyed Mr. Head and Nelson. It occurred to Mr. Head that since the streetcar ran on tracks, they could simply follow the tracks. He gave Nelson a slight push and explained that they would follow the tracks on into the railroad station, walking, and they set off.

Presently to their great relief they began to see white people again and Nelson sat down on the sidewalk against the wall of a building. "I got to rest myself some," he said. "You lost the sack and the direction. You can just wait on me to rest myself."

"There's the tracks in front of us," Mr. Head said. "All we got to do is keep them in sight and you could have remembered the sack as good as me. This is where you were born. This is your old home town. This is your second trip. You ought to know how to do," and he squatted down and continued in this vein but the boy, easing his burning feet out of his shoes, did not answer.

"And standing their grinning like a chim-pan-zee while a nigger woman gives you direction. Great Gawd!" Mr. Head said.

"I never said I was nothing but born here," the boy said in a shaky voice. "I never said I would or wouldn't like it. I never said I wanted to come. I only said I was born here and I never had nothing to do with that. I want to go home. I never wanted to come in the first place. It was all your big idea. How you know you ain't following the tracks in the wrong direction?"

This last had occurred to Mr. Head too. "All these people are white," he said.

"We ain't passed here before," Nelson said. This was a neighborhood of brick buildings that might have been lived in or might not. A few empty automobiles were parked along the curb and there was an occasional passerby. The heat of the pavement came up through Nelson's thin suit. His eyelids began to droop, and after a few minutes his head tilted forward. His shoulders twitched once or twice and then he fell over on his side and lay sprawled in an exhausted fit of sleep.

Mr. Head watched him silently. He was very tired himself but they could not both sleep at the same time and he could not have slept anyway because he did not know where he was. In a few minutes Nelson would wake up, refreshed by his sleep and very cocky, and would begin complaining that he had lost the sack and the way. You'd have a mighty sorry time if I wasn't here, Mr. Head thought; and then another idea occurred to him. He looked at the sprawled figure for several minutes; presently he stood up. He justified what he was going to do on the grounds that it is sometimes necessary to teach a child a lesson he won't forget, particularly when the child is always reasserting his position with some new impudence. He walked without a sound to the corner about twenty feet away and sat down on a covered garbage can in the alley where he could look out and watch Nelson wake up alone.

The boy was dozing fitfully, half conscious of vague noises and black forms moving up from some dark part of him into the light. His face worked in his sleep and he had pulled his knees up under his chin. The sun shed a dull dry light on the narrow street; everything looked like exactly what it was. After a while Mr. Head, hunched like an old monkey on the garbage can lid, decided that if Nelson didn't wake up soon, he would make a loud noise by bamming his foot against the can. He looked at his watch and discovered that it was two o'clock. Their train left at six and the possibility of missing it was too awful for him to think of. He kicked his foot backwards on the can and a hollow boom reverberated in the alley.

Nelson shot up onto his feet with a shout. He looked where his grandfather should have been and stared. He seemed to whirl several times and then, picking up his feet and throwing his head back, he dashed down the street like a wild maddened pony. Mr. Head jumped off the can and galloped after but the child was almost out of sight. He saw a streak of gray disappearing diagonally a block ahead. He ran as fast as he could, looking both ways down every intersection, but without sight of him again. Then as he passed the third intersection, completely winded, he saw about half a block down the street a scene that stopped him altogether. He crouched behind a trash box to watch and get his bearings.

Nelson was sitting with both legs spread out and by his side lay an elderly woman, screaming. Groceries were scattered about the sidewalk. A crowd of women had already gathered to see justice done and Mr. Head distinctly heard the old woman on the pavement shout, "You've broken my ankle and your daddy'll pay for it! Every nickel! Police! Police!" Several of the women were plucking at Nelson's shoulder but the boy seemed too dazed to get up.

Something forced Mr. Head from behind the trash box and forward, but only at a creeping pace. He had never in his life been accosted by a policeman. The women were milling around Nelson as if they might suddenly all dive on him at once and tear him to pieces, and the old woman continued to scream that her ankle was broken and to call for an officer. Mr. Head came on so slowly that he could have been taking a backward step after each forward one, but when he was about ten feet away, Nelson saw him and sprang. The child caught him around the hips and clung panting against him.

The women all turned on Mr. Head. The injured one sat up and shouted, "You sir! You'll pay every penny of my doctor's bill that your boy has caused. He's a juve-nile delinquent! Where is an officer? Somebody take this man's name and address!"

Mr. Head was trying to detach Nelson's fingers from the flesh in the back of his legs. The old man's head had lowered itself into his collar like a turtle's; his eyes were glazed with fear and caution.

"Your boy has broken my ankle!" the old woman shouted. "Police!"

Mr. Head sensed the approach of the policeman from behind. He stared straight ahead at the women who were massed in their fury like a solid wall to block his escape. "This is not my boy," he said. "I never seen him before."

He felt Nelson's fingers fall out of his flesh.

The women dropped back, staring at him with horror,

as if they were so repulsed by a man who would deny his own image and likeness that they could not bear to lay hands on him. Mr. Head walked on, through a space they silently cleared, and left Nelson behind. Ahead of him he saw nothing but a hollow tunnel that had once been the street.

The boy remained standing where he was, his neck craned forward and his hands hanging by his sides. His hat was jammed on his head so that there were no longer any creases in it. The injured woman got up and shook her fist at him and the others gave him pitying looks, but he didn't notice any of them. There was no policeman in sight.

In a minute he began to move mechanically, making no effort to catch up with his grandfather but merely following at about twenty paces. They walked on for five blocks in this way. Mr. Head's shoulders were sagging and his neck hung forward at such an angle that it was not visible from behind. He was afraid to turn his head. Finally he cut a short hopeful glance over his shoulder. Twenty feet behind him, he saw two small eyes piercing into his back like pitchfork prongs.

The boy was not of a forgiving nature but this was the first time he had ever had anything to forgive. Mr. Head had never disgraced himself before. After two more blocks, he turned and called over his shoulder in a high desperately gay voice, "Let's us go get us a Co' Cola somewheres!"

Nelson, with a dignity he had never shown before, turned and stood with his back to his grandfather.

Mr. Head began to feel the depth of his denial. His face as they walked on became all hollows and bare ridges. He saw nothing they were passing but he perceived that they had lost the car tracks. There was no dome to be seen anywhere and the afternoon was advancing. He knew that if dark overtook them in the city, they would be beaten and robbed. The speed of God's justice was only what he expected for himself, but he could not stand to think that his sins would be visited upon Nelson and that even now, he was leading the boy to his doom.

They continued to walk on block after block through an endless section of small brick houses until Mr. Head almost fell over a water spigot sticking up about six inches off the edge of a grass plot. He had not had a drink of water since early morning but he felt he did not deserve it now. Then he thought that Nelson would be thirsty and they would both drink and be brought together. He squatted down and put his mouth to the nozzle and turned a cold stream of water into his throat. Then he called out in the high desperate voice, "Come on and getcher some water!"

This time the child stared through him for nearly sixty seconds. Mr. Head got up and walked on as if he had drunk poison. Nelson, though he had not had water since some he had drunk out of a paper cup on the train, passed by the spigot, disdaining to drink where his grandfather had. When Mr. Head realized this, he lost all hope. His face in the waning afternoon light looked ravaged and abandoned. He could feel the boy's steady hate, traveling at an even pace behind him and he knew that (if by some miracle they escaped being murdered in the city) it would continue just that way for the rest of his life. He knew that now he was wandering into a black strange place where nothing was like it had ever been before, a long old age without respect and an end that would be welcome because it would be the end.

As for Nelson, his mind had frozen around his grandfather's treachery as if he were trying to preserve it intact to present at the final judgment. He walked without looking to one side or the other, but every now and then his mouth would twitch and this was when he felt, from some remote place inside himself, a black mysterious form reach up as if it would melt his frozen vision in one hot grasp.

The sun dropped down behind a row of houses and hardly noticing, they passed into an elegant suburban section where mansions were set back from the road by lawns with birdbaths on them. Here everything was entirely deserted. For blocks they didn't pass even a dog. The big white houses were like partially submerged icebergs in the distance. There were no sidewalks, only drives, and these wound around and around in endless ridiculous circles. Nelson made no move to come nearer to Mr. Head. The old man felt that if he saw a sewer entrance he would drop down into it and let himself be carried away; and he could imagine the boy standing by, watching with only a slight interest, while he disappeared.

A loud bark jarred him to attention and he looked up to see a fat man approaching with two bulldogs. He waved both arms like someone shipwrecked on a desert island. "I'm lost!" he called. "I'm lost and can't find my way and me and this boy have got to catch this train and I can't find the station. Oh Gawd I'm lost! Oh hep me Gawd I'm lost!"

The man, who was bald-headed and had on golf knickers, asked him what train he was trying to catch and Mr.

Head began to get out his tickets, trembling so violently he could hardly hold them. Nelson had come up to within fifteen feet and stood watching.

"Well," the fat man said, giving him back the tickets, "you won't have time to get back to town to make this but you can catch it at the suburb stop. That's three blocks from here," and he began explaining how to get there.

Mr. Head stared as if he were slowly returning from the dead and when the man had finished and gone off with the dogs jumping at his heels, he turned to Nelson and said breathlessly, "We're going to get home!"

The child was standing about ten feet away, his face bloodless under the gray hat. His eyes were triumphantly cold. There was no light in them, no feeling, no interest. He was merely there, a small figure, waiting. Home was nothing to him.

Mr. Head turned slowly. He felt he knew now what time would be like without seasons and what heat would be like without light and what man would be like without salvation. He didn't care if he never made the train and if it had not been for what suddenly caught his attention, like a cry out of the gathering dusk, he might have forgotten there was a station to go to.

He had not walked five hundred yards down the road when he saw, within reach of him, the plaster figure of a Negro sitting bent over on a low yellow brick fence that curved around a wide lawn. The Negro was about Nelson's size and he was pitched forward at an unsteady angle because the putty that held him to the wall had cracked. One of his eyes was entirely white and he held a piece of brown watermelon.

Mr. Head stood looking at him silently until Nelson stopped at a little distance. Then as the two of them stood there, Mr. Head breathed, "An artificial nigger!"

It was not possible to tell if the artificial Negro were meant to be young or old; he looked too miserable to be either. He was meant to look happy because his mouth was stretched up at the corners but the chipped eye and the angle he was cocked at gave him a wild look of misery instead.

"An artificial nigger!" Nelson repeated in Mr. Head's exact tone.

The two of them stood there with their necks forward at almost the same angle and their shoulders curved in almost exactly the same way and their hands trembling identically in their pockets. Mr. Head looked like an ancient child and Nelson like a miniature old man. They stood gazing at the artificial Negro as if they were faced with some great mystery, some monument to another's victory that brought them together in their common defeat. They could both feel it dissolving their differences like an action of mercy. Mr. Head had never known before what mercy felt like because he had been too good to deserve any, but he felt he knew now. He looked at Nelson and understood that he must say something to the child to show that he was still wise and in the look the boy returned he saw a hungry need for that assurance. Nelson's eyes seemed to implore him to explain once and for all the mystery of existence.

Mr. Head opened his lips to make a lofty statement and heard himself say, "They ain't got enough real ones here. They got to have an artificial one."

After a second, the boy nodded with a strange shivering about his mouth, and said, "Let's go home before we get ourselves lost again."

Their train glided into the suburb stop just as they reached the station and they boarded it together, and ten minutes before it was due to arrive at the junction, they went to the door and stood ready to jump off if it did not stop; but it did, just as the moon, restored to its full splendor, sprang from a cloud and flooded the clearing with light. As they stepped off, the sage grass was shivering gently in shades of silver and the clinkers under their feet glittered with a fresh black light. The treetops, fencing the junction like the protecting walls of a garden, were darker than the sky which was hung with gigantic white clouds illuminated like lanterns.

Mr. Head stood very still and felt the action of mercy touch him again but this time he knew that there were no words in the world that could name it. He understood that it grew out of agony, which is not denied to any man and which is given in strange ways to children. He understood it was all a man could carry into death to give his Maker and he suddenly burned with shame that he had so little of it to take with him. He stood appalled, judging himself with the thoroughness of God, while the action of mercy covered his pride like a flame and consumed it. He had never thought himself a great sinner before but he saw now that his true depravity had been hidden from him lest it cause him despair. He realized that he was forgiven for sins from the beginning of time, when he had conceived in his own heart the sin of Adam, until the present, when he had denied poor Nelson. He saw that no sin was too monstrous for him to claim as his own, and since God loved in proportion as He forgave, he felt ready at that instant to enter Paradise.

Nelson, composing his expression under the shadow of his hat brim, watched him with a mixture of fatigue and suspicion, but as the train glided past them and disappeared like a frightened serpent into the woods, even his face lightened and he muttered, "I'm glad I've went once, but I'll never go back again!"

Sometimes the last line of trees was a solid gray-blue wall a little darker than the sky but this afternoon it was almost black and behind it the sky was a livid glaring white. "You know that woman that had that baby in that iron lung?" Mrs. Pritchard said. She and the child's mother were underneath the window the child was looking down from. Mrs. Pritchard was leaning against the chimney, her arms folded on a shelf of stomach, one foot crossed and the toe pointed into the ground. She was a large woman with a small pointed face and steady ferreting eyes. Mrs. Cope was the opposite, very small and trim, with a large round face and black eyes that seemed to be enlarging all the time behind her glasses as if she were continually being astonished. She was squatting down pulling grass out of the border beds around the house. Both women had on sunhats that had once been identical but now Mrs. Pritchard's was faded and out of shape while Mrs. Cope's was still stiff and bright green.

"I read about her," she said.

"She was a Pritchard that married a Brookins and so's kin to me—about my seventh or eighth cousin by marriage."

"Well, well," Mrs. Cope muttered and threw a large clump of nut grass behind her. She worked at the weeds and nut grass as if they were an evil sent directly by the devil to destroy the place.

"Beinst she was kin to us, we gone to see the body," Mrs. Pritchard said. "Seen the little baby too."

Mrs. Cope didn't say anything. She was used to these calamitous stories; she said they wore her to a frazzle. Mrs. Pritchard would go thirty miles for the satisfaction of seeing anybody laid away. Mrs. Cope always changed the subject to something cheerful but the child had observed that this only put Mrs. Pritchard in a bad humor.

The child thought the blank sky looked as if it were pushing against the fortress wall, trying to break through. The trees across the near field were a patchwork of gray and yellow greens. Mrs. Cope was always worrying about fires in her woods. When the nights were very windy, she would say to the child, "Oh Lord, do pray there won't be any fires, it's so windy," and the child would grunt from behind her book or not answer at all because she heard it so often. In the evenings in the summer when they sat on the porch, Mrs. Cope would say to the child who was reading fast to catch the last light, "Get up and look at the sunset, it's gorgeous. You ought to get up and look at it," and the child would scowl and not answer or glare up once across the lawn and two front pastures to the gray-blue sentinel line of trees and then begin to read again with no change of expression, sometimes muttering for meanness, "It looks like a fire. You better get up and smell around and see if the woods ain't on fire."

"She had her arm around it in the coffin," Mrs. Pritchard went on, but her voice was drowned out by the sound of the tractor that the Negro, Culver, was driving up the road from the barn. The wagon was attached and another Negro was sitting in the back, bouncing, his feet jogging about a foot from the ground. The one on the tractor drove it past the gate that led into the field on the left.

Mrs. Cope turned her head and saw that he had not gone through the gate because he was too lazy to get off and open it. He was going the long way around at her expense. "Tell him to stop and come here!" she shouted.

Mrs. Pritchard heaved herself from the chimney and waved her arm in a fierce circle but he pretended not to hear. She stalked to the edge of the lawn and screamed, "Get off, I toljer! She wants you!"

He got off and started toward the chimney, pushing his head and shoulders forward at each step to give the appearance of hurrying. His head was thrust up to the top in a white cloth hat streaked with different shades of sweat. The brim was down and hid all but the lower parts of his reddish eyes.

Mrs. Cope was on her knees, pointing the trowel into the ground. "Why aren't you going through the gate there?" she asked and waited, her eyes shut and her mouth stretched flat as if she were prepared for any ridiculous answer.

"Got to raise the blade on the mower if we do," he said and his gaze bore just to the left of her. Her Negroes were as destructive and impersonal as the nut grass.

Her eyes, as she opened them, looked as if they would keep on enlarging until they turned her wrongsideout. "Raise it," she said and pointed across the road with the trowel.

He moved off.

"It's nothing to them," she said. "They don't have the

responsibility. I thank the Lord all these things don't come at once. They'd destroy me."

"Yeah, they would," Mrs. Pritchard shouted against the sound of the tractor. He opened the gate and raised the blade and drove through and down into the field; the noise diminished as the wagon disappeared. "I don't see myself how she had it *in* it," she went on in her normal voice.

Mrs. Cope was bent over, digging fiercely at the nut grass again. "We have a lot to be thankful for," she said. "Every day you should say a prayer of thanksgiving. Do you do that?"

"Yes'm," Mrs. Pritchard said. "See she was in it four months before she even got thataway. Look like to me if I was in one of them, I would leave off . . . how you reckon they . . . ?"

"Every day I say a prayer of thanksgiving," Mrs. Cope said. "Think of all we have. Lord," she said and sighed, "we have everything," and she looked around at her rich pastures and hills heavy with timber and shook her head as if it might all be a burden she was trying to shake off her back.

Mrs. Pritchard studied the woods. "All I got is four abscess teeth," she remarked.

"Well, be thankful you don't have five," Mrs. Cope snapped and threw back a clump of grass. "We might all be destroyed by a hurricane. I can always find something to be thankful for."

Mrs. Pritchard took up a hoe resting against the side of the house and struck lightly at a weed that had come up between two bricks in the chimney. "I reckon *you* can," she said, her voice a little more nasal than usual with contempt.

"Why, think of all those poor Europeans," Mrs. Cope went on, "that they put in boxcars like cattle and rode them to Siberia. Lord," she said, "we ought to spend half our time on our knees."

"I know if I was in an iron lung there would be some things I wouldn't do," Mrs. Pritchard said, scratching her bare ankle with the end of the hoe.

"Even that poor woman had plenty to be thankful for," Mrs. Cope said.

"She could be thankful she wasn't dead."

"Certainly," Mrs. Cope said, and then she pointed the trowel up at Mrs. Pritchard and said, "I have the best kept place in the county and do you know why? Because I work. I've had to work to save this place and work to keep it." She emphasized each word with the trowel. "I don't let anything get ahead of me and I'm not always looking for trouble. I take it as it comes."

"If it all come at oncet sometime," Mrs. Pritchard began.

"It doesn't all come at once," Mrs. Cope said sharply.

The child could see over to where the dirt road joined the highway. She saw a pick-up truck stop at the gate and let off three boys who started walking up the pink dirt road. They walked single file, the middle one bent to the side carrying a black pig-shaped valise.

"Well, if it ever did," Mrs. Pritchard said, "it wouldn't be nothing you could do but fling up your hands."

Mrs. Cope didn't even answer this. Mrs. Pritchard folded her arms and gazed down the road as if she could easily enough see all these fine hills flattened to nothing. She saw the three boys who had almost reached the front walk by now. "Lookit yonder," she said. "Who you reckon they are?"

Mrs. Cope leaned back and supported herself with one hand behind her and looked. The three came toward them but as if they were going to walk on through the side of the house. The one with the suitcase was in front now. Finally about four feet from her, he stopped and set it down. The three boys looked something alike except that the middle-sized one wore silver-rimmed spectacles and carried the suitcase. One of his eyes had a slight cast to it so that his gaze seemed to be coming from two directions at once as if it had them surrounded. He had on a sweat shirt with a faded destroyer printed on it but his chest was so hollow that the destroyer was broken in the middle and seemed on the point of going under. His hair was stuck to his forehead with sweat. He looked to be about thirteen. All three boys had white penetrating stares. "I don't reckon you remember me, Mrs. Cope," he said.

"Your face is certainly familiar," she murmured, scrutinizing him. "Now let's see . . ."

"My daddy used to work here," he hinted.

"Boyd?" she said. "Your father was Mr. Boyd and you're J.C.?"

"Nome, I'm Powell, the secont one, only I've growed some since then and my daddy he's daid now. Done died."

"Dead. Well I declare," Mrs. Cope said as if death were always an unusual thing. "What was Mr. Boyd's trouble?"

One of Powell's eyes seemed to be making a circle of the place, examining the house and the white water tower behind it and the chicken houses and the pastures that rolled away on either side until they met the first line of woods. The other eye looked at her. "Died in Florda," he said and began kicking the valise.

"Well I declare," she murmured. After a second she said, "And how is your mother?"

"Mah'd again." He kept watching his foot kick the suitcase. The other two boys stared at her impatiently.

"And where do you all live now?" she asked.

"Atlanta," he said. "You know, out to one of them developments."

"Well I see," she said, "I see." After a second she said it again. Finally she asked, "And who are these other boys?" and smiled at them.

"Garfield Smith him, and W. T. Harper him," he said, nodding his head backward first in the direction of the large boy and then the small one.

"How do you boys do?" Mrs. Cope said. "This is Mrs. Pritchard. Mr. and Mrs. Pritchard work here now."

They ignored Mrs. Pritchard who watched them with steady beady eyes. The three seemed to hang there, waiting, watching Mrs. Cope.

"Well well," she said, glancing at the suitcase, "it's nice of you to stop and see me. I think that was real sweet of you."

Powell's stare seemed to pinch her like a pair of tongs. "Come back to see how you was doing," he said hoarsely.

"Listen here," the smallest boy said, "all the time we been knowing him he's been telling us about this here place. Said it was everything here. Said it was horses here. Said he had the best time of his entire life right here on this here place. Talks about it all the time."

"Never shuts his trap about this place," the big boy grunted, drawing his arm across his nose as if to muffle his words.

"Always talking about them horses he rid here," the small one continued, "and said he would let us ride them too. Said it was one name Gene."

Mrs. Cope was always afraid someone would get hurt on her place and sue her for everything she had. "They aren't shod," she said quickly. "There was one named Gene but he's dead now but I'm afraid you boys can't ride the horses because you might get hurt. They're dangerous," she said, speaking very fast.

The large boy sat down on the ground with a noise of disgust and began to finger rocks out of his tennis shoe. The small one darted looks here and there and Powell fixed her with his stare and didn't say anything.

After a minute the little boy said, "Say, lady, you know

what he said one time? He said when he died he wanted
to come here!"

For a second Mrs. Cope looked blank; then she blushed;
then a peculiar look of pain came over her face as she
realized that these children were hungry. They were staring
because they were hungry! She almost gasped in their
faces and then she asked them quickly if they would have
something to eat. They said they would but their expressions,
composed and unsatisfied, didn't lighten any. They looked
as if they were used to being hungry and it was no business
of hers.

The child upstairs had grown red in the face with excitement. She was kneeling down by the window so that only
her eyes and forehead showed over the sill. Mrs. Cope
told the boys to come around on the other side of the house
where the lawn chairs were and she led the way and Mrs.
Pritchard followed. The child moved from the right bedroom
across the hall and over into the left bedroom and looked
down on the other side of the house where there were
three white lawn chairs and a red hammock strung between
two hazelnut trees. She was a pale fat girl of twelve with
a frowning squint and a large mouth full of silver bands.
She knelt down at the window.

The three boys came around the corner of the house
and the large one threw himself into the hammock and
lit a stub of cigarette. The small boy tumbled down on
the grass next to the black suitcase and rested his head
on it and Powell sat down on the edge of one of the chairs
and looked as if he were trying to enclose the whole place
in one encircling stare. The child heard her mother and
Mrs. Pritchard in a muted conference in the kitchen. She
got up and went out into the hall and leaned over the banisters.

Mrs. Cope's and Mrs. Pritchard's legs were facing each
other in the back hall. "Those poor children are hungry,"
Mrs. Cope said in a dead voice.

"You seen that suitcase?" Mrs. Pritchard asked. "What
if they intend to spend the night with you?"

Mrs. Cope gave a slight shriek. "I can't have three boys
in here with only me and Sally Virginia," she said. "I'm
sure they'll go when I feed them."

"I only know they got a suitcase," Mrs. Pritchard said.

The child hurried back to the window. The large boy
was stretched out in the hammock with his wrists crossed
under his head and the cigarette stub in the center of
his mouth. He spit it out in an arc just as Mrs. Cope came

around the corner of the house with a plate of crackers. She stopped instantly as if a snake had been slung in her path. "Ashfield!" she said. "Please pick that up. I'm afraid of fires."

"Gawfield!" the little boy shouted indignantly. "Gawfield!"

The large boy raised himself without a word and lumbered for the butt. He picked it up and put it in his pocket and stood with his back to her, examining a tattooed heart on his forearm. Mrs. Pritchard came up holding three Coca-Colas by the necks in one hand and gave one to each of them.

"I remember everything about this place," Powell said, looking down the opening of his bottle.

"Where did you all go when you left here?" Mrs. Cope asked and put the plate of crackers on the arm of his chair.

He looked at it but didn't take one. He said, "I remember it was one name Gene and it was one name George. We gone to Florda and my daddy he, you know, died, and then we gone to my sister's and then my mother she, you know, mah'd, and we been there ever since."

"There are some crackers," Mrs. Cope said and sat down in the chair across from him.

"He don't like it in Atlanta," the little boy said, sitting up and reaching indifferently for a cracker. "He ain't ever satisfied with where he's at except this place here. Lemme tell you what he'll do, lady. We'll be playing ball, see, on this here place in this development we got to play ball on, see, and he'll quit playing and say, 'Goddam, it was a horse down there name Gene and if I had him here I'd bust this concrete to hell riding him!' "

"I'm sure Powell doesn't use words like that, do you, Powell?" Mrs. Cope said.

"No, mam," Powell said. His head was turned completely to the side as if he were listening for the horses in the field.

"I don't like them kind of crackers," the little boy said and returned his to the plate and got up.

Mrs. Cope shifted in her chair. "So you boys live in one of those nice new developments," she said.

"The only way you can tell your own is by smell," the small boy volunteered. "They're four stories high and there's ten of them, one behind the other. Let's go see them horses," he said.

Powell turned his pinching look on Mrs. Cope. "We thought we would just spend the night in your barn," he said. "My uncle brought us this far on his pick-up truck and he's going to stop for us again in the morning."

There was a moment in which she didn't say a thing and the child in the window thought: she's going to fly out of that chair and hit the tree.

"Well, I'm afraid you can't do that," she said, getting up suddenly. "The barn's full of hay and I'm afraid of fire from your cigarettes."

"We won't smoke," he said.

"I'm afraid you can't spend the night in there just the same," she repeated as if she were talking politely to a gangster.

"Well, we can camp out in the woods then," the little boy said. "We brought our own blankets anyways. That's what we got in thatere suitcase. Come on."

"In the woods!" she said. "Oh no! The woods are very dry now, I can't have people smoking in my woods. You'll have to camp out in the field, in this field here next to the house, where there aren't any trees."

"Where she can keep her eye on you," the child said under her breath.

"Her woods," the large boy muttered and got out of the hammock.

"We'll sleep in the field," Powell said but not particularly as if he were talking to her. "This afternoon I'm going to show them about this place." The other two were already walking away and he got up and bounded after them and the two women sat with the black suitcase between them.

"Not no thank you, not no nothing," Mrs. Pritchard remarked.

"They only played with what we gave them to eat," Mrs. Cope said in a hurt voice.

Mrs. Pritchard suggested that they might not like *soft* drinks.

"They certainly *looked* hungry," Mrs. Cope said.

About sunset they appeared out of the woods, dirty and sweating, and came to the back porch and asked for water. They did not ask for food but Mrs. Cope could tell that they wanted it. "All I have is some cold guinea," she said. "Would you boys like some guinea and some sandwiches?"

"I wouldn't eat nothing bald-headed like a guinea," the little boy said. "I would eat a chicken or a turkey but not no guinea."

"Dog wouldn't eat one of them," the large boy said. He had taken off his shirt and stuck it in the back of his trousers like a tail. Mrs. Cope carefully avoided looking at him. The little boy had a cut on his arm.

"You boys haven't been riding the horses when I asked you not to, have you?" she asked suspiciously and they all said, "No mam!" at once in loud enthusiastic voices like the Amens are said in country churches.

She went into the house and made them sandwiches and, while she did it, she held a conversation with them from inside the kitchen, asking what their fathers did and how many brothers and sisters they had and where they went to school. They answered in short explosive sentences, pushing each other's shoulders and doubling up with laughter as if the questions had meanings she didn't know about. "And do you have men teachers or lady teachers at your school?" she asked.

"Some of both and some you can't tell which," the big boy hooted.

"And does your mother work, Powell?" she asked quickly.

"She ast you does your mother work!" the little boy yelled. "His mind's affected by them horses he only looked at," he said. "His mother she works at a factory and leaves him to mind the rest of them only he don't mind them much. Lemme tell you, lady, one time he locked his little brother in a box and set it on fire."

"I'm sure Powell wouldn't do a thing like that," she said, coming out with the plate of sandwiches and setting it down on the step. They emptied the plate at once and she picked it up and stood holding it, looking at the sun which was going down in front of them, almost on top of the tree line. It was swollen and flame-colored and hung in a net of ragged cloud as if it might burn through any second and fall into the woods. From the upstairs window the child saw her shiver and catch both arms to her sides. "We have so much to be thankful for," she said suddenly in a mournful marveling tone. "Do you boys thank God every night for all He's done for you? Do you thank Him for everything?"

This put an instant hush over them. They bit into the sandwiches as if they had lost all taste for food.

"Do you?" she persisted.

They were as silent as thieves hiding. They chewed without a sound.

"Well, I know I do," she said at length and turned and went back to the house and the child watched their shoulders drop. The large one stretched his legs out as if he were releasing himself from a trap. The sun burned so fast that it seemed to be trying to set everything in sight on fire. The white water tower was glazed pink and the grass was an unnatural green as if it were turning to glass. The child suddenly stuck her head far out the window and said, "Ugggghhrhh," in a loud voice, crossing her eyes and hanging her tongue out as far as possible as if she were going to vomit.

The large boy looked up and stared at her. "Jesus," he growled, "another woman."

She dropped back from the window and stood with her back against the wall, squinting fiercely as if she had been slapped in the face and couldn't see who had done it. As soon as they left the steps, she came down into the kitchen where Mrs. Cope was washing the dishes. "If I had that big boy down I'd beat the daylight out of him," she said.

"You keep away from those boys," Mrs. Cope said, turning sharply. "Ladies don't beat the daylight out of people. You keep out of their way. They'll be gone in the morning."

But in the morning they were not gone.

When she went out on the porch after breakfast, they were standing around the back door, kicking the steps. They were smelling the bacon she had had for her breakfast. "Why boys!" she said. "I thought you were going to meet your uncle." They had the same look of hardened hunger that had pained her yesterday but today she felt faintly provoked.

The big boy turned his back at once and the small one squatted down and began to scratch in the sand. "We ain't, though," Powell said.

The big boy turned his head just enough to take in a small section of her and said, "We ain't bothering nothing of yours."

He couldn't see the way her eyes enlarged but he could take note of the significant silence. After a minute she said in an altered voice, "Would you boys care for some breakfast?"

"We got plenty of our own food," the big boy said. "We don't want nothing of yours."

She kept her eyes on Powell. His thin white face seemed to confront but not actually to see her. "You boys know that I'm glad to have you," she said, "but I expect you to behave. I expect you to act like gentlemen."

They stood there, each looking in a different direction, as if they were waiting for her to leave. "After all," she said in a suddenly high voice, "this is my place."

The big boy made some ambiguous noise and they

turned and walked off toward the barn, leaving her there
with a shocked look as if she had had a searchlight thrown
on her in the middle of the night.

In a little while Mrs. Pritchard came over and stood
in the kitchen door with her cheek against the edge of
it. "I reckon you know they rode them horses all yesterday
afternoon," she said. "Stole a bridle out the saddle room
and rode bareback because Hollis seen them. He runnum
out the barn at nine o'clock last night and then he runnum
out the milk room this morning and there was milk all
over their mouths like they had been drinking out the cans."

"I cannot have this," Mrs. Cope said and stood at the
sink with both fists knotted at her sides. "I cannot have
this," and her expression was the same as when she tore
at the nut grass.

"There ain't a thing you can do about it," Mrs. Pritchard
said. "What I expect is you'll have them for a week or
so until school begins. They just figure to have themselves
a vacation in the country and there ain't nothing you can
do but fold your hands."

"I do not fold my hands," Mrs. Cope said. "Tell Mr.
Pritchard to put the horses up in the stalls."

"He's already did that. You take a boy thirteen year
old is equal in meanness to a man twict his age. It's no
telling what he'll think up to do. You never know where
he'll strike next. This morning Hollis seen them behind
the bull pen and that big one ast if it wasn't some place
they could wash at and Hollis said no it wasn't and that
you didn't want no boys dropping cigarette butts in your
woods and he said, 'She don't own them woods,' and
Hollis said, 'She does too,' and that there little one he
said, 'Man, Gawd owns them woods and her too,' and that
there one with the glasses said, 'I reckon she owns the
sky over this place too,' and that there littlest one says,
'Owns the sky and can't no airplane go over here without
she says so,' and then the big one says, 'I never seen a
place with so many damn women on it, how do you stand
it here?' and Hollis said he had done had enough of their
big talk by then and he turned and walked off without giving
no reply one way or the other."

"I'm going out there and tell those boys they can get
a ride away from here on the milk truck," Mrs. Cope said
and she went out the back door, leaving Mrs. Pritchard
and the child together in the kitchen.

"Listen," the child said. "I could handle them quicker
than that."

"Yeah?" Mrs. Pritchard murmured, giving her a long leering look. "How'd you handle them?"

The child gripped both hands together and made a contorted face as if she were strangling someone.

"They'd handle you," Mrs. Pritchard said with satisfaction.

The child retired to the upstairs window to get out of her way and looked down where her mother was walking off from the three boys who were squatting under the water tower, eating something out of a cracker box. She heard her come in the kitchen door and say, "They say they'll go on the milk truck, and no wonder they aren't hungry—they have that suitcase half full of food."

"Likely stole every bit of it too," Mrs. Pritchard said.

When the milk truck came, the three boys were nowhere in sight, but as soon as it left without them their three faces appeared, looking out of the opening in the top of the calf barn. "Can you beat this?" Mrs. Cope said, standing at one of the upstairs windows with her hands at her hips. "It's not that I wouldn't be glad to have them—it's their attitude."

"You never like nobody's attitude," the child said. "I'll go tell them they got five minutes to leave here in."

"You are not to go anywhere near those boys, do you hear me?" Mrs. Cope said.

"Why?" the child asked.

"I'm going out there and give them a piece of my mind," Mrs. Cope said.

The child took over the position in the window and in a few minutes she saw the stiff green hat catching the glint of the sun as her mother crossed the road toward the calf barn. The three faces immediately disappeared from the opening, and in a second the large boy dashed across the lot, followed an instant later by the other two. Mrs. Pritchard came out and the two women started for the grove of trees the boys had vanished into. Presently the two sunhats disappeared in the woods and the three boys came out at the left side of it and ambled across the field and into another patch of woods. By the time Mrs. Cope and Mrs. Pritchard reached the field, it was empty and there was nothing for them to do but come home again.

Mrs. Cope had not been inside long before Mrs. Pritchard came running toward the house, shouting something. "They've let out the bull!" she hollered. "Let out the bull!" And in a second she was followed by the bull himself, ambling, black and leisurely, with four geese hissing at his heels. He was not mean until hurried and it took Mr. Pritchard and the two Negroes a half-hour to ease him back to his pen. While the men were engaged in this, the boys let the oil out of the three tractors and then disappeared again into the woods.

Two blue veins had come out on either side of Mrs. Cope's forehead and Mrs. Pritchard observed them with satisfaction. "Like I toljer," she said, "there ain't a thing you can do about it."

Mrs. Cope ate her dinner hastily, not conscious that she had her sunhat on. Every time she heard a noise, she jumped up. Mrs. Pritchard came over immediately after dinner and said, "Well, you want to know where they are now?" and smiled in an omniscient rewarded way.

"I want to know at once," Mrs. Cope said, coming to an almost military attention.

"Down to the road, throwing rocks at your mailbox," Mrs. Pritchard said, leaning comfortably in the door. "Done already about knocked it off its stand."

"Get in the car," Mrs. Cope said.

The child got in too and the three of them drove down the road to the gate. The boys were sitting on the embankment on the other side of the highway, aiming rocks across the road at the mailbox. Mrs. Cope stopped the car almost directly beneath them and looked up out of her window. The three of them stared at her as if they had never seen her before, the large boy with a sullen glare, the small one glint-eyed and unsmiling, and Powell with his two-sided glassed gaze hanging vacantly over the crippled destroyer on his shirt.

"Powell," she said, "I'm sure your mother would be ashamed of you," and she stopped and waited for this to make its effect. His face seemed to twist slightly but he continued to look through her at nothing in particular.

"Now I've put up with this as long as I can," she said. "I've tried to be nice to you boys. Haven't I been nice to you boys?"

They might have been three statues except that the big one, barely opening his mouth, said, "We're not even on your side the road, lady."

"There ain't a thing you can do about it," Mrs. Pritchard hissed loudly. The child was sitting on the back seat close to the side. She had a furious outraged look on her face but she kept her head drawn back from the window so that they couldn't see her.

Mrs. Cope spoke slowly, emphasizing every word. "I think I have been very nice to you boys. I've fed you twice.

Now I'm going into town and if you're still here when I come back, I'll call the sheriff," and with this, she drove off. The child, turning quickly so that she could see out the back window, observed that they had not moved; they had not even turned their heads.

"You done angered them now," Mrs. Pritchard said, "and it ain't any telling what they'll do."

"They'll be gone when we get back," Mrs. Cope said.

Mrs. Pritchard could not stand an anticlimax. She required the taste of blood from time to time to keep her equilibrium. "I known a man oncet that his wife was poisoned by a child she had adopted out of pure kindness," she said. When they returned from town, the boys were not on the embankment and she said, "I would rather to see them than not to see them. When you see them you know what they're doing."

"Ridiculous," Mrs. Cope muttered. "I've scared them and they've gone and now we can forget them."

"I ain't forgetting them," Mrs. Pritchard said. "I wouldn't be none surprised if they didn't have a gun in that there suitcase."

Mrs. Cope prided herself on the way she handled the type of mind that Mrs. Pritchard had. When Mrs. Pritchard saw signs and omens, she exposed them calmly for the figments of imagination that they were, but this afternoon her nerves were taut and she said, "Now I've had about enough of this. Those boys are gone and that's that."

"Well, we'll wait and see," Mrs. Pritchard said.

Everything was quiet for the rest of the afternoon but at supper time, Mrs. Pritchard came over to say that she had heard a high vicious laugh pierce out of the bushes near the hog pen. It was an evil laugh, full of calculated meanness, and she had heard it come three times, herself, distinctly.

"I haven't heard a thing," Mrs. Cope said.

"I look for them to strike just after dark," Mrs. Pritchard said.

That night Mrs. Cope and the child sat on the porch until nearly ten o'clock and nothing happened. The only sounds came from tree frogs and from one whippoorwill who called faster and faster from the same spot of darkness. "They've gone," Mrs. Cope said, "poor things," and she began to tell the child how much they had to be thankful for, for she said they might have had to live in a development themselves or they might have been Negroes or they might have been in iron lungs or they might have been Europeans ridden in boxcars like cattle, and she began a litany of her blessings, in a stricken voice, that the child, straining her attention for a sudden shriek in the dark, didn't listen to.

There was no sign of them the next morning either. The fortress line of trees was a hard granite blue, the wind had risen overnight and the sun had come up a pale gold. The season was changing. Even a small change in the weather made Mrs. Cope thankful, but when the seasons changed she seemed almost frightened at her good fortune in escaping whatever it was that pursued her. As she sometimes did when one thing was finished and another about to begin, she turned her attention to the child who had put on a pair of overalls over her dress and had pulled a man's old felt hat down as far as it would go on her head and was arming herself with two pistols in a decorated holster that she had fastened around her waist. The hat was very tight and seemed to be squeezing the redness into her face. It came down almost to the tops of her glasses. Mrs. Cope watched her with a tragic look. "Why do you have to look like an idiot?" she asked. "Suppose company were to come? When are you going to grow up? What's going to become of you? I look at you and I want to cry! Sometimes you look like you might belong to Mrs. Pritchard!"

"Leave me be," the child said in a high irritated voice. "Leave me be. Just leave me be. I ain't you," and she went off to the woods as if she were stalking out an enemy, her head thrust forward and each hand gripped on a gun.

Mrs. Pritchard came over, sour-humored, because she didn't have anything calamitous to report. "I got the misery in my face today," she said, holding on to what she could salvage. "Theseyer teeth. They each one feel like an individual boil."

The child crashed through the woods, making the fallen leaves sound ominous under her feet. The sun had risen a little and was only a white hole like an opening for the wind to escape through in a sky a little darker than itself, and the tops of the trees were black against the glare. "I'm going to get you," she said. "I'm going to get you one by one and beat you black and blue. Line up. LINE UP!" she said and waved one of the pistols at a cluster of long bare-trunked pines, four times her height, as she passed them. She kept moving, muttering and growling to herself and occasionally hitting out with one of the guns at a branch that got in her way. From time to time she stopped to remove the thorn vine that caught in her shirt and she would say, "Leave me be, I told you. Leave me be," and give it a crack with the pistol and then stalk on.

Presently she sat down on a stump to cool off but she planted both feet carefully and firmly on the ground. She lifted them and put them down several times, grinding them fiercely into the dirt as if she were crushing something under her heels. Suddenly she heard a laugh.

She sat up, prickle-skinned. It came again. She heard the sound of splashing and she stood up, uncertain which way to run. She was not far from where this patch of woods ended and the back pasture began. She eased toward the pasture, careful not to make a sound, and coming suddenly to the edge of it, she saw the three boys, not twenty feet away, washing in the cow trough. Their clothes were piled against the black valise out of reach of the water that flowed over the side of the tank. The large boy was standing up and the small one was trying to climb onto his shoulders. Powell was sitting down looking straight ahead through glasses that were splashed with water. He was not paying any attention to the other two. The trees must have looked like green waterfalls through his wet glasses. The child stood partly hidden behind a pine trunk, the side of her face pressed into the bark.

"I wish I lived here!" the little boy shouted, balancing with his knees clutched around the big one's head.

"I'm goddam glad I don't," the big boy panted, and jumped up to dislodge him.

Powell sat without moving, without seeming to know that the other two were behind him, and looked straight ahead like a ghost sprung upright in his coffin. "If this place was not here any more," he said, "you would never have to think of it again."

"Listen," the big boy said, sitting down quietly in the water with the little one still moored to his shoulders, "it don't belong to nobody."

"It's ours," the little boy said.

The child behind the tree did not move.

Powell jumped out of the trough and began to run. He ran all the way around the field as if something were after him and as he passed the tank again, the other two jumped out and raced with him, the sun glinting on their long wet bodies. The big one ran the fastest and was the leader. They dashed around the field twice and finally dropped down by their clothes and lay there with their ribs moving up and down. After a while, the big one said hoarsely, "Do you know what I would do with this place if I had the chance?"

"No, what?" the little boy said and sat up to give him his full attention.

"I'd build a big parking lot on it, or something," he muttered.

They began to dress. The sun made two white spots on Powell's glasses and blotted out his eyes. "I know what let's do," he said. He took something small from his pocket and showed it to them. For almost a minute they sat looking at what he had in his hand. Then without any more discussion, Powell picked up the suitcase and they got up and moved past the child and entered the woods not ten feet from where she was standing, slightly away from the tree now, with the imprint of the bark embossed red and white on the side of her face.

She watched with a dazed stare as they stopped and collected all the matches they had between them and began to set the brush on fire. They began to whoop and holler and beat their hands over their mouths and in a few seconds there was a narrow line of fire widening between her and them. While she watched, it reached up from the brush, snatching and biting at the lowest branches of the trees. The wind carried rags of it higher and the boys disappeared shrieking behind it.

She turned and tried to run across the field but her legs were too heavy and she stood there, weighted down with some new unplaced misery that she had never felt before. But finally she began to run.

Mrs. Cope and Mrs. Pritchard were in the field behind the barn when Mrs. Cope saw smoke rising from the woods across the pasture. She shrieked and Mrs. Pritchard pointed up the road to where the child came loping heavily, screaming, "Mama, Mama, they're going to build a parking lot here!"

Mrs. Cope began to scream for the Negroes while Mrs. Pritchard, charged now, ran down the road shouting. Mr. Pritchard came out of the open end of the barn and the two Negroes stopped filling the manure spreader in the lot and started toward Mrs. Cope with their shovels. "Hurry, hurry!" she shouted. "Start throwing dirt on it!" They passed her almost without looking at her and headed off slowly across the field toward the smoke. She ran after them a little way, shrilling, "Hurry, hurry, don't you see it! Don't you see it!"

"It'll be there when we git there," Culver said and they thrust their shoulders forward a little and went on at the same pace.

The child came to a stop beside her mother and stared up at her face as if she had never seen it before. It was the face of the new misery she felt, but on her mother it looked old and it looked as if it might have belonged to anybody, a Negro or a European or to Powell himself. The child turned her head quickly, and past the Negroes' ambling figures she could see the column of smoke rising and widening unchecked inside the granite line of trees. She stood taut, listening, and could just catch in the distance a few wild high shrieks of joy as if the prophets were dancing in the fiery furnace, in the circle the angel had cleared for them.

A LATE ENCOUNTER WITH THE ENEMY

General Sash was a hundred and four years old. He lived with his granddaughter, Sally Poker Sash, who was sixty-two years old and who prayed every night on her knees that he would live until her graduation from college. The General didn't give two slaps for her graduation but he never doubted he would live for it. Living had got to be such a habit with him that he couldn't conceive of any other condition. A graduation exercise was not exactly his idea of a good time, even if, as she said, he would be expected to sit on the stage in his uniform. She said there would be a long procession of teachers and students in their robes but that there wouldn't be anything to equal *him* in his uniform. He knew this well enough without her telling him, and as for the damn procession, it could march to hell and back and not cause him a quiver. He liked parades with floats full of Miss Americas and Miss Daytona Beaches and Miss Queen Cotton Products. He didn't have any use for processions and a procession full of schoolteachers was about as deadly as the River Styx to his way of thinking. However, he was willing to sit on the stage in his uniform so that they could see him.

Sally Poker was not as sure as he was that he would live until her graduation. There had not been any perceptible change in him for the last five years, but she had the sense that she might be cheated out of her triumph because she so often was. She had been going to summer school every year for the past twenty because when she started teaching, there were no such things as degrees. In those times, she said, everything was normal but nothing had been normal since she was sixteen, and for the past twenty summers, when she should have been resting, she had had to take a trunk in the burning heat to the state teacher's college; and though when she returned in the fall, she always taught in the exact way she had been taught not to teach, this was a mild revenge that didn't satisfy her sense of justice. She wanted the General at her graduation because she wanted to show what she stood for, or, as she said, "what all was behind her," and was not behind them. This *them*

233

was not anybody in particular. It was just all the upstarts who had turned the world on its head and unsettled the ways of decent living.

She meant to stand on that platform in August with the General sitting in his wheel chair on the stage behind her and she meant to hold her head very high as if she were saying, "See him! See him! My kin, all you upstarts! Glorious upright old man standing for the old traditions! Dignity! Honor! Courage! See him!" One night in her sleep she screamed, "See him! See him!" and turned her head and found him sitting in his wheel chair behind her with a terrible expression on his face and with all his clothes off except the general's hat and she had waked up and had not dared to go back to sleep again that night.

For his part, the General would not have consented even to attend her graduation if she had not promised to see to it that he sit on the stage. He liked to sit on any stage. He considered that he was still a very handsome man. When he had been able to stand up, he had measured five feet four inches of pure game cock. He had white hair that reached to his shoulders behind and he would not wear teeth because he thought his profile was more striking without them. When he put on his full-dress general's uniform, he knew well enough that there was nothing to match him anywhere.

This was not the same uniform he had worn in the War between the States. He had not actually been a general in that war. He had probably been a foot soldier; he didn't remember what he had been; in fact, he didn't remember that war at all. It was like his feet, which hung down now shriveled at the very end of him, without feeling, covered with a blue-gray afghan that Sally Poker had crocheted when she was a little girl. He didn't remember the Spanish-American War in which he had lost a son; he didn't even remember the son. He didn't have any use for history because he never expected to meet it again. To his mind, history was connected with processions and life with parades and he liked parades. People were always asking him if he remembered this or that—a dreary black procession of questions about the past. There was only one event in the past that had any significance for him and that he cared to talk about: that was twelve years ago when he had received the general's uniform and had been in the premiere.

"I was in that preemy they had in Atlanta," he would tell visitors sitting on his front porch. "Surrounded by beautiful guls. It wasn't a thing local about it. It was nothing

local about it. Listen here. It was a nashnul event and they
had me in it—up onto the stage. There was no bob-tails
at it. Every person at it had paid ten dollars to get in
and had to wear his tuxseeder. I was in this uniform. A
beautiful gul presented me with it that afternoon in a
hotel room."

"It was in a suite in the hotel and I was in it too, Papa,"
Sally Poker would say, winking at the visitors. "You weren't
alone with any young lady in a hotel room."

"Was, I'd a known what to do," the old General would
say with a sharp look and the visitors would scream with
laughter. "This was a Hollywood, California, gul," he'd
continue. "She was from Hollywood, California, and didn't
have any part in the pitcher. Out there they have so many
beautiful guls that they don't need that they call them a
extra and they don't use them for nothing but presenting
people with things and having their pitchers taken. They
took my pitcher with her. No, it was two of them. One
on either side and me in the middle with my arms around
each of them's waist and their waist ain't any bigger than
a half a dollar."

Sally Poker would interrupt again. "It was Mr. Govisky
that gave you the uniform, Papa, and he gave me the most
exquisite corsage. Really, I wish you could have seen
it. It was made with gladiola petals taken off and painted
gold and put back together to look like a rose. It was exquisite. I wish you could have seen it, it was . . ."

"It was as big as her head," the General would snarl.
"I was tellin it. They gimme this uniform and they gimme
this soward and they say, 'Now General, we don't want
you to start a war on us. All we want you to do is march
right up on that stage when you're innerduced tonight
and answer a few questions. Think you can do that?' 'Think
I can do it!' I say. 'Listen here. I was doing things before
you were born,' and they hollered."

"He was the hit of the show," Sally Poker would say,
but she didn't much like to remember the premiere on
account of what had happened to her feet at it. She had
bought a new dress for the occasion—a long black crepe
dinner dress with a rhinestone buckle and a bolero—and
a pair of silver slippers to wear with it, because she was
supposed to go up on the stage with him to keep him from
falling. Everything was arranged for them. A real limousine
came at ten minutes to eight and took them to the theater.
It drew up under the marquee at exactly the right time,
after the big stars and the director and the author and the
governor and the mayor and some less important stars.

The police kept traffic from jamming and there were ropes to keep the people off who couldn't go. All the people who couldn't go watched them step out of the limousine into the lights. Then they walked down the red and gold foyer and an usherette in a Confederate cap and little short skirt conducted them to their special seats. The audience was already there and a group of UDC members began to clap when they saw the General in his uniform and that started everybody to clap. A few more celebrities came after them and then the doors closed and the lights went down.

A young man with blond wavy hair who said he represented the motion-picture industry came out and began to introduce everybody and each one who was introduced walked up on the stage and said how really happy he was to be here for this great event. The General and his granddaughter were introduced sixteenth on the program. He was introduced as General Tennessee Flintrock Sash of the Confederacy, though Sally Poker had told Mr. Govisky that his name was George Poker Sash and that he had only been a major. She helped him up from his seat but her heart was beating so fast she didn't know whether she'd make it herself.

The old man walked up the aisle slowly with his fierce white head high and his hat held over his heart. The orchestra began to play the Confederate Battle Hymn very softly and the UDC members rose as a group and did not sit down again until the General was on the stage. When he reached the center of the stage with Sally Poker just behind him guiding his elbow, the orchestra burst out in a loud rendition of the Battle Hymn and the old man, with real stage presence, gave a vigorous trembling salute and stood at attention until the last blast had died away. Two of the usherettes in Confederate caps and short skirts held a Confederate and a Union flag crossed behind them.

The General stood in the exact center of the spotlight and it caught a weird moon-shaped slice of Sally Poker—the corsage, the rhinestone buckle and one hand clenched around a white glove and handkerchief. The young man with the blond wavy hair inserted himself into the circle of light and said he was *really* happy to have here tonight for this great event, one, he said, who had fought and bled in the battles they would soon see daringly re-acted on the screen, and "Tell me, General," he asked, "how old are you?"

"Niiiiiinnttty-two!" the General screamed.

The young man looked as if this were just about the most impressive thing that had been said all evening. "Ladies and gentlemen," he said, "let's give the General the biggest hand we've got!" and there was applause immediately and the young man indicated to Sally Poker with a motion of his thumb that she could take the old man back to his seat now so that the next person could be introduced; but the General had not finished. He stood immovable in the exact center of the spotlight, his neck thrust forward, his mouth slightly open, and his voracious gray eyes drinking in the glare and the applause. He elbowed his granddaughter roughly away. "How I keep so young," he screeched, "I kiss all the pretty guls!"

This was met with a great din of spontaneous applause and it was at just that instant that Sally Poker looked down at her feet and discovered that in the excitement of getting ready she had forgotten to change her shoes: two brown Girl Scout oxfords protruded from the bottom of her dress. She gave the General a yank and almost ran with him off the stage. He was very angry that he had not got to say how glad he was to be here for this event and on the way back to his seat, he kept saying as loud as he could, "I'm glad to be here at this preemy with all these beautiful guls!" but there was another celebrity going up the other aisle and nobody paid any attention to him. He slept through the picture, muttering fiercely every now and then in his sleep.

Since then, his life had not been very interesting. His feet were completely dead now, his knees worked like old hinges, his kidneys functioned when they would, but his heart persisted doggedly to beat. The past and the future were the same thing to him, one forgotten and the other not remembered; he had no more notion of dying than a cat. Every year on Confederate Memorial Day, he was bundled up and lent to the Capitol City Museum where he was displayed from one to four in a musty room full of old photographs, old uniforms, old artillery, and historic documents. All these were carefully preserved in glass cases so that children would not put their hands on them. He wore his general's uniform from the premiere and sat, with a fixed scowl, inside a small roped area. There was nothing about him to indicate that he was alive except an occasional movement in his milky gray eyes, but once when a bold child touched his sword, his arm shot forward and slapped the hand off in an instant. In the spring when the old homes were opened for pilgrimages, he was invited to wear his uniform and sit in some conspicuous spot and lend atmosphere to the scene. Some of these times he only snarled at the visitors but sometimes he told about the premiere and the beautiful girls.

If he had died before Sally Poker's graduation, she thought she would have died herself. At the beginning of the summer term, even before she knew if she would pass, she told the Dean that her grandfather, General Tennessee Flintrock Sash of the Confederacy, would attend her graduation and that he was a hundred and four years old and that his mind was still clear as a bell. Distinguished visitors were always welcome and could sit on the stage and be introduced. She made arrangements with her nephew, John Wesley Poker Sash, a Boy Scout, to come wheel the General's chair. She thought how sweet it would be to see the old man in his courageous gray and the young boy in his clean khaki—the old and the new, she thought appropriately—they would be behind her on the stage when she received her degree.

Everything went almost exactly as she had planned. In the summer while she was away at school, the General stayed with other relatives and they brought him and John Wesley, the Boy Scout, down to the graduation. A reporter came to the hotel where they stayed and took the General's picture with Sally Poker on one side of him and John Wesley on the other. The General, who had had his picture taken with beautiful girls, didn't think much of this. He had forgotten precisely what kind of event this was he was going to attend but he remembered that he was to wear his uniform and carry the sword.

On the morning of the graduation, Sally Poker had to line up in the academic procession with the B.S.'s in Elementary Education and she couldn't see to getting him on the stage herself—but John Wesley, a fat blond boy of ten with an executive expression, guaranteed to take care of everything. She came in her academic gown to the hotel and dressed the old man in his uniform. He was as frail as a dried spider. "Aren't you just thrilled, Papa?" she asked. "I'm just thrilled to death!"

"Put the soward acrost my lap, damm you," the old man said, "where it'll shine."

She put it there and then stood back looking at him. "You look just grand," she said.

"God damm it," the old man said in a slow monotonous certain tone as if he were saying it to the beating of his heart. "God damm every goddam thing to hell."

"Now, now," she said and left happily to join the procession.

The graduates were lined up behind the Science building and she found her place just as the line started to move. She had not slept much the night before and when she had, she had dreamed of the exercises, murmuring, "See him, see him?" in her sleep but waking up every time just before she turned her head to look at him behind her. The graduates had to walk three blocks in the hot sun in their black wool robes and as she plodded stolidly along she thought that if anyone considered this academic procession something impressive to behold, they need only wait until they saw that old General in his courageous gray and that clean young Boy Scout stoutly wheeling his chair across the stage with the sunlight catching the sword. She imagined that John Wesley had the old man ready now behind the stage.

The black procession wound its way up the two blocks and started on the main walk leading to the auditorium. The visitors stood on the grass, picking out their graduates. Men were pushing back their hats and wiping their foreheads and women were lifting their dresses slightly from the shoulders to keep them from sticking to their backs. The graduates in their heavy robes looked as if the last beads of ignorance were being sweated out of them. The sun blazed off the fenders of automobiles and beat from the columns of the buildings and pulled the eye from one spot of glare to another. It pulled Sally Poker's toward the big red Coca-Cola machine that had been set up by the side of the auditorium. Here she saw the General parked, scowling and hatless in his chair in the blazing sun while John Wesley, his blouse loose behind, his hip and cheek pressed to the red machine, was drinking a Coca-Cola. She broke from the line and galloped to them and snatched the bottle away. She shook the boy and thrust in his blouse and put the hat on the old man's head. "Now get him in there!" she said, pointing one rigid finger to the side door of the building.

For his part the General felt as if there were a little hole beginning to widen in the top of his head. The boy wheeled him rapidly down a walk and up a ramp and into a building and bumped him over the stage entrance and into position where he had been told and the General glared in front of him at heads that all seemed to flow together and eyes that moved from one face to another. Several figures in black robes came and picked up his hand and shook it. A black procession was flowing up each aisle and forming to stately music in a pool in front of him. The music seemed to be entering his head through the little hole and he thought for a second that the procession would try to enter it too.

He didn't know what procession this was but there was something familiar about it. It must be familiar to him since it had come to meet him, but he didn't like a black procession. Any procession that came to meet him, he thought irritably, ought to have floats with beautiful guls on them like the floats before the preemy. It must be something connected with history like they were always having. He had no use for any of it. What happened then wasn't anything to a man living now and he was living now.

When all the procession had flowed into the black pool, a black figure began orating in front of it. The figure was telling something about history and the General made up his mind he wouldn't listen, but the words kept seeping in through the little hole in his head. He heard his own name mentioned and his chair was shuttled forward roughly and the Boy Scout took a big bow. They called his name and the fat brat bowed. Goddam you, the old man tried to say, get out of my way, I can stand up!—but he was jerked back again before he could get up and take the bow. He supposed the noise they made was for him. If he was over, he didn't intend to listen to any more of it. If it hadn't been for the little hole in the top of his head, none of the words would have got to him. He thought of putting his finger up there into the hole to block them but the hole was a little wider than his finger and it felt as if it were getting deeper.

Another black robe had taken the place of the first one and was talking now and he heard his name mentioned again but they were not talking about him, they were still talking about history. "If we forget our past," the speaker was saying, "we won't remember our future and it will be as well for we won't have one." The General heard some of these words gradually. He had forgotten history and he didn't intend to remember it again. He had forgotten the name and face of his wife and the names and faces of his children or even if he had a wife and children, and he had forgotten the names of places and the places themselves and what had happened at them.

He was considerably irked by the hole in his head. He had not expected to have a hole in his head at this event. It was the slow black music that had put it there and though most of the music had stopped outside, there was still a little of it in the hole, going deeper and moving around in his thoughts, letting the words he heard into the dark places of his brain. He heard the words, Chickamauga, Shiloh, Johnston, Lee, and he knew he was inspiring all these words that meant nothing to him. He wondered if he had been a general at Chickamauga or at Lee. Then he tried to see himself and the horse mounted in the middle of a float full of beautiful girls, being driven slowly through downtown Atlanta. Instead, the old words began to stir in his head as if they were trying to wrench themselves out of place and come to life.

The speaker was through with that war and had gone on to the next one and now he was approaching another and all his words, like the black procession, were vaguely familiar and irritating. There was a long finger of music in the General's head, probing various spots that were words, letting in a little light on the words and helping them to live. The words began to come toward him and he said, Dammit! I ain't going to have it! and he started edging backwards to get out of the way. Then he saw the figure in the black robe sit down and there was a noise and the black pool in front of him began to rumble and to flow toward him from either side to the black slow music, and he said, Stop dammit! I can't do but one thing at a time! He couldn't protect himself from the words and attend to the procession too and the words were coming at him fast. He felt that he was running backwards and the words were coming at him like musket fire, just escaping him but getting nearer and nearer. He turned around and began to run as fast as he could but he found himself running toward the words. He was running into a regular volley of them and meeting them with quick curses. As the music swelled toward him, the entire past opened up on him out of nowhere and he felt his body riddled in a hundred places with sharp stabs of pain and he fell down, returning a curse for every hit. He saw his wife's narrow face looking at him critically through her round gold-rimmed glasses; he saw one of his squinting bald-headed sons; and his mother ran toward him with an anxious look; then a succession of places—Chickamauga, Shiloh, Marthasville—rushed at him as if the past were the only future now and he had to endure it. Then suddenly he saw that the black procession was almost on him. He recognized it, for it had been dogging all his days. He made such a desperate effort to see over it and find out what comes after the past that his hand clenched the sword until the blade touched bone.

The graduates were crossing the stage in a long file to receive their scrolls and shake the president's hand. As Sally Poker, who was near the end, crossed, she glanced at the General and saw him sitting fixed and fierce, his eyes wide open, and she turned her head forward again and held it a perceptible degree higher and received her scroll. Once it was all over and she was out of the auditorium in the sun again, she located her kin and they waited together on a bench in the shade for John Wesley to wheel the old man out. That crafty scout had bumped him out the back way and rolled him at high speed down a flagstone path and was waiting now, with the corpse, in the long line at the Coca-Cola machine.

GOOD COUNTRY PEOPLE

Besides the neutral expression that she wore when she was alone, Mrs. Freeman had two others, forward and reverse, that she used for all her human dealings. Her forward expression was steady and driving like the advance of a heavy truck. Her eyes never swerved to left or right but turned as the story turned as if they followed a yellow line down the center of it. She seldom used the other expression because it was not often necessary for her to retract a statement, but when she did, her face came to a complete stop, there was an almost imperceptible movement of her black eyes, during which they seemed to be receding, and then the observer would see that Mrs. Freeman, though she might stand there as real as several grain sacks thrown on top of each other, was no longer there in spirit. As for getting anything across to her when this was the case, Mrs. Hopewell had given it up. She might talk her head off. Mrs. Freeman could never be brought to admit herself wrong on any point. She would stand there and if she could be brought to say anything, it was something like, "Well, I wouldn't of said it was and I wouldn't of said it wasn't," or letting her gaze range over the top kitchen shelf where there was an assortment of dusty bottles, she might remark, "I see you ain't ate many of them figs you put up last summer."

They carried on their most important business in the kitchen at breakfast. Every morning Mrs. Hopewell got up at seven o'clock and lit her gas heater and Joy's. Joy was her daughter, a large blonde girl who had an artificial leg. Mrs. Hopewell thought of her as a child though she was thirty-two years old and highly educated. Joy would get up while her mother was eating and lumber into the bathroom and slam the door, and before long, Mrs. Freeman would arrive at the back door. Joy would hear her mother call, "Come on in," and then they would talk for a while in low voices that were indistinguishable in the bathroom. By the time Joy came in, they had usually finished the weather report and were on one or the other of Mrs. Freeman's daughters, Glynese or Carramae. Joy called them Glycerin and Caramel. Glynese, a redhead, was eighteen and had many admirers; Carramae, a blonde, was only fifteen but already married and pregnant. She could not keep anything on her stomach. Every morning Mrs. Freeman told Mrs. Hopewell how many times she had vomited since the last report.

Mrs. Hopewell liked to tell people that Glynese and Carramae were two of the finest girls she knew and that Mrs. Freeman was a *lady* and that she was never ashamed to take her anywhere or introduce her to anybody they might meet. Then she would tell how she had happened to hire the Freemans in the first place and how they were a godsend to her and how she had had them four years. The reason for her keeping them so long was that they were not trash. They were good country people. She had telephoned the man whose name they had given as a reference and he had told her that Mr. Freeman was a good farmer but that his wife was the nosiest woman ever to walk the earth. "She's got to be into everything," the man said. "If she don't get there before the dust settles, you can bet she's dead, that's all. She'll want to know all your business. I can stand him real good," he had said, "but me nor my wife neither could have stood that woman one more minute on this place." That had put Mrs. Hopewell off for a few days.

She had hired them in the end because there were no other applicants but she had made up her mind beforehand exactly how she would handle the woman. Since she was the type who had to be into everything, then, Mrs. Hopewell had decided, she would not only let her be into everything, she would *see to it* that she was into everything—she would give her the responsibility of everything, she would put her in charge. Mrs. Hopewell had no bad qualities of her own but she was able to use other people's in such a constructive way that she never felt the lack. She had hired the Freemans and she had kept them four years.

Nothing is perfect. This was one of Mrs. Hopewell's favorite sayings. Another was: that is life! And still another, the most important, was: well, other people have their opinions too. She would make these statements, usually at the table, in a tone of gentle insistence as if no one held them but her, and the large hulking Joy, whose constant outrage had obliterated every expression from her face, would stare just a little to the side of her, her eyes icy blue, with the look of someone who has achieved blindness by an act of will and means to keep it.

When Mrs. Hopewell said to Mrs. Freeman that life

was like that, Mrs. Freeman would say, "I always said so myself." Nothing had been arrived at by anyone that had not first been arrived at by her. She was quicker than Mr. Freeman. When Mrs. Hopewell said to her after they had been on the place a while, "You know, you're the wheel behind the wheel," and winked, Mrs. Freeman had said, "I know it. I've always been quick. It's some that are quicker than others."

"Everybody is different," Mrs. Hopewell said.

"Yes, most people is," Mrs. Freeman said.

"It takes all kinds to make the world."

"I always said it did myself."

The girl was used to this kind of dialogue for breakfast and more of it for dinner; sometimes they had it for supper too. When they had no guest they ate in the kitchen because that was easier. Mrs. Freeman always managed to arrive at some point during the meal and to watch them finish it. She would stand in the doorway if it were summer but in the winter she would stand with one elbow on top of the refrigerator and look down on them, or she would stand by the gas heater, lifting the back of her skirt slightly. Occasionally she would stand against the wall and roll her head from side to side. At no time was she in any hurry to leave. All this was very trying on Mrs. Hopewell but she was a woman of great patience. She realized that nothing is perfect and that in the Freemans she had good country people and that if, in this day and age, you get good country people, you had better hang onto them.

She had had plenty of experience with trash. Before the Freemans she had averaged one tenant family a year. The wives of these farmers were not the kind you would want to be around you for very long. Mrs. Hopewell, who had divorced her husband long ago, needed someone to walk over the fields with her; and when Joy had to be impressed for these services, her remarks were usually so ugly and her face so glum that Mrs. Hopewell would say, "If you can't come pleasantly, I don't want you at all," to which the girl, standing square and rigid-shouldered with her neck thrust slightly forward, would reply, "If you want me, here I am—LIKE I AM."

Mrs. Hopewell excused this attitude because of the leg (which had been shot off in a hunting accident when Joy was ten). It was hard for Mrs. Hopewell to realize that her child was thirty-two now and that for more than twenty years she had had only one leg. She thought of her still as a child because it tore her heart to think instead of the poor stout girl in her thirties who had never danced a step or had any *normal* good times. Her name was really Joy but as soon as she was twenty-one and away from home, she had had it legally changed. Mrs. Hopewell was certain that she had thought and thought until she had hit upon the ugliest name in any language. Then she had gone and had the beautiful name, Joy, changed without telling her mother until after she had done it. Her legal name was Hulga.

When Mrs. Hopewell thought the name, Hulga, she thought of the broad blank hull of a battleship. She would not use it. She continued to call her Joy to which the girl responded but in a purely mechanical way.

Hulga had learned to tolerate Mrs. Freeman who saved her from taking walks with her mother. Even Glynese and Carramae were useful when they occupied attention that might otherwise have been directed at her. At first she had thought she could not stand Mrs. Freeman for she had found that it was not possible to be rude to her. Mrs. Freeman would take on strange resentments and for days together she would be sullen but the source of her displeasure was always obscure; a direct attack, a positive leer, blatant ugliness to her face—these never touched her. And without warning one day, she began calling her Hulga.

She did not call her that in front of Mrs. Hopewell who would have been incensed but when she and the girl happened to be out of the house together, she would say something and add the name Hulga to the end of it, and the big spectacled Joy-Hulga would scowl and redden as if her privacy had been intruded upon. She considered the name her personal affair. She had arrived at it first purely on the basis of its ugly sound and then the full genius of its fitness had struck her. She had a vision of the name working like the ugly sweating Vulcan who stayed in the furnace and to whom, presumably, the goddess had to come when called. She saw it as the name of her highest creative act. One of her major triumphs was that her mother had not been able to turn her dust into Joy, but the greater one was that she had been able to turn it herself into Hulga. However, Mrs. Freeman's relish for using the name only irritated her. It was as if Mrs. Freeman's beady steel-pointed eyes had penetrated far enough behind her face to reach some secret fact. Something about her seemed to fascinate Mrs. Freeman and then one day Hulga realized that it was the artificial leg. Mrs. Freeman had a special fondness for the details of secret infections, hidden deformities, assaults upon children. Of diseases, she preferred the lingering or incurable. Hulga had heard Mrs. Hopewell give her the details of the hunting accident, how the leg had been literally blasted off, how she had never lost consciousness. Mrs. Freeman could listen to it any time as if it had happened an hour ago.

When Hulga stumped into the kitchen in the morning (she could walk without making the awful noise but she made it—Mrs. Hopewell was certain—because it was ugly-sounding), she glanced at them and did not speak. Mrs. Hopewell would be in her red kimono with her hair tied around her head in rags. She would be sitting at the table, finishing her breakfast and Mrs. Freeman would be hanging by her elbow outward from the refrigerator, looking down at the table. Hulga always put her eggs on the stove to boil and then stood over them with her arms folded, and Mrs. Hopewell would look at her—a kind of indirect gaze divided between her and Mrs. Freeman—and would think that if she would only keep herself up a little, she wouldn't be so bad looking. There was nothing wrong with her face that a pleasant expression wouldn't help. Mrs. Hopewell said that people who looked on the bright side of things would be beautiful even if they were not.

Whenever she looked at Joy this way, she could not help but feel that it would have been better if the child had not taken the Ph.D. It had certainly not brought her out any and now that she had it, there was no more excuse for her to go to school again. Mrs. Hopewell thought it was nice for girls to go to school to have a good time but Joy had "gone through." Anyhow, she would not have been strong enough to go again. The doctors had told Mrs. Hopewell that with the best of care, Joy might see forty-five. She had a weak heart. Joy had made it plain that if it had not been for this condition, she would be far from these red hills and good country people. She would be in a university lecturing to people who knew what she was talking about. And Mrs. Hopewell could very well picture her there, looking like a scarecrow and lecturing to more of the same. Here she went about all day in a six-year-old skirt and a yellow sweat shirt with a faded cowboy on a horse embossed on it. She thought this was funny; Mrs. Hopewell thought it was idiotic and showed simply that she was still a child. She was brilliant but she didn't have a grain of sense. It seemed to Mrs. Hopewell that every year she grew less like other people and more like herself—bloated, rude, and squint-eyed. And she said such strange things! To her own mother she had said—without warning, without excuse, standing up in the middle of a meal with her face purple and her mouth half full—"Woman! do you ever look inside? Do you ever look inside and see what you are *not?* God!" she had cried sinking down again and staring at her plate, "Malebranche was right: we are not our own light. We are not our own light!" Mrs. Hopewell had no idea to this day what brought that on. She had only made the remark, hoping Joy would take it in, that a smile never hurt anyone.

The girl had taken the Ph.D. in philosophy and this left Mrs. Hopewell at a complete loss. You could say, "My daughter is a nurse," or "My daughter is a school teacher," or even, "My daughter is a chemical engineer." You could not say, "My daughter is a philosopher." That was something that had ended with the Greeks and Romans. All day Joy sat on her neck in a deep chair, reading. Sometimes she went for walks but she didn't like dogs or cats or birds or flowers or nature or nice young men. She looked at nice young men as if she could smell their stupidity.

One day Mrs. Hopewell had picked up one of the books the girl had just put down and opening it at random, she read, "Science, on the other hand, has to assert its soberness and seriousness afresh and declare that it is concerned solely with what-is. Nothing—how can it be for science anything but a horror and a phantasm? If science is right, then one thing stands firm: science wishes to know nothing of nothing. Such is after all the strictly scientific approach to Nothing. We know it by wishing to know nothing of Nothing." These words had been underlined with a blue pencil and they worked on Mrs. Hopewell like some evil incantation in gibberish. She shut the book quickly and went out of the room as if she were having a chill.

This morning when the girl came in, Mrs. Freeman was on Carramae. "She thrown up four times after supper," she said, "and was up twict in the night after three o'clock. Yesterday she didn't do nothing but ramble in the bureau drawer. All she did. Stand up there and see what she could run up on."

"She's got to eat," Mrs. Hopewell muttered, sipping her coffee, while she watched Joy's back at the stove. She was wondering what the child had said to the Bible salesman. She could not imagine what kind of a conversation she could possibly have had with him.

He was a tall gaunt hatless youth who had called yesterday to sell them a Bible. He had appeared at the door, carrying a large black suitcase that weighted him so heavily on one side that he had to brace himself against the door facing. He seemed on the point of collapse but he said in a cheerful voice, "Good morning, Mrs. Cedars!" and set the suitcase down on the mat. He was not a bad-looking young man though he had on a bright blue suit and yellow socks that were not pulled up far enough. He had prominent face bones and a streak of sticky-looking brown hair falling across his forehead.

"I'm Mrs. Hopewell," she said.

"Oh!" he said, pretending to look puzzled but with his eyes sparkling, "I saw it said 'The Cedars,' on the mailbox so I thought you was Mrs. Cedars!" and he burst out in a pleasant laugh. He picked up the satchel and under cover of a pant, he fell forward into her hall. It was rather as if the suitcase had moved first, jerking him after it. "Mrs. Hopewell!" he said and grabbed her hand. "I hope you are well!" and he laughed again and then all at once his face sobered completely. He paused and gave her a straight earnest look and said, "Lady, I've come to speak of serious things."

"Well, come in," she muttered, none too pleased because her dinner was almost ready. He came into the parlor and sat down on the edge of a straight chair and put the suitcase between his feet and glanced around the room as if he were sizing her up by it. Her silver gleamed on the two sideboards; she decided he had never been in a room as elegant as this.

"Mrs. Hopewell," he began, using her name in a way that sounded almost intimate, "I know you believe in Christian service."

"Well yes," she murmured.

"I know," he said and paused, looking very wise with his head cocked on one side, "that you're a good woman. Friends have told me."

Mrs. Hopewell never liked to be taken for a fool. "What are you selling?" she asked.

"Bibles," the young man said and his eye raced around the room before he added, "I see you have no family Bible in your parlor, I see that is the one lack you got!"

Mrs. Hopewell could not say, "My daughter is an atheist and won't let me keep the Bible in the parlor." She said, stiffening slightly, "I keep my Bible by my bedside." This was not the truth. It was in the attic somewhere.

"Lady," he said, "the word of God ought to be in the parlor."

"Well, I think that's a matter of taste," she began. "I think . . ."

"Lady," he said, "for a Christian, the word of God

ought to be in every room in the house besides in his heart. I know you're a Chrustian because I can see it in every line of your face."

She stood up and said, "Well, young man, I don't want to buy a Bible and I smell my dinner burning."

He didn't get up. He began to twist his hands and looking down at them, he said softly, "Well lady, I'll tell you the truth—not many people want to buy one nowadays and besides, I know I'm real simple. I don't know how to say a thing but to say it. I'm just a country boy." He glanced up into her unfriendly face. "People like you don't like to fool with country people like me!"

"Why!" she cried, "good country people are the salt of the earth! Besides, we all have different ways of doing, it takes all kinds to make the world go 'round. That's life!"

"You said a mouthful," he said.

"Why, I think there aren't enough good country people in the world!" she said, stirred. "I think that's what's wrong with it!"

His face had brightened. "I didn't inraduce myself," he said. "I'm Manley Pointer from out in the country around Willohobie, not even from a place, just from near a place."

"You wait a minute," she said. "I have to see about my dinner." She went out to the kitchen and found Joy standing near the door where she had been listening.

"Get rid of the salt of the earth," she said, "and let's eat."

Mrs. Hopewell gave her a pained look and turned the heat down under the vegetables. "*I* can't be rude to anybody," she murmured and went back into the parlor.

He had opened the suitcase and was sitting with a Bible on each knee.

"You might as well put those up," she told him. "I don't want one."

"I appreciate your honesty," he said. "You don't see any more real honest people unless you go way out in the country."

"I know," she said, "real genuine folks!" Through the crack in the door she heard a groan.

"I guess a lot of boys come telling you they're working their way through college," he said, "but I'm not going to tell you that. Somehow," he said, "I don't want to go to college. I want to devote my life to Chrustian service. See," he said, lowering his voice, "I got this heart condition. I may not live long. When you know it's something wrong

with you and you may not live long, well then, lady . . ."
He paused, with his mouth open, and stared at her.

He and Joy had the same condition! She knew that
her eyes were filling with tears but she collected herself
quickly and murmured, "Won't you stay for dinner? We'd
love to have you!" and was sorry the instant she heard
herself say it.

"Yes mam," he said in an abashed voice, "I would sher
love to do that!"

Joy had given him one look on being introduced to
him and then throughout the meal had not glanced at
him again. He had addressed several remarks to her,
which she had pretended not to hear. Mrs. Hopewell could
not understand deliberate rudeness, although she lived with
it, and she felt she had always to overflow with hospitality
to make up for Joy's lack of courtesy. She urged him to
talk about himself and he did. He said he was the seventh
child of twelve and that his father had been crushed under
a tree when he himself was eight year old. He had been
crushed very badly, in fact, almost cut in two and was practically not recognizable. His mother had got along the best
she could by hard working and she had always seen that
her children went to Sunday School and that they read
the Bible every evening. He was now nineteen year old
and he had been selling Bibles for four months. In that
time he had sold seventy-seven Bibles and had the promise
of two more sales. He wanted to become a missionary because
he thought that was the way you could do most for people.
"He who losest his life shall find it," he said simply and
he was so sincere, so genuine and earnest that Mrs. Hopewell
would not for the world have smiled. He prevented his
peas from sliding onto the table by blocking them with
a piece of bread which he later cleaned his plate with.
She could see Joy observing sidewise how he handled his
knife and fork and she saw too that every few minutes,
the boy would dart a keen appraising glance at the girl
as if he were trying to attract her attention.

After dinner Joy cleared the dishes off the table and
disappeared and Mrs. Hopewell was left to talk with him.
He told her again about his childhood and his father's
accident and about various things that had happened to
him. Every five minutes or so she would stifle a yawn. He
sat for two hours until finally she told him she must go
because she had an appointment in town. He packed his
Bibles and thanked her and prepared to leave, but in
the doorway he stopped and wrung her hand and said

that not on any of his trips had he met a lady as nice as her and he asked if he could come again. She had said she would always be happy to see him.

Joy had been standing in the road, apparently looking at something in the distance, when he came down the steps toward her, bent to the side with his heavy valise. He stopped where she was standing and confronted her directly. Mrs. Hopewell could not hear what he said but she trembled to think what Joy would say to him. She could see that after a minute Joy said something and that then the boy began to speak again, making an excited gesture with his free hand. After a minute Joy said something else at which the boy began to speak once more. Then to her amazement, Mrs. Hopewell saw the two of them walk off together, toward the gate. Joy had walked all the way to the gate with him and Mrs. Hopewell could not imagine what they had said to each other, and she had not yet dared to ask.

Mrs. Freeman was insisting upon her attention. She had moved from the refrigerator to the heater so that Mrs. Hopewell had to turn and face her in order to seem to be listening. "Glynese gone out with Harvey Hill again last night," she said. "She had this sty."

"Hill," Mrs. Hopewell said absently, "is that the one who works in the garage?"

"Nome, he's the one that goes to chiropracter school," Mrs. Freeman said. "She had this sty. Been had it two days. So she says when he brought her in the other night he says, 'Lemme get rid of that sty for you,' and she says, 'How?' and he says, 'You just lay yourself down acrost the seat of that car and I'll show you.' So she done it and he popped her neck. Kept on a-popping it several times until she made him quit. This morning," Mrs. Freeman said, "she ain't got no sty. She ain't got no traces of a sty."

"I never heard of that before," Mrs. Hopewell said.

"He ast her to marry him before the Ordinary," Mrs. Freeman went on, "and she told him she wasn't going to be married in no *office*."

"Well, Glynese is a fine girl," Mrs. Hopewell said. "Glynese and Carramae are both fine girls."

"Carramae said when her and Lyman was married Lyman said it sure felt sacred to him. She said he said he wouldn't take five hundred dollars for being married by a preacher."

"How much would he take?" the girl asked from the stove.

"He said he wouldn't take five hundred dollars," Mrs. Freeman repeated.

"Well we all have work to do," Mrs. Hopewell said.

"Lyman said it just felt more sacred to him," Mrs. Freeman said. "The doctor wants Carramae to eat prunes. Says instead of medicine. Says them cramps is coming from pressure. You know where I think it is?"

"She'll be better in a few weeks," Mrs. Hopewell said.

"In the tube," Mrs. Freeman said. "Else she wouldn't be as sick as she is."

Hulga had cracked her two eggs into a saucer and was bringing them to the table along with a cup of coffee that she had filled too full. She sat down carefully and began to eat, meaning to keep Mrs. Freeman there by questions if for any reason she showed an inclination to leave. She could perceive her mother's eye on her. The first round-about question would be about the Bible salesman and she did not wish to bring it on. "How did he pop her neck?" she asked.

Mrs. Freeman went into a description of how he had popped her neck. She said he owned a '55 Mercury but that Glynese said she would rather marry a man with only a '36 Plymouth who would be married by a preacher. The girl asked what if he had a '32 Plymouth and Mrs. Freeman said what Glynese had said was a '36 Plymouth.

Mrs. Hopewell said there were not many girls with Glynese's common sense. She said what she admired in those girls was their common sense. She said that reminded her that they had had a nice visitor yesterday, a young man selling Bibles. "Lord," she said, "he bored me to death but he was so sincere and genuine I couldn't be rude to him. He was just good country people, you know," she said, "—just the salt of the earth."

"I seen him walk up," Mrs. Freeman said, "and then later—I seen him walk off," and Hulga could feel the slight shift in her voice, the slight insinuation, that he had not walked off alone, had he? Her face remained expressionless but the color rose into her neck and she seemed to swallow it down with the next spoonful of egg. Mrs. Freeman was looking at her as if they had a secret together.

"Well, it takes all kinds of people to make the world go 'round," Mrs. Hopewell said. "It's very good we aren't all alike."

"Some people are more alike than others," Mrs. Freeman said.

Hulga got up and stumped, with about twice the noise

that was necessary, into her room and locked the door. She was to meet the Bible salesman at ten o'clock at the gate. She had thought about it half the night. She had started thinking of it as a great joke and then she had begun to see profound implications in it. She had lain in bed imagining dialogues for them that were insane on the surface but that reached below to depths that no Bible salesman would be aware of. Their conversation yesterday had been of this kind.

He had stopped in front of her and had simply stood there. His face was bony and sweaty and bright, with a little pointed nose in the center of it, and his look was different from what it had been at the dinner table. He was gazing at her with open curiosity, with fascination, like a child watching a new fantastic animal at the zoo, and he was breathing as if he had run a great distance to reach her. His gaze seemed somehow familiar but she could not think where she had been regarded with it before. For almost a minute he didn't say anything. Then on what seemed an insuck of breath, he whispered, "You ever ate a chicken that was two days old?"

The girl looked at him stonily. He might have just put this question up for consideration at the meeting of a philosophical association. "Yes," she presently replied as if she had considered it from all angles.

"It must have been mighty small!" he said triumphantly and shook all over with little nervous giggles, getting very red in the face, and subsiding finally into his gaze of complete admiration, while the girl's expression remained exactly the same.

"How old are you?" he asked softly.

She waited some time before she answered. Then in a flat voice she said, "Seventeen."

His smiles came in succession like waves breaking on the surface of a little lake. "I see you got a wooden leg," he said. "I think you're real brave. I think you're real sweet."

The girl stood blank and solid and silent.

"Walk to the gate with me," he said. "You're a brave sweet little thing and I liked you the minute I seen you walk in the door."

Hulga began to move forward.

"What's your name?" he asked, smiling down on the top of her head.

"Hulga," she said.

"Hulga," he murmured, "Hulga. Hulga. I never heard

of anybody name Hulga before. You're shy, aren't you, Hulga?" he asked.

She nodded, watching his large red hand on the handle of the giant valise.

"I like girls that wear glasses," he said. "I think a lot. I'm not like these people that a serious thought don't ever enter their heads. It's because I may die."

"I may die too," she said suddenly and looked up at him. His eyes were very small and brown, glittering feverishly.

"Listen," he said, "don't you think some people was meant to meet on account of what all they got in common and all? Like they both think serious thoughts and all?" He shifted the valise to his other hand so that the hand nearest her was free. He caught hold of her elbow and shook it a little. "I don't work on Saturday," he said. "I like to walk in the woods and see what Mother Nature is wearing. O'er the hills and far away. Pic-nics and things. Couldn't we go on a pic-nic tomorrow? Say yes, Hulga," he said and gave her a dying look as if he felt his insides about to drop out of him. He had even seemed to sway slightly toward her.

During the night she had imagined that she seduced him. She imagined that the two of them walked on the place until they came to the storage barn beyond the two back fields and there, she imagined, that things came to such a pass that she very easily seduced him and that then, of course, she had to reckon with his remorse. True genius can get an idea across even to an inferior mind. She imagined that she took his remorse in hand and changed it into a deeper understanding of life. She took all his shame away and turned it into something useful.

She set off for the gate at exactly ten o'clock, escaping without drawing Mrs. Hopewell's attention. She didn't take anything to eat, forgetting that food is usually taken on a picnic. She wore a pair of slacks and a dirty white shirt, and as an afterthought, she had put some Vapex on the collar of it since she did not own any perfume. When she reached the gate no one was there.

She looked up and down the empty highway and had the furious feeling that she had been tricked, that he had only meant to make her walk to the gate after the idea of him. Then suddenly he stood up, very tall, from behind a bush on the opposite embankment. Smiling, he lifted his hat which was new and wide-brimmed. He had not worn it yesterday and she wondered if he had bought it for the occasion. It was toast-colored with a red and white band around it and was slightly too large for him. He stepped from behind the bush still carrying the black valise. He had on the same suit and the same yellow socks sucked down in his shoes from walking. He crossed the highway and said, "I knew you'd come!"

The girl wondered acidly how he had known this. She pointed to the valise and asked, "Why did you bring your Bibles?"

He took her elbow, smiling down on her as if he could not stop. "You can never tell when you'll need the word of God, Hulga," he said. She had a moment in which she doubted that this was actually happening and then they began to climb the embankment. They went down into the pasture toward the woods. The boy walked lightly by her side, bouncing on his toes. The valise did not seem to be heavy today; he even swung it. They crossed half the pasture without saying anything and then, putting his hand easily on the small of her back, he asked softly, "Where does your wooden leg join on?"

She turned an ugly red and glared at him and for an instant the boy looked abashed. "I didn't mean you no harm," he said. "I only meant you're so brave and all. I guess God takes care of you."

"No," she said, looking forward and walking fast, "I don't even believe in God."

At this he stopped and whistled. "No!" he exclaimed as if he were too astonished to say anything else.

She walked on and in a second he was bouncing at her side, fanning with his hat. "That's very unusual for a girl," he remarked, watching her out of the corner of his eye. When they reached the edge of the wood, he put his hand on her back again and drew her against him without a word and kissed her heavily.

The kiss, which had more pressure than feeling behind it, produced that extra surge of adrenalin in the girl that enables one to carry a packed trunk out of a burning house, but in her, the power went at once to the brain. Even before he released her, her mind, clear and detached and ironic anyway, was regarding him from a great distance, with amusement but with pity. She had never been kissed before and she was pleased to discover that it was an unexceptional experience and all a matter of the mind's control. Some people might enjoy drain water if they were told it was vodka. When the boy, looking expectant but uncertain, pushed her gently away, she turned and walked on, saying nothing as if such business, for her, were common enough.

He came along panting at her side, trying to help her

when he saw a root that she might trip over. He caught and held back the long swaying blades of thorn vine until she had passed beyond them. She led the way and he came breathing heavily behind her. Then they came out on a sunlit hillside, sloping softly into another one a little smaller. Beyond, they could see the rusted top of the old barn where the extra hay was stored.

The hill was sprinkled with small pink weeds. "Then you ain't saved?" he asked suddenly, stopping.

The girl smiled. It was the first time she had smiled at him at all. "In my economy," she said, "I'm saved and you are damned but I told you I didn't believe in God."

Nothing seemed to destroy the boy's look of admiration. He gazed at her now as if the fantastic animal at the zoo had put its paw through the bars and given him a loving poke. She thought he looked as if he wanted to kiss her again and she walked on before he had the chance.

"Ain't there somewheres we can sit down sometime?" he murmured, his voice softening toward the end of the sentence.

"In that barn," she said.

They made for it rapidly as if it might slide away like a train. It was a large two-story barn, cool and dark inside. The boy pointed up the ladder that led into the loft and said, "It's too bad we can't go up there."

"Why can't we?" she asked.

"Yer leg," he said reverently.

The girl gave him a contemptuous look and putting both hands on the ladder, she climbed it while he stood below, apparently awestruck. She pulled herself expertly through the opening and then looked down at him and said, "Well, come on if you're coming," and he began to climb the ladder, awkwardly bringing the suitcase with him.

"We won't need the Bible," she observed.

"You never can tell," he said, panting. After he had got into the loft, he was a few seconds catching his breath. She had sat down in a pile of straw. A wide sheath of sunlight, filled with dust particles, slanted over her. She lay back against a bale, her face turned away, looking out the front opening of the barn where hay was thrown from a wagon into the loft. The two pink-speckled hillsides lay back against a dark ridge of woods. The sky was cloudless and cold blue. The boy dropped down by her side and put one arm under her and the other over her and began methodically kissing her face, making little noises like a fish. He did not remove his hat but it was pushed far enough back not to interfere. When her glasses got in his way, he took them off of her and slipped them into his pocket.

The girl at first did not return any of the kisses but presently she began to and after she had put several on his cheek, she reached his lips and remained there, kissing him again and again as if she were trying to draw all the breath out of him. His breath was clear and sweet like a child's and the kisses were sticky like a child's. He mumbled about loving her and about knowing when he first seen her that he loved her, but the mumbling was like the sleepy fretting of a child being put to sleep by his mother. Her mind, throughout this, never stopped or lost itself for a second to her feelings. "You ain't said you loved me none," he whispered finally, pulling back from her. "You got to say that."

She looked away from him off into the hollow sky and then down at a black ridge and then down farther into what appeared to be two green swelling lakes. She didn't realize he had taken her glasses but this landscape could not seem exceptional to her for she seldom paid any close attention to her surroundings.

"You got to say it," he repeated. "You got to say you love me."

She was always careful how she committed herself. "In a sense," she began, "if you use the word loosely, you might say that. But it's not a word I use. I don't have illusions. I'm one of those people who see *through* to nothing."

The boy was frowning. "You got to say it. I said it and you got to say it," he said.

The girl looked at him almost tenderly. "You poor baby," she murmured. "It's just as well you don't understand," and she pulled him by the neck, face-down, against her. "We are all damned," she said, "but some of us have taken off our blindfolds and see that there's nothing to see. It's a kind of salvation."

The boy's astonished eyes looked blankly through the ends of her hair. "Okay," he almost whined, "but do you love me or don'tcher?"

"Yes," she said and added, "in a sense. But I must tell you something. There mustn't be anything dishonest between us." She lifted his head and looked him in the eye. "I am thirty years old," she said. "I have a number of degrees."

The boy's look was irritated but dogged. "I don't care," he said. "I don't care a thing about what all you done. I just want to know if you love me or don'tcher?" and he caught her to him and wildly planted her face with kisses until she said, "Yes, yes."

"Okay then," he said, letting her go. "Prove it."

She smiled, looking dreamily out on the shifty landscape. She had seduced him without even making up her mind to try. "How?" she asked, feeling that he should be delayed a little.

He leaned over and put his lips to her ear. "Show me where your wooden leg joins on," he whispered.

The girl uttered a sharp little cry and her face instantly drained of color. The obscenity of the suggestion was not what shocked her. As a child she had sometimes been subject to feelings of shame but education had removed the last traces of that as a good surgeon scrapes for cancer; she would no more have felt it over what he was asking than she would have believed in his Bible. But she was as sensitive about the artificial leg as a peacock about his tail. No one ever touched it but her. She took care of it as someone else would his soul, in private and almost with her own eyes turned away. "No," she said.

"I known it," he muttered, sitting up. "You're just playing me for a sucker."

"Oh no no!" she cried. "It joins on at the knee. Only at the knee. Why do you want to see it?"

The boy gave her a long penetrating look. "Because," he said, "it's what makes you different. You ain't like anybody else."

She sat staring at him. There was nothing about her face or her round freezing-blue eyes to indicate that this had moved her; but she felt as if her heart had stopped and left her mind to pump her blood. She decided that for the first time in her life she was face to face with real innocence. This boy, with an instinct that came from beyond wisdom, had touched the truth about her. When after a minute, she said in a hoarse high voice, "All right," it was like surrendering to him completely. It was like losing her own life and finding it again, miraculously, in his.

Very gently he began to roll the slack leg up. The artificial limb, in a white sock and brown flat shoe, was bound in a heavy material like canvas and ended in an ugly jointure where it was attached to the stump. The boy's face and his voice were entirely reverent as he uncovered it and said, "Now show me how to take it off and on."

She took it off for him and put it back on again and then he took it off himself, handling it as tenderly as if it were a real one. "See!" he said with a delighted child's face. "Now I can do it myself!"

"Put it back on," she said. She was thinking that she would run away with him and that every night he would take the leg off and every morning put it back on again. "Put it back on," she said.

"Not yet," he murmured, setting it on its foot out of her reach. "Leave it off for a while. You got me instead."

She gave a little cry of alarm but he pushed her down and began to kiss her again. Without the leg she felt entirely dependent on him. Her brain seemed to have stopped thinking altogether and to be about some other function that it was not very good at. Different expressions raced back and forth over her face. Every now and then the boy, his eyes like two steel spikes, would glance behind him where the leg stood. Finally she pushed him off and said, "Put it back on me now."

"Wait," he said. He leaned the other way and pulled the valise toward him and opened it. It had a pale blue spotted lining and there were only two Bibles in it. He took one of these out and opened the cover of it. It was hollow and contained a pocket flask of whiskey, a pack of cards, and a small blue box with printing on it. He laid these out in front of her one at a time in an evenly-spaced row, like one presenting offerings at the shrine of a goddess. He put the blue box in her hand. THIS PRODUCT TO BE USED ONLY FOR THE PREVENTION OF DISEASE, she read, and dropped it. The boy was unscrewing the top of the flask. He stopped and pointed, with a smile, to the deck of cards. It was not an ordinary deck but one with an obscene picture on the back of each card. "Take a swig," he said, offering her the bottle first. He held it in front of her, but like one mesmerized, she did not move.

Her voice when she spoke had an almost pleading sound. "Aren't you," she murmured, "aren't you just good country people?"

The boy cocked his head. He looked as if he were just beginning to understand that she might be trying to insult him. "Yeah," he said, curling his lip slightly, "but it ain't held me back none. I'm as good as you any day in the week."

"Give me my leg," she said.

He pushed it farther away with his foot. "Come on now, let's begin to have us a good time," he said coaxingly. "We ain't got to know one another good yet."

"Give me my leg!" she screamed and tried to lunge for it but he pushed her down easily.

"What's the matter with you all of a sudden?" he asked, frowning as he screwed the top on the flask and put it quickly back inside the Bible. "You just a while ago said you didn't believe in nothing. I thought you was some girl!"

Her face was almost purple. "You're a Christian!" she hissed. "You're a fine Christian! You're just like them all—say one thing and do another. You're a perfect Christian, you're . . ."

The boy's mouth was set angrily. "I hope you don't think," he said in a lofty indignant tone, "that I believe in that crap! I may sell Bibles but I know which end is up and I wasn't born yesterday and I know where I'm going!"

"Give me my leg!" she screeched. He jumped up so quickly that she barely saw him sweep the cards and the blue box back into the Bible and throw the Bible into the valise. She saw him grab the leg and then she saw it for an instant slanted forlornly across the inside of the suitcase with a Bible at either side of its opposite ends. He slammed the lid shut and snatched up the valise and swung it down the hole and then stepped through himself.

When all of him had passed but his head, he turned and regarded her with a look that no longer had any admiration in it. "I've gotten a lot of interesting things," he said. "One time I got a woman's glass eye this way. And you needn't to think you'll catch me because Pointer ain't really my name. I use a different name at every house I call at and don't stay nowhere long. And I'll tell you another thing, Hulga," he said, using the name as if he didn't think much of it, "you ain't so smart. I been believing in nothing ever since I was born!" and then the toast-colored hat disappeared down the hole and the girl was left, sitting on the straw in the dusty sunlight. When she turned her churning face toward the opening, she saw his blue figure struggling successfully over the green speckled lake.

Mrs. Hopewell and Mrs. Freeman, who were in the back pasture, digging up onions, saw him emerge a little later from the woods and head across the meadow toward the highway. "Why, that looks like that nice dull young man that tried to sell me a Bible yesterday," Mrs. Hopewell said, squinting. "He must have been selling them to the Negroes back in there. He was so simple," she said, "but I guess the world would be better off if we were all that simple."

Mrs. Freeman's gaze drove forward and just touched him before he disappeared under the hill. Then she returned her attention to the evil-smelling onion shoot she was lifting from the ground. "Some can't be that simple," she said. "I know I never could."

THE DISPLACED PERSON

The peacock was following Mrs. Shortley up the road to the hill where she meant to stand. Moving one behind the other, they looked like a complete procession. Her arms were folded and as she mounted the prominence, she might have been the giant wife of the countryside, come out at some sign of danger to see what the trouble was. She stood on two tremendous legs, with the grand self-confidence of a mountain, and rose, up narrowing bulges of granite, to two icy blue points of light that pierced forward, surveying everything. She ignored the white afternoon sun which was creeping behind a ragged wall of cloud as if it pretended to be an intruder and cast her gaze down the red clay road that turned off from the highway.

The peacock stopped just behind her, his tail—glittering green-gold and blue in the sunlight—lifted just enough so that it would not touch the ground. It flowed out on either side like a floating train and his head on the long blue reed-like neck was drawn back as if his attention were fixed in the distance on something no one else could see.

Mrs. Shortley was watching a black car turn through the gate from the highway. Over by the toolshed, about fifteen feet away, the two Negroes, Astor and Sulk, had stopped work to watch. They were hidden by a mulberry tree but Mrs. Shortley knew they were there.

Mrs. McIntyre was coming down the steps of her house to meet the car. She had on her largest smile but Mrs. Shortley, even from her distance, could detect a nervous slide in it. These people who were coming were only hired help, like the Shortleys themselves or the Negroes. Yet here was the owner of the place out to welcome them. Here she was, wearing her best clothes and a string of beads, and now bounding forward with her mouth stretched.

The car stopped at the walk just as she did and the priest was the first to get out. He was a long-legged black-suited old man with a white hat on and a collar that he wore backwards, which, Mrs. Shortley knew, was what priests did who wanted to be known as priests. It was this priest who had arranged for these people to come here. He opened the back door of the car and out jumped two children, a boy and a girl, and then, stepping more slowly, a woman in brown, shaped like a peanut. Then the front door opened and out stepped the man, the Displaced Person. He was short and a little sway-backed and wore gold-rimmed spectacles.

Mrs. Shortley's vision narrowed on him and then widened to include the woman and the two children in a group picture. The first thing that struck her as very peculiar was that they looked like other people. Every time she had seen them in her imagination, the image she had got was of the three bears, walking single file, with wooden shoes on like Dutchmen and sailor hats and bright coats with a lot of buttons. But the woman had on a dress she might have worn herself and the children were dressed like anybody from around. The man had on khaki pants and a blue shirt. Suddenly, as Mrs. McIntyre held out her hand to him, he bobbed down from the waist and kissed it.

Mrs. Shortley jerked her own hand up toward her mouth and then after a second brought it down and rubbed it vigorously on her seat. If Mr. Shortley had tried to kiss her hand, Mrs. McIntyre would have knocked him into the middle of next week, but then Mr. Shortley wouldn't have kissed her hand anyway. He didn't have time to mess around.

She looked closer, squinting. The boy was in the center of the group, talking. He was supposed to speak the most English because he had learned some in Poland and so he was to listen to his father's Polish and say it in English and then listen to Mrs. McIntyre's English and say that in Polish. The priest had told Mrs. McIntyre his name was Rudolph and he was twelve and the girl's name was Sledgewig and she was nine. Sledgewig sounded to Mrs. Shortley like something you would name a bug, or vice versa, as if you named a boy Bollweevil. All of them's last name was something that only they themselves and the priest could pronounce. All she could make out of it was Gobblehook. She and Mrs. McIntyre had been calling them the Gobblehooks all week while they got ready for them.

There had been a great deal to do to get ready for them because they didn't have anything of their own, not a stick of furniture or a sheet or a dish, and everything had had to be scraped together out of things that Mrs. McIntyre couldn't use any more herself. They had collected a piece of odd furniture here and a piece there and they had taken some flowered chicken feed sacks and made curtains for

the windows, two red and one green, because they had
not had enough of the red sacks to go around. Mrs. McIntyre
said she was not made of money and she could not afford
to buy curtains. "They can't talk," Mrs. Shortley said.
"You reckon they'll know what colors even is?" and Mrs.
McIntyre had said that after what those people had been
through, they should be grateful for anything they could
get. She said to think how lucky they were to escape from
over there and come to a place like this.

Mrs. Shortley recalled a newsreel she had seen once
of a small room piled high with bodies of dead naked people
all in a heap, their arms and legs tangled together, a head
thrust in here, a head there, a foot, a knee, a part that
should have been covered up sticking out, a hand raised
clutching nothing. Before you could realize that it was real
and take it into your head, the picture changed and a
hollow-sounding voice was saying, "Time marches on!"
This was the kind of thing that was happening every day
in Europe where they had not advanced as in this country,
and watching from her vantage point, Mrs. Shortley had
the sudden intuition that the Gobblehooks, like rats with
typhoid fleas, could have carried all those murderous ways
over the water with them directly to this place. If they
had come from where that kind of thing was done to
them, who was to say they were not the kind that would
also do it to others? The width and breadth of this question
nearly shook her. Her stomach trembled as if there had
been a slight quake in the heart of the mountain and automatically she moved down from her elevation and went
forward to be introduced to them, as if she meant to find
out at once what they were capable of.

She approached, stomach foremost, head back, arms
folded, boots flopping gently against her large legs. About fifteen feet from the gesticulating group, she stopped and made
her presence felt by training her gaze on the back of Mrs.
McIntyre's neck. Mrs. McIntyre was a small woman of
sixty with a round wrinkled face and red bangs that came
almost down to two high orange-colored penciled eyebrows.
She had a little doll's mouth and eyes that were a soft
blue when she opened them wide but more like steel or
granite when she narrowed them to inspect a milk can.
She had buried one husband and divorced two and Mrs.
Shortley respected her as a person nobody had put anything
over on yet—except, ha, ha, perhaps the Shortleys. She
held out her arm in Mrs. Shortley's direction and said
to the Rudolph boy, "And this is Mrs. Shortley. Mr. Shortley
is my dairyman. Where's Mr. Shortley?" she asked as

is wife began to approach again, her arms still folded. I want him to meet the Guizacs."

Now it was Guizac. She wasn't calling them Gobblehook o their face. "Chancey's at the barn," Mrs. Shortley said. He don't have time to rest himself in the bushes like hem niggers over there."

Her look first grazed the tops of the displaced people's heads and then revolved downwards slowly, the way a buzzard glides and drops in the air until it alights on the carcass. She stood far enough away so that the man would not be able to kiss her hand. He looked directly at her with little green eyes and gave her a broad grin that was toothless on one side. Mrs. Shortley, without smiling, turned her attention to the little girl who stood by the mother, swinging her shoulders from side to side. She had long braided hair in two looped pigtails and there was no denying he was a pretty child even if she did have a bug's name. She was better looking than either Annie Maude or Sarah Mae, Mrs. Shortley's two girls going on fifteen and seventeen but Annie Maude had never got her growth and Sarah Mae had a cast in her eye. She compared the foreign boy to her son, H.C., and H.C. came out far ahead. H.C. was twenty years old with her build and eyeglasses. He was going to Bible school now and when he finished he was going to start him a church. He had a strong sweet voice for hymns and could sell anything. Mrs. Shortley looked at the priest and was reminded that these people did not have an advanced religion. There was no telling what all they believed since none of the foolishness had been reformed out of it. Again she saw the room piled high with bodies.

The priest spoke in a foreign way himself, English but as if he had a throatful of hay. He had a big nose and a bald rectangular face and head. While she was observing him, his large mouth dropped open and with a stare behind her, he said, "Arrrrrrr!" and pointed.

Mrs. Shortley spun around. The peacock was standing a few feet behind her, with his head slightly cocked.

"What a beauti-ful birdrrrd!" the priest murmured.

"Another mouth to feed," Mrs. McIntyre said, glancing in the peafowl's direction.

"And when does he raise his splendid tail?" asked the priest.

"Just when it suits him," she said. "There used to be twenty or thirty of those things on the place but I've let them die off. I don't like to hear them scream in the middle of the night."

"So beauti-ful," the priest said. "A tail full of suns,"

and he crept forward on tiptoe and looked down on th
bird's back where the polished gold and green design begar
The peacock stood still as if he had just come down fror
some sun-drenched height to be a vision for them al
The priest's homely red face hung over him, glowing wit
pleasure.

Mrs. Shortley's mouth had drawn acidly to one side
"Nothing but a peachicken," she muttered.

Mrs. McIntyre raised her orange eyebrows and exchange
a look with her to indicate that the old man was in hi
second childhood. "Well, we must show the Guizacs thei
new home," she said impatiently and she herded then
into the car again. The peacock stepped off toward th
mulberry tree where the two Negroes were hiding and th
priest turned his absorbed face away and got in the ca
and drove the displaced people down to the shack the
were to occupy.

Mrs. Shortley waited until the car was out of sight an
then she made her way circuitously to the mulberry tre
and stood about ten feet behind the two Negroes, one ar
old man holding a bucket half full of calf feed and the
other a yellowish boy with a short woodchuck-like head
pushed into a rounded felt hat. "Well," she said slowly
"yawl have looked long enough. What you think about
them?"

The old man, Astor, raised himself. "We been watching,"
he said as if this would be news to her. "Who they now?"

"They come from over the water," Mrs. Shortley said
with a wave of her arm. "They're what is called Displaced
Persons."

"Displaced Persons," he said. "Well now. I declare. What
do that mean?"

"It means they ain't where they were born at and there's
nowhere for them to go—like if you was run out of here
and wouldn't nobody have you."

"It seem like they here, though," the old man said in
a reflective voice. "If they here, they somewhere."

"Sho is," the other agreed. "They here."

The illogic of Negro-thinking always irked Mrs. Shortley.
"They ain't where they belong to be at," she said. "They
belong to be back over yonder where everything is still
like they been used to. Over here it's more advanced than
where they come from. But yawl better look out now,"
she said and nodded her head. "There's about ten million
billion more just like them and I know what Mrs. McIntyre
said."

"Say what?" the young one asked.

"Places are not easy to get nowadays, for white or black, but I reckon I heard what she stated to me," she said in a sing-song voice.

"You liable to hear most anything," the old man remarked, leaning forward as if he were about to walk off but holding himself suspended.

"I heard her say, 'This is going to put the Fear of the Lord into those shiftless niggers!' " Mrs. Shortley said in a ringing voice.

The old man started off. "She say something like that every now and then," he said. "Ha. Ha. Yes indeed."

"You better get on in that barn and help Mr. Shortley," she said to the other one. "What you reckon she pays you for?"

"He the one sont me out," the Negro muttered. "He the one gimme something else to do."

"Well you better get to doing it then," she said and stood there until he moved off. Then she stood a while longer, reflecting, her unseeing eyes directly in front of the peacock's tail. He had jumped into the tree and his tail hung in front of her, full of fierce planets with eyes that were each ringed in green and set against a sun that was gold in one second's light and salmon-colored in the next. She might have been looking at a map of the universe but she didn't notice it any more than she did the spots of sky that cracked the dull green of the tree. She was having an inner vision instead. She was seeing the ten million billion of them pushing their way into new places over here and herself, a giant angel with wings as wide as a house, telling the Negroes that they would have to find another place. She turned herself in the direction of the barn, musing on this, her expression lofty and satisfied.

She approached the barn from an oblique angle that allowed her a look in the door before she could be seen herself. Mr. Chancey Shortley was adjusting the last milking machine on a large black and white spotted cow near the entrance, squatting at her heels. There was about a half-inch of cigarette adhering to the center of his lower lip. Mrs. Shortley observed it minutely for half a second. "If she seen or heard of you smoking in this barn, she would blow a fuse," she said.

Mr. Shortley raised a sharply rutted face containing a washout under each cheek and two long crevices eaten down both sides of his blistered mouth. "You gonter be the one to tell her?" he asked.

"She's got a nose of her own," Mrs. Shortley said.

Mr. Shortley, without appearing to give the feat any

consideration, lifted the cigarette stub with the sharp en of his tongue, drew it into his mouth, closed his lips tightly rose, stepped out, gave his wife a good round appreciativ stare, and spit the smoldering butt into the grass.

"Aw Chancey," she said, "haw haw," and she dug little hole for it with her toe and covered it up. This tric of Mr. Shortley's was actually his way of making lov to her. When he had done his courting, he had not brough a guitar to strum or anything pretty for her to keep, bu had sat on her porch steps, not saying a word, imitatin a paralyzed man propped up to enjoy a cigarette. Whe the cigarette got the proper size, he would turn his eye to her and open his mouth and draw in the butt and the sit there as if he had swallowed it, looking at her wit the most loving look anybody could imagine. It nearly drove her wild and every time he did it, she wanted t pull his hat down over his eyes and hug him to death.

"Well," she said, going into the barn after him, "the Gobblehooks have come and she wants you to meet them says, 'Where's Mr. Shortley?' and I says, 'He don't hav time...'"

"Tote up them weights," Mr. Shortley said, squatting to the cow again.

"You reckon he can drive a tractor when he don't know English?" she asked. "I don't think she's going to get he money's worth out of them. That boy can talk but he looks delicate. The one can work can't talk and the one can talk can't work. She ain't any better off than if she had more niggers."

"I rather have a nigger if it was me," Mr. Shortley said.

"She says it's ten million more like them, Displaced Persons, she says that there priest can get her all she wants."

"She better quit messin with that there priest," Mr. Shortley said.

"He don't look smart," Mrs. Shortley said, "—kind of foolish."

"I ain't going to have the Pope of Rome tell me how to run no dairy," Mr. Shortley said.

"They ain't Eye-talians, they're Poles," she said. "From Poland where all them bodies were stacked up at. You remember all them bodies?"

"I give them three weeks here," Mr. Shortley said.

Three weeks later Mrs. McIntyre and Mrs. Shortley drove to the cane bottom to see Mr. Guizac start to operate the silage cutter, a new machine that Mrs. McIntyre had just bought because she said, for the first time, she had

omebody who could operate it. Mr. Guizac could drive
a tractor, use the rotary hay-baler, the silage cutter, the
combine, the letz mill, or any other machine she had on
the place. He was an expert mechanic, a carpenter, and
a mason. He was thrifty and energetic. Mrs. McIntyre said
she figured he would save her twenty dollars a month on
repair bills alone. She said getting him was the best day's
work she had ever done in her life. He could work milking
machines and he was scrupulously clean. He did not smoke.

She parked her car on the edge of the cane field and
they got out. Sulk, the young Negro, was attaching the
wagon to the cutter and Mr. Guizac was attaching the
cutter to the tractor. He finished first and pushed the colored
boy out of the way and attached the wagon to the cutter
himself, gesticulating with a bright angry face when he
wanted the hammer or the screwdriver. Nothing was done
quick enough to suit him. The Negroes made him nervous.

The week before, he had come upon Sulk at the dinner
hour, sneaking with a croker sack into the pen where the
young turkeys were. He had watched him take a frying-size
turkey from the lot and thrust it in the sack and put the
sack under his coat. Then he had followed him around the
barn, jumped on him, dragged him to Mrs. McIntyre's
back door and had acted out the entire scene for her,
while the Negro muttered and grumbled and said God
might strike him dead if he had been stealing any turkey,
he had only been taking it to put some black shoe polish
on its head because it had the sorehead. God might strike
him dead if that was not the truth before Jesus. Mrs. McIntyre
told him to go put the turkey back and then she was a
long time explaining to the Pole that all Negroes would
steal. She finally had to call Rudolph and tell him in English
and have him tell his father in Polish, and Mr. Guizac
had gone off with a startled disappointed face.

Mrs. Shortley stood by hoping there would be trouble
with the silage machine but there was none. All of Mr.
Guizac's motions were quick and accurate. He jumped on
the tractor like a monkey and maneuvered the big orange
cutter into the cane; in a second the silage was spurting
in a green jet out of the pipe into the wagon. He went
jolting down the row until he disappeared from sight and
the noise became remote.

Mrs. McIntyre sighed with pleasure. "At last," she said,
"I've got somebody I can depend on. For years I've been
fooling with sorry people. Sorry people. Poor white trash
and niggers," she muttered. "They've drained me dry.
Before you all came I had Ringfields and Collins and Jarrells

and Perkins and Pinkins and Herrins and God knows what all else and not a one of them left without taking something off this place that didn't belong to them. Not a one!"

Mrs. Shortley could listen to this with composure because she knew that if Mrs. McIntyre had considered her trash, they couldn't have talked about trashy people together. Neither of them approved of trash. Mrs. McIntyre continued with the monologue that Mrs. Shortley had heard oftentimes before. "I've been running this place for thirty years," she said, looking with a deep frown out over the field, "and always just barely making it. People think you're made of money. I have the taxes to pay. I have the insurance to keep up. I have the repair bills. I have the feed bills." It all gathered up and she stood with her chest lifted and her small hands gripped around her elbows. "Ever since the Judge died," she said, "I've barely been making ends meet and they all take something when they leave. The niggers don't leave—they stay and steal. A nigger thinks anybody is rich he can steal from and that white trash thinks anybody is rich who can afford to hire people as sorry as they are. And all I've got is the dirt under my feet!"

You hire and fire, Mrs. Shortley thought, but she didn't always say what she thought. She stood by and let Mrs. McIntyre say it all out to the end but this time it didn't end as usual. "But at last I'm saved!" Mrs. McIntyre said. "One fellow's misery is the other fellow's gain. That man there," and she pointed where the Displaced Person had disappeared, "—he has to work! He wants to work!" She turned to Mrs. Shortley with her bright wrinkled face. "That man is my salvation!" she said.

Mrs. Shortley looked straight ahead as if her vision penetrated the cane and the hill and pierced through to the other side. "I would suspicion salvation got from the devil," she said in a slow detached way.

"Now what do you mean by that?" Mrs. McIntyre asked, looking at her sharply.

Mrs. Shortley wagged her head but would not say anything else. The fact was she had nothing else to say for this intuition had only at that instant come to her. She had never given much thought to the devil for she felt that religion was essentially for those people who didn't have the brains to avoid evil without it. For people like herself, for people of gumption, it was a social occasion providing the opportunity to sing; but if she had ever given it much thought, she would have considered the devil the head of it and God the hanger-on. With the coming of these displaced people, she was obliged to give new thought to a good many things.

"I know what Sledgewig told Annie Maude," she said, and when Mrs. McIntyre carefully did not ask her what but reached down and broke off a sprig of sassafras to chew, she continued in a way to indicate she was not telling all, "that they wouldn't be able to live long, the four of them, on seventy dollars a month."

"He's worth raising," Mrs. McIntyre said. "He saves me money."

This was as much as to say that Chancey had never saved her money. Chancey got up at four in the morning to milk her cows, in winter wind and summer heat, and he had been doing it for the last two years. They had been with her the longest she had ever had anybody. The gratitude they got was these hints that she hadn't been saved any money.

"Is Mr. Shortley feeling better today?" Mrs. McIntyre asked.

Mrs. Shortley thought it was about time she was asking that question. Mr. Shortley had been in bed two days with an attack. Mr. Guizac had taken his place in the dairy in addition to doing his own work. "No he ain't," she said. "That doctor said he was suffering from over-exhaustion."

"If Mr. Shortley is over-exhausted," Mrs. McIntyre said, "then he must have a second job on the side," and she looked at Mrs. Shortley with almost closed eyes as if she were examining the bottom of a milk can.

Mrs. Shortley did not say a word but her dark suspicion grew like a black thunder cloud. The fact was that Mr. Shortley did have a second job on the side and that, in a free country, this was none of Mrs. McIntyre's business. Mr. Shortley made whisky. He had a small still back in the farthest reaches of the place, on Mrs. McIntyre's land to be sure, but on land that she only owned and did not cultivate, on idle land that was not doing anybody any good. Mr. Shortley was not afraid of work. He got up at four in the morning and milked her cows and in the middle of the day when he was supposed to be resting, he was off attending to his still. Not every man would work like that. The Negroes knew about his still but he knew about theirs so there had never been any disagreeableness between them. But with foreigners on the place, with people who were all eyes and no understanding, who had come from a place continually fighting, where the religion had not been reformed—with this kind of people, you had to be on the lookout every minute. She thought there ought to be a law against them. There was no reason they couldn't stay over there and take the places of some of the people who had been killed in their wars and butcherings.

"What's furthermore," she said suddenly, "Sledgewig said as soon as her papa saved the money, he was going to buy him a used car. Once they get them a used car, they'll leave you."

"I can't pay him enough for him to save money," Mrs. McIntyre said. "I'm not worrying about that. Of course," she said then, "if Mr. Shortley got incapacitated, I would have to use Mr. Guizac in the dairy all the time and I would have to pay him more. He doesn't smoke," she said, and it was the fifth time within the week that she had pointed this out.

"It is no man," Mrs. Shortley said emphatically, "that works as hard as Chancey, or is as easy with a cow, or is more of a Christian," and she folded her arms and her gaze pierced the distance. The noise of the tractor and cutter increased and Mr. Guizac appeared coming around the other side of the cane row. "Which can not be said about everybody," she muttered. She wondered whether, if the Pole found Chancey's still, he would know what it was. The trouble with these people was, you couldn't tell what they knew. Every time Mr. Guizac smiled, Europe stretched out in Mrs. Shortley's imagination, mysterious and evil, the devil's experiment station.

The tractor, the cutter, the wagon passed, rattling and rumbling and grinding before them. "Think how long that would have taken with men and mules to do it," Mrs. McIntyre shouted. "We'll get this whole bottom cut within two days at this rate."

"Maybe," Mrs. Shortley muttered, "if don't no terrible accident occur." She thought how the tractor had made mules worthless. Nowadays you couldn't give away a mule. The next thing to go, she reminded herself, will be niggers.

In the afternoon she explained what was going to happen to them to Astor and Sulk who were in the cow lot, filling the manure spreader. She sat down next to the block of salt under a small shed, her stomach in her lap, her arms on top of it. "All you colored people better look out," she said. "You know how much you can get for a mule."

"Nothing, no indeed," the old man said, "not one thing."

"Before it was a tractor," she said, "it could be a mule. And before it was a Displaced Person, it could be a nigger. The time is going to come," she prophesied, "when it won't be no more occasion to speak of a nigger."

The old man laughed politely. "Yes indeed," he said. "Ha ha."

The young one didn't say anything. He only looked sullen but when she had gone in the house, he said, "Big Belly act like she know everything."

"Never mind," the old man said, "your place too low for anybody to dispute with you for it."

She didn't tell her fears about the still to Mr. Shortley until he was back on the job in the dairy. Then one night after they were in bed, she said, "That man prowls."

Mr. Shortley folded his hands on his bony chest and pretended he was a corpse.

"Prowls," she continued and gave him a sharp kick in the side with her knee. "Who's to say what they know and don't know? Who's to say if he found it he wouldn't go right to her and tell? How you know they don't make liquor in Europe? They drive tractors. They got them all kinds of machinery. Answer me."

"Don't worry me now," Mr. Shortley said. "I'm a dead man."

"It's them little eyes of his that's foreign," she muttered. "And that way he's got of shrugging." She drew her shoulders up and shrugged several times. "How come he's got anything to shrug about?" she asked.

"If everybody was as dead as I am, nobody would have no trouble," Mr. Shortley said.

"That priest," she muttered and was silent for a minute. Then she said, "In Europe they probably got some different way to make liquor but I reckon they know all the ways. They're full of crooked ways. They never have advanced or reformed. They got the same religion as a thousand years ago. It could only be the devil responsible for that. Always fighting amongst each other. Disputing. And then get us into it. Ain't they got us into it twict already and we ain't got no more sense than to go over there and settle it for them and then they come on back over here and snoop around and find your still and go straight to her. And liable to kiss her hand any minute. Do you hear me?"

"No," Mr. Shortley said.

"And I'll tell you another thing," she said. "I wouldn't be a tall surprised if he don't know everything you say, whether it be in English or not."

"I don't speak no other language," Mr. Shortley murmured.

"I suspect," she said, "that before long there won't be no more niggers on this place. And I tell you what. I'd rather have niggers than them Poles. And what's furthermore,

I aim to take up for the niggers when the time comes. When Gobblehook first come here, you recollect how he shook their hands, like he didn't know the difference, like he might have been as black as them, but when it come to finding out Sulk was taking turkeys, he gone on and told her. I known he was taking turkeys. I could have told her myself."

Mr. Shortley was breathing softly as if he were asleep.

"A nigger don't know when he has a friend," she said. "And I'll tell you another thing. I get a heap out of Sledgewig. Sledgewig said that in Poland they lived in a brick house and one night a man come and told them to get out of it before daylight. Do you believe they ever lived in a brick house?

"Airs," she said. "That's just airs. A wooden house is good enough for me. Chancey," she said, "turn thisaway. I hate to see niggers mistreated and run out. I have a heap of pity for niggers and poor folks. Ain't I always had?" she asked. "I say ain't I always been a friend to niggers and poor folks?

"When the time comes," she said, "I'll stand up for the niggers and that's that. I ain't going to see that priest drive out all the niggers."

Mrs. McIntyre bought a new drag harrow and a tractor with a power lift because she said, for the first time, she had someone who could handle machinery. She and Mrs. Shortley had driven to the back field to inspect what he had harrowed the day before. "That's been done beautifully!" Mrs. McIntyre said, looking out over the red undulating ground.

Mrs. McIntyre had changed since the Displaced Person had been working for her and Mrs. Shortley had observed the change very closely: she had begun to act like somebody who was getting rich secretly and she didn't confide in Mrs. Shortley the way she used to. Mrs. Shortley suspected that the priest was at the bottom of the change. They were very slick. First he would get her into his Church and then he would get his hand in her pocketbook. Well, Mrs. Shortley thought, the more fool she! Mrs. Shortley had a secret herself. She knew something the Displaced Person was doing that would floor Mrs. McIntyre. "I still say he ain't going to work forever for seventy dollars a month," she murmured. She intended to keep her secret to herself and Mr. Shortley.

"Well," Mrs. McIntyre said, "I may have to get rid of some of this other help so I can pay him more."

Mrs. Shortley nodded to indicate she had known this for some time. "I'm not saying those niggers ain't had it coming," she said. "But they do the best they know how. You can always tell a nigger what to do and stand by until he does it."

"That's what the Judge said," Mrs. McIntyre said and looked at her with approval. The Judge was her first husband, the one who had left her the place. Mrs. Shortley had heard that she had married him when she was thirty and he was seventy-five, thinking she would be rich as soon as he died, but the old man was a scoundrel and when his estate was settled, they found he didn't have a nickel. All he left her were the fifty acres and the house. But she always spoke of him in a reverent way and quoted his sayings, such as, "One fellow's misery is the other fellow's gain," and "The devil you know is better than the devil you don't."

"However," Mrs. Shortley remarked, "the devil you know is better than the devil you don't," and she had to turn away so that Mrs. McIntyre would not see her smile. She had found out what the Displaced Person was up to through the old man, Astor, and she had not told anybody but Mr. Shortley. Mr. Shortley had risen straight up in bed like Lazarus from the tomb.

"Shut your mouth!" he had said.

"Yes," she had said.

"Naw!" Mr. Shortley had said.

"Yes," she had said.

Mr. Shortley had fallen back flat.

"The Pole don't know any better," Mrs. Shortley had said. "I reckon that priest is putting him up to it is all. I blame the priest."

The priest came frequently to see the Guizacs and he would always stop in and visit Mrs. McIntyre too and they would walk around the place and she would point out her improvements and listen to his rattling talk. It suddenly came to Mrs. Shortley that he was trying to persuade her to bring another Polish family onto the place. With two of them here, there would be almost nothing spoken but Polish! The Negroes would be gone and there would be the two families against Mr. Shortley and herself! She began to imagine a war of words, to see the Polish words and the English words coming at each other, stalking forward, not sentences, just words, gabble gabble gabble, flung out high and shrill and stalking forward and then grappling with each other. She saw the Polish words, dirty and all-knowing and unreformed, flinging mud on the clean English words until everything was equally dirty. She saw them all piled up in a room, all the dead dirty words, theirs and hers too, piled up like the naked bodies in the newsreel. God save me! she cried silently, from the stinking power of Satan! And she started from that day to read her Bible with a new attention. She poured over the Apocalypse and began to quote from the Prophets and before long she had come to a deeper understanding of her existence. She saw plainly that the meaning of the world was a mystery that had been planned and she was not surprised to suspect that she had a special part in the plan because she was strong. She saw that the Lord God Almighty had created the strong people to do what had to be done and she felt that she would be ready when she was called. Right now she felt that her business was to watch the priest.

His visits irked her more and more. On the last one, he went about picking up feathers off the ground. He found two peacock feathers and four or five turkey feathers and an old brown hen feather and took them off with him like a bouquet. This foolish-acting did not deceive Mrs. Shortley any. Here he was: leading foreigners over in hoards to places that were not theirs, to cause disputes, to uproot niggers, to plant the Whore of Babylon in the midst of the righteous! Whenever he came on the place, she hid herself behind something and watched until he left.

It was on a Sunday afternoon that she had her vision. She had gone to drive in the cows for Mr. Shortley who had a pain in his knee and she was walking slowly through the pasture, her arms folded, her eyes on the distant low-lying clouds that looked like rows and rows of white fish washed up on a great blue beach. She paused after an incline to heave a sigh of exhaustion for she had an immense weight to carry around and she was not as young as she used to be. At times she could feel her heart, like a child's fist, clenching and unclenching inside her chest, and when the feeling came, it stopped her thought altogether and she would go about like a large hull of herself, moving for no reason; but she gained this incline without a tremor and stood at the top of it, pleased with herself. Suddenly while she watched, the sky folded back in two pieces like the curtain to a stage and a gigantic figure stood facing her. It was the color of the sun in the early afternoon, white-gold. It was of no definite shape but there were fiery wheels with fierce dark eyes in them, spinning rapidly all around it. She was not able to tell if the figure was going forward or backward because its magnificence was so great. She shut her eyes in order to look at it and it turned blood-red and the wheels turned white. A voice, very resonant, said the one word, "Prophesy!"

She stood there, tottering slightly but still upright, her eyes shut tight and her fists clenched and her straw sun hat low on her forehead. "The children of wicked nations will be butchered," she said in a loud voice. "Legs where arms should be, foot to face, ear in the palm of hand. Who will remain whole? Who will remain whole? Who?"

Presently she opened her eyes. The sky was full of white fish carried lazily on their sides by some invisible current and pieces of the sun, submerged some distance beyond them, appeared from time to time as if they were being washed in the opposite direction. Woodenly she planted one foot in front of the other until she had crossed the pasture and reached the lot. She walked through the barn like one in a daze and did not speak to Mr. Shortley. She continued up the road until she saw the priest's car parked in front of Mrs. McIntyre's house. "Here again," she muttered. "Come to destroy."

Mrs. McIntyre and the priest were walking in the yard. In order not to meet them face to face, she turned to the left and entered the feed house, a single-room shack piled on one side with flowered sacks of scratch feed. There were spilled oyster shells in one corner and a few old dirty calendars on the wall, advertising calf feed and various patent medicine remedies. One showed a bearded gentleman in a frock coat, holding up a bottle, and beneath his feet was the inscription, "I have been made regular by this marvelous discovery!" Mrs. Shortley had always felt close to this man as if he were some distinguished person she was acquainted with but now her mind was on nothing but the dangerous presence of the priest. She stationed herself at a crack between two boards where she could look out and see him and Mrs. McIntyre strolling toward the turkey brooder, which was placed just outside the feed house.

"Arrrrr!" he said as they approached the brooder. "Look at the little biddies!" and he stooped and squinted through the wire.

Mrs. Shortley's mouth twisted.

"Do you think the Guizacs will want to leave me?" Mrs. McIntyre asked. "Do you think they'll go to Chicago or some place like that?"

"And why should they do that now?" asked the priest, wiggling his finger at a turkey, his big nose close to the wire.

"Money," Mrs. McIntyre said.

"Arrrr, give them some morrre then," he said indifferently. "They have to get along."

"So do I," Mrs. McIntyre muttered. "It means I'm going to have to get rid of some of these others."

"And arrre the Shortleys satisfactory?" he inquired, paying more attention to the turkeys than to her.

"Five times in the last month I've found Mr. Shortley smoking in the barn," Mrs. McIntyre said. "Five times."

"And arrre the Negroes any better?"

"They lie and steal and have to be watched all the time," she said.

"Tsk, tsk," he said. "Which will you discharge?"

"I've decided to give Mr. Shortley his month's notice tomorrow," Mrs. McIntyre said.

The priest scarcely seemed to hear her he was so busy wiggling his finger inside the wire. Mrs. Shortley sat down on an open sack of laying mash with a dead thump that sent feed dust clouding up around her. She found herself looking straight ahead at the opposite wall where the gentleman on the calendar was holding up his marvelous discovery but she didn't see him. She looked ahead as if she saw nothing whatsoever. Then she rose and ran to her house. Her face was an almost volcanic red.

She opened all the drawers and dragged out boxes and old battered suitcases from under the bed. She began to unload the drawers into the boxes, all the time without pause, without taking off the sunhat she had on her head. She set the two girls to doing the same. When Mr. Shortley came in, she did not even look at him but merely pointed one arm at him while she packed with the other. "Bring the car around to the back door," she said. "You ain't waiting to be fired!"

Mr. Shortley had never in his life doubted her omniscience. He perceived the entire situation in half a second and, with only a sour scowl, retreated out the door and went to drive the automobile around to the back.

They tied the two iron beds to the top of the car and the two rocking chairs inside the beds and rolled the two mattresses up between the rocking chairs. On top of this they tied a crate of chickens. They loaded the inside of the car with the old suitcases and boxes, leaving a small space for Annie Maude and Sarah Mae. It took them the rest of the afternoon and half the night to do this but Mrs. Shortley was determined that they would leave before four o'clock in the morning, that Mr. Shortley should not adjust another milking machine on this place. All the time she had been working, her face was changing rapidly from red to white and back again.

Just before dawn, as it began to drizzle rain, they were ready to leave. They all got in the car and sat there cramped up between boxes and bundles and rolls of bedding. The square black automobile moved off with more than its customary grinding noises as if it were protesting the load. In the back, the two long bony yellow-haired girls were sitting on a pile of boxes and there was a beagle hound puppy and a cat with two kittens somewhere under the blankets. The car moved slowly, like some overfreighted leaking ark, away from their shack and past the white house where Mrs. McIntyre was sleeping soundly—hardly guessing that her cows would not be milked by Mr. Shortley that morning—and past the Pole's shack on top of the hill and on down the road to the gate where the two Negroes were walking, one behind the other, on their way to help with the milking. They looked straight at the car and its occupants but even as the dim yellow headlights lit up their faces, they politely did not seem to see anything, or anyhow, to attach significance to what was there. The loaded car might have been passing mist in the early morning half-light. They continued up the road at the same even pace without looking back.

A dark yellow sun was beginning to rise in a sky that was the same slick dark gray as the highway. The fields stretched away, stiff and weedy, on either side. "Where we goin?" Mr. Shortley asked for the first time.

Mrs. Shortley sat with one foot on a packing box so that her knee was pushed into her stomach. Mr. Shortley's elbow was almost under her nose and Sarah Mae's bare left foot was sticking over the front seat, touching her ear.

"Where we goin?" Mr. Shortley repeated and when she didn't answer again, he turned and looked at her.

Fierce heat seemed to be swelling slowly and fully into her face as if it were welling up now for a final assault. She was sitting in an erect way in spite of the fact that one leg was twisted under her and one knee was almost into her neck, but there was a peculiar lack of light in her icy blue eyes. All the vision in them might have been turned around, looking inside her. She suddenly grabbed Mr. Shortley's elbow and Sarah Mae's foot at the same time and began to tug and pull on them as if she were trying to fit the two extra limbs onto herself.

Mr. Shortley began to curse and quickly stopped the car and Sarah Mae yelled to quit but Mrs. Shortley apparently intended to rearrange the whole car at once. She thrashed forward and backward, clutching at everything she could get her hands on and hugging it to herself, Mr. Shortley's head, Sarah Mae's leg, the cat, a wad of white bedding, her own big moon-like knee; then all at once her fierce expression faded into a look of astonishment and her grip on what she had loosened. One of her eyes drew near to the other and seemed to collapse quietly and she was still.

The two girls, who didn't know what had happened to her, began to say, "Where we goin, Ma? Where we goin?" They thought she was playing a joke and that their father, staring straight ahead at her, was imitating a dead man. They didn't know that she had had a great experience or ever been displaced in the world from all that belonged to her. They were frightened by the gray slick road before them and they kept repeating in higher and higher voices, "Where we goin, Ma? Where we goin?" while their mother, her huge body rolled back still against the seat and her eyes like blue-painted glass, seemed to contemplate for the first time the tremendous frontiers of her true country.

II

"Well," Mrs. McIntyre said to the old Negro, "we can get along without them. We've seen them come and seen them go—black and white." She was standing in the calf barn while he cleaned it and she held a rake in her hand and now and then pulled a corn cob from a corner or pointed to a soggy spot that he had missed. When she discovered the Shortleys were gone, she was delighted as it meant she wouldn't have to fire them. The people she hired always left her—because they were that kind of people. Of all the families she had had, the Shortleys were the best if she didn't count the Displaced Person. They had been not quite trash; Mrs. Shortley was a good woman, and she would miss her but as the Judge used to say, you couldn't have your pie and eat it too, and she was satisfied with the D.P. "We've seen them come and seen them go," she repeated with satisfaction.

"And me and you," the old man said, stooping to drag his hoe under a feed rack, "is still here."

She caught exactly what he meant her to catch in his tone. Bars of sunlight fell from the cracked ceiling across his back and cut him in three distinct parts. She watched his long hands clenched around the hoe and his crooked old profile pushed close to them. You might have been here *before* I was, she said to herself, but it's mighty likely

I'll be here when you're gone. "I've spent half my life fooling with worthless people," she said in a severe voice, "but now I'm through."

"Black and white," he said, "is the same."

"I am through," she repeated and gave her dark smock that she had thrown over her shoulders like a cape a quick snatch at the neck. She had on a broad-brimmed black straw hat that had cost her twenty dollars twenty years ago and that she used now for a sunhat. "Money is the root of all evil," she said. "The Judge said so every day. He said he deplored money. He said the reason you niggers were so uppity was because there was so much money in circulation."

The old Negro had known the Judge. "Judge say he long for the day when he be too poor to pay a nigger to work," he said. "Say when that day come, the world be back on its feet."

She leaned forward, her hands on her hips and her neck stretched and said, "Well that day has almost come around here and I'm telling each and every one of you: you better look sharp. I don't have to put up with foolishness any more. I have somebody now who *has* to work!"

The old man knew when to answer and when not. At length he said, "We seen them come and we seen them go."

"However, the Shortleys were not the worst by far," she said. "I well remember those Garrits."

"They was before them Collinses," he said.

"No, before the Ringfields."

"Sweet Lord, them Ringfields!" he murmured.

"None of that kind *want* to work," she said.

"We seen them come and we seen them go," he said as if this were a refrain. "But we ain't never had one before," he said, bending himself up until he faced her, "like what we got now." He was cinnamon-colored with eyes that were so blurred with age that they seemed to be hung behind cobwebs.

She gave him an intense stare and held it until, lowering his hands on the hoe, he bent down again and dragged a pile of shavings alongside the wheelbarrow. She said stiffly, "He can wash out that barn in the time it took Mr. Shortley to make up his mind he had to do it."

"He from Pole," the old man muttered.

"From Poland."

"In Pole it ain't like it is here," he said. "They got different ways of doing," and he began to mumble unintelligibly.

"What are you saying?" she said. "If you have anything

to say about him, say it and say it aloud."

He was silent, bending his knees precariously and edging the rake along the underside of the trough.

"If you know anything he's done that he shouldn't, I expect you to report it to me," she said.

"It warn't like it was what he should ought or oughtn't," he muttered. "It was like what nobody else don't do."

"You don't have anything against him," she said shortly, "and he's here to stay."

"We ain't never had one like him before is all," he murmured and gave his polite laugh.

"Times are changing," she said. "Do you know what's happening to this world? It's swelling up. It's getting so full of people that only the smart thrifty energetic ones are going to survive," and she tapped the words, smart, thrifty, and energetic out on the palm of her hand. Through the far end of the stall she could see down the road to where the Displaced Person was standing in the open barn door with the green hose in his hand. There was a certain stiffness about his figure that seemed to make it necessary for her to approach him slowly, even in her thoughts. She had decided this was because she couldn't hold an easy conversation with him. Whenever she said anything to him, she found herself shouting and nodding extravagantly and she would be conscious that one of the Negroes was leaning behind the nearest shed, watching.

"No indeed!" she said, sitting down on one of the feed racks and folding her arms, "I've made up my mind that I've had enough trashy people on this place to last me a lifetime and I'm not going to spend my last years fooling with Shortleys and Ringfields and Collins when the world is full of people who *have* to work."

"Howcome they so many extra?" he asked.

"People are selfish," she said. "They have too many children. There's no sense in it any more."

He had picked up the wheelbarrow handles and was backing out the door and he paused, half in the sunlight and half out, and stood there chewing his gums as if he had forgotten which direction he wanted to move in.

"What you colored people don't realize," she said, "is that I'm the one around here who holds all the strings together. If you don't work, I don't make any money and I can't pay you. You're all dependent on me but you each and every one act like the shoe is on the other foot."

It was not possible to tell from his face if he heard her. Finally he backed out with the wheelbarrow. "Judge say the devil he know is better than the devil he don't," he said in a clear mutter and trundled off.

She got up and followed him, a deep vertical pit appearing suddenly in the center of her forehead, just under the red bangs. "The Judge has long since ceased to pay the bills around here," she called in a piercing voice.

He was the only one of her Negroes who had known the Judge and he thought this gave him title. He had had a low opinion of Mr. Crooms and Mr. McIntyre, her other husbands, and in his veiled polite way, he had congratulated her after each of her divorces. When he thought it necessary, he would work under a window where he knew she was sitting and talk to himself, a careful roundabout discussion, question and answer and then refrain. Once she had got up silently and slammed the window down so hard that he had fallen backwards off his feet. Or occasionally he spoke with the peacock. The cock would follow him around the place, his steady eye on the ear of corn that stuck up from the old man's back pocket or he would sit near him and pick himself. Once from the open kitchen door, she had heard him say to the bird, "I remember when it was twenty of you walking about this place and now it's only you and two hens. Crooms it was twelve. McIntyre it was five. You and two hens now."

And that time she had stepped out of the door onto the porch and said, "MISTER Crooms and MISTER McIntyre! And I don't want to hear you call either of them anything else again. And you can understand this: when that peachicken dies there won't be any replacements."

She kept the peacock only out of a superstitious fear of annoying the Judge in his grave. He had liked to see them walking around the place for he said they made him feel rich. Of her three husbands, the Judge was the one most present to her although he was the only one she had buried. He was in the family graveyard, a little space fenced in the middle of the back cornfield, with his mother and father and grandfather and three great aunts and two infant cousins. Mr. Crooms, her second, was forty miles away in the state asylum and Mr. McIntyre, her last, was intoxicated, she supposed, in some hotel room in Florida. But the Judge, sunk in the cornfield with his family, was always at home.

She had married him when he was an old man and because of his money but there had been another reason that she would not admit then, even to herself: she had liked him. He was a dirty snuff-dipping Court House figure, famous all over the county for being rich, who wore hightop shoes, a string tie, a gray suit with a black stripe in it, and a yellowed panama hat, winter and summer. His teeth and hair were tobacco-colored and his face a clay pink pitted and tracked with mysterious prehistoric-looking marks as if he had been unearthed among fossils. There had been a peculiar odor about him of sweaty fondled bills but he never carried money on him or had a nickel to show. She was his secretary for a few months and the old man with his sharp eye had seen at once that here was a woman who admired him for himself. The three years that he lived after they married were the happiest and most prosperous of Mrs. McIntyre's life, but when he died his estate proved to be bankrupt. He left her a mortgaged house and fifty acres that he had managed to cut the timber off before he died. It was as if, as the final triumph of a successful life, he had been able to take everything with him.

But she had survived. She had survived a succession of tenant farmers and dairymen that the old man himself would have found hard to outdo, and she had been able to meet the constant drain of a tribe of moody unpredictable Negroes, and she had even managed to hold her own against the incidental bloodsuckers, the cattle dealers and lumber men and the buyers and sellers of anything who drove up in pieced-together trucks and honked in the yard.

She stood slightly reared back with her arms folded under her smock and a satisfied expression on her face as she watched the Displaced Person turn off the hose and disappear inside the barn. She was sorry that the poor man had been chased out of Poland and run across Europe and had had to take up in a tenant shack in a strange country, but she had not been responsible for any of this. She had had a hard time herself. She knew what it was to struggle. People ought to have to struggle. Mr. Guizac had probably had everything given to him all the way across Europe and over here. He had probably not had to struggle enough. She had given him a job. She didn't know if he was grateful or not. She didn't know anything about him except that he did the work. The truth was that he was not very real to her yet. He was a kind of miracle that she had seen happen and that she talked about but that she still didn't believe.

She watched as he came out of the barn and motioned to Sulk, who was coming around the back of the lot. He gesticulated and then took something out of his pocket and the two of them stood looking at it. She started down the lane toward them. The Negro's figure was slack and tall and he was craning his round head forward in his usual idiotic way. He was a little better than half-witted but when they were like that they were always good workers. The Judge had said always hire you a half-witted nigger because they don't have sense enough to stop working. The Pole was gesticulating rapidly. He left something with the colored boy and then walked off and before she rounded the turn in the lane, she heard the tractor crank up. He was on his way to the field. The Negro was still hanging there, gaping at whatever he had in his hand.

She entered the lot and walked through the barn, looking with approval at the wet spotless concrete floor. It was only nine-thirty and Mr. Shortley had never got anything washed until eleven. As she came out at the other end, she saw the Negro moving very slowly in a diagonal path across the road in front of her, his eyes still on what Mr. Guizac had given him. He didn't see her and he paused and dipped his knees and leaned over his hand, his tongue describing little circles. He had a photograph. He lifted one finger and traced it lightly over the surface of the picture. Then he looked up and saw her and seemed to freeze, his mouth in a half-grin, his finger lifted.

"Why haven't you gone to the field?" she asked.

He raised one foot and opened his mouth wider while the hand with the photograph edged toward his back pocket.

"What's that?" she said.

"It ain't nothin," he muttered and handed it to her automatically.

It was a photograph of a girl of about twelve in a white dress. She had blond hair with a wreath in it and she looked forward out of light eyes that were bland and composed. "Who is this child?" Mrs. McIntyre asked.

"She his cousin," the boy said in a high voice.

"Well what are you doing with it?" she asked.

"She going to mah me," he said in an even higher voice.

"Marry you!" she shrieked.

"I pays half to get her over here," he said. "I pays him three dollar a week. She bigger now. She his cousin. She don't care who she mah she so glad to get away from there." The high voice seemed to shoot up like a nervous jet of sound and then fall flat as he watched her face. Her eyes were the color of blue granite when the glare falls on it, but she was not looking at him. She was looking down the road where the distant sound of the tractor could be heard.

"I don't reckon she goin to come nohow," the boy murmured.

"I'll see that you get every cent of your money back,"

she said in a toneless voice and turned and walked off, holding the photograph bent in two. There was nothing about her small stiff figure to indicate that she was shaken.

As soon as she got in the house, she lay down on her bed and shut her eyes and pressed her hand over her heart as if she were trying to keep it in place. Her mouth opened and she made two or three dry little sounds. Then after a minute she sat up and said aloud, "They're all the same. It's always been like this," and she fell back flat again. "Twenty years of being beaten and done in and they even robbed his grave!" and remembering that, she began to cry quietly, wiping her eyes every now and then with the hem of her smock.

What she had thought of was the angel over the Judge's grave. This had been a naked granite cherub that the old man had seen in the city one day in a tombstone store window. He had been taken with it at once, partly because its face reminded him of his wife and partly because he wanted a genuine work of art over his grave. He had come home with it sitting on the green plush train seat beside him. Mrs. McIntyre had never noticed the resemblance to herself. She had always thought it hideous but when the Herrins stole it off the old man's grave, she was shocked and outraged. Mrs. Herrin had thought it very pretty and had walked to the graveyard frequently to see it, and when the Herrins left the angel left with them, all but its toes, for the ax old man Herrin had used to break it off with had struck slightly too high. Mrs. McIntyre had never been able to afford to have it replaced.

When she had cried all she could, she got up and went into the back hall, a closet-like space that was dark and quiet as a chapel and sat down on the edge of the Judge's black mechanical chair with her elbow on his desk. This was a giant roll-top piece of furniture pocked with pigeon holes full of dusty papers. Old bankbooks and ledgers were stacked in the half-open drawers and there was a small safe, empty but locked, set like a tabernacle in the center of it. She had left this part of the house unchanged since the old man's time. It was a kind of memorial to him, sacred because he had conducted his business here. With the slightest tilt one way or the other, the chair gave a rusty skeletal groan that sounded something like him when he had complained of his poverty. It had been his first principle to talk as if he were the poorest man in the world and she followed it, not only because he had but because it was true. When she sat with her intense constricted face turned toward the empty safe, she knew there was nobody poorer in the world than she was.

She sat motionless at the desk for ten or fifteen minutes and then as if she had gained some strength, she got up and got in her car and drove to the cornfield.

The road ran through a shadowy pine thicket and ended on top of a hill that rolled fan-wise down and up again in a broad expanse of tasseled green. Mr. Guizac was cutting from the outside of the field in a circular path to the center where the graveyard was all but hidden by the corn, and she could see him on the high far side of the slope, mounted on the tractor with the cutter and wagon behind him. From time to time, he had to get off the tractor and climb in the wagon to spread the silage because the Negro had not arrived. She watched impatiently, standing in front of her black coupe with her arms folded under her smock, while he progressed slowly around the rim of the field, gradually getting close enough for her to wave to him to get down. He stopped the machine and jumped off and came running forward, wiping his red jaw with a piece of grease rag.

"I want to talk to you," she said and beckoned him to the edge of the thicket where it was shady. He took off the cap and followed her, smiling, but his smile faded when she turned and faced him. Her eyebrows, thin and fierce as a spider's leg, had drawn together ominously and the deep vertical pit had plunged down from under the red bangs into the bridge of her nose. She removed the bent picture from her pocket and handed it to him silently. Then she stepped back and said, "Mr. Guizac! You would bring this poor innocent child over here and try to marry her to a half-witted thieving black stinking nigger! What kind of a monster are you!"

He took the photograph with a slowly returning smile. "My cousin," he said. "She twelve here. First Communion. Six-ten now."

Monster! she said to herself and looked at him as if she were seeing him for the first time. His forehead and skull were white where they had been protected by his cap but the rest of his face was red and bristled with short yellow hairs. His eyes were like two bright nails behind his gold-rimmed spectacles that had been mended over the nose with haywire. His whole face looked as if it might have been patched together out of several others. "Mr. Guizac," she said, beginning slowly and then speaking faster until she ended breathless in the middle of a word, "that nigger cannot have a white wife from Europe. You can't talk to a nigger that way. You'll excite him and besides it can't be done. Maybe it can be done in Poland but it can't be done here and you'll have to stop. It's all foolishness. That nigger don't have a grain of sense and you'll excite . . ."

"She in camp three year," he said.

"Your cousin," she said in a positive voice, "cannot come over here and marry one of my Negroes."

"She six-ten year," he said. "From Poland. Mamma die, pappa die. She wait in camp. Three camp." He pulled a wallet from his pocket and fingered through it and took out another picture of the same girl, a few years older, dressed in something dark and shapeless. She was standing against a wall with a short woman who apparently had no teeth. "She mamma," he said, pointing to the woman. "She die in two camp."

"Mr. Guizac," Mrs. McIntyre said, pushing the picture back at him, "I will not have my niggers upset. I cannot run this place without my niggers. I can run it without you but not without them and if you mention this girl to Sulk again, you won't have a job with me. Do you understand?"

His face showed no comprehension. He seemed to be piecing all these words together in his mind to make a thought.

Mrs. McIntyre remembered Mrs. Shortley's words: "He understands everything, he only pretends he don't so as to do exactly as he pleases," and her face regained the look of shocked wrath she had begun with. "I cannot understand how a man who calls himself a Christian," she said, "could bring a poor innocent girl over here and marry her to something like that. I cannot understand it. I cannot!" and she shook her head and looked into the distance with a pained blue gaze.

After a second he shrugged and let his arms drop as if he were tired. "She no care black," he said. "She in camp three year."

Mrs. McIntyre felt a peculiar weakness behind her knees. "Mr. Guizac," she said, "I don't want to have to speak to you about this again. If I do, you'll have to find another place yourself. Do you understand?"

The patched face did not say. She had the impression that he didn't see her there. "This is my place," she said. "I say who will come here and who won't."

"Ya," he said and put back on his cap.

"I am not responsible for the world's misery," she said as an afterthought.

"Ya," he said.

"You have a good job. You should be grateful to be here," she added, "but I'm not sure you are."

"Ya," he said and gave his little shrug and turned back to the tractor.

She watched him get on and maneuver the machine into the corn again. When he had passed her and rounded the turn, she climbed to the top of the slope and stood with her arms folded and looked out grimly over the field. "They're all the same," she muttered, "whether they come from Poland or Tennessee. I've handled Herrins and Ringfields and Shortleys and I can handle a Guizac," and she narrowed her gaze until it closed entirely around the diminishing figure on the tractor as if she were watching him through a gunsight. All her life she had been fighting the world's overflow and now she had it in the form of a Pole. "You're just like all the rest of them," she said, "—only smart and thrifty and energetic but so am I. And this is my place," and she stood there, a small black-hatted, black-smocked figure with an aging cherubic face, and folded her arms as if she were equal to anything. But her heart was beating as if some interior violence had already been done to her. She opened her eyes to include the whole field so that the figure on the tractor was no larger than a grasshopper in her widened view.

She stood there for some time. There was a slight breeze and the corn trembled in great waves on both sides of the slope. The big cutter, with its monotonous roar, continued to shoot it pulverized into the wagon in a steady spurt of fodder. By nightfall, the Displaced Person would have worked his way around and around until there would be nothing on either side of the two hills but the stubble, and down in the center, risen like a little island, the graveyard where the Judge lay grinning under his desecrated monument.

III

The priest, with his long bland face supported on one finger, had been talking for ten minutes about Purgatory while Mrs. McIntyre squinted furiously at him from an opposite chair. They were drinking ginger ale on her front porch and she kept rattling the ice in her glass, rattling her beads, rattling her bracelet like an impatient pony jingling its harness. There is no moral obligation to keep him, she was saying under her breath, there is absolutely no moral obligation. Suddenly she lurched up and her voice fell across his brogue like a drill into a mechanical saw.

"Listen!" she said, "I'm not theological. I'm practical! I want to talk to you about something practical!"

"Arrrrrrr," he groaned, grating to a halt.

She had put at least a finger of whisky in her own ginger ale so that she would be able to endure his full-length visit and she sat down awkwardly, finding the chair closer to her than she had expected. "Mr. Guizac is not satisfactory," she said.

The old man raised his eyebrows in mock wonder.

"He's extra," she said. "He doesn't fit in. I have to have somebody who fits in."

The priest carefully turned his hat on his knees. He had a little trick of waiting a second silently and then swinging the conversation back into his own paths. He was about eighty. She had never known a priest until she had gone to see this one on the business of getting her the Displaced Person. After he had got her the Pole, he had used the business introduction to try to convert her—just as she had supposed he would.

"Give him time," the old man said. "He'll learn to fit in. Where is that beautiful birrrrd of yours?" he asked and then said, "Arrrrr, I see him!" and stood up and looked out over the lawn where the peacock and the two hens were stepping at a strained attention, their long necks ruffled, the cock's violent blue and the hens' silver-green, glinting in the late afternoon sun.

"Mr. Guizac," Mrs. McIntyre continued, bearing down with a flat steady voice, "is very efficient. I'll admit that. But he doesn't understand how to get on with my niggers and they don't like him. I can't have my niggers run off. And I don't like his attitude. He's not the least grateful for being here."

The priest had his hand on the screen door and he opened it, ready to make his escape. "Arrrr, I must be off," he murmured.

"I tell you if I had a white man who understood the Negroes, I'd have to let Mr. Guizac go," she said and stood up again.

He turned then and looked her in the face. "He has nowhere to go," he said. Then he said, "Dear lady, I know you well enough to know you wouldn't turn him out for a trifle!" and without waiting for an answer, he raised his hand and gave her his blessing in a rumbling voice.

She smiled angrily and said, "I didn't create his situation, of course."

The priest let his eyes wander toward the birds. They had reached the middle of the lawn. The cock stopped suddenly and curving his neck backwards, he raised his tail and spread it with a shimmering timbrous noise. Tiers of small pregnant suns floated in a green-gold haze over his head. The priest stood transfixed, his jaw slack. Mrs. McIntyre wondered where she had ever seen such an idiotic old man. "Christ will come like that!" he said in a loud gay voice and wiped his hand over his mouth and stood there, gaping.

Mrs. McIntyre's face assumed a set puritanical expression and she reddened. Christ in the conversation embarrassed her the way sex had her mother. "It is not my responsibility that Mr. Guizac has nowhere to go," she said. "I don't find myself responsible for all the extra people in the world."

The old man didn't seem to hear her. His attention was fixed on the cock who was taking minute steps backward, his head against the spread tail. "The Transfiguration," he murmured.

She had no idea what he was talking about. "Mr. Guizac didn't have to come here in the first place," she said, giving him a hard look.

The cock lowered his tail and began to pick grass.

"He didn't have to come in the first place," she repeated, emphasizing each word.

The old man smiled absently. "He came to redeem us," he said and blandly reached for her hand and shook it and said he must go.

If Mr. Shortley had not returned a few weeks later, she would have gone out looking for a new man to hire. She had not wanted him back but when she saw the familiar black automobile drive up the road and stop by the side of the house, she had the feeling that she was the one returning, after a long miserable trip, to her own place. She realized all at once that it was Mrs. Shortley she had been missing. She had had no one to talk to since Mrs. Shortley left, and she ran to the door, expecting to see her heaving herself up the steps.

Mr. Shortley stood there alone. He had on a black felt hat and a shirt with red and blue palm trees designed in it but the hollows in his long bitten blistered face were deeper than they had been a month ago.

"Well!" she said. "Where is Mrs. Shortley?"

Mr. Shortley didn't say anything. The change in his face seemed to have come from the inside; he looked like a man who had gone for a long time without water. "She was God's own angel," he said in a loud voice. "She was the sweetest woman in the world."

"Where is she?" Mrs. McIntyre murmured.

"Daid," he said. "She had herself a stroke on the day she left out of here." There was a corpse-like composure about his face. "I figure that Pole killed her," he said. "She seen through him from the first. She known he come from the devil. She told me so."

It took Mrs. McIntyre three days to get over Mrs. Shortley's death. She told herself that anyone would have thought they were kin. She rehired Mr. Shortley to do farm work though actually she didn't want him without his wife. She told him she was going to give thirty days' notice to the Displaced Person at the end of the month and that then he could have his job back in the dairy. Mr. Shortley preferred the dairy job but he was willing to wait. He said it would give him some satisfaction to see the Pole leave the place, and Mrs. McIntyre said it would give her a great deal of satisfaction. She confessed that she should have been content with the help she had in the first place and not have been reaching into other parts of the world for it. Mr. Shortley said he never had cared for foreigners since he had been in the first world's war and seen what they were like. He said he had seen all kinds then but that none of them were like us. He said he recalled the face of one man who had thrown a hand-grenade at him and that the man had had little round eye-glasses exactly like Mr. Guizac's.

"But Mr. Guizac is a Pole, he's not a German," Mrs. McIntyre said.

"It ain't a great deal of difference in them two kinds," Mr. Shortley had explained.

The Negroes were pleased to see Mr. Shortley back. The Displaced Person had expected them to work as hard as he worked himself, whereas Mr. Shortley recognized their limitations. He had never been a very good worker himself with Mrs. Shortley to keep him in line, but without her, he was even more forgetful and slow. The Pole worked as fiercely as ever and seemed to have no inkling that he was about to be fired. Mrs. McIntyre saw jobs done in a short time that she had thought would never get done at all. Still she was resolved to get rid of him. The sight of his small stiff figure moving quickly here and there had come to be the most irritating sight on the place for her, and she felt she had been tricked by the old priest. He had said there was no legal obligation for her to keep the Displaced Person if he was not satisfactory, but then he had brought up the moral one.

She meant to tell him that *her* moral obligation was to

her own people, to Mr. Shortley, who had fought in the world war for his country and not to Mr. Guizac who had merely arrived here to take advantage of whatever he could. She felt she must have this out with the priest before she fired the Displaced Person. When the first of the month came and the priest hadn't called, she put off giving the Pole notice for a little longer.

Mr. Shortley told himself that he should have known all along that no woman was going to do what she said she was when she said she was. He didn't know how long he could afford to put up with her shilly-shallying. He thought himself that she was going soft and was afraid to turn the Pole out for fear he would have a hard time getting another place. He could tell her the truth about this: that if she let him go, in three years he would own his own house and have a television aerial sitting on top of it. As a matter of policy, Mr. Shortley began to come to her back door every evening to put certain facts before her. "A white man sometimes don't get the consideration a nigger gets," he said, "but that don't matter because he's still white, but sometimes," and here he would pause and look off into the distance, "a man that's fought and bled and died in the service of his native land don't get the consideration of one of them like them he was fighting. I ast you: is that right?" When he asked her such questions he could watch her face and tell he was making an impression. She didn't look too well these days. He noticed lines around her eyes that hadn't been there when he and Mrs. Shortley had been the only white help on the place. Whenever he thought of Mrs. Shortley, he felt his heart go down like an old bucket into a dry well.

The old priest kept away as if he had been frightened by his last visit but finally, seeing that the Displaced Person had not been fired, he ventured to call again to take up giving Mrs. McIntyre instructions where he remembered leaving them off. She had not asked to be instructed but he instructed anyway, forcing a little definition of one of the sacraments or of some dogma into each conversation he had, no matter with whom. He sat on her porch, taking no notice of her partly mocking, partly outraged expression as she sat shaking her foot, waiting for an opportunity to drive a wedge into his talk. "For," he was saying, as if he spoke of something that had happened yesterday in town, "when God sent his Only Begotten Son, Jesus Christ Our Lord"—he slightly bowed his head—"as a Redeemer to mankind, He . . ."

"Father Flynn!" she said in a voice that made him jump.

"I want to talk to you about something serious!"

The skin under the old man's right eye flinched.

"As far as I'm concerned," she said and glared at him fiercely, "Christ was just another D.P."

He raised his hands slightly and let them drop on his knees. "Arrrrrr," he murmured as if he were considering this.

"I'm going to let that man go," she said. "I don't have any obligation to him. My obligation is to the people who've done something for their country, not to the ones who've just come over to take advantage of what they can get," and she began to talk rapidly, remembering all her arguments. The priest's attention seemed to retire to some private oratory to wait until she got through. Once or twice his gaze roved out onto the lawn as if he were hunting some means of escape but she didn't stop. She told him how she had been hanging onto this place for thirty years, always just barely making it against people who came from nowhere and were going nowhere, who didn't want anything but an automobile. She said she had found out they were the same whether they came from Poland or Tennessee. When the Guizacs got ready, she said, they would not hesitate to leave her. She told him how the people who looked rich were the poorest of all because they had the most to keep up. She asked him how he thought she paid her feed bills. She told him she would like to have her house done over but she couldn't afford it. She couldn't even afford to have the monument restored over her husband's grave. She asked him if he would like to guess what her insurance amounted to for the year. Finally she asked him if he thought she was made of money and the old man suddenly let out a great ugly bellow as if this were a comical question.

When the visit was over, she felt let down, though she had clearly triumphed over him. She made up her mind now that on the first of the month, she would give the Displaced Person his thirty days' notice and she told Mr. Shortley so.

Mr. Shortley didn't say anything. His wife had been the only woman he was ever acquainted with who was never scared off from doing what she said. She said the Pole had been sent by the devil and the priest. Mr. Shortley had no doubt that the priest had got some peculiar control over Mrs. McIntyre and that before long she would start attending his Masses. She looked as if something was wearing her down from the inside. She was thinner and more fidgety and not as sharp as she used to be. She would look at a milk can now and not see how dirty it was and he had seen her lips move when she was not talking. The Pole never did anything the wrong way but all the same he was very irritating to her. Mr. Shortley himself did things as he pleased—not always her way—but she didn't seem to notice. She had noticed though that the Pole and all his family were getting fat; she pointed out to Mr. Shortley that the hollows had come out of their cheeks and that they saved every cent they made. "Yes'm, and one of these days he'll be able to buy and sell you out," Mr. Shortley had ventured to say, and he could tell that the statement had shaken her.

"I'm just waiting for the first," she had said.

Mr. Shortley waited too and the first came and went and she didn't fire him. He could have told anybody how it would be. He was not a violent man but he hated to see a woman done in by a foreigner. He felt that that was one thing a man couldn't stand by and see happen.

There was no reason Mrs. McIntyre should not fire Mr. Guizac at once but she put it off from day to day. She was worried about her bills and about her health. She didn't sleep at night or when she did she dreamed about the Displaced Person. She had never discharged anyone before; they had all left her. One night she dreamed that Mr. Guizac and his family were moving into her house and that she was moving in with Mr. Shortley. This was too much for her and she woke up and didn't sleep again for several nights; and one night she dreamed that the priest came to call and droned on and on, saying, "Dear lady, I know your tender heart won't suffer you to turn the porrrrr man out. Think of the thousands of them, think of the ovens and the boxcars and the camps and the sick children and Christ Our Lord."

"He's extra and he's upset the balance around here," she said, "and I'm a logical practical woman and there are no ovens here and no camps and no Christ Our Lord and when he leaves, he'll make more money. He'll work at the mill and buy a car and don't talk to me—all they want is a car."

"The ovens and the boxcars and the sick children," droned the priest, "and our dear Lord."

"Just one too many," she said.

The next morning, she made up her mind while she was eating her breakfast that she would give him his notice at once, and she stood up and walked out of the kitchen and down the road with her table napkin still in her hand. Mr. Guizac was spraying the barn, standing in his swaybacked way with one hand on his hip. He turned off the hose and gave her an impatient kind of attention as if she were interfering with his work. She had not thought of what she would say to him, she had merely come. She stood in the barn door, looking severely at the wet spotless floor and the dripping stanchions. "Ya goot?" he said.

"Mr. Guizac," she said, "I can barely meet my obligations now." Then she said in a louder, stronger voice, emphasizing each word, "I have bills to pay."

"I too," Mr. Guizac said. "Much bills, little money," and he shrugged.

At the other end of the barn, she saw a long beak-nosed shadow glide like a snake halfway up the sunlit open door and stop; and somewhere behind her, she was aware of a silence where the sound of the Negroes shoveling had come a minute before. "This is my place," she said angrily. "All of you are extra. Each and every one of you are extra!"

"Ya," Mr. Guizac said and turned on the hose again.

She wiped her mouth with the napkin she had in her hand and walked off, as if she had accomplished what she came for.

Mr. Shortley's shadow withdrew from the door and he leaned against the side of the barn and lit half of a cigarette that he took out of his pocket. There was nothing for him to do now but wait on the hand of God to strike, but he knew one thing: he was not going to wait with his mouth shut.

Starting that morning, he began to complain and to state his side of the case to every person he saw, black or white. He complained in the grocery store and at the courthouse and on the street corner and directly to Mrs. McIntyre herself, for there was nothing underhanded about him. If the Pole could have understood what he had to say, he would have said it to him too. "All men was created free and equal," he said to Mrs. McIntyre, "and I risked my life and limb to prove it. Gone over there and fought and bled and died and come back on over here and find out who's got my job—just exactly who I been fighting. It was a hand-grenade come that near to killing me and I seen who throwed it—little man with eye-glasses just like his. Might have bought them at the same store. Small world," and he gave a bitter little laugh. Since he didn't have Mrs. Shortley to do the talking any more, he had started doing it himself and had found that he had a gift for it. He had the power of making other people see his logic. He talked a good deal to the Negroes.

"Whyn't you go back to Africa?" he asked Sulk one morning as they were cleaning out the silo. "That's your country, ain't it?"

"I ain't goin there," the boy said. "They might eat me up."

"Well, if you behave yourself it isn't any reason you can't stay here," Mr. Shortley said kindly. "Because you didn't run away from nowhere. Your granddaddy was brought. He didn't have a thing to do with coming. It's the people that run away from where they come from that I ain't got any use for."

"I never felt no need to travel," the Negro said.

"Well," Mr. Shortley said, "if I was going to travel again, it would be to either China or Africa. You go to either of them two places and you can tell right away what the difference is between you and them. You go to these other places and the only way you can tell is if they say something. And then you can't always tell because about half of them know the English language. That's where we make our mistake," he said, "—letting all them people onto English. There'd be a heap less trouble if everybody only knew his own language. My wife said knowing two languages was like having eyes in the back of your head. You couldn't put nothing over on her."

"You sho couldn't," the boy muttered, and then he added, "She was fine. She was sho fine. I never known a finer white woman than her."

Mr. Shortley turned in the opposite direction and worked silently for a while. After a few minutes he leaned up and tapped the colored boy on the shoulder with the handle of his shovel. For a second he only looked at him while a great deal of meaning gathered in his wet eyes. Then he said softly, "Revenge is mine, saith the Lord."

Mrs. McIntyre found that everybody in town knew Mr. Shortley's version of her business and that everyone was critical of her conduct. She began to understand that she had a moral obligation to fire the Pole and that she was shirking it because she found it hard to do. She could not stand the increasing guilt any longer and on a cold Saturday morning, she started off after breakfast to fire him. She walked down to the machine shed where she heard him cranking up the tractor.

There was a heavy frost on the ground that made the fields look like the rough backs of sheep; the sun was almost silver and the woods stuck up like dry bristles on the sky line. The countryside seemed to be receding from the little circle of noise around the shed. Mr. Guizac was squatting on the ground beside the small tractor, putting in a part. Mrs. McIntyre hoped to get the fields turned over while he still had thirty days to work for her. The colored boy was standing by with some tools in his hand and Mr. Shortley was under the shed about to get up on the large tractor and back it out. She meant to wait until he and the Negro got out of the way before she began her unpleasant duty.

She stood watching Mr. Guizac, stamping her feet on the hard ground, for the cold was climbing like a paralysis up her feet and legs. She had on a heavy black coat and a red head-kerchief with her black hat pulled down on top of it to keep the glare out of her eyes. Under the black brim her face had an abstracted look and once or twice her lips moved silently. Mr. Guizac shouted over the noise of the tractor for the Negro to hand him a screwdriver and when he got it, he turned over on his back on the icy ground and reached up under the machine. She could not see his face, only his feet and legs and trunk sticking impudently out from the side of the tractor. He had on rubber boots that were cracked and splashed with mud. He raised one knee and then lowered it and turned himself slightly. Of all the things she resented about him, she resented most that he hadn't left of his own accord.

Mr. Shortley had got on the large tractor and was backing it out from under the shed. He seemed to be warmed by it as if its heat and strength sent impulses up through him that he obeyed instantly. He had headed it toward the small tractor but he braked it on a slight incline and jumped off and turned back toward the shed. Mrs. McIntyre was looking fixedly at Mr. Guizac's legs lying flat on the ground now. She heard the brake on the large tractor slip and, looking up, she saw it move forward, calculating its own path. Later she remembered that she had seen the Negro jump silently out of the way as if a spring in the earth had released him and that she had seen Mr. Shortley turn his head with incredible slowness and stare silently over his shoulder and that she had started to shout to the Displaced Person but that she had not. She had felt her eyes and Mr. Shortley's eyes and the Negro's eyes come together in one look that froze them in collusion forever, and she had heard the little noise the Pole made as the tractor wheel broke his backbone. The two men ran forward to help and she fainted.

She remembered, when she came to, running somewhere, perhaps into the house and out again but she could not remember what for or if she had fainted again when she got there. When she finally came back to where the tractors were, the ambulance had arrived. Mr. Guizac's body was covered with the bent bodies of his wife and two children and by a black one which hung over him, murmuring words she didn't understand. At first she thought this must be the doctor but then with a feeling of annoyance she recognized the priest, who had come with the ambulance and was slipping something into the crushed man's mouth. After a minute he stood up and she looked first at his bloody pants legs and then at his face which was not averted from her but was as withdrawn and expressionless as the rest of the countryside. She only stared at him for she was too shocked by her experience to be quite herself. Her mind was not taking hold of all that was happening. She felt she was in some foreign country where the people bent over the body were natives, and she watched like a stranger while the dead man was carried away in the ambulance.

That evening Mr. Shortley left without notice to look for a new position and the Negro, Sulk, was taken with a sudden desire to see more of the world and set off for the southern part of the state. The old man Astor could not work without company. Mrs. McIntyre hardly noticed that she had no help left for she came down with a nervous affliction and had to go to the hospital. When she came back, she saw that the place would be too much for her to run now and she turned her cows over to a professional auctioneer (who sold them at a loss) and retired to live on what she had, while she tried to save her declining health. A numbness developed in one of her legs and her hands and head began to jiggle and eventually she had to stay in bed all the time with only a colored woman to wait on her. Her eyesight grew steadily worse and she lost her voice altogether. Not many people remembered to come out to the country to see her except the old priest. He came regularly once a week with a bag of breadcrumbs and, after he had fed these to the peacock, he would come in and sit by the side of her bed and explain the doctrines of the Church.

THE VIOLENT
BEAR IT AWAY

for Edward Francis O'Connor
1896—1941

"FROM THE DAYS OF JOHN THE BAPTIST UNTIL NOW,
THE KINDGOM OF HEAVEN SUFFERETH VIOLENCE, AND
THE VIOLENT BEAR IT AWAY."

Matthew 11:12

PART

I

CHAPTER ONE

Francis Marion Tarwater's uncle had been dead for only half a day when the boy got too drunk to finish digging his grave and a Negro named Buford Munson, who had come to get a jug filled, had to finish it and drag the body from the breakfast table where it was still sitting and bury it in a decent and Christian way, with the sign of its Saviour at the head of the grave and enough dirt on top to keep the dogs from digging it up. Buford had come along about noon and when he left at sundown, the boy, Tarwater, had never returned from the still.

The old man had been Tarwater's great-uncle, or said he was, and they had always lived together so far as the child knew. His uncle had said he was seventy years of age at the time he had rescued and undertaken to bring him up; he was eighty-four when he died. Tarwater figured this made his own age fourteen. His uncle had taught him Figures, Reading, Writing, and History beginning with Adam expelled from the Garden and going on down through the presidents to Herbert Hoover and on in speculation toward the Second Coming and the Day of Judgment. Besides giving him a good education, he had rescued him from his only other connection, old Tarwater's nephew, a schoolteacher who had no child of his own at the time and wanted this one of his dead sister's to raise according to his own ideas.

The old man was in a position to know what his ideas were. He had lived for three months in the nephew's house on what he had thought at the time was Charity but what he said he had found out was not Charity or anything like it. All the time he had lived there, the nephew had secretly been making a study of him. The nephew, who had taken him in under the name of Charity, had at the same time been creeping into his soul by the back door, asking him questions that meant more than one thing, planting traps around the house and watching him fall into them, and finally coming up with a written study of him for a schoolteacher magazine. The stench of his behavior had reached heaven and the Lord Himself had rescued the old man.

He had sent him a rage of vision, had told him to fly with the orphan boy to the farthest part of the backwoods and raise him up to justify his Redemption. The Lord had assured him a long life and he had snatched the baby from under the schoolteacher's nose and taken him to live in the clearing, Powderhead, that he had a title to for his lifetime.

The old man, who said he was a prophet, had raised the boy to expect the Lord's call himself and to be prepared for the day he would hear it. He had schooled him in the evils that befall prophets; in those that come from the world, which are trifling, and those that come from the Lord and burn the prophet clean; for he himself had been burned clean and burned clean again. He had learned by fire.

He had been called in his early youth and had set out for the city to proclaim the destruction awaiting a world that had abandoned its Saviour. He proclaimed from the midst of his fury that the world would see the sun burst in blood and fire and while he raged and waited, it rose every morning, calm and contained in itself, as if not only the world, but the Lord Himself had failed to hear the prophet's message. It rose and set, rose and set on a world that turned from green to white and green to white and green to white again. It rose and set and he despaired of the Lord's listening. Then one morning he saw to his joy a finger of fire coming out of it and before he could turn, before he could shout, the finger had touched him and the destruction he had been waiting for had fallen in his own brain and his own body. His blood had been burned dry and not the blood of the world.

Having learned much by his own mistakes, he was in a position to instruct Tarwater—when the boy chose to listen—in the hard facts of serving the Lord. The boy, who had ideas of his own, listened with an impatient conviction that he would not make any mistakes himself when the time came and the Lord called him.

That was not the last time the Lord had corrected the old man with fire, but it had not happened since he had taken Tarwater from the schoolteacher. That time his rage of vision had been clear. He had known what he was saving the boy from and it was saving and not destruction he was seeking. He had learned enough to hate the destruction that had to come and not all that was going to be destroyed.

Rayber, the schoolteacher, had shortly discovered where they were and had come out to the clearing to get the baby back. He had had to leave his car on the dirt road and walk a mile through the woods on a path that appeared and disappeared before he came to the corn patch with the gaunt two-story shack standing in the middle of it. The old man had been fond of recalling for Tarwater the red sweating bitten face of his nephew bobbing up and down through the corn and behind it the pink flowered hat of a welfare-woman he had brought along with him. The corn was planted up to four feet from the porch that year and as the nephew came out of it, the old man appeared in the door with his shotgun and shouted that he would shoot any foot that touched his step and the two stood facing each other while the welfare-woman bristled out of the corn, ruffled like a peahen upset on the nest. The old man said if it hadn't been for the welfare-woman, his nephew wouldn't have taken a step. Both their faces were scratched and bleeding from thorn bushes and a switch of blackberry bush hung from the sleeve of the welfare-woman's blouse.

She had only to let out her breath slowly as if she were releasing the last patience on earth and the nephew lifted his foot and planted it on the step and the old man shot him in the leg. He recalled for the boy's benefit the nephew's expression of outraged righteousness, a look that had so infuriated him that he had raised the gun slightly higher and shot him again, this time taking a wedge out of his right ear. The second shot flushed the righteousness off his face and left it blank and white, revealing that there was nothing underneath it, revealing, the old man sometimes admitted, his own failure as well, for he had tried and failed, long ago, to rescue the nephew. He had kidnapped him when the child was seven and had taken him to the backwoods and baptized him and instructed him in the facts of his Redemption, but the instruction had lasted only for a few years; in time the child had set himself a different course. There were moments when the thought that he might have helped the nephew on to his new course himself became so heavy in the old man that he would stop telling the story to Tarwater, stop and stare in front of him as if he were looking into a pit which had opened up before his feet.

At such times he would wander into the woods and leave Tarwater alone in the clearing, occasionally for days, while he thrashed out his peace with the Lord, and when he returned, bedraggled and hungry, he would look the way the boy thought a prophet ought to look. He would look as if he had been wrestling a wildcat, as if his head were still full of the visions he had seen in its eyes, wheels of light and strange beasts with giant wings of fire and four heads turned to the four points of the universe. These were the times that Tarwater knew that when he was called, he would say, "Here I am, Lord, ready!" At other times when there was no fire in his uncle's eye and he spoke only of the sweat and stink of the cross, of being born again to die, and of spending eternity eating the bread of life, the boy would let his mind wander off to other subjects.

The old man's thought did not always move at the same rate of speed through every point in his story. Sometimes, as if he did not want to think of it, he would speed over the part where he shot the nephew and race on, telling how the two of them, the nephew and the welfare-woman (whose very name was comical—Bernice Bishop) had scuttled off, making a disappearing rattle in the corn, and how the welfare-woman had screamed, "Why didn't you tell me? You knew he was crazy!" and how when they came out of the corn on the other side, he had noted from the upstairs window where he had run that she had her arm around the nephew and was holding him up while he hopped into the woods. Later he learned that he had married her though she was twice his age and he could only possibly get one child out of her. She had never let him come back again.

And the Lord, the old man said, had preserved the one child he had got out of her from being corrupted by such parents. He had preserved him in the only possible way: the child was dim-witted. The old man would pause here and let the weight of this mystery sink in on Tarwater. He had made, since he learned of that child's existence, several trips into town to try to kidnap him so that he could baptize him, but each time he had come back unsuccessful. The schoolteacher was on his guard and the old man was too fat and stiff now to make an agile kidnapper.

"If by the time I die," he had said to Tarwater, "I haven't got him baptized, it'll be up to you. It'll be the first mission the Lord sends you."

The boy doubted very much that his first mission would be to baptize a dim-witted child. "Oh no it won't be," he said. "He don't mean for me to finish up your leavings. He has other things in mind for me." And he thought of Moses who struck water from a rock, of Joshua who made the sun stand still, of Daniel who stared down lions in the pit.

"It's no part of your job to think for the Lord," his great-uncle said. "Judgment may rack your bones."

The morning the old man died, he came down and cooked the breakfast as usual and died before he got the first spoonful to his mouth. The downstairs of their house was all kitchen, large and dark, with a wood stove at one end of it and a board table drawn up to the stove. Sacks of feed and mash were stacked in the corners and scrapmetal, woodshavings, old rope, ladders, and other tinder were wherever he or Tarwater had let them fall. They had slept in the kitchen until a bobcat sprang in the window one night and frightened his uncle into carrying the bed upstairs where there were two empty rooms. The old man prophesied at the time that the stairsteps would take ten years off his life. At the moment of his death, he sat down to his breakfast and lifted his knife in one square red hand halfway to his mouth, and then with a look of complete astonishment, he lowered it until the hand rested on the edge of the plate and tilted it up off the table.

He was a bull-like old man with a short head set directly into his shoulders and silver protruding eyes that looked like two fish straining to get out of a net of red threads. He had on a putty-colored hat with the brim turned up all around and over his undershirt a grey coat that had once been black. Tarwater, sitting across the table from him, saw red ropes appear in his face and a tremor pass over him. It was like the tremor of a quake that had begun at his heart and run outward and was just reaching the surface. His mouth twisted down sharply on one side and he remained exactly as he was, perfectly balanced, his back a good six inches from the chair back and his stomach caught just under the edge of the table. His eyes, dead silver, were focussed on the boy across from him.

Tarwater felt the tremor transfer itself and run lightly over him. He knew the old man was dead without touching him and he continued to sit across the table from the corpse, finishing his breakfast in a kind of sullen embarrassment as if he were in the presence of a new personality and couldn't think of anything to say. Finally he said in a querulous tone, "Just hold your horses. I already told you I would do it right." The voice sounded like a stranger's voice, as if the death had changed him instead of his great-uncle.

He got up and took his plate out the back door and set

it down on the bottom step and two long-legged black game roosters tore across the yard and finished what was on it. He sat down on a long pine box on the back porch and his hands began absently to unravel a length of rope while his long face stared ahead beyond the clearing over the woods that ran in grey and purple folds until they touched the light blue fortress line of trees set against the empty morning sky.

Powderhead was not simply off the dirt road but off the wagon track and footpath, and the nearest neighbors, colored not white, still had to walk through the woods, pushing plum branches out of their way to get to it. Once there had been two houses; now there was only the one house with the dead owner inside and the living owner outside on the porch, waiting to bury him. The boy knew he would have to bury the old man before anything would begin. It was as if there would have to be dirt over him before he would be thoroughly dead. The thought seemed to give him respite from something that pressed on him.

A few weeks before, the old man had started an acre of corn to the left and had run it beyond the fenceline almost up to the house on one side. The two strands of barbed-wire ran through the middle of the patch. A line of fog, hump-shaped, was creeping toward it like a white hound dog ready to crouch under and crawl across the yard.

"I'm going to move that fence," Tarwater said. "I ain't going to have any fence I own in the middle of a patch." The voice was loud and strange and disagreeable. Inside his head it continued: you ain't the owner. The schoolteacher owns it.

I own it, Tarwater said, because I'm here and can't nobody get me off. If any schoolteacher comes to claim the property, I'll kill him.

The Lord may send you off, he thought. There was a complete stillness over everything and the boy felt his heart begin to swell. He held his breath as if he were about to hear a voice from on high. After a few moments he heard a hen scratching beneath him under the porch. He ran his arm fiercely under his nose and gradually his face paled again.

He had on a faded pair of overalls and a grey hat pulled down over his ears like a cap. He followed his uncle's custom of never taking off his hat except in bed. He had always followed his uncle's customs up to this date but: if I want to move that fence before I bury him, it wouldn't be a soul to hinder me, he thought; no voice will be uplifted.

Bury him first and get it over with, the loud stranger's

disagreeable voice said. He got up and went to look for the shovel.

The pine box he had been sitting on was his uncle's coffin but he didn't intend to use it. The old man was too heavy for a thin boy to hoist over the side of a box and though old Tarwater had built it himself a few years before, he had said that if it wasn't feasible to get him into it when the time came, then just to put him in the hole as he was, only to be sure the hole was deep. He wanted it ten foot, he said, not just eight. He had worked on the box a long time and when he finished it, he had scratched on the lid, MASON TARWATER, WITH GOD, and had climbed into it where it stood on the back porch, and had lain there some time, nothing showing but his stomach which rose over the top like over-leavened bread. The boy had stood at the side of the box, studying him. "This is the end of us all," the old man said with satisfaction, his gravel voice hearty in the coffin.

"It's too much of you for the box," Tarwater said. "I'll have to sit on the lid to press you down or wait until you rot a little."

"Don't wait," old Tarwater had said. "Listen. If it ain't feasible to use the box when the time comes, if you can't lift it or whatever, just get me in the hole but I want it deep. I want it ten foot, not just eight, ten. You can roll me to it if nothing else. I'll roll. Get two boards and set them down the steps and start me rolling and dig where I stop and don't let me roll over into it until it's deep enough. Prop me with some bricks so I won't roll into it and don't let the dogs nudge me over the edge before it's finished. You better pen up the dogs," he said.

"What if you die in bed?" the boy asked. "How'm I going to get you down the stairs?"

"I ain't going to die in bed," the old man said. "As soon as I hear the summons, I'm going to run downstairs. I'll get as close to the door as I can. If I should get stuck up there, you'll have to roll me down the stairs, that's all."

"My Lord," the child said.

The old man sat up in the box and brought his fist down on the edge of it. "Listen," he said. "I never asked much of you. I taken you and raised you and saved you from that ass in town and now all I'm asking in return is when I die to get me in the ground where the dead belong and set up a cross over me to show I'm there. That's all in the world I'm asking you to do. I ain't even asking you to go for the niggers and try to get me in the plot with my daddy. I could ask you that but I ain't. I'm doing everything to make it easy for you. All I'm asking you is to get me in the ground and set up a cross."

"I'll be doing good if I get you in the ground," Tarwater said. "I'll be too wore out to set up any cross. I ain't bothering with trifles."

"Trifles!" his uncle hissed. "You'll learn what a trifle is on the day those crosses are gathered! Burying the dead right may be the only honor you ever do yourself. I brought you out here to raise you a Christian, and more than a Christian, a prophet!" he hollered, "and the burden of it will be on you!"

"If I don't have the strength to do it," the child said, watching him with a careful detachment, "I'll notify my uncle in town and he can come out and take care of you. The schoolteacher," he drawled, observing that the pockmarks in his uncle's face had already turned pale against the purple. "He'll tend to you."

The threads that restrained the old man's eyes thickened. He gripped both sides of the coffin and pushed forward as if he were going to drive it off the porch. "He'd burn me," he said hoarsely. "He'd have me cremated in an oven and scatter my ashes. 'Uncle,' he said to me, 'you're a type that's almost extinct!' He'd be willing to pay the undertaker to burn me to be able to scatter my ashes," he said. "He don't believe in the Resurrection. He don't believe in the Last Day. He don't believe in the bread of life . . ."

"The dead don't bother with particulars," the boy interrupted.

The old man grabbed the front of his overalls and pulled him up against the side of the box and glared into his pale face. "The world was made for the dead. Think of all the dead there are," he said, and then as if he had conceived the answer for all the insolence in the world, he said, "There's a million times more dead than living and the dead are dead a million times longer than the living are alive," and he released him with a laugh.

The boy had shown only by a slight quiver that he was shaken by this, and after a minute he had said, "The schoolteacher is my uncle. The only blood connection with good sense I'll have and a living man and if I wanted to go to him, I'd go; now."

The old man looked at him silently for what seemed a full minute. Then he slammed his hands flat on the sides of the box and roared, "Whom the plague beckons, to the plague! Whom the sword to the sword! Whom fire to fire!" And the child trembled visibly.

"I saved you to be free, your own self!" he had shouted,

"and not a piece of information inside his head! If you were living with him, you'd be information right now, you'd be inside his head, and what's furthermore," he said, "you'd be going to school."

The boy grimaced. The old man had always impressed on him his good fortune in not being sent to school. The Lord had seen fit to guarantee the purity of his up-bringing, to preserve him from contamination, to preserve him as His elect servant, trained by a prophet for prophesy. While other children his age were herded together in a room to cut out paper pumpkins under the direction of a woman, he was left free for the pursuit of wisdom, the companions of his spirit Abel and Enoch and Noah and Job, Abraham and Moses, King David and Solomon, and all the prophets, from Elijah who escaped death, to John whose severed head struck terror from a dish. The boy knew that escaping school was the surest sign of his election.

The truant officer had come only once. The Lord had told the old man to expect it and what to do and old Tarwater had instructed the boy in his part against the day when, as the devil's emissary, the officer would appear. When the time came and they saw him cutting across the field, they were ready. The child got behind the house and the old man sat on the steps and waited. When the officer, a thin bald-headed man with red galluses, stepped out of the field onto the packed dirt of the yard, he greeted old Tarwater warily and commenced his business as if he had not come for it. He sat down on the steps and spoke of poor weather and poor health. Finally, gazing out over the field, he said, "You got a boy, don't you, that ought to be in school?"

"A fine boy," the old man said, "and I wouldn't stand in his way if anybody thought they could teach him. You boy!" he called. The boy didn't come at once. "Oh you boy!" the old man shouted.

In a few minutes Tarwater appeared from around the side of the house. His eyes were open but not well-focused. His head rolled uncontrollably on his slack shoulders and his tongue lolled in his open mouth.

"He ain't bright," the old man said, "but he's a mighty good boy. He knows to come when you call him."

"Yes," the truant officer said, "well yes, but it might be best to leave him in peace."

"I don't know, he might take to schooling," the old man said. "He ain't had a fit for going on two months."

"I speck he better stay at home," the officer said. "I wouldn't want to put a strain on him," and he commenced

to speak of other things. Shortly he took his leave and
the two of them watched with satisfaction as the diminishing
figure moved back across the field and the red galluses
were finally lost to view.

If the schoolteacher had got hold of him, right now he
would have been in school, one among many, indistinguishable
from the herd, and in the schoolteacher's head, he would
be laid out in parts and numbers. "That's where he wanted
me," the old man said, "and he thought once he had me
in that schoolteacher magazine, I would be as good as
in his head." The schoolteacher's house had had little
in it but books and papers. The old man had not known
when he went there to live that every living thing that
passed through the nephew's eyes into his head was turned
by his brain into a book or a paper or a chart. The schoolteacher had appeared to have a great interest in his being
a prophet, chosen by the Lord, and had asked numerous
questions, the answers to which he had sometimes scratched
down on a pad, his little eyes lighting every now and then
as if in some discovery.

The old man had fancied he was making progress in
convincing the nephew again of his Redemption, for he
at least listened though he did not *say* he believed. He
seemed to delight to talk about the things that interested
his uncle. He questioned him at length about his early
life, which old Tarwater had practically forgotten. The
old man had thought this interest in his forebears would
bear fruit, but what it bore, what it bore, stench and shame,
were dead words. What it bore was a dry and seedless
fruit, incapable even of rotting, dead from the beginning.
From time to time, the old man would spit out of his mouth,
like gobbets of poison, some of the idiotic sentences from
the schoolteacher's piece. Wrath had burned them on
his memory, word for word. "His fixation of being called
by the Lord had its origin in insecurity. He needed the
assurance of a call, and so he called himself."

"Called myself!" the old man would hiss, "called myself!"
This so enraged him that half the time he could do nothing
but repeat it. "Called myself. I called myself. I, Mason
Tarwater, called myself! Called myself to be beaten and
tied up. Called myself to be spit on and snickered at.
Called myself to be struck down in my pride. Called myself
to be torn by the Lord's eye. Listen boy," he would say
and grab the child by the straps of his overalls and shake
him slowly, "even the mercy of the Lord burns." He
would let go the straps and allow the boy to fall back into

the thorn bed of that thought, while he continued to hiss and groan.

"Where he wanted me was inside that schoolteacher magazine. He thought once he got me in there, I'd be as good as inside his head and done for and that would be that, that would be the end of it. Well, that wasn't the end of it! Here I sit. And there you sit. In freedom. Not inside anybody's head!" and his voice would run away from him as if it were the freest part of his free self and were straining ahead of his heavy body to be off. Something of his great-uncle's glee would take hold of Tarwater at that point and he would feel that he had escaped some mysterious prison. He even felt he could smell his freedom, pine-scented, coming out of the woods, until the old man would continue, "You were born into bondage and baptized into freedom, into the death of the Lord, into the death of the Lord Jesus Christ."

Then the child would feel a sullenness creeping over him, a slow warm rising resentment that this freedom had to be connected with Jesus and that Jesus had to be the Lord.

"Jesus is the bread of life," the old man said.

The boy, disconcerted, would look off into the distance over the dark blue treeline where the world stretched out, hidden and at its ease. In the darkest, most private part of his soul, hanging upsidedown like a sleeping bat, was the certain, undeniable knowledge that he was not hungry for the bread of life. Had the bush flamed for Moses, the sun stood still for Joshua, the lions turned aside before Daniel only to prophesy the bread of life? Jesus? He felt a terrible disappointment in that conclusion, a dread that it was true. The old man said that as soon as he died, he would hasten to the banks of the Lake of Galilee to eat the loaves and fishes that the Lord had multiplied.

"Forever?" the horrified boy asked.

"Forever," the old man said.

The boy sensed that this was the heart of his great-uncle's madness, this hunger, and what he was secretly afraid of was that it might be passed down, might be hidden in the blood and might strike some day in him and then he would be torn by hunger like the old man, the bottom split out of his stomach so that nothing would heal or fill it but the bread of life.

He tried when possible to pass over these thoughts, to keep his vision located on an even level, to see no more than what was in front of his face and to let his eyes stop at the surface of that. It was as if he were afraid that if he let his eye rest for an instant longer than was needed to place something—a spade, a hoe, the mule's hind quarters before his plow, the red furrow under him—that the thing would suddenly stand before him, strange and terrifying, demanding that he name it and name it justly and be judged for the name he gave it. He did all he could to avoid this threatened intimacy of creation. When the Lord's call came, he wished it to be a voice from out of a clear and empty sky, the trumpet of the Lord God Almighty, untouched by any fleshly hand or breath. He expected to see wheels of fire in the eyes of unearthly beasts. He had expected this to happen as soon as his great-uncle died. He turned his mind off this quickly and went to get the shovel. The schoolteacher is a living man, he thought as he went, but he'd better not come out here and try to get me off this property because I'll kill him. Go to him and be damned, his uncle had said. I've saved you from him this far and if you go to him the minute I'm in the ground there's nothing I can do about it.

The shovel lay against the side of the hen house. "I'll never set my foot in the city again," the boy said to himself aloud. I'll never go to him. Him nor nobody else will ever get me off this place.

He decided to dig the grave under the fig tree because the old man would be good for the figs. The ground was sandy on top and solid brick underneath and the shovel made a clanging sound when he struck it in the sand. Two hundred pounds of dead mountain to bury, he thought, and stood with one foot on the shovel, leaning forward, studying the white sky through the leaves of the tree. It would take all day to get a hole big enough out of this rock and the schoolteacher would burn him in a minute.

Tarwater had seen the schoolteacher once from a distance of about twenty feet and he had seen the dim-witted child closer up. The little boy somewhat resembled old Tarwater except for his eyes which were grey like the old man's but clear, as if the other side of them went down and down into two pools of light. It was plain to look at him that he did not have any sense. The old man had been so shocked by the likeness and the unlikeness that the time he and Tarwater had gone there, he had only stood in the door, staring at the little boy and rolling his tongue around outside his mouth as if he had no sense himself. That had been the first time he had seen the child and he could not forget him. "Married her and got one child out of her and that without sense," he would murmur. "The

Lord preserved him and now He means to see he's baptized."

"Well whyn't you get on with it then?" the boy asked, for he wanted something to happen, wanted to see the old man in action, wanted him to kidnap the child and have the schoolteacher have to come after him so that he could get a closer look at his other uncle. "What ails you?" he asked. "What makes you tarry so long? Why don't you make haste and steal him?"

"I take my directions from the Lord God," the old man said, "Who moves in His own time. I don't take them from you."

The white fog had eased through the yard and disappeared into the next bottom and the air was clear and blank. His mind continued to dwell on the schoolteacher's house. "Three months there," his great-uncle had said. "It shames me. Betrayed for three months in the house of my own kin and if when I'm dead you want to turn me over to my betrayer and see my body burned, go ahead! Go ahead, boy," he had shouted, sitting up splotch-faced in his box. "Go ahead and let him burn me but watch out for the Lord's lion after that. Remember the Lord's lion set in the path of the false prophet! I been leavened by the yeast he don't believe in," he had said, "and I won't be burned! And when I'm gone, you'll be better off in these woods by yourself with just as much light as the sun wants to let in than you'll be in the city with him."

He kept on digging but the grave did not get any deeper. "The dead are poor," he said in the voice of the stranger. You can't be any poorer than dead. He'll have to take what he gets. Nobody to bother me, he thought. Ever. No hand uplifted to hinder me from anything; except the Lord's and He ain't said anything. He ain't even noticed me yet.

A sand-colored hound beat its tail on the ground nearby and a few black chickens scratched in the raw clay he was turning up. The sun had slipped over the blue line of trees and circled by a haze of yellow was moving slowly across the sky. "Now I can do anything I want to," he said, softening the stranger's voice so that he could stand it. Could kill off all those chickens if I had a mind to, he thought, watching the worthless black game bantams that his uncle had been fond of keeping.

He favored a lot of foolishness, the stranger said. The truth is he was childish. Why, that schoolteacher never did him any harm. You take, all he did was to watch him and write down what he seen and heard and put it in a paper for schoolteachers to read. Now what was wrong in that? Why nothing. Who cares what a schoolteacher reads? And the old fool acted like he had been killed in his very soul. Well he wasn't so near dead as he thought he was. Lived on fourteen years and raised up a boy to bury him, suitable to his own taste.

As Tarwater slashed at the ground with the shovel, the stranger's voice took on a kind of restrained fury and he kept repeating, you got to bury him whole and completely by hand and that schoolteacher would burn him in a minute.

After he had dug for an hour or more, the grave was only a foot deep, not as deep yet as the corpse. He sat down on the edge of it for a while. The sun was like a furious white blister in the sky.

The dead are a heap more trouble than the living, the stranger said. That schoolteacher wouldn't consider for a minute that on the last day all the bodies marked by crosses will be gathered. In the rest of the world they do things different than what you been taught.

"I been there once," Tarwater muttered. "Nobody has to tell me."

His uncle two or three years before had gone to call on the lawyers to try to get the property unentailed so that it would skip the schoolteacher and go to Tarwater. Tarwater had sat at the lawyer's twelfth-story window and looked down into the pit of the street while his uncle transacted the business. On the way from the railroad station he had walked tall in the mass of moving metal and concrete speckled with the very small eyes of people. The glitter of his own eyes was shaded under the stiff roof-like brim of a new gray hat, balanced perfectly straight on his buttressing ears. Before coming he had read facts in the almanac and he knew that there were 75,000 people here who were seeing him for the first time. He wanted to stop and shake hands with each of them and say his name was F. M. Tarwater and that he was here only for the day to accompany his uncle on business at a lawyers. His head jerked backwards after each passing figure until they began to pass too thickly and he observed that their eyes didn't grab at you like the eyes of country people. Several people bumped into him and this contact that should have made an acquaintance for life, made nothing because the hulks shoved on with ducked heads and muttered apologies that he would have accepted if they had waited.

Then he had realized, almost without warning, that this place was evil—the ducked heads, the muttered words, the hastening away. He saw in a burst of light that these people were hastening away from the Lord God Almighty. It was to the city that the prophets came and he was here in the midst of it. He was here enjoying what should have repelled him. His lids narrowed with caution and he looked at his uncle who was rolling on ahead of him, no more concerned with it all than a bear in the woods. "What kind of prophet are you?" the boy hissed.

His uncle paid him no attention, did not stop.

"Call yourself a prophet!" he continued in a high rasping carrying voice.

His uncle stopped and turned. "I'm here on bidnis," he said mildly.

"You always said you were a prophet," Tarwater said. "Now I see what kind of prophet you are. Elijah would think a heap of you."

His uncle thrust his head forward and his eyes began to bulge. "I'm here on bidnis," he said. "If you been called by the Lord, then be about your own mission."

The boy paled slightly and his gaze shifted. "I ain't been called *yet*," he muttered. "It's you that's been called."

"And I know what times I'm called and what times I ain't," his uncle said and turned and paid him no more attention.

At the lawyer's window, he knelt down and let his face hang out upsidedown over the floating speckled street moving like a river of tin below and watched the glints on it from the sun which drifted pale in a pale sky, too far away to ignite anything. When he was called, on that day when he returned, he would set the city astir, he would return with fire in his eyes. You have to do something particular here to make them look at you, he thought. They ain't going to look at you just because you're here. He considered his uncle with renewed disgust. When I come for good, he said to himself, I'll do something to make every eye stick on me, and leaning forward, he saw his new hat drop down gently, lost and casual, dallied slightly by the breeze on its way to be smashed in the tin river below. He clutched at his bare head and fell back inside the room.

His uncle was in argument with the lawyer, both hitting the desk that separated them, bending their knees and hitting their fists at the same time. The lawyer, a tall dome-headed man with an eagle's nose, kept repeating in a restrained shriek, "But I didn't make the will. I didn't make the law," and his uncle's gravel voice grated, "I can't help it. My daddy wouldn't have seen a fool inherit his property. That's not how he intended it."

"My hat is gone," Tarwater said.

The lawyer threw himself backwards into his chair and screaked it toward Tarwater and saw him without interest from pale blue eyes and screaked it forward again and said to his uncle, "There's nothing I can do. You're wasting your time and mine. You might as well resign yourself to this will."

"Listen," old Tarwater said, "at one time I thought I was finished, old and sick and about to die and no money, nothing, and I accepted his hospitality because he was my closest blood connection and you could have called it his duty to take me, only I thought it was Charity, I thought . . ."

"I can't help what you thought or did or what your connection thought or did," the lawyer said and closed his eyes.

"My hat fell," Tarwater said.

"I'm only a lawyer," the lawyer said, letting his glance rove over the lines of clay-colored books of law that fortressed his office.

"A car is liable to have run over it by now."

"Listen," his uncle said, "all the time he was studying me for this paper. Taking secret tests on me, his own kin, crawling into my soul through the back door and then says to me, 'Uncle, you're a type that's almost extinct!' Almost extinct!" the old man piped, barely able to force a thread of sound from his throat. "You see how extinct I am!"

The lawyer closed his eyes again and smiled into one cheek.

"Other lawyers," the old man growled and they had left and visited three more, without stopping, and Tarwater had counted eleven men who might have had on his hat or might not. Finally when they came out of the fourth lawyer's office, they sat down on the window ledge of a bank building and his uncle felt in his pocket for some biscuits he had brought and handed one to Tarwater. The old man unbuttoned his coat and allowed his stomach to ease forward and rest on his lap while he ate. His face worked wrathfully; the skin between the pockmarks appeared to jump from one spot to another. Tarwater was very pale and his eyes glittered with a peculiar hollow depth. He had an old work kerchief tied around his head, knotted at the four corners. He didn't observe the passing people who observed him now. "Thank God we're finished and can go home," he muttered.

"We ain't finished here," the old man said and got up abruptly and started down the street.

"My Lord!" the boy groaned, jumping to catch up with him. "Can't we sit down for one minute? Ain't you got any sense? They all tell you the same thing. It's only one law and it's nothing you can do about it. I got sense enough to get that; why ain't you? What's the matter with you?"

The old man strode on with his head thrust forward as if he were smelling out an enemy.

"Where we going?" Tarwater asked after they had walked out of the business streets and were passing between rows of grey bulbous houses with sooty porches that overhung the sidewalks. "Listen," he said, hitting at his uncle's hip, "I never ast to come."

"You would have ast to come soon enough," the old man muttered. "Get your fill now."

"I never ast for no fill. I never ast to come at all. I'm here before I knew this here was here."

"Just remember," the old man said, "just remember that I told you to remember when you ast to come that you never liked it when you were here," and they kept on going, crossing one length of sidewalk after another, row after row of overhanging houses with half-open doors that let a little dried light fall on the stained passageways inside. Finally they came out into another section where the houses were clean and squat and almost identical and each had a square of grass in front of it. After a few blocks Tarwater dropped down on the sidewalk and said, "I ain't going no further. I don't even know where I'm going and I ain't going no further." His uncle didn't stop or look back. In a second he jumped up and followed him again in a panic lest he be left.

The old man kept straining forward as if his blood scent were leading him closer and closer to the place where his enemy was hiding. He suddenly turned up the short walk of a pale yellow brick house and moved rigidly to the white door, his heavy shoulders hunched as if he were going to crash through it. He struck the wood with his fist, ignoring a polished brass knocker. At that instant Tarwater realized that this was where the schoolteacher lived, and he stopped where he was and remained rigid, his eye on the door. He knew by some obscure instinct that the door was going to open and reveal his destiny. In his mind's eye, he saw the schoolteacher about to appear in it, lean and evil, waiting to engage whom the Lord would send to conquer him. The boy clamped his teeth together to keep them from chattering. The door opened.

A small pink-faced boy stood in it with his mouth hung in a silly smile. He had white hair and a knobby forehead. He wore steel-rimmed spectacles and had pale silver eyes like the old man's except that they were clear and empty. He was gnawing on a brown apple core.

The old man stared at him, his lips parting slowly until his mouth hung open. He looked as if he beheld an unspeakable mystery. The little boy made an unintelligible noise and pushed the door almost shut, hiding himself all but one spectacled eye.

Suddenly a tremendous indignation seized Tarwater. He eyed the small face peering from the crack. He searched his mind fiercely for the right word to hurl at it. Finally he said in a slow emphatic voice, "Before you was here, *I* was here."

The old man caught his shoulder and pulled him back. "He don't have good sense," he said. "Can't you see he don't have good sense? He don't know what you're talking about."

The boy grew more furious than ever. He swung around on his heel to leave.

"Wait," his uncle said and caught him. "Get behind that hedge yonder and hide yourself. I'm going in there and baptize him."

Tarwater's mouth was agape.

"Get behind there like I told you," he said and gave him a push toward the hedge. Then the old man braced himself. He turned and went back to the door. Just as he reached it, it was flung open and a lean young man with heavy black-rimmed spectacles stood in it, his head thrust forward, glaring at him.

Old Tarwater raised his fist. "The Lord Jesus Christ sent me to baptize that boy!" he shouted. "Stand aside. I mean to do it!"

Tarwater's head popped up from behind the hedge. Breathlessly he took the schoolteacher in—the narrow boney face slanting backwards from the jutting jaw, the hair that receded from the high forehead, the eyes encircled in glass. The white-haired child had caught hold of his father's leg and was hanging onto it. The schoolteacher pushed him back inside the house. Then he stepped outside and slammed the door behind him and continued to glare at the old man as if he dared him to take a step.

"That boy cries out for his baptism," the old man said. "Precious in the sight of the Lord even an idiot!"

"Get off my property," the nephew said in a tight voice

as if he were keeping it calm by force. "If you don't, I'll have you put back in the asylum where you belong."

"You can't touch the servant of the Lord!" the old man hollered.

"You get away from here!" the nephew shouted, losing control of his voice. "Ask the Lord why He made him an idiot in the first place, uncle. Tell him I want to know why!"

The boy's heart was beating so fast he was afraid it was going to gallop out of his chest and disappear forever. He was head and shoulders out of the shrubbery.

"Yours not to ask!" the old man shouted. "Yours not to question the mind of the Lord God Almighty. Yours not to grind the Lord into your head and spit out a number!"

"Where's the boy?" the nephew asked, looking around suddenly as if he had just thought of it. "Where's the boy you were going to raise into a prophet to burn my eyes clean?" and he laughed.

Tarwater lowered his head into the bush again, instantly disliking the schoolteacher's laugh which seemed to reduce him to the least importance.

"His day is going to come," the old man said. "Either him or me is going to baptize that child. If not me in my day, him in his."

"You'll never lay a hand on him," the schoolteacher said. "You could slosh water on him for the rest of his life and he'd still be an idiot. Five years old for all eternity, useless forever. Listen," he said, and the boy heard his taut voice turn low with a kind of subdued intensity, a passion equal and opposite to the old man's, "he'll never be baptized—just as a matter of principle, nothing else. As a gesture of human dignity, he'll never be baptized."

"Time will discover the hand that baptizes him," the old man said.

"Time will discover it," the nephew said and opened the door behind him and stepped back inside and slammed it on himself.

The boy had risen from the shrubbery, his head swirling with excitement. He had never been back there again, never seen his cousin again, never seen the schoolteacher again, and he hoped to God, he told the stranger digging the grave along with him now, that he would never see him again though he had nothing against him himself and he would dislike to have to kill him but if he came out here, messing in what was none of his business except by law, then he would be obliged to.

Listen, the stranger said, what would he want to come

out here for—where there's nothing?

Tarwater didn't answer. He didn't search out the stranger's face but he knew by now that it was sharp and friendly and wise, shadowed under a stiff broad-brimmed panama hat that obscured the color of his eyes. He had lost his dislike for the thought of the voice. Only every now and then it sounded like a stranger's voice to him. He began to feel that he was only just now meeting himself, as if as long as his uncle had lived, he had been deprived of his own acquaintance. I ain't denying the old man was a good one, his new friend said, but like you said: you can't be any poorer than dead. They have to take what they can get. His soul is off this mortal earth now and his body is not going to feel the pinch, of fire or anything else.

"It was the last day he was thinking of," Tarwater murmured.

Well now, the stranger said, don't you think any cross you set up in the year 1952 would be rotted out by the year the Day of Judgment comes in? Rotted to as much dust as his ashes if you reduced him to ashes? And lemme ast you this: what's God going to do with sailors drowned at sea that the fish have et and the fish that et them et by other fish and they et by yet others? And what about people that get burned up naturally in house fires? Burnt up one way or another or lost in machines until they're pulp? And all those sojers blasted to nothing? What about all those that there's nothing left of to burn or bury?

If I burnt him, Tarwater said, it wouldn't be natural, it would be deliberate.

Oh I see, the stranger said. It ain't the Day of Judgment for him you're worried about. It's the Day of Judgment for you.

That's my bidnis, Tarwater said.

I ain't buttin into your bidnis, the stranger said. It don't mean a thing to me. You're left by yourself in this empty place. Forever by yourself in this empty place with just as much light at that dwarf sun wants to let in. You don't mean a thing to a soul as far as I can see.

"Redeemed," Tarwater muttered.

Do you smoke? the stranger asked.

Smoke if I want to and don't if I don't, Tarwater said. Bury if need be and don't if don't.

Go take a look at him and see if he's fell off his chair, his friend suggested.

Tarwater let the shovel drop in the grave and returned to the house. He opened the front door a crack and put his face to it. His uncle glared slightly to the side of him like a judge intent upon some terrible evidence. The boy shut the door quickly and went back to the grave, cold in spite of the sweat that stuck his shirt to his back. He began digging again.

The schoolteacher was too smart for him, that's all, the stranger said presently. You remember well enough how he said he kidnapped him when the schoolteacher was seven years of age. Gone to town and persuaded him out of his own backyard and brought him out here and baptized him. And what come of it? Nothing. The schoolteacher don't care now if he's baptized or if he ain't. It don't mean a thing to him one way or the other. Don't care if he's Redeemed or not neither. He only spent four days out here; you've spent fourteen years and now got to spend the rest of your life.

You see he was crazy all along, he continued. Wanted to make a prophet out of that schoolteacher too, but the schoolteacher was too smart for him. He got away.

He had somebody to come for him, Tarwater said. His daddy came and got him back. Nobody came and got me back.

The schoolteacher himself come after you, the stranger said, and got shot in the leg and the ear for his trouble.

I was not yet one year old, Tarwater said. A baby can't walk off and leave.

You ain't a baby now, his friend said.

The grave did not appear to get any deeper though he continued to dig. Look at the big prophet, the stranger jeered, and watched him from the shade of the speckled tree shadows. Lemme hear you prophesy something. The truth is the Lord ain't studying about you. You ain't entered His Head.

Tarwater turned around abruptly and worked from the other side and the voice continued from behind him. Anybody that's a prophet has got to have somebody to prophesy to. Unless you're just going to prophesy to yourself, he amended—or go baptize that dim-witted child, he added in a tone of high sarcasm.

The truth is, he said after a minute, the truth is that you're just as smart, if you ain't actually smarter, than the schoolteacher. Because he had somebody—his daddy and his mother—to tell him the old man was crazy, whereas you ain't had anybody and yet you've figured it out for yourself. Of course, it's taken you longer, but you've come to the right conclusion: you know he was a crazy man even when he wasn't in the asylum, even those last years.

Or if he wasn't actually crazy, he was the same thing in a different way: he didn't have but one thing on his mind. He was a one-notion man. Jesus. Jesus this and Jesus that. Ain't you in all your fourteen years of supporting his foolishness fed up and sick to the roof of your mouth with Jesus? My Lord and Saviour, the stranger sighed, I am if you ain't.

After a pause he continued. The way I see it, he said, you can do one of two things. One of them, not both. Nobody can do both of two things without straining themselves. You can do one thing or you can do the opposite.

Jesus or the devil, the boy said.

No no no, the stranger said, there ain't no such thing as a devil. I can tell you that from my own self-experience. I know that for a fact. It ain't Jesus or the devil. It's Jesus or *you.*

Jesus or me, Tarwater repeated. He put the shovel down for a rest and thought: he said the schoolteacher was glad to come. He said all he had to do was go out in the schoolteacher's back yard where he was playing and say, Let's you and me go to the country for a while—you have to be born again. The Lord Jesus Christ sent me to see to it. And the schoolteacher got up and took hold of his hand without a word and came with him and all the four days while he was out here he said the schoolteacher was hoping they wouldn't come for him.

Well that's all the sense a seven-year-old boy's got, the stranger said. You can't expect no more from a child. He learned better as soon as he got back to town; his daddy told him the old man was crazy and not to believe a word of what all he had learnt him.

There's not the way he told it, Tarwater said. He said that when the schoolteacher was seven years old, he had good sense but later it dried up. His daddy was an ass and not fit to raise him and his mother was a whore. She ran away from here when she was eighteen years old.

It took her that long? the stranger said in an incredulous tone. My, she was kind of an ass herself.

My great-uncle said he hated to admit it that his own sister was a whore but he had to say it to say the truth, the boy said.

Shaw, you know yourself that it give him great satisfaction to admit she was a whore, the stranger said. He was always admitting somebody was an ass or a whore. That's all a prophet is good for—to admit somebody else is an

ass or a whore. And anyway, he asked slyly, what do
you know about whores? Where have you ever run up
on one of them?

Certainly I know what one of them is, the boy said.

The Bible is full of them. He knew what they were and
to what they were liable to come, and just as Jezebel was
discovered by dogs, an arm here and a foot there, so
said his great-uncle, it had almost been with his own mother
and grandmother. The two of them, along with his grandfather, had been killed in an automobile crash, leaving
only the schoolteacher alive in that family, and Tarwater
himself, for his mother (unmarried and shameless) had
lived just long enough after the crash for him to be born.
He had been born at the scene of the wreck.

The boy was very proud that he had been born in a
wreck. He had always felt that it set his existence apart
from the ordinary one and he had understood from it
that the plans of God for him were special, even though
nothing of consequence had happened to him so far.
Often when he walked in the woods and came upon some
bush a little removed from the rest, his breath would catch
in his throat and he would stop and wait for the bush to
burst into flame. It had not done it yet.

His uncle had never seemed to be aware of the importance
of the way he had been born, only of how he had been
born again. He would often ask him why he thought the
Lord had rescued him out of the womb of a whore and
let him see the light of day at all, and then why, having
done it once, He had gone and done it again, allowing him
to be baptized by his great-uncle into the death of Christ,
and then having done it twice, gone on and done it
a third time, allowing him to be rescued by his great-uncle
from the schoolteacher and brought to the backwoods
and given a chance to be brought up according to the
truth. It was because, his uncle said, the Lord meant him
to be trained for a prophet, even though he was a bastard,
and to take his great-uncle's place when he died. The
old man compared their situation to that of Elijah and
Elisha.

All right, the stranger said, I suppose you know what
one of them is. But there's a heap else you don't know.
You go ahead and put your feet in his shoes. Elisha after
Elijah like he said. But just lemme ast you this: where
is the voice of the Lord? I haven't heard it. Who's called
you this morning? Or any morning? Have you been
told what to do? You ain't even heard the sound of natural

thunder this morning. There ain't a cloud in the sky. The trouble with you, I see, he concluded, is that you ain't got but just enough sense to believe every word he told you.

The sun was directly overhead, apparently dead still, holding its breath, waiting out the noontime. The grave was about two feet deep. Ten foot now, remember, the stranger said and laughed. Old men are selfish. You got to expect the least of them. The least of everybody, he added and let out a flat sigh that was like a gust of sand raised and dropped suddenly by the wind.

Tarwater looked up and saw two figures cutting across the field, a colored man and woman, each dangling an empty vinegar jug by a finger. The woman, tall and Indianlike, had on a green sun hat. She stooped under the fence without pausing and came on across the yard toward the grave; the man held the wire down and swung his leg over and followed at her elbow. They kept their eyes on the hole and stopped at the edge of it, looking down into the raw ground with shocked satisfied expressions. The man, Buford, had a crinkled face, darker than his hat. "Old man passed," he said.

The woman lifted her head and let out a slow sustained wail, piercing and formal. She set her jug down on the ground and crossed her arms and then lifted them in the air and wailed again.

"Tell her to shut up that," Tarwater said. "I'm in charge here now and I don't want no nigger-mourning."

"I seen his spirit for two nights," she said. "Seen him two nights and he was unrested."

"He ain't been dead but since this morning," Tarwater said. "If you all want your jugs filled, give them to me and dig while I'm gone."

"He'd been predicting his passing for many years," Buford said. "She seen him in her dream several nights and he wasn't rested. I known him well. I known him very well indeed."

"Poor sweet sugar boy," the woman said to Tarwater, "what you going to do here now by yourself in this lonesome place?"

"Mind my bidnis," the boy said, jerking the jug out of her hand. He started off so quickly that he almost fell. He stalked across the back field toward the rim of trees that surrounded the clearing.

The birds had gone into the deep woods to escape the noon sun and one thrush, hidden some distance ahead of him, called the same four notes again and again, stopping each time after them to make a silence. Tarwater began to walk faster, then he began to lope, and in a second he was running like something hunted, sliding down slopes waxed with pine needles and grasping the limbs of trees to pull himself, panting, up the slippery inclines. He crashed through a wall of honeysuckle and leapt across a sandy near-dry stream bed and fell down against the high clay bank that formed the back wall of a cove where the old man kept his extra liquor hidden. He hid it in a hollow of the bank, covered with a large stone. Tarwater began to fight at the stone to pull it away, while the stranger stood over his shoulder panting, He was crazy! He was crazy! That's the long and short of it, he was crazy!

Tarwater got the stone away and pulled out a black jug and sat down against the bank with it. Crazy! the stranger hissed, collapsing by his side.

The sun appeared, a furious white, edging its way secretly behind the tops of the trees that rose over the hiding place.

Any man, seventy years of age, to bring a baby out into the backwoods to raise him right! Suppose he had died when you were four years old instead of fourteen? Could you have toted mash to the still then and supported yourself? I never heard of no four-year-old running a still.

Never did I hear of that, he continued. You weren't anything to him but something that would grow big enough to bury him when the time came and now that he's dead, he's shut of you but you got two hundred and fifty pounds of him to put below the face of the earth. And don't think he wouldn't heat up like a coal stove to see you take a drop of liquor, he added. Though he had a weakness for it himself. When he couldn't stand the Lord one instant longer, he got drunk, prophet or no prophet. Hah. He might say it would hurt you but what he meant was you might get so much you wouldn't be in no fit condition to bury him. He said he brought you out here to raise you according to principle and that was the principle: that you should be fit when the time came to bury him so he would have a cross to mark where he was at.

A prophet with a still! He's the only prophet I ever heard of making liquor for a living.

After a minute he said in a softer tone as the boy took a long swallow from the black jug, well, a little won't interfere. Moderation never hurt no one.

A burning arm slid down Tarwater's throat as if the

devil were already reaching inside him to finger his soul. He squinted at the angry sun creeping behind the topmost fringe of trees.

Take it easy, his friend said. Do you remember them nigger gospel singers you saw one time, all drunk, all singing, all dancing around that black Ford automobile? Jesus, they wouldn't have · been near so glad they were Redeemed if they hadn't had that liquor in them. I wouldn't pay too much attention to my Redemption if I was you. Some people take everything too hard.

Tarwater drank more slowly. He had been drunk only one time before and that time his uncle had beat him with a piece of crate for it, saying liquor would dissolve a child's gut, another of his lies because his gut had not dissolved.

It should be clear to you, his kind friend said, how all your life you been tricked by that old man. You could have been a city slicker for the last fourteen years. Instead, you been deprived of any company but his, you been living in a two-story barn in the middle of this earth's bald patch, following behind a mule and plow since you were seven. And how do you know the education he give you is true to the facts? Maybe he taught you a system of figures nobody else uses? How do you know that two added to two makes four? Four added to four makes eight? Maybe other people don't think so. How do you know if there was an Adam or if Jesus eased your situation any when He redeemed you? Or how do you know if He actually done it? Nothing but that old man's word and it ought to be obvious to you by now that he was crazy. And as for Judgment Day, the stranger said, every day is Judgment Day.

Ain't you old enough to have learnt that yet for yourself? Don't everything you do, everything you have ever done, work itself out right or wrong before your eye and usually before the sun has set? Have you ever got by with anything? No you ain't nor ever thought you would. You might as well drink all that liquor since you've already drunk so much. Once you pass the moderation mark you've passed it, and that gyration you feel working down from the top of your brain, he said, that's the Hand of God laying a blessing on you. He has given you your release. That old man was the stone before your door and the Lord has rolled it away. He ain't rolled it quite far enough, of course. You got to finish up yourself but He's done the main part. Praise Him.

Tarwater had ceased to have any feelings in his legs. He dozed for a while, his head hanging to the side and his mouth open and the liquor trickling slowly down the side of his overalls where the jug had overturned in his lap. Eventually there was only a drip at the neck of the bottle, forming and filling and dropping, silent and measured and sun-colored. The bright even sky began to fade, coarsening with clouds until every shadow had gone in. He woke with a wrench forward, his eyes focussing and unfocussing on something that looked like a burnt rag hanging close to his face.

Buford said, "This ain't no way for you to act. Old man don't deserve this. There's no rest until the dead is buried." He was squatting on his heels, one hand gripped around Tarwater's arm. "I gone yonder to the door and seen him sitting there at the table, not even laid out on a cooling board. He ought to be laid out and have some salt on his bosom if you mean to keep him overnight."

The boy's lids pinched together to hold the image steady and in a second he made out two small red blistered eyes.

"He deserves to lie in a grave that fits him," Buford said. "He was deep in this life, he was deep in Jesus' misery."

"Nigger," the child said, working his strange swollen tongue, "take your hand off me."

Buford lifted his hand. "He needs to be rested," he said.

"He'll be rested all right when I get through with him," Tarwater said vaguely. "Go on and lea' me to my bidnis."

"Nobody going to bother you," Buford said, standing up. He waited a minute, bent, looking down at the limp figure sprawled against the bank. The boy's head was tilted backwards over a root that jutted out of the clay wall. His mouth hung open and his turned-up hat had cut a straight line across his forehead, just over his half-open unseeing eyes. His cheekbones protruded, narrow and thin like the arms of a cross, and the hollows under them had an ancient look as if the child's skeleton beneath were as old as the world. "Nobody going to bother you," the Negro muttered, pushing through the wall of honeysuckle without looking back. "That going to be your trouble."

Tarwater closed his eyes again.

Some night bird complaining close by woke him up. It was not a screeching noise, only an intermittent hump-hump as if the bird had to recall his grievance each time before he repeated it. Clouds were moving convulsively across a black sky and there was a pink unsteady moon that appeared to be jerked up a foot or so and then dropped and jerked up again. This was because, as he observed in an instant, the sky was lowering, coming down fast to smother him. The bird screeched and flew off in time and Tarwater lurched into the middle of the stream bed and crouched on his hands and knees. The moon was reflected like pale fire in the few spots of water in the sand. He sprang at the wall of honeysuckle and began to tear through it, confusing the sweet familiar odor with the weight coming down on him. When he stood up on the other side, the black ground swung slowly and threw him down again. A flare of pink lightning lit the woods and he saw the black shapes of trees pierce out of the ground all around him. The night bird began to hump again from a thicket where he had settled.

He got up and began to move in the direction of the clearing, feeling his way from tree to tree, the trunks very cold and dry to his touch. There was distant thunder and a continuous flicker of pale lightning firing one section of woods and then another. Finally he saw the shack, standing gaunt-black and tall in the middle of the clearing, with the pink moon trembling directly over it. His eyes glittered like open pits of light as he moved across the sand, dragging his crushed shadow behind him. He didn't turn his head to that side of the yard where he had started the grave. He stopped at the far back corner of the house and squatted down on the ground and looked underneath at the litter there, chicken crates and barrels and old rags and boxes. He had a small box of wooden matches in his pocket.

He crawled under and began to set small fires, building one from another, and working his way out at the front porch, leaving the fire behind him eating greedily at the dry tinder and the floor boards of the house. He crossed the front side of the yard and went through the rutted field without looking back until he reached the edge of the opposite woods. Then he glanced over his shoulder and saw that the pink moon had dropped through the roof of the shack and was bursting and he began to run, forced on through the woods by two bulging silver eyes that grew in immense astonishment in the center of the fire behind him. He could hear it moving up through the black night like a whirling chariot.

Toward midnight he came out on the highway and

caught a ride with a salesman who was a manufacturer's representative, selling copper flues throughout the Southeast, and who gave the silent boy what he said was the best advice he could give any young fellow setting out to find himself a place in the world. While they sped forward on the black untwisting highway, watched on either side by a dark wall of trees, the salesman said that it had been his personal experience that you couldn't sell a copper flue to a man you didn't love. He was a thin fellow with a narrow face that appeared to have been worn down to the sharpest possible depressions. He wore a broad-brimmed stiff grey hat of the kind used by businessmen who would like to look like cowboys. He said love was the only policy that worked 95% of the time. He said when he went to sell a man a flue, he asked first about that man's wife's health and how his children were. He said he had a book that he kept the names of his customers' families in and what was wrong with them. A man's wife had cancer, he put her name down in the book and wrote *cancer* after it and inquired about her every time he went to that man's hardware store until she died; then he scratched out the word *cancer* and wrote *dead* there. "And I say thank God when they're dead," the salesman said; "that's one less to remember."

"You don't owe the dead anything," Tarwater said in a loud voice, speaking for almost the first time since he had got in the car.

"Nor they you," said the stranger. "And that's the way it ought to be in this world—nobody owing nobody nothing."

"Look," Tarwater said suddenly, sitting forward, his face close to the windshield, "we're headed in the wrong direction. We're going back where we came from. There's the fire again. There's the fire we left!"

Ahead of them in the sky there was a faint glow, steady, and not made by lightning. "That's the same fire we came from!" the boy said in a high voice.

"Boy, you must be nuts," the salesman said. "That's the city we're coming to. That's the glow from the city lights. I reckon this is your first trip anywhere."

"You're turned around," the child said; "it's the same fire."

The stranger twisted his rutted face sharply. "I've never been turned around in my life," he said. "And I didn't come from any fire. I come from Mobile. And I know where I'm going. What's the matter with you?"

Tarwater sat staring at the glow in front of him. "I

was asleep," he muttered. "I'm just now waking up."

"You should have been listening to me," the salesman said. "I been telling you things you ought to know."

CHAPTER TWO

If the boy had actually trusted his new friend, Meeks, the copper flue salesman, he would have accepted Meeks' offer to take him directly to his uncle's door and let him out. Meeks had turned on the car light and told him to climb over onto the back seat and root around until he found the telephone book and when Tarwater had climbed back with it, he had showed him how to find his uncle's name in the book. Tarwater wrote the address and the telephone number down on the back of one of Meeks' cards. Meeks' telephone number was on the other side and he said any time Tarwater wanted to contact him for a little loan or any assistance, not to be afraid to use it. What Meeks had decided after about a half hour of the boy was that he was just enough off in the head and just ignorant enough to be a very hard worker, and he wanted a very ignorant energetic boy to work for him. But Tarwater was evasive. "I got to contact this uncle of mine, my only blood connection," he said.

Meeks could look at this boy and tell that he was running away from home, that he had left a mother and probably a sot-father and probably four or five brothers and sisters in a two-room shack set in a brush-swept bare-ground clearing just off the highway and that he was hightailing it for the big world, having first, from the way he reeked, fortified himself with stump liquor. He didn't for a minute believe he had any uncle at any such respectable address. He thought the boy had set his finger down on the name, Rayber, by chance and said, "That's him. A schoolteacher. My uncle."

"I'll take you right to his door," Meeks had said, fox-like. "We pass there going through town. We pass right by there."

"No," Tarwater said. He was sitting forward on the seat, looking out the window at a hill covered with old used-car bodies. In the indistinct darkness, they seemed to be drowning into the ground, to be about half-submerged already. The city hung in front of them on the side of the mountain as if it were a larger part of the same pile.

not yet buried so deep. The fire had gone out of it and it appeared settled into its unbreakable parts.

The boy did not intend to go to the schoolteacher's until daylight and when he went he intended to make it plain that he had not come to be beholden or to be studied for a schoolteacher magazine. He began trying to remember the schoolteacher's face so that he could stare him down in his mind before he actually faced him. He felt that the more he could recall about him, the less advantage the new uncle would have over him. The face had not been one that held together in his mind, though he remembered the sloping jaw and the black-rimmed glasses. What he could not picture were the eyes behind the glasses. He had no memory of them and there was every kind of contradiction in the rubble of his great-uncle's descriptions. Sometimes the old man had said the nephew's eyes were black and sometimes brown. The boy kept trying to find eyes that fit mouth, nose that fit chin, but every time he thought he had a face put together, it fell apart and he had to begin on a new one. It was as if the schoolteacher, like the devil, could take on any look that suited him.

Meeks was telling him about the value of work. He said that it had been his personal experience that if you wanted to get ahead, you had to work. He said this was the law of life and it was no way to get around it because it was inscribed on the human heart like love thy neighbor. He said these two laws were the team that worked together to make the world go round and that any individual who wanted to be a success and win the pursuit of happiness, that was all he needed to know.

The boy was beginning to see a consistent image for the schoolteacher's eyes and was not listening to this advice. He saw them dark gray, shadowed with knowledge, and the knowledge moved like tree reflections in a pond where far below the surface shadows a snake may glide and disappear. He had made a habit of catching his great-uncle in contradictions about the schoolteacher's appearance.

"I forget what color eyes he's got," the old man would say, irked. "What difference does the color make when I know the look? I know what's behind it."

"What's behind it?"

"Nothing. He's full of nothing."

"He knows a heap," the boy said. "I don't reckon it's anything he don't know."

"He don't know it's anything he can't know," the

old man said. "That's his trouble. He thinks if it's something he can't know then somebody smarter than him can tell him about it and he can know it just the same. And if you were to go there, the first thing he would do would be to test your head and tell you what you were thinking and howcome you were thinking it and what you ought to be thinking instead. And before long you wouldn't belong to your self no more, you would belong to him."

The boy had no intention of allowing this to happen. He knew enough about the schoolteacher to be on his guard. He knew two complete histories, the history of the world, beginning with Adam, and the history of the schoolteacher, beginning with his mother, old Tarwater's own and only sister who had run away from Powderhead when she was eighteen years old and had become—the old man said he would mince no words, even with a child—a whore, until she had found a man by the name of Rayber who was willing to marry one. At least once a week, beginning at the beginning, the old man had reviewed this history through to the end.

His sister and this Rayber had brought two children into the world, one the schoolteacher and one a girl who had turned out to be Tarwater's mother and who, the old man said, had followed in the natural footsteps of her own mother, being already a whore by the time she was eighteen.

The old man had a great deal to say about Tarwater's conception, for the schoolteacher had told him that he himself had got his sister this first (and last) lover because he thought it would contribute to her *self-confidence*. The old man would say this, imitating the schoolteacher's voice and making it sillier than the boy felt it probably was. The old man was thrown into a fury of exasperation that there was not enough scorn in the world to cast upon this idiocy. Finally he would give up trying. The lover had shot himself after the accident, which was a relief to the schoolteacher for he wanted to bring up the baby himself.

The old man said that with the devil having such a heavy role in his beginning, it was little wonder that he should have an eye on the boy and keep him under close surveillance during his time on earth, in order that the soul he had helped call into being might serve him forever in hell. "You are the kind of boy," the old man said, "that the devil is always going to be offering to assist, to give you a smoke or a drink or a ride, and to ask you your bidnis. You had better mind how you take up with strangers. And keep your bidnis to yourself." It was to foil the devil's plans for him that the Lord had seen to his upbringing.

"What line you going to get into?" Meeks asked.

The boy didn't appear to hear.

Whereas the schoolteacher had led his sister into evil, with success, old Tarwater had made every attempt to lead his own sister to repentance, without success. Through one means or another, he had managed to keep up with her after she ran away from Powderhead; but even after she married, she would not listen to any word that had to do with her salvation. He had twice been thrown out of her house by her husband—each time with the assistance of the police because the husband was a man of no force —but the Lord had prompted him constantly to go back, even in the face of going to jail. When he could not get inside the house, he would stand outside it and shout and then she would let him in lest he attract the attention of the neighbors. The neighborhood children would gather to listen to him and she would have to let him in.

It was not to be wondered at, the old man would say, that the schoolteacher was no better than he was with such a father as he had. The man, an insurance salesman, wore a straw hat on the side of his head and smoked a cigar and when you told him his soul was in danger, he offered to sell you a policy against any contingency. He said he was a prophet too, a prophet of life insurance, for every right-thinking Christian, he said, knew that it was his Christian duty to protect his family and provide for them in the event of the unexpected. There was no use treating with him, the old man said; his brain was as slick as his eyeballs and the truth would no more soak into it than rain would penetrate tin. The schoolteacher, with Tarwater blood in him, at least had his father's strain diluted. "Good blood flows in his veins," the old man said. "And good blood knows the Lord and there ain't a thing he can do about having it. There ain't a way in the world he can get rid of it."

Meeks abruptly poked the boy in the side with his elbow. He said if it was one thing a person needed to learn it was to pay attention to older people than him when they gave him good advice. He said he himself had graduated from the School of Experience with an H.L.L. degree. He asked the boy if he knew what was an H.L.L. degree. Tarwater shook his head. Meeks said the H.L.L. degree was the Hard Lesson from Life degree. He said it was the quickest got and that it stayed learnt the longest

The boy turned his head to the window.

One day the old man's sister had worked a perfidy on him. He had been in the habit of going on Wednesday afternoon because on that afternoon the husband played a golf game and he could find her alone. On this particular Wednesday, she did not open the door but he knew she was inside because he heard footsteps. He beat on the door a few times to warn her and when she wouldn't open it, he began to shout, for her and for all who would hear.

While he was telling this to Tarwater, he would jump up and begin to shout and prophesy there in the clearing the same way he had done it in front of her door. With no one to hear but the boy, he would flail his arms and roar, "Ignore the Lord Jesus as long as you can! Spit out the bread of life and sicken on honey. Whom work beckons, to work! Whom blood to blood! Whom lust to lust! Make haste, make haste. Fly faster and faster. Spin yourselves in a frenzy, the time is short! The Lord is preparing a prophet. The Lord is preparing a prophet with fire in his hand and eye and the prophet is moving toward the city with his warning. The prophet is coming with the Lord's message. 'Go warn the children of God,' saith the Lord, 'of the terrible speed of justice.' Who will be left? Who will be left when the Lord's mercy strikes?"

He might have been shouting to the silent woods that encircled them. While he was in his frenzy, the boy would take up the shotgun and hold it to his eye and sight along the barrel, but sometimes as his uncle grew more and more wild, he would lift his face from the gun for a moment with a look of uneasy alertness, as if while he had been inattentive, the old man's words had been dropping one by one into him and now, silent, hidden in his bloodstream, were moving secretly toward some goal of their own.

His uncle would prophesy until he exhausted himself and then he would fall with a thud on the sway-back step and sometimes it would be five or ten minutes before he could go on and relate how the sister had worked the perfidy on him.

Whenever he came to this part of the story, his breath would at once come short as if he were struggling to run up a hill. His face would get redder and his voice thinner and sometimes it would give out completely and he would sit there on the step, beating the porch floor with his fist while he moved his lips and no sound came out. Finally he would pipe, "They grabbed me. Two. From behind. The door behind. Two."

His sister had had two men and a doctor behind the door, listening, and the papers made out to commit him to the asylum if the doctor thought he was crazy. When he understood what was happening, he had raged through her house like a blinded bull, everything crashing behind him, and it had taken two of them and the doctor and two neighbors to get him down. The doctor had said he was not only crazy but dangerous and they had taken him to the asylum in a strait jacket.

"Ezekiel was in the pit for forty days," he would say, "but I was in it for four years," and he would stop at that point and warn Tarwater that the servants of the Lord Jesus could expect the worse. The boy could see that this was so. But no matter how little they had now, his uncle said, their reward in the end was the Lord Jesus Himself, the bread of life!

The boy would have a hideous vision of himself sitting forever with his great-uncle on a green bank, full and sick, staring at a broken fish and a multiplied loaf.

His uncle had been in the asylum four years because it had taken him four years to understand that the way for him to get out was to stop prophesying on the ward. It had taken him four years to discover what the boy felt he himself would have discovered in no time at all. But at least in the asylum the old man had learned caution and when he got out, he put everything he had learned to the service of his cause. He proceeded about the Lord's business like an experienced crook. He had given the sister up but he intended to help her boy. He planned to kidnap the child and keep him long enough to baptize him and instruct him in the facts of his Redemption and he mapped out his plan to the last detail and carried it out exactly.

Tarwater liked this part best because in spite of himself he had to admire his uncle's craft. The old man had persuaded Buford Munson to send his daughter in to get a job cooking for the sister and with the girl once in the house, he had been able to find out what he needed to know. He learned that there were two children now instead of one and that his sister sat in her nightgown all day drinking whiskey out of a medicine bottle. While Luella Munson washed and cooked and took care of the children, his sister lay on the bed sipping from the bottle and reading books that she had to buy fresh every night from the drugstore. But the principle reason the kidnapping had been so easy was because his great-uncle had had the full cooperation of the schoolteacher himself, a thin boy with a boney pale face and a pair of gold-rimmed spectacles that were always falling down his nose.

The two of them, the old man said, had liked each other from the first. The day he had gone to do the kidnapping, the husband was away on business and the sister, shut up in her room with the bottle, didn't even know the time of day. All the old man had done was to walk in and tell Luella Munson that his nephew was going off to spend a few days with him in the country and then he had gone out to the back yard and spoken to the schoolteacher who had been digging holes and lining them with broken glass.

He and the schoolteacher had taken the train as far as the junction and had walked the rest of the way to Powderhead. The old man had explained to him that he was not taking him on this trip for pleasure but because the Lord had sent him to do it, to see that he was born again and instructed in his Redemption. All these facts were new to the schoolteacher, for his parents had never taught him anything, old Tarwater said, except not to wet the bed.

In four days the old man taught him what was necessary to know and baptized him. He made him understand that his true father was the Lord and not the simpleton in town and that he would have to lead a secret life in Jesus until the day came when he would be able to bring the rest of his family around to repentance. He had made him understand that on the last day it would be his destiny to rise in glory in the Lord Jesus. Since this was the first time anybody had bothered to tell these facts to the schoolteacher, he could not hear too much of them, and as he had never seen woods before or been in a boat or caught a fish or walked on roads that were not paved, they did all those things too and, his uncle said, he even allowed him to plow. His sallow face had become bright in four days. At this point Tarwater would begin to weary of the story.

The schoolteacher had spent four days in the clearing because his mother had not missed him for three days and when Luella Munson had mentioned where he had gone, she had to wait another day before his father came home and she could send him after the child. She would not come herself, the old man said, for fear the wrath of God would strike her at Powderhead and she would not be able to get back to the city again. She had wired the schoolteacher's father and when the simpleton arrived at the clearing, the schoolteacher was in despair at having to leave. The light had left his eyes. He had gone but the old man insisted that he had been able to tell by the look on his face that he would never be the same boy again.

"If he didn't say he didn't want to go, you can't be sure he didn't," Tarwater would say contentiously.

"Then why did he try to come back?" the old man asked. "Answer me that. Why one week later did he run away and try to find his way back and got his picture in the paper when the state patrol found him in the woods? I ask you why. Tell me that if you know so much."

"Because here was less bad than there," Tarwater said. "Less bad don't mean good, it only means better-than."

"He tried to come back," his uncle said slowly, emphasizing each word, "to hear more about God his Father, more about Jesus Christ Who had died to redeem him and more of the Truth I could tell him."

"Well go on," Tarwater would say irritably, "get on with the rest of it." The story always had to be taken to completion. It was like a road that the boy had travelled on so often that half the time he didn't look where they were going, and when at certain points he would become aware where they were, he would be surprised to see that the old man had not got farther on with it. Sometimes his uncle would lag at one point as if he didn't want to face what was coming and then when he finally came to it, he would try to get past it in a rush. At such points, Tarwater plagued him for details. "Tell about when he came when he was fourteen years old and had already decided none of it was true and he give you all that sass."

"Bah," the old man would say. "He was living in confusion. I don't say it was his fault then. They told him I was a crazy man. But I'll tell you one thing: he never believed them neither. They kept him from believing me but I kept him from believing them and he never took on none of their ways though he took on worse ones. And when he got shut of the three of them in that crash, nobody was gladder than he was. Then he turned his mind to raising you. Said he was going to give you every advantage, every advantage." The old man snorted. "You have me to thank for saving you from those advantages."

The boy looked off into the distance as though he were staring blankly at his invisible advantages.

"When he got shut of the three of them in that crash, this was the first place he came. On the very day they were killed he came out here to tell me. Straight out here

Yes sir," the old man said with the greatest satisfaction, "straight out here. He hadn't seen me in years but this is where he came. I was the one he came to. I was the one he wanted to see. Me. I had never left his mind. I had taken my seat in it."

"You skipped all that part about how he came when he was fourteen and give you all that sass," Tarwater said.

"It was sass he got from them," the old man said. "Just parrot-mouthing all they had ever said about how I was a crazy man. The truth was even if they told him not to believe what I had taught him, he couldn't forget it. He never could forget that there was a chance that that simpleton was not his only father. I planted the seed in him and it was there for good. Whether anybody liked it or not."

"It fell amongst cockles," Tarwater said. "Say the sass."

"It fell in deep," the old man said, "or else after that crash he wouldn't have come out here hunting me."

"He only wanted to see if you were still crazy," the boy offered.

"The day may come," his great-uncle said slowly, "when a pit opens up inside you and you know some things you never known before," and he would give him such a prescient piercing look that the child would turn his face away, scowling fiercely.

His great-uncle had gone to live with the schoolteacher and as soon as he had got there, he had baptized Tarwater, practically under the schoolteacher's nose and the schoolteacher had made a blasphemous joke of it. But the old man could never tell this straight through. He always had to back up and tell why he had gone to live with the schoolteacher in the first place. He had gone for three reasons. One, he said, because he knew the schoolteacher wanted him. He was the only person in the schoolteacher's life who had ever taken two steps out of his way in his behalf. And two, because his nephew was the proper person to bury him and he wanted to have it understood with him how he wanted it done. And three, because the old man meant to see that Tarwater was baptized.

"I know all that," the boy would say, "get on with the rest of it."

"After the three of them perished and the house was his, he cleared it out," old Tarwater said. "He moved every stick of furniture out of it except a table and a chair or two and a bed or two and the crib he bought for you. Taken down all the pictures and all the curtains and taken up all the rugs. Even burned up all his mother's and sister's and the simpleton's clothes, didn't want a thing of theirs around. It wasn't anything left but books and papers that he had collected. Papers everywhere," the old man said. "Every room looked like the inside of a bird's nest. I came a few days after the crash and when he saw me standing there, he was glad to see me. His eyes lit up. He was glad to see me. 'Ha,' he said, 'my house is swept and garnished and here are the seven other devils, all rolled into one!' " The old man slapped his knee with pleasure.

"It don't sound to me like . . ."

"No, he didn't say so," the uncle said, "but I ain't an idiot."

"If he didn't say so you can't be sure."

"I'm as sure," his uncle said, "as I am that this here," and he held up his hand, every short thick finger stretched rigid in front of Tarwater's face, "is my hand and not yours." There was something final in this that always made the boy's impudence subside.

"Well get on with it," he would say. "If you don't make haste, you'll never get to where he blasphemed at."

"He was glad to see me," his uncle said. "He opened the door with all that house full of paper-trash behind him and there I stood and he was glad to see me. It was all underneath his face."

"What did he say?" Tarwater asked.

"He looked at my satchel," the old man said, "and he said, 'Uncle, you can't live with me. I know exactly what you want but I'm going to raise this child my way.' "

These words of the schoolteacher's had always caused a quick charge of excitement to race through Tarwater, an almost sensuous satisfaction. "It might have sounded to you like he was glad to see you," he said. "It don't sound that way to me."

"He wasn't but twenty-four years old," the old man said. "His expression hadn't even set on his face yet. I could still see the seven-year-old boy that had gone off with me, except that now he had a pair of black-rimmed glasses and a nose big enough to hold them up. The size of his eyes had shrunk because his face had grown but it was the same face all right. You could see behind it to what he really wanted to say. When he came out here later to get you back after I had stolen you, it was already set. It was as set then as the outside of a penitentiary but not now when I'm telling you about. Then it wasn't set and I could see he wanted me. Else why had he come out to Powderhead to tell me they were all dead? I ask you that? He could have let me alone."

The boy couldn't answer.

"Anyway," the old man said, "what all he gone on and done proved he wanted me right then because he took me in. He looked at my satchel and I said, 'I'm on your charity,' and he said, 'I'm sorry, Uncle. You can't live with me and ruin another child's life. This one is going to be brought up to live in the real world. He's going to be brought up to expect exactly what he can do for himself. He's going to be his own saviour. He's going to be free!' " The old man turned his head to the side and spit. "Free," he said. "He was full of such-like phrases. But then I said it. I said what changed his mind."

The boy sighed at this. The old man considered it his master stroke. He had said, "I never come to live with you. I come to die!"

"And you should have seen his face," he said. "He looked like he'd been pushed all of a sudden from behind. He hadn't cared if the other three were wiped out but when he thought of me going, it was like he was losing somebody for the first time. He stood there staring at me." And once, only once, the old man had leaned forward and said to Tarwater, in a voice that could no longer contain the pleasure of its secret, "He loved me like a daddy and he was ashamed of it!"

The boy's face had remained unmoved. "Yes," he said, "and you had told him a bare-face lie. You never had no intention of dying."

"I was sixty-nine years of age," his uncle said. "I could have died the next day as well as not. No man knows the hour of his death. I didn't have my life in front of me. It was not a lie, it was only a speculation. I told him, I said, 'I may live two months or two days.' And I had on my clothes that I bought to be buried in—all new."

"Ain't it that same suit you got on now?" the boy asked indignantly, pointing to the threadbare knee. "Ain't it that one you got on yourself right now?"

"I may live two months or two days, I said to him," his uncle said.

Or ten years or twenty, Tarwater thought.

"Oh it was a shock to him," the old man said.

It might have been a shock, the boy thought, but he wasn't all that sorry about it. The schoolteacher had merely said, "So I'm to put you away, Uncle? All right, I'll put you away. I'll do it with pleasure. I'll put you away for good and all," but the old man insisted that his words were one thing and his actions and the look on his face another.

His great-uncle had not been in the nephew's house ten minutes before he had baptized Tarwater. They had gone into the room where the crib was with Tarwater in it and as the old man looked at him for the first time—a wizened grey-faced scrawny sleeping baby—the voice of the Lord had come to him and said: HERE IS THE PROPHET TO TAKE YOUR PLACE. BAPTIZE HIM.

That? the old man had asked, that wizened grey-faced . . . and then as he wondered how he could baptize him with the nephew standing there, the Lord had sent the paper boy to knock on the door and the schoolteacher had gone to answer it.

When he came back in a few minutes, his uncle was holding Tarwater in one hand and with the other he was pouring water over his head out of the bottle that had been on the table by the crib. He had pulled off the nipple and stuck it in his pocket. He was just finishing the words of baptism as the schoolteacher came back in the door and he had had to laugh when he looked up and saw his nephew's face. It looked hacked, the old man said. Not even angry at first, just hacked.

Old Tarwater had said, "He's been born again and there ain't a thing you can do about it," and then he had seen the rage rise in the nephew's face and had seen him try to conceal it.

"Time has passed you by, Uncle," the nephew said. "That can't even irritate me. That only makes me laugh," and he laughed, a short forced bark, but the old man said his face was mottled. "Just as well you did it now," he said. "If you had got me when I was seven days instead of seven years, you might not have ruined my life."

"If it's ruined," the old man said, "it wasn't me that ruined it."

"Oh yes it was," the nephew said, advancing across the room, his face very red. "You're too blind to see what you did to me. A child can't defend himself. Children are cursed with believing. You pushed me out of the real world and I stayed out of it until I didn't know which was which. You infected me with your idiot hopes, your foolish violence. I'm not always myself, I'm not al . . ." but he stopped. He wouldn't admit what the old man knew. "There's nothing wrong with me," he said. "I've straightened the tangle you made. Straightened it by pure will power. I've made myself straight."

"You see," the old man said, "he admitted himself the seed was still in him."

Old Tarwater had laid the baby back in the crib but the nephew took him out again, a peculiar smile, the old man said, stiffening on his face. "If one baptism is good, two will be better," he said and he had turned Tarwater over and poured what was left in the bottle over his bottom and said the words of baptism again. Old Tarwater had stood there, aghast at this blasphemy. "Now Jesus has a claim on both ends," the nephew said.

The old man had roared, "Blasphemy never changed a plan of the Lord's!"

"And the Lord hasn't changed any of mine either," said the nephew coolly and put the baby back.

"And what did I do?" Tarwater asked.

"You didn't do nothing," the old man said as if what he did or didn't do was of no consequence whatsoever.

"It was me that was the prophet," the boy said sullenly.

"You didn't even know what was going on," his uncle said.

"Oh yes I did," the child said. "I was laying there thinking."

His uncle would ignore this and go on. He had thought for a while that by living with the schoolteacher, he might convince him again of all that he had convinced him of when he had kidnapped him as a child and he had had hope of it up until the time when the schoolteacher showed him the study he had written of him for the magazine. Then the old man had realized at last that there was no hope of his doing anything for the schoolteacher. He had failed the schoolteacher's mother and he had failed the schoolteacher, and now there was nothing to do but try to save Tarwater from being brought up by a fool. In this he had not failed.

The boy felt that the schoolteacher could have made more of an effort to get him back. He had come out and got shot in the leg and the ear but if he had used his head, he might have avoided that and got him back at the same time. "Why didn't he bring the law out here and get me back?" he had asked.

"You want to know why?" his uncle said. "Well I'll tell you why. I'll tell you exactly why. It was because he found you a heap of trouble. He wanted it all in his head. You can't change a child's pants in your head."

The boy would think: but if the schoolteacher hadn't written that piece on him, we might all three be living in town right now.

When the old man had read the piece in the schoolteacher magazine, he had at first not recognized who it was the schoolteacher was writing about, who the type was that was almost extinct. He had sat down to read the piece, full of pride that his nephew had succeeded in having a composition printed in a magazine. He had handed it carelessly to his uncle and said he might want to glance over it and the old man had sat down at once at the kitchen table and commenced to read it. He recalled that the schoolteacher had kept passing by the kitchen door to witness how he was taking the piece.

About the middle of it, old Tarwater had begun to think that he was reading about someone he had once known or at least someone he had dreamed about, for the figure was strangely familiar. "This fixation of being called by the Lord had its origin in insecurity. He needed the assurance of a call and so he called himself," he read. The schoolteacher kept passing by the door, passing and repassing, and finally he came in and sat down quietly on the other side of the small white metal table. When the old man looked up, the schoolteacher smiled. It was a very slight smile, the slightest that would do for any occasion. The old man knew from the smile who it was he had been reading about.

For the length of a minute, he could not move. He felt he was tied hand and foot inside the schoolteacher's head, a space as bare and neat as the cell in the asylum, and was shrinking, drying up to fit it. His eyeballs swerved from side to side as if he were pinned in a strait jacket again. Jonah, Ezekiel, Daniel, he was at that moment all of them—the swallowed, the lowered, the enclosed.

The nephew, his smile still fixed, reached across the table and put his hand on the old man's wrist in a gesture of pity. "You've got to be born again, Uncle," he said, "by your own efforts, back to the real world where there's no saviour but yourself."

The old man's tongue lay in his mouth like a stone but his heart began to swell. His prophet's blood surged in him, surged to floodtide for a miraculous release, though his face remained shocked, expressionless. The nephew patted his huge clenched fist and got up and left the kitchen, bearing away his smile of triumph.

The next morning when he went to the crib to give the baby his bottle, he found nothing in it but the blue magazine with the old man's message scrawled on the back of it: THE PROPHET I RAISE UP OUT OF THIS BOY WILL BURN YOUR EYES CLEAN.

"It was me could act," the old man said, "not him. He could never take action. He could only get everything inside his head and grind it to nothing. But I acted. And because I acted, you sit here in freedom, you sit here a rich man, knowing the Truth, in the freedom of the Lord Jesus Christ."

The boy would move his thin shoulder blades irritably as if he were shifting the burden of Truth like a cross on his back. "He came out here and got shot to get me back," he said obstinately.

"If he had really wanted you back, he could have got you," the old man said. "He could have had the law out here after me or got me put back in the asylum. There was plenty he could have done, but what happened to him was that welfare-woman. She persuaded him to have one of his own and let you go, and he was easy persuaded. And that one," the old man would say, beginning to brood on the schoolteacher's child again, "that one—the Lord gave him one he couldn't corrupt." And then he would grip the boy's shoulder and put a fierce pressure on it. "And if I don't get him baptized, it'll be for you to do," he said. "I enjoin you to do it, boy."

Nothing irritated the boy so much as this. "I take my orders from the Lord," he would say in an ugly voice, trying to pry the fingers out of his shoulder. "Not from you."

"The Lord will give them to you," the old man said, gripping his shoulder tighter.

"He had to change that one's pants and he done it," Tarwater muttered.

"He had the welfare-woman to do it for him," his uncle said. "She had to be good for something, but you can bet she ain't still around there. Bernice Bishop!" he said as if he found this the most idiotic name in the language. "Bernice Bishop!"

The boy had sense enough to know that he had been betrayed by the schoolteacher and he did not mean to go to his house until daylight, when he could see behind and before him. "I ain't going there until daylight," he said suddenly to Meeks. "You needn't to stop there because I ain't getting out there."

Meeks leaned casually against the door of the car, driving with half his attention and giving the other half to Tarwater. "Son," he said, "I'm not going to be a preacher to you. I'm not going to tell you not to lie. I ain't going to tell you nothing impossible. All I'm going to tell you is this: don't lie when you don't have to. Else when you do have to, nobody'll believe you. You don't have to lie to me. I know exactly what you done." A shaft of light plunged through the car window and he looked to the side and saw the white face beside him, staring up with soot-colored eyes.

"How do you know?" the boy asked.

Meeks smiled with pleasure. "Because I done the same thing myself once," he said.

Tarwater caught hold of the sleeve of the salesman's coat and gave it a quick pull. "On the Day of Judgment," he said, "me and you will rise and say we done it!"

Meeks looked at him again with one eyebrow cocked at the same angle he wore his hat. "Will we?" he asked. Then he said, "What line you gonna get into, boy?"

"What line?"

"What you going to do? What kind of *work?*"

"I know everything but the machines," Tarwater said, sitting back again. "My great-uncle learnt me everything but first I have to find out how much of it is true." They were entering the dilapidated outskirts of the city where wooden buildings leaned together and an occasional dim light lit up a faded sign advertising some remedy or other.

"What line was your great-uncle in?" Meeks asked.

"He was a prophet," the boy said.

"Is that right?" Meeks asked and his shoulders jumped several times as if they were going to leap over his head. "Who'd he prophesy to?"

"To me," Tarwater said. "Nobody else would listen to him and there wasn't anybody else for me to listen to. He grabbed me away from this other uncle, my only blood connection now, so as to save me from running to doom."

"You were a captive audience," Meeks said. "And now you're coming to town to run to doom with the rest of us, huh?"

The boy didn't answer at once. Then he said in a guarded tone, "I ain't said what I'm going to do."

"You ain't sure about what all this great-uncle of yours told you, are you?" Meeks asked. "You figure he might have got aholt to some misinformation."

Tarwater looked away, out the window, at the brittle forms of the houses. He was holding both arms close to his sides as if he were cold. "I'll find out," he said.

"Well how now?" Meeks asked.

The dark city was unfolding on either side of them and they were approaching a low circle of light in the distance. "I mean to wait and see what happens," he said after a moment.

"And suppose nothing don't happen?" Meeks asked.

The circle of light became huge and they swung into the center of it and stopped. It was a gaping concrete mouth with two red gas pumps set in front of it and a small glass office toward the back. "I say suppose nothing don't happen?" Meeks repeated.

The boy looked at him darkly, remembering the silence after his great-uncle's death.

"Well?" Meeks said.

"Then I'll make it happen," he said. "I can act."

"Attaboy," Meeks said. He opened the car door and put his leg out while he continued to observe his rider. Then he said, "Wait a minute. I got to call my girl."

A man was asleep in a chair tilted against the outside wall of the glass office and Meeks went inside without waking him up. For a minute Tarwater only craned his neck out the window. Then he got out and went to the office door to watch Meeks use the machine. It sat, small and black, in the center of a cluttered desk which Meeks sat down on as if it had been his own. The room was lined with automobile tires and had a concrete and rubber smell. Meeks took the machine in two parts and held one part to his head while he circled with his finger on the other part. Then he sat waiting, swinging his foot, while the horn buzzed in his ear. After a minute an acid smile began to eat at the corners of his mouth and he said, drawing in his breath, "Heythere, Sugar, hyer you?" and Tarwater, from where he stood in the door, heard an actual woman's voice, like one coming from beyond the grave, say, "Why Sugar, is that reely you?" and Meeks said it was him in the same old flesh and made an appointment with her in ten minutes.

Tarwater stood awestruck in the doorway. Meeks put the telephone together and then he said in a sly voice, "Now why don't you call your uncle?" and watched the boy's face change, the eyes swerve suspiciously to the side and the flesh drop around the boney mouth.

"I'll speak with him soon enough," he muttered, but he kept looking at the black coiled machine, fascinated. "How do you use it?" he asked.

"You dial it like I did. Call your uncle," Meeks urged.

"No, that woman is waiting on you," Tarwater said.

"Let 'er wait," Meeks said. "That's what she knows how to do best."

The boy approached it, taking out the card he had written

the number on. He put his finger on the dial and began
gingerly to turn it.

"Great God," Meeks said and took the receiver off
the hook and put it in his hand and thrust his hand to
his ear. He dialed the number for him and then pushed
him down in the office chair to wait but Tarwater stood
up again, slightly crouched, holding the buzzing horn
to his head, while his heart began to kick viciously at
his chest wall.

"It don't speak," he murmured.

"Give him time," Meeks said, "maybe he don't like
to get up in the middle of the night."

The buzzing continued for a minute and then stopped
abruptly. Tarwater stood speechless, holding the earpiece
tight against his head, his face rigid as if he were afraid
that the Lord might be about to speak to him over the
machine. All at once he heard what sounded like heavy
breathing in his ear.

"Ask for your party," Meeks prompted. "How do you
expect to get your party if you don't ask for him?"

The boy remained exactly as he was, saying nothing.

"I told you to ask for your party," Meeks said irritably.
"Ain't you got good sense?"

"I want to speak with my uncle," Tarwater whispered.

There was a silence over the telephone but it was not
a silence that seemed to be empty. It was the kind where
the breath is drawn in and held. Suddenly the boy realized
that it was the schoolteacher's child on the other side
of the machine. The white-haired, blunted face rose before
him. He said in a furious shaking voice, "I want to speak
with my uncle. Not you!"

The heavy breathing began again as if in answer. It
was a kind of bubbling noise, the kind of noise someone
would make who was struggling to breathe in water.
In a second it faded away. The horn of the machine dropped
out of Tarwater's hand. He stood there blankly as if
he had received a revelation he could not yet decipher.
He seemed to have been stunned by some deep internal
blow that had not yet made its way to the surface of
his mind.

Meeks picked up the earpiece and listened but there
was no sound. He put it back on the hook and said, "Come
on. I ain't got this kind of time." He gave the stupefied
boy a shove and they left, driving off into the city again.
Meeks told him to learn to work every machine he saw.
The greatest invention of man, he said, was the wheel
and he asked Tarwater if he had ever thought how things

were before it was a wheel, but the boy didn't answer him. He didn't even appear to be listening. He sat slightly forward and from time to time his lips moved as if he were speaking silently with himself.

"Well, it was terrible," Meeks said sourly. He knew the boy didn't have any uncle at any such respectable address and to prove it, he turned down the street the uncle was supposed to live on and drove slowly past the small shapes of squat houses until he found the number, visible in phosphorescent letters on a small stick set on the edge of the grass plot. He stopped the car and said, "Okay, kiddo, that's it."

"That's what?" Tarwater mumbled.

"That's your uncle's house," Meeks said.

The boy grabbed the edge of the window with both hands and stared out at what appeared to be only a black shape crouched in a greater darkness a little distance away. "I told you I wasn't going there until daylight," he said angrily; "go on."

"You're going there right now," Meeks said. "Because I ain't getting stuck with you. You can't go with me where I'm going."

"I ain't getting out here," the boy said.

Meeks reached across him and opened the car door. "So long, son," he said, "if you get real hungry by next week, you can contack me from that card and we might make a deal."

The boy gave him one white-faced outraged look and flung himself from the car. He moved up the short concrete walk to the doorstep and sat down abruptly, absorbed into the darkness. Meeks pulled the car door shut. His face hung for a moment watching the barely visible outline of the boy's shape on the step. Then he drew back and drove on. He won't come to no good end, he said to himself.

CHAPTER THREE

Tarwater sat in the corner of the doorstep, scowling in the dark as the car disappeared down the block. He did not look up at the sky but he was unpleasantly aware of the stars. They seemed to be holes in his skull through which some distant unmoving light was watching him. It was as if he were alone in the presence of an immense silent eye. He had an intense desire to make himself known to the schoolteacher at once, to tell him what he had done and why and to be congratulated by him. At the same time, his deep suspicion of the man continued to work in him. He tried to bring the schoolteacher's face again to mind, but all he could manage was the face of the seven-year-old boy the old man had kidnapped. He stared at it boldly, hardening himself for the encounter.

Then he rose and faced the heavy brass knocker on the door. He touched it and jerked his hand away, burnt by a metallic coldness. He looked quickly over his shoulder. The houses across the street formed a dark jagged wall. The quiet seemed palpable, waiting. It seemed almost to be waiting patiently, biding its time until it should reveal itself and demand to be named. He turned back to the cold knocker and grabbed it and shattered the silence as if it were a personal enemy. The noise filled his head. He was aware of nothing but the racket he was making.

He beat louder and louder, bamming at the same time with his free fist until he felt he was shaking the house. The empty street echoed with his blows. He stopped once to get his breath and then began again, kicking the door frenziedly with the blunt toe of his heavy work shoe. Nothing happened. Finally he stopped and the implacable silence descended around him, immune to his fury. A mysterious dread filled him. His whole body felt hollow as if he had been lifted like Habakkuk by the hair of his head, borne swiftly through the night and set down in the place of his mission. He had a sudden foreboding that he was about to step into a trap laid for him by the old man. He half-turned to run.

At once the glass panels on either side of the door

filled with light. There was a click and the knob turned. Tarwater jerked his hands up automatically as if he were pointing an invisible gun and his uncle, who had opened the door, jumped back at the sight of him.

The image of the seven-year-old boy disappeared forever from Tarwater's mind. His uncle's face was so familiar to him that he might have seen it every day of his life. He steadied himself and shouted, "My great-uncle is dead and burnt, just like you would have burnt him yourself!"

The schoolteacher remained absolutely still as if he thought that by looking long enough his hallucination would disappear. He had been roused by the vibration in the house and had run, half-asleep, to the door. His face was like the face of a sleep-walker who wakes and sees some horror of his dreams take shape before him. After a moment he muttered, "Wait here, deaf," and turned and went quickly out of the hall. He was barefooted and in his pajamas. He came back almost at once, plugging something into his ear. He had thrust on the black-rimmed glasses and he was sticking a metal box into the waist-band of his pajamas. This was joined by a cord to the plug in his ear. For an instant the boy had the thought that his head ran by electricity. He caught Tarwater by the arm and pulled him into the hall under a lantern-shaped light that hung from the ceiling. The boy found himself scrutinized by two small drill-like eyes set in the depths of twin glass caverns. He drew away. Already he felt his privacy imperilled.

"My great-uncle is dead and burnt," he said again. "I was the only one there to do it and I done it. I done your work for you," and as he said the last, a perceptible trace of scorn crossed his face.

"Dead?" the schoolteacher said. "My uncle? The old man's dead?" he asked in a blank unbelieving tone. He caught Tarwater abruptly by the arms and stared into his face. In the depths of his eyes, the boy, shocked, saw an instant's stricken look, plain and awful. It vanished at once. The straight line of the schoolteacher's mouth began turning into a smile. "And how did he go—with his fist in the air?" he asked. "Did the Lord arrive for him in a chariot of fire?"

"He didn't have no warning," Tarwater said, suddenly breathless. "He was eating his breakfast and I never moved him from the table. I set him on fire where he was and the house with him."

The schoolteacher said nothing but the boy read in his look a doubt that this had happened, a suspicion that he dealt with an interesting liar.

"You can go there and see for yourself," Tarwater said. "He was too big to bury. I done it the quickest way."

His uncle's eyes had the look now of being trained on a fascinating problem. "How did you get here? How did you know this was where you belonged?" he asked.

The boy had expended all his energy announcing himself. He was suddenly blank and stunned and he remained stupidly silent. He had never been this tired before. He felt he was about to fall.

The schoolteacher waited, searching his face impatiently. Then his expression changed again. He tightened his grip on Tarwater's arm and his eyes turned, glowering, toward the front door, which was still open. "Is he out there?" he asked in a low enraged voice. "Is this one of his tricks? Is he out there waiting to sneak in a window and baptize Bishop while you're here baiting me? Is that his senile game this time?"

The boy blanched. In his mind's eye he saw the old man, a dark shape standing behind the corner of the house, restraining his wheezing breath while he waited impatiently for him to baptize the dim-witted child. He stared shocked at the schoolteacher's face. There was a wedge-shaped gash in his new uncle's ear. The sight of it brought old Tarwater so close that the boy thought he could hear him laugh. With a terrible clarity he saw that the schoolteacher was no more than a decoy the old man had set up to lure him to the city to do his unfinished business.

His eyes began to burn in his fierce fragile face. A new energy seized him. "He's dead," he said. "You can't be any deader than he is. He's reduced to ashes. He don't even have a cross set up over him. If it's anything left of him, the buzzards wouldn't have it and the bones the dogs'll carry off. That's how dead he is."

The schoolteacher winced, but almost at once he was smiling again. He held Tarwater's arms tightly and peered into his face as if he were beginning to see a solution, one that intrigued him with its symmetry and rightness. "It's a perfect irony," he murmured, "a perfect irony that you should have taken care of the matter in that way. He got what he deserved."

The boy's pride swelled. "I done the needful," he said.

"Everything he touched he warped," the schoolteacher said. "He lived a long and useless life and he did you a great injustice. It's a blessing he's dead at last. You could have had everything and you've had nothing. All that can be changed now. Now you belong to someone who can help you and understand you." His eyes were alight with pleasure. "It's not too late for me to make a man of you!"

The boy's face darkened. His expression hardened until it was a fortress wall to keep his thoughts from being exposed; but the schoolteacher did not notice any change. He gazed through the actual insignificant boy before him to an image of him that he held fully developed in his mind.

"You and I will make up for lost time," he said. "We'll get you started now in the right direction."

Tarwater was not looking at him. His neck had suddenly snapped forward and he was staring straight ahead over the schoolteacher's shoulder. He heard a faint familiar sound of heavy breathing. It was closer to him than the beating of his own heart. His eyes widened and an inner door in them opened in preparation for some inevitable vision.

The small white-haired boy shambled into the back of the hall and stood peering forward at the stranger. He had on the bottoms to a pair of blue pajamas drawn up as high as they would go, the string tied over his chest and then again, harness-like, around his neck to keep them on. His eyes were slightly sunken beneath his forehead and his cheekbones were lower than they should have been. He stood there, dim and ancient, like a child who had been a child for centuries.

Tarwater clenched his fists. He stood like one condemned, waiting at the spot of execution. Then the revelation came, silent, implacable, direct as a bullet. He did not look into the eyes of any fiery beast or see a burning bush. He only knew, with a certainty sunk in despair, that he was expected to baptize the child he saw and begin the life his great-uncle had prepared him for. He knew that he was called to be a prophet and that the ways of his prophecy would not be remarkable. His black pupils, glassy and still, reflected depth on depth his own stricken image of himself, trudging into the distance in the bleeding stinking mad shadow of Jesus, until at last he received his reward, a broken fish, a multiplied loaf. The Lord out of dust had created him, had made him blood and nerve and mind, had made him to bleed and weep and think, and set him in a world of loss and fire all to baptize one idiot child that He need not have created in the first place and to cry out a gospel just as foolish. He tried to shout, "NO!" but it was like trying to shout in his sleep. The sound was saturated in silence, lost.

His uncle put a hand on his shoulder and shook him slightly to penetrate his inattention. "Listen boy," he said, "getting out from under the old man is just like coming out of the darkness into the light. You're going to have a chance now for the first time in your life. A chance to develop into a useful man, a chance to use your talents, to do what you want to do and not what he wanted—whatever idiocy it was."

The boy's eyes were focussed beyond him, the pupils dilated. The schoolteacher turned his head to see what it was that was keeping him from being responsive. His own face tightened. The little boy was creeping forward, grinning.

"That's only Bishop," he said. "He's not all right. Don't mind him. All he can do is stare at you and he's very friendly. He stares at everything that way." His hand tightened on the boy's shoulder and his mouth stretched painfully. "All the things that I would do for him—if it were any use—I'll do for you," he said. "Now do you see why I'm so glad to have you here?"

The boy heard nothing he said. The muscles in his neck stood out like cables. The dim-witted child was not five feet from him and was coming every instant closer with his lop-sided smile. Suddenly he knew that the child *recognized* him, that the old man himself had primed him from on high that here was the forced servant of God come to see that he was born again. The little boy was sticking out his hand to touch him.

"Git!" Tarwater screamed. His arm shot out like a whip and knocked the hand away. The child let out a bellow startlingly loud. He clambered up his father's leg, pulling himself up by the schoolteacher's pajama coat until he was almost on his shoulder.

"All right, all right," the schoolteacher said, "there, there, shut up, it's all right, he didn't mean to hit you," and he righted the child on his back and tried to slide him off but the little boy hung on, thrusting his head against his father's neck and never taking his eyes off Tarwater.

The boy had a vision of the schoolteacher and his child as inseparably joined. The schoolteacher's face was red and pained. The child might have been a deformed part of himself that had been accidentally revealed.

"You'll get used to him," he said.

"No!" the boy shouted.

It was like a shout that had been waiting, straining to burst out. "I won't get used to him! I won't have anything to do with him!" He clenched his fist and lifted it. "I won't have anything to do with him!" he shouted and the words were clear and positive and defiant like a challenge hurled in the face of his silent adversary.

PART

2

CHAPTER FOUR

After four days of Tarwater, the schoolteacher's enthusiasm had passed. He would admit no more than that. It had passed the first day and had been succeeded by determination, and while he knew that determination was a less powerful tool, he thought that in this case, it was the one best fitted for the job. It had taken him barely half a day to find out that the old man had made a wreck of the boy and that what was called for was a monumental job of reconstruction. The first day enthusiasm had given him energy but ever since, determination had exhausted him.

Although it was only eight o'clock in the evening, he had put Bishop to bed and had told the boy that he could go to his room and read. He had bought him books, among other things still ignored. Tarwater had gone to his room and had closed the door, not saying whether he intended to read or not, and Rayber was in bed for the night, lying too exhausted to sleep, watching the late evening light fade through the hedge that grew in front of his window. He had left his hearing aid on so that if the boy tried to escape, he would hear and could go after him. For the last two days he had looked poised to leave, and not simply to leave but to be gone, silently and in the night when he would not be followed. This was the fourth night and the schoolteacher lay thinking, with a wry expression on his face, how it differed from the first.

The first night he had sat until daylight by the side of the bed where, still dressed, the boy had fallen. He had sat there, his eyes shining, like a man who sits before a treasure he is not yet convinced is real. His eyes had moved over and over the sprawled thin figure which had appeared lost in an exhaustion so profound that it seemed doubtful it would ever move again. As he followed the outline of the face, he had realized with an intense stab of joy that his nephew looked enough like him to be his son. The heavy work shoes, the worn overalls, the atrocious stained hat filled him with pain and pity. He thought of his poor sister. The only real pleasure she had had in her life was the time she had had the lover who had given

363

her this child, the hollow-cheeked boy who had come from the country to study divinity but whose mind Rayber (a graduate student at the time) had seen at once was too good for that. He had befriended him, and helped him to discover himself and then to discover her. He had engineered their meeting purposely and then had observed to his delight how it prospered and how the relationship developed them both. If there had been no accident, he felt sure the boy would have become completely stable. As it was, after the calamity he had killed himself, a prey to morbid guilt. He had come to Rayber's apartment and had stood confronting him with the gun. He saw again the long brittle face as raw red as if a blast of fire had singed the skin off it and the eyes that had seemed burnt too. He had not felt they were entirely human eyes. They were the eyes of repentance and lacked all dignity. The boy had looked at him for what seemed an age but was perhaps only a second, then he had turned without a word and left and killed himself as soon as he reached his own room.

When Rayber had first opened the door in the middle of the night and had seen Tarwater's face—white, drawn by some unfathomable hunger and pride—he had remained for an instant frozen before what might have been a mirror thrust toward him in a nightmare. The face before him was his own, but the eyes were not his own. They were the student's eyes, singed with guilt. He had left the door hurriedly to get his glasses and his hearing aid.

As he sat that first night by the bed, he had recognized something rigid and recalcitrant about the boy even in repose. He lay with his teeth bared and the hat clenched in his fist like a weapon. Rayber's conscience smote him that all these years he had left him to his fate, that he had not gone back and saved him. His throat had tightened, his eyes had begun to ache. He had vowed to make it up to him now, to lavish on him everything he would have lavished on his own child if he had had one who would have known the difference.

The next morning while Tarwater was still asleep, he had rushed out and bought him a decent suit, a plaid shirt, socks, and a red leather cap. He wanted him to have new clothes to wake up to, new clothes to indicate a new life.

After four days they were still untouched in the box on a chair in the room. The boy had looked at them as if the suggestion he put them on were equal to asking that he appear naked.

It was apparent from everything he did and said exactly who had brought him up. At every turn an almost un-

controllable fury would rise in Rayber at the brand of
independence the old man had wrought—not a constructive
independence but one that was irrational, backwoods, and
ignorant. After Rayber had rushed back with the clothes,
he had gone to the bed and put his hand on the still sleeping
boy's forehead and decided that he had a fever and should
not get up. He had prepared a breakfast on a tray and
brought it to the room. When he appeared in the door with
it, Bishop at his side, Tarwater was sitting up in the bed, in
the act of shaking out his hat and putting it on. Rayber had
said, "Don't you want to hang up your hat and stay a while?"
and had given him such a smile of welcome and good
will as he thought had possibly never been turned on him
before.

The boy, with no look of appreciation or even interest,
had pulled the hat down farther on his head. His gaze
had turned with a peculiar glare of recognition to Bishop.
The child had on a black cowboy hat and he was gaping
over the top of a trashbasket that he clasped to his stomach.
He kept a rock in it. Rayber remembered that Bishop had
caused the boy some disturbance the night before and he
pushed him back with his free hand so that he could not
get in. Then stepping into the room, he closed the door
and locked it. Tarwater looked at the closed door darkly
as if he continued to see the child through it, still clasping
his trashbasket.

Rayber set the tray down across his knees and stood
back scrutinizing him. The boy seemed barely aware that
he was in the room. "That's your breakfast," his uncle
said as if he might not be able to identify it. It was a
bowl of dry cereal and a glass of milk. "I thought you'd
better stay in bed today," he said. "You don't look too
chipper." He pulled up a straight chair and sat down. "Now
we can have a real talk," he said, his smile spreading. "It's
high time we got to know each other."

No expression of approval or pleasure lightened the
boy's face. He glanced at the breakfast but did not pick
up the spoon. He began to look around the room. The
walls were an insistent pink, the color chosen by Rayber's
wife. He used it now for a store room. There were trunks
in the corners with crates piled on top of them. On the
mantel, besides medicine bottles and dead electric lightbulbs
and some old match boxes, was a picture of her. The
boy's attention paused there and the corner of his mouth
twitched slightly as if in some kind of comic recognition.
"The welfare woman," he said.

His uncle reddened. The tone he detected under this

was old Tarwater's exactly. Without warning, irritation mounted in him. The old man might suddenly have obtruded his presence between them. He felt the same familiar fantastic anger, out of all proportion to its cause, that his uncle had always been able to stir in him. With an effort, he forced it out of his way. "That's my wife," he said, "but she doesn't live with us anymore. This is her old room you're in."

The boy picked up the spoon. "My great-uncle said she wouldn't hang around long," he said and began to eat rapidly as if he had established enough independence by this remark to eat somebody else's food. It was apparent from his expression that he found the quality of it poor.

Rayber sat and watched him, saying to himself in an effort to calm his irritation: this child hasn't had a chance, remember he hasn't had a chance. "God only knows what the old fool has told you and taught you!" he said with a sudden explosive force. "God only knows!"

The boy stopped eating and looked at him sharply. Then after a second he said, "He ain't had no effect on me," and returned to his eating.

"He did you a terrible injustice," Rayber said, wishing to impress this on him as often as he could. "He kept you from having a normal life, from getting a decent education. He filled your head with God knows what rot!"

Tarwater continued to eat. Then with a stony deliberateness, he looked up and his gaze fastened on the gash in his uncle's ear. Somewhere in the depths of his eyes a glint appeared. "Shot yer, didn't he?" he said.

Rayber took a package of cigarets from his shirt pocket and lit one, his motions inordinately slow from the effort he was making to calm himself. He blew the smoke straight into the boy's face. Then he tilted back in the chair and gave him a long hard look. The cigaret hanging from the corner of his mouth trembled. "Yes, he shot me," he said.

The glint in the boy's eyes followed the wires of the hearing aid down to the metal box stuck in his belt. "What you wired for?" he drawled. "Does your head light up?"

Rayber's jaw snapped and then relaxed. After a moment, after extending his arm stiffly and knocking the ash off his cigaret onto the floor, he replied that his head did not light up. "This is a hearing aid," he said patiently. "After the old man shot me I began to lose my hearing. I didn't have a gun when I went to get you back. If I'd stayed he would have killed me and I wouldn't have done you any good dead."

The boy continued to study the machine. His uncle's

face might have been only an appendage to it. "You ain't done me no good neither," he remarked.

"Do you understand me?" Rayber persisted. "I didn't have a gun. He would have killed me. He was a mad man. The time when I can do you good is beginning now, and I want to help you. I want to make up for all these years."

For an instant the boy's eyes left the hearing aid and rested on his uncle's eyes. "Could have got you a gun and come back terreckly," he said.

Stricken by the distinct sound of betrayal in his voice, Rayber could not say a word. He looked at him helplessly. The boy returned to his eating.

Finally Rayber said, "Listen." He took hold of the fist with the spoon in it and held it. "I want you to understand. He was crazy and if he had killed me, you wouldn't have this place to come to now. I'm no fool. I don't believe in senseless sacrifice. A dead man is not going to do you any good, don't you know that? Now I can do something for you. Now I can make up for all the time we've lost. I can help correct what he's done to you, help you to correct it yourself." He kept hold of the fist all the while it was being drawn insistently back. "This is our problem together," he said, seeing himself so clearly in the face before him that he might have been beseeching his own image.

With a quick yank, Tarwater managed to free his hand. Then he gave the schoolteacher a long appraising look, tracing the line of his jaw, the two creases on either side of his mouth, the forehead extending into skull until it reached the pie-shaped hairline. He gazed briefly at the pained eyes behind his uncle's glasses, appearing to abandon a search for something that could not possibly be there. The glint in his eye fell on the metal box half-sticking out of Rayber's shirt. "Do you think in the box," he asked, "or do you think in your head?"

His uncle had wanted to tear the machine out of his ear and fling it against the wall. "It's because of you I can't hear!" he said, glaring at the impassive face. "It's because once I tried to help you!"

"You never helped me none."

"I can help you now," he said.

After a second he sank back in his chair. "Perhaps you're right," he said, letting his hands fall in a helpless gesture. "It was my mistake. I should have gone back and killed him or let him kill me. Instead I let something in you be killed."

The boy put down his milk glass. "Nothing in me has

been killed," he said in a positive voice, and then he added, "And you needn't to worry. I done your work for you. I tended to him. It was me put him away. I was drunk as a coot and I tended to him." He said it as if he were recalling the most vivid point in his history.

Rayber heard his own heart, magnified by the hearing aid, suddenly begin to pound like the works of a gigantic machine in his chest. The boy's delicate defiant face, his glowering eyes still shocked by some violent memory, brought back instantly to him the vision of himself when he was fourteen and had found his way to Powderhead to shout imprecations at the old man.

An insight came to him that he was not to question until the end. He understood that the boy was held in bondage by his great-uncle, that he suffered a terrible false guilt for burning and not burying him, and he saw that he was engaged in a desperate heroic struggle to free himself from the old man's ghostly grasp. He leaned forward and said in a voice so full of feeling that it was barely balanced, "Listen, listen Frankie," he said, "you're not alone any more. You have a friend. You have more than a friend now." He swallowed. "You have a father."

The boy turned very white. His eyes were blackened by the shadow of some unspeakable outrage. "I ain't ast for no father," he said and the sentence struck like a whip across his uncle's face. "I ain't ast for no father," he repeated. "I'm out of the womb of a whore. I was born in a wreck." He flung this forth as if he were declaring a royal birth. "And my name ain't Frankie. I go by Tarwater and . . ."

"Your mother was not a whore," the schoolteacher said angrily. "That's just some rot he's taught you. She was a good healthy American girl, just beginning to find herself when she was struck down. She was . . ."

"I ain't fixing to hang around here," the boy said, looking about him as if he might throw over the breakfast tray and jump out the window. "I only come to find out a few things and when I find them out, then I'm going."

"What did you come to find out?" the schoolteacher asked evenly. "I can help you. All I want to do is help you any way I can."

"I don't need noner yer help," the boy said, looking away.

His uncle felt something tightening around him like an invisible strait jacket. "How do you mean to find out if you don't have help?"

"I'll wait," he said, "and see what happens."

"And suppose," his uncle asked, "nothing happens?"

An odd smile, like some strange inverted sign of grief, came over the boy's face. "Then I'll make it happen," he said, "like I done before."

In four days nothing had happened and nothing had been made to happen. They had simply covered—the three of them—the entire city, walking, and all night Rayber rewalked the same territory backwards in his sleep. It would not have been so tiring if he had not had Bishop. The child dragged backwards on his hand, always attracted by something they had already passed. Every block or so he would squat down to pick up a stick or a piece of trash and have to be pulled up and along. Whereas Tarwater was always slightly in advance of them, pushing forward on the scent of something. In four days they had been to the art gallery and the movies, they had toured department stores, ridden escalators, visited the supermarkets, inspected the water works, the post office, the railroad yards and the city hall. Rayber had explained how the city was run and detailed the duties of a good citizen. He had talked as much as he had walked, and the boy for all the interest he showed might have been the one who was deaf. Silent, he viewed everything with the same noncommittal eye as if he found nothing here worth holding his attention but must keep moving, must keep searching for whatever it was that appeared just beyond his vision.

Once he had paused at a window where a small red car turned slowly on a revolving platform. Seizing on the display of interest, Rayber had said that perhaps when he was sixteen, he could have a car of his own. It might have been the old man who had replied that he could walk on his two feet for nothing without being beholden. Rayber had never, even when old Tarwater had lived under his roof, been so conscious of the old man's presence.

Once the boy had stopped suddenly in front of a tall building and had stood glaring up at it with a peculiar ravaged look of recognition. Puzzled, Rayber said, "You look as if you've been here before."

"I lost my hat there," he muttered.

"Your hat is on your head," Rayber said. He could not look at the object without irritation. He wished to God there were some way to get it off him.

"My first hat," the boy said. "It fell," and he had rushed on, away from the place as if he could not stand to be near it.

Only one other time had he shown a particular interest. He had stopped with a kind of lurch backwards in front of a large grimy garage-like structure with two yellow and blue painted windows in the front of it, and had stood there, precariously balanced as if he were arresting himself in the middle of a fall. Rayber recognized the place for some kind of pentecostal tabernacle. Over the door was a paper banner bearing the words, UNLESS YE BE BORN AGAIN YE SHALL NOT HAVE EVERLASTING LIFE. Beneath it a poster showed a man and woman and child holding hands. "Hear the Carmodys for Christ!" it said. "Thrill to the Music, Message, and Magic of this team!"

Rayber was well enough aware of the boy's trouble to understand the sinister pull such a place would have on his mind. "Does this interest you?" he asked drily. "Does it remind you of something in particular?"

Tarwater was very pale. "Horse manure," he whispered.

Rayber smiled. Then he laughed. "All such people have in life," he said, "is the conviction they'll rise again."

The boy steadied himself, his eyes still on the banner but as if he had reduced it to a small spot a great distance away.

"They won't rise again?" he said. The statement had the lilt of a question and Rayber realized with an intense thrill of pleasure that his opinion, for the first time, was being called for.

"No," he said simply, "they won't rise again." There was a profound finality in his tone. The grimy structure might have been the carcass of a beast he had just brought down. He put his hand experimentally on the boy's shoulder. It was suffered to remain there.

In a voice unsteady with the sudden return of enthusiasm he said, "That's why I want you to learn all you can. I want you to be educated so that you can take your place as an intelligent man in the world. This fall when you start school . . ."

The shoulder was roughly withdrawn and the boy, throwing him one dark look, removed himself to the farthest edge of the sidewalk.

He wore his isolation like a mantle, wrapped it around himself as if it were a garment signifying the elect. Rayber had intended to keep notes on him and write up his most important observations but each night his energy had been too depleted to permit him to do any work. He had dropped off every night into a restless sleep, afraid that he would wake up and find the boy gone. He felt he had hastened his urge to leave by confronting him with the test. He had intended giving him the standard ones, intelligence and aptitude, and then going on to some he had perfected himself dealing with emotional factors. He had thought that in this way he could ferret to the center of the emotional infection. He had laid a simple aptitude test out on the kitchen table—the printed book and a few newly sharpened pencils. "This is a kind of game," he said. "Sit down and see what you can make of it. I'll help you begin."

The expression that came over the boy's face was very peculiar. His eyelids lowered just slightly; his mouth failed a smile by only a fraction; his look was compounded of fury and superiority. "Play with it yourself," he said. "I ain't taking no *test*," and he spit the word out as if it were not fit to pass between his lips.

Rayber sized up the situation. Then he said, "Maybe you don't really know how to read and write. Is that the trouble?"

The boy thrust his head forward. "I'm free," he hissed. "I'm outside your head. I ain't in it. I ain't in it and I ain't about to be."

His uncle laughed. "You don't know what freedom is," he said, "you don't . . ." but the boy turned and strode off.

It was no use. He could no more be reasoned with than a jackal. Nothing gave him pause—except Bishop, and Rayber knew that the reason Bishop gave him pause was because the child reminded him of the old man. Bishop looked like the old man grown backwards to the lowest form of innocence, and Rayber observed that the boy strictly avoided looking him in the eye. Wherever the child happened to be standing or sitting or walking seemed to be for Tarwater a dangerous hole in space that he must keep away from at all costs. Rayber was afraid that Bishop would drive him away with his friendliness. He was always creeping up to touch him and when the boy was aware of his being near, he would draw himself up like a snake ready to strike and hiss, "Git!" and Bishop would scurry off to watch him again from behind the nearest piece of furniture.

The schoolteacher understood this too. Every problem the boy had he had had himself and had conquered, or had for the most part conquered, for he had not conquered the problem of Bishop. He had only learned to live with it and had learned too that he could not live without it.

When he had got rid of his wife, he and the child had begun living together in a quiet automatic fashion like two bachelors whose habits were so smoothly connected that they no longer needed to take notice of each other. In the winter he sent him to a school for exceptional children and he had made great strides. He could wash himself, dress himself, feed himself, go to the toilet by himself and make peanut butter sandwiches though sometimes he put the bread inside. For the most part Rayber lived with him without being painfully aware of his presence but the moments would still come when, rushing from some inexplicable part of himself, he would experience a love for the child so outrageous that he would be left shocked and depressed for days, and trembling for his sanity. It was only a touch of the curse that lay in his blood.

His normal way of looking on Bishop was as an x signifying the general hideousness of fate. He did not believe that he himself was formed in the image and likeness of God but that Bishop was he had no doubt. The little boy was part of a simple equation that required no further solution, except at the moments when with little or no warning he would feel himself overwhelmed by the horrifying love. Anything he looked at too long could bring it on. Bishop did not have to be around. It could be a stick or a stone, the line of a shadow, the absurd old man's walk of a starling crossing the sidewalk. If, without thinking, he lent himself to it, he would feel suddenly a morbid surge of the love that terrified him—powerful enough to throw him to the ground in an act of idiot praise. It was completely irrational and abnormal.

He was not afraid of love in general. He knew the value of it and how it could be used. He had seen it transform in cases where nothing else had worked, such as with his poor sister. None of this had the least bearing on his situation. The love that would overcome him was of a different order entirely. It was not the kind that could be used for the child's improvement or his own. It was love without reason, love for something futureless, love that appeared to exist only to be itself, imperious and all demanding, the kind that would cause him to make a fool of himself in an instant. And it only began with Bishop. It began with Bishop and then like an avalanche covered everything his reason hated. He always felt with it a rush of longing to have the old man's eyes—insane, fish-colored, violent with their impossible vision of a world transfigured—turned on him once again. The longing was like an undertow in his blood dragging him backwards to what he knew to be madness.

The affliction was in the family. It lay hidden in the line of blood that touched them, flowing from some ancient source, some desert prophet or polesitter, until, its power unabated, it appeared in the old man and him and, he surmised, in the boy. Those it touched were condemned to fight it constantly or be ruled by it. The old man had been ruled by it. He, at the cost of a full life, staved it off. What the boy would do hung in the balance.

He had kept it from gaining control over him by what amounted to a rigid ascetic discipline. He did not look at anything too long, he denied his senses unnecessary satisfactions. He slept in a narrow iron bed, worked sitting in a straight-backed chair, ate frugally, spoke little, and cultivated the dullest for friends. At his high school he was the expert on testing. All his professional decisions were prefabricated and did not involve his participation. He was not deceived that this was a whole or a full life, he only knew that it was the way his life had to be lived if it were going to have any dignity at all. He knew that he was the stuff of which fanatics and madmen are made and that he had turned his destiny as if with his bare will. He kept himself upright on a very narrow line between madness and emptiness, and when the time came for him to lose his balance, he intended to lurch toward emptiness and fall on the side of his choice. He recognized that in silent ways he lived an heroic life. The boy would go either his way or old Tarwater's and he was determined to save him for the better course. Although Tarwater claimed to believe nothing the old man had taught him, Rayber could see clearly that there was still a backdrag of belief and fear in him keeping his responses locked.

By virtue of kinship and similarity and experience, Rayber was the person to save him, yet something in the boy's very look drained him, something in his very look, something starved in it, seemed to feed on him. With Tarwater's eyes on him, he felt subjected to a pressure that killed his energy before he had a chance to exert it. The eyes were the eyes of the crazy student father, the personality was the old man's, and somewhere between the two, Rayber's own image was struggling to survive and he was not able to reach it. After three days of walking, he was numb with fatigue and plagued with a sense of his own ineffectiveness. All day his sentences had not quite connected with his thought.

That night they had eaten at an Italian restaurant, dark and not crowded, and he had ordered ravioli for them because Bishop liked it. After each meal the boy removed a piece of paper and a stub of pencil from his pocket and wrote down a figure—his estimate of what the meal was worth. In time he would pay back the total sum, he had said, as he did not intend to be beholden. Rayber would have liked to see the figures and learn what his meals were valued at—the boy never asked the price. He was a finicky eater, pushing the food around on his plate before he ate it and putting each forkful in his mouth as if he suspected it was poisoned. He had pushed the ravioli about, his face drawn. He ate a little of it and then put the fork down.

"Don't you like that?" Rayber had asked. "You can have something else if you don't."

"It all come out the same slop bucket," the boy said.

"Bishop is eating his," Rayber said. Bishop had it smeared all over his face. Occasionally he would feed a spoonful into the sugar bowl or touch the tip of his tongue to the dish.

"That's what I said," Tarwater said, and his glance grazed the top of the child's head, "—a hog might like it."

The schoolteacher put his fork down.

Tarwater was glaring at the dark walls of the room. "He's like a hog," he said. "He eats like a hog and he don't think no more than a hog and when he dies, he'll rot like a hog. Me and you too," he said, looking back at the schoolteacher's mottled face, "will rot like hogs. The only difference between me and you and a hog is me and you can calculate, but there ain't any difference between him and one."

Rayber appeared to be gritting his teeth. Finally he said, "Just forget Bishop exists. You haven't been asked to have anything to do with him. He's just a mistake of nature. Try not even to be aware of him."

"He ain't my mistake," the boy muttered. "I ain't having a thing to do with him."

"Forget him," Rayber said in a short harsh voice.

The boy looked at him oddly as if he were beginning to perceive his secret affliction. What he saw or thought he saw seemed grimly to amuse him. "Let's leave out of here," he said, "and get to walking again."

"We are not going to walk tonight," Rayber said. "We are going home and go to bed." He said it with a firmness and finality he had not used before. The boy had only shrugged.

As Rayber lay watching the window darken, he felt that all his nerves were stretched through him like high tension wire. He began trying to relax one muscle at a time as the books recommended, beginning with those in the back of his neck. He emptied his mind of everything but the just visible pattern of the hedge against the screen. Still he was alert for any sound. Long after he lay in complete darkness, he was still alert, unrelaxed, ready to spring up at the least creak of a floor board in the hall. All at once he sat up, wide awake. A door opened and closed. He leapt up and ran across the hall into the opposite room. The boy was gone. He ran back to his own room and pulled his trousers on over his pajamas. Then grabbing his coat, he went out the house by way of the kitchen, barefooted, his jaw set.

CHAPTER FIVE

Keeping close to his side of the hedge, he crept through the dark damp grass toward the street. The night was close and very still. A light went on in a window of the next house and revealed, at the end of the hedge, the hat. It turned slightly and Rayber saw the sharp profile beneath it, the set thrust of a jaw very like his own. The boy was stopped still, most likely taking his bearings, deciding which direction to walk in.

He turned again and again. Rayber saw only the hat, intransigently ground upon his head, fierce-looking even in the dim light. It had the boy's own defiant quality, as if its shape had been formed over the years by his personality. It had been the first thing that Rayber had seen must go. It suddenly moved out of the light and vanished.

Rayber slipped through the hedge and followed, soundless on his bare feet. Nothing cast a shadow. He could barely make out the boy a quarter of a block in front of him, except when occasionally light from a window outlined him briefly. Since Rayber didn't know whether he thought he was leaving for good or only going for a walk on his own, he decided not to shout and stop him but to follow silently and observe. He turned off his hearing aid and pursued the dim figure as if in a dream. The boy walked even faster at night than in the day time and was always on the verge of vanishing.

Rayber felt the accelerated beat of his heart. He took a handkerchief out of his pocket and wiped his forehead and inside the neck of his pajama top. He walked over something sticky on the sidewalk and shifted hurriedly to the other side, cursing under his breath. Tarwater was heading toward town. Rayber thought it likely he was returning to see something that had secretly interested him. He might discover tonight what he would have found by testing if the boy had not been so pig-headed. He felt the insidious pleasure of revenge and checked it.

A patch of sky blanched, revealing for a moment the outlines of the housetops. Tarwater turned suddenly to the right. Rayber cursed himself for not stopping long enough to get his shoes. They had come into a neighborhood of large ramshackle boarding houses with porches that abutted the sidewalks. On some of them late sitters were rocking and watching the street. He felt eyes in the darkness move on him and he turned on the hearing aid again. On one porch a woman rose and leaned over the banister. She stood with her hands on her hips, looking him over, taking in his bare feet, the striped pajama coat under his seersucker suit. Irritated, he glanced back at her. The thrust of her neck indicated a conclusion formed. He buttoned his coat and hurried on.

The boy stopped on the next corner. His lean shadow made by a street light slanted to the side of him. The hat's shadow, like a knob at the top of it, turned to the right and then the left. He appeared to be considering his direction. Rayber's muscles felt suddenly weighted. He was not conscious of his fatigue until the pace slackened.

Tarwater turned to the left and Rayber began angrily to move again. They went down a street of dilapidated stores. When Rayber turned the next corner, the gaudy cave of a movie house yawned to the side of him. A knot of small boys stood in front of it. "Forgot yer shoes!" one of them chirruped. "Forgot yer shirt!"

He began a kind of limping lope.

The chorus followed him down the block. "Hi yo Silverwear, Tonto's lost his underwear! What in the heck do we care?"

He kept his eye wrathfully on Tarwater who was turning to the right. When he reached the corner and turned, he saw the boy stopped in the middle of the block, looking in a store window. He slipped into a narrow entrance a few yards farther on where a flight of steps led upward into darkness. Then he looked out.

Tarwater's face was strangely lit from the window he was standing before. Rayber watched curiously for a few moments. It looked to him like the face of someone starving who sees a meal he can't reach laid out before him. At last, something he *wants*, he thought, and determined that tomorrow he would return and buy it. Tarwater reached out and touched the glass and then drew his hand back slowly. He hung there as if he could not take his eyes off what it was he wanted. A pet shop, perhaps, Rayber thought. Maybe he wants a dog. A dog might make all the difference. Abruptly the boy broke away and moved on.

Rayber stepped out of the entrance and made for the window he had left. He stopped with a shock of disappointment. The place was only a bakery. The window was empty except for a loaf of bread pushed to the side that must have been overlooked when the shelf was cleaned for the night. He stared, puzzled, at the empty window for a second before he started after the boy again. Everything a false alarm, he thought with disgust. If he had eaten his dinner, he wouldn't be hungry. A man and woman strolling past looked with interest at his bare feet. He glared at them, then glanced to the side and saw his bloodless wired reflection in the glass of a shoe shop. The boy disappeared all at once into an alley. My God, Rayber thought, how long is this going on?

He turned into the alley, which was unpaved and so dark that he could not see Tarwater in it at all. He was certain that any minute he would cut his feet on broken glass. A garbage can materialized in his path. There was a noise like the collapse of a tin house and he found himself sitting up with his hand and one foot in something unidentifiable. He scrambled up and limped on, hearing his own curses like the voice of a stranger broadcast through his hearing aid. At the end of the alley, he saw the lean figure in the middle of the next block, and with a sudden fury he began to run.

The boy turned into another alley. Doggedly Rayber ran on. At the end of the second alley, the boy turned to the left. When Rayber reached the street, Tarwater was standing still in the middle of the next block. With a furtive look around him, he vanished, apparently into the building he had been facing. Rayber dashed forward. As he reached the place, singing burst flatly against his eardrums. Two blue and yellow windows glared at him in the darkness like the eyes of some Biblical beast. He stopped in front of the banner and read the mocking words, UNLESS YE BE BORN AGAIN. . . .

That the boy's corruption was this deep did not surprise him. What unstrung him was the thought that what Tarwater carried into the atrocious temple was his own imprisoned image. Enraged, he started around the building to locate a window he could look through and see the boy's face among the crowd. When he saw him, he would roar at him to come out. The windows near the front were all too high but toward the back, he found a lower one. He pushed through a straggly shrub beneath it and, his chin just above the ledge, looked into what appeared to be a small ante-room. A door on the other side of it opened onto a stage and there a man in a bright blue suit was standing in a spotlight, leading a hymn. Rayber could not see into the main body of the building where the people were. He was about to move away when the man brought the hymn to a close and began to speak.

"Friends," he said, "the time has come. The time we've all been waiting for this evening. Jesus said suffer the little children to come unto Him and forbid them not and maybe it was because He knew that it would be the little children that would call others to Him, maybe He knew, friends, maybe He hadda hunch."

Rayber listened angrily, too exhausted to move away once he had stopped.

"Friends," the preacher said, "Lucette has travelled the world over telling people about Jesus. She's been to India and China. She's spoken to all the rulers of the world. Jesus is wonderful, friends. He teaches us wisdom out of the mouths of babes!"

Another child exploited, Rayber thought furiously. It was the thought of a child's mind warped, of a child led away from reality, that always enraged him, bringing back to him his own childhood's seduction. Glaring at the spotlight, he saw the man there as a blur which he looked through, down the length of his life until what confronted him were the old man's fish-colored eyes. He saw himself taking the offered hand and innocently walking out of his own yard, innocently walking into six or seven years of unreality. Any other child would have thrown off the spell in a week. He could not have. He had analysed his case and closed it. Still, every now and then he would live over the five minutes it had taken his father to snatch him away from Powderhead. Through the blur of the man on the stage, as if he were looking into a transparent nightmare, he had the experience again. He and his uncle sat on the steps of the house at Powderhead watching his father emerge from the woods and sight them across the field. His uncle leaned forward, squinting, his hand cupped over his eyes, and he sat with his hands clenched between his knees, his heart threshing from side to side as his father moved closer and closer.

"Lucette travels with her mother and daddy and I want you to meet them because a mother and daddy have to be unselfish to share their only child with the world," the preacher said. "Here they are, friends—Mr. and Mrs. Carmody!"

While a man and woman moved into the light, Rayber had a clear vision of plowed ground, of the shaded red ridges that separated him from the lean figure approaching. He had let himself imagine that the field had an undertow that would drag his father backwards and suck him under, but he came on inexorably, only stopping every now and then to put a finger in his shoe and push out a clod of dirt.

"He's going to take me back with him," he said.

"Back with him where?" his uncle growled. "He ain't got any place to take you back to."

"He can't take me back with him?"

"Not where you were before."

"He can't take me back to town?"

"I never said nothing about town," his uncle said.

He saw vaguely that the man in the spotlight had sat down but that the woman was still standing. She became a blur and he saw his father again, getting closer and closer and he had one impulse to dart up and run through his uncle's house and tear out the back to the woods. He would have raced along the path, familiar to him then, and sliding and slipping over the waxy pine needles, he would have run down and down until he reached the thicket of bamboo and would have pushed through it and out onto the other side and would have fallen into the stream and lain there, panting and wheezing and safe where he had been born again, where his head had been thrust by his uncle into the water and brought up again into a new life. Sitting on the step, his leg muscles twitched as if they were ready for him to spring up but he remained absolutely still. He could see the line of his father's mouth, the line that had gone past the point of exasperation, past the point of loud wrath to a kind of stoked rage that would feed him for months.

While the woman evangelist, tall and raw-boned, was speaking of the hardships she had endured, he watched his father as he reached the edge of the yard and stepped onto the packed dirt, his face a slick pink from the exertion of crossing a field. He was drawing short hard breaths. For an instant he seemed about to reach forward and snatch him but he remained where he was. His pale eyes moved carefully over the rock-like figure watching him steadily from the steps, at the red hands knotted on the heavy thighs and then at the gun lying on the porch. He said, "His mother wants him back, Mason. I don't know why. For my part you could have him but you know how she is."

"A drunken whore," his uncle growled.

"Your sister, not mine," his father said, and then said, "All right boy, snap it up," and nodded curtly to him.

He explained in a high reedy voice the exact reason

he could not go back, "I've been born again."

"Great," his father said, "great." He took a step forward and grabbed his arm and yanked him to his feet. "Glad you got him fixed up, Mason," he said. "One bath more or less won't hurt the bugger."

He had had no chance to see his uncle's face. His father had already lept into the plowed field and was dragging him across the furrows while the pellets pierced the air over their heads. His shoulders, just under the window ledge, jumped. He shook his head to clear it.

"For ten years I was a missionary in China," the woman was saying, "for five years I was a missionary in Africa, and one year I was a missionary in Rome where minds are still chained in priestly darkness; but for the last six years, my husband and I have travelled the world over with our daughter. They have been years of trial and pain, years of hardship and suffering." She had on a long dramatic cape, one side of which was turned backward over her shoulder to reveal a red lining.

His father's face was suddenly very close to his own. "Back to the real world, boy," he was saying, "back to the real world. And that's me and not him, see? Me and not him," and he heard himself screaming, "It's him! Him! Him and not you! And I've been born again and there's not a thing you can do about it!"

"Christ in hell," his father said, "believe it if you want to. Who cares? You'll find out soon enough."

The woman's tone had changed. The sound of something grasping drew his attention again. "We have not had an easy time. We have been a hard-working team for Christ. People have not always been generous to us. Only here are the people really generous. I am from Texas and my husband is from Tennessee but we have travelled the world over. We know," she said in a deepened softened voice, "where the people are really generous."

Rayber forgot himself and listened. He felt a relief from his pain, recognizing that the woman was only after money. He could hear the beginning click of coins falling in a plate.

"Our little girl began to preach when she was six. We saw that she had a mission, that she had been called. We saw that we could not keep her to ourselves and so we have endured many hardships to give her to the world, to bring her to you tonight. To us," she said, "you are as important as the great rulers of the world!" Here she lifted the end of her cape and holding it out as a magician would make a low bow. After a moment she lifted her head, gazed in front of her as if at some grand vista, and disappeared from view. A little girl hobbled into the spotlight.

Rayber cringed. Simply by the sight of her he could tell that she was not a fraud, that she was only exploited. She was eleven or twelve with a small delicate face and a head of black hair that looked too thick and heavy for a frail child to support. A cape like her mother's was turned back over one shoulder and her skirt was short as if better to reveal the thin legs twisted from the knees. She held her arms over her head for a moment. "I want to tell you people the story of the world," she said in a loud high child's voice. "I want to tell you why Jesus came and what happened to Him. I want to tell you how He'll come again. I want to tell you to be ready. Most of all," she said, "I want to tell you to be ready so that on the last day you'll rise in the glory of the Lord."

Rayber's fury encompassed the parents, the preacher, all the idiots he could not see who were sitting in front of the child, parties to her degradation. She believed it, she was locked tight in it, chained hand and foot, exactly as he had been, exactly as only a child could be. He felt the taste of his own childhood pain laid again on his tongue like a bitter wafer.

"Do you know who Jesus is?" she cried. "Jesus is the word of God and Jesus is love. The Word of God is love and do you know what love is, you people? If you don't know what love is you won't know Jesus when He comes. You won't be ready. I want to tell you people the story of the world, how it never known when love come, so when love comes again, you'll be ready."

She moved back and forth across the stage, frowning as if she were trying to see the people through the fierce circle of light that followed her. "Listen to me, you people," she said, "God was angry with the world because it always wanted more. It wanted as much as God had and it didn't know what God had but it wanted it and more. It wanted God's own breath, it wanted His very Word and God said, 'I'll make my Word Jesus, I'll give them my Word for a king, I'll give them my very breath for theirs.'

"Listen you people," she said and flung her arms wide, "God told the world He was going to send it a king and the world waited. The world thought, a golden fleece will do for His bed. Silver and gold and peacock tails, a thousand suns in a peacock's tail will do for His sash. His mother will ride on a four-horned white beast and use the sunset for a cape. She'll trail it behind her over the ground and let the world pull it to pieces, a new one every evening."

To Rayber she was like one of those birds blinded to make it sing more sweetly. Her voice had the tone of a glass bell. His pity encompassed all exploited children—himself when he was a child, Tarwater exploited by the old man, this child exploited by parents, Bishop exploited by the very fact he was alive.

"The world said, 'How long, Lord, do we have to wait for this?' And the Lord said, 'My Word is coming, my Word is coming from the house of David, the king.' " She paused and turned her head to the side, away from the fierce light. Her dark gaze moved slowly until it rested on Rayber's head in the window. He stared back at her. Her eyes remained on his face for a moment. A deep shock went through him. He was certain that the child had looked directly into his heart and seen his pity. He felt that some mysterious connection was established between them.

" 'My Word is coming,' " she said, turning back to face the glare, " 'my Word is coming from the house of David, the king.' "

She began again in a dirge-like tone. "Jesus came on cold straw. Jesus was warmed by the breath of an ox. 'Who is this?' the world said, 'who is this blue-cold child and this woman, plain as the winter? Is this the Word of God, this blue-cold child? Is this His will, this plain winter-woman?'

"Listen you people!" she cried, "the world knew in its heart, the same as you know in your hearts and I know in my heart. The world said, 'Love cuts like the cold wind and the will of God is plain as the winter. Where is the summer will of God? Where are the green seasons of God's will? Where is the spring and summer of God's will?'

"They had to flee into Egypt," she said in a low voice and turned her head again and this time her eyes moved directly to Rayber's face in the window and he knew they sought it. He felt himself caught up in her look, held there before the judgment seat of her eyes.

"You and I know," she said turning again, "what the world hoped then. The world hoped old Herod would slay the right child, the world hoped old Herod wouldn't waste those children, but he wasted them. He didn't get the right one. Jesus grew up and raised the dead."

Rayber felt his spirit borne aloft. But not those dead!

he cried, not the innocent children, not you, not me when I was a child, not Bishop, not Frank! and he had a vision of himself moving like an avenging angel through the world, gathering up all the children that the Lord, not Herod, had slain.

"Jesus grew up and raised the dead," she cried, "and the world shouted, 'Leave the dead lie. The dead are dead and can stay that way. What do we want with the dead alive?' Oh you people!" she shouted, "they nailed Him to a cross and run a spear through His side and then they said, 'Now we can have some peace, now we can ease our minds.' And they hadn't but only said it when they wanted Him to come again. Their eyes were opened and they saw the glory they had killed.

"Listen world," she cried, flinging up her arms so that the cape flew out behind her, "Jesus is coming again! The mountains are going to lie down like hounds at His feet, the stars are going to perch on His shoulder and when He calls it, the sun is going to fall like a goose for His feast. Will you know the Lord Jesus then? The mountains will know Him and bound forward, the stars will light on His head, the sun will drop down at His feet, but will you know the Lord Jesus then?"

Rayber saw himself fleeing with the child to some enclosed garden where he would teach her the truth, where he would gather all the exploited children of the world and let the sunshine flood their minds.

"If you don't know Him now, you won't know Him then. Listen to me, world, listen to this warning. The Holy Word is in my mouth!

"The Holy Word is in my mouth!" she cried and turned her eyes again on his face in the window. This time there was a lowering concentration in her gaze. He had drawn her attention entirely away from the congregation.

Come away with me! he silently implored, and I'll teach you the truth, I'll save you, beautiful child!

Her eyes still fixed on him, she cried, "I've seen the Lord in a tree of fire! The Word of God is a burning Word to burn you clean!" She was moving in his direction, the people in front of her forgotten. Rayber's heart began to race. He felt some miraculous communication between them. The child alone in the world was meant to understand him. "Burns the whole world, man and child," she cried, her eye on him, "none can escape." She stopped a little distance from the end of the stage and stood silent, her whole attention directed across the small room to his face on the ledge. Her eyes were large and dark and fierce.

He felt that in the space between them, their spirits had broken the bonds of age and ignorance and were mingling in some unheard of knowledge of each other. He was transfixed by the child's silence. Suddenly she raised her arm and pointed toward his face. "Listen you people," she shrieked, "I see a damned soul before my eye! I see a dead man Jesus hasn't raised. His head is in the window but his ear is deaf to the Holy Word!"

Rayber's head, as if it had been struck by an invisible bolt, dropped from the ledge. He crouched on the ground, his furious spectacled eyes glittering behind the shrubbery. Inside she continued to shriek, "Are you deaf to the Lord's Word? The Word of God is a burning Word to burn you clean, burns man and child, man and child the same, you people! Be saved in the Lord's fire or perish in your own! Be saved in . . ."

He was groping fiercely about him, slapping at his coat pockets, his head, his chest, not able to find the switch that would cut off the voice. Then his hand touched the button and he snapped it. A silent dark relief enclosed him like shelter after a tormenting wind. For a while he sat limp behind the bush. Then the reason for his being here returned to him and he experienced a moment of loathing for the boy that earlier would have made him shudder. He wanted nothing but to get back home and sink into his own bed, whether the boy returned or not.

He got out of the shrubbery and started toward the front of the building. As he turned onto the sidewalk, the door of the tabernacle flew open and Tarwater flung himself out. Rayber stopped abruptly.

The boy stood confronting him, his face strangely mobile as if successive layers of shock were settling on it to form a new expression. After a moment he raised his arm in an uncertain gesture of greeting. The sight of Rayber seemed to afford him relief amounting to rescue.

Rayber's face had the wooden look it wore when his hearing aid was off. He did not see the boy's expression at all. His rage obliterated all but the general lines of his figure and he saw them moulded in an irreversible shape of defiance. He grabbed him roughly by the arm and started down the block with him. Both of them walked rapidly as if neither could leave the place fast enough. When they were well down the block, Rayber stopped and swung him around and glared into his face. Through his fury he could not discern that for the first time the boy's eyes were submissive. He snapped on his hearing aid and said fiercely, "I hope you enjoyed the show."

Tarwater's lips moved convulsively. Then he murmured, "I only gone to spit on it."

The schoolteacher continued to glare at him. "I'm not so sure of that."

The boy said nothing. He seemed to have suffered some shock inside the building that had permanently slowed his tongue.

Rayber turned and they walked away in silence. At any point along the way, he could have put his hand on the shoulder next to his and it would not have been withdrawn, but he made no gesture. His head was churning with old rages. The afternoon he had learned the full extent of Bishop's future had sprung to his mind. He saw himself rigidly facing the doctor, a man who had made him think of a bull, impassive, insensitive, his brain already on the next case. He had said, "You should be grateful his health is good. In addition to this, I've seen them born blind as well, some without arms and legs, and one with a heart outside."

He had lurched up, almost ready to strike the man. "How can I be grateful," he had hissed, "when one—just one—is born with a heart outside?"

"You'd better try," the doctor had said.

Tarwater walked slightly behind him and Rayber did not cast a glance back at him. His fury seemed to be stirring from buried depths that had lain quiet for years and to be working upward, closer and closer, toward the slender roots of his peace. When they reached the house he went in and straight to his bed without turning to look at the boy's white face which, drained but expectant, lingered a moment at the threshold of his door as if waiting for an invitation to enter.

CHAPTER SIX

The next day, too late, he had the sense of opportunity missed. Tarwater's face had hardened again and the steely gleam in his eye was like the glint of a metal door sealed against an intruder. Rayber felt afflicted with a peculiar chilling clarity of mind in which he saw himself divided in two—a violent and a rational self. The violent self inclined him to see the boy as an enemy and he knew that nothing would hinder his progress with the case so much as giving in to such an inclination. He had waked up after a wild dream in which he chased Tarwater through an interminable alley that twisted suddenly back on itself and reversed the roles of pursuer and pursued. The boy had overtaken him, given him a thunderous blow on the head, and then disappeared. And with his disappearance there had come such an overwhelming feeling of release that Rayber had waked up with a pleasant anticipation that his guest would be gone. He was at once ashamed of the feeling. He settled on a rational, tiring plan for the day and by ten o'clock the three of them were on their way to the natural history museum. He intended to stretch the boy's mind by introducing him to his ancestor, the fish, and to all the great wastes of unexplored time.

They passed part of the territory they had walked over the night before but nothing was said about that trip. Except for the circles under Rayber's eyes, there was nothing about either of them to indicate it had been made. Bishop stumped along, squatting every now and then to pick up something off the sidewalk, while Tarwater, to avoid contamination with them, walked a good four feet to the other side and slightly in advance. I must have infinite patience, I must have infinite patience, Rayber kept repeating to himself.

The museum lay on the other side of the city park which they had not crossed before. As they approached it, the boy paled as if he were shocked to find a wood in the middle of the city. Once inside the park, he stopped and stood glaring about him at the huge trees whose ancient rustling branches intermingled overhead. Patches of light sifting through them spattered the concrete walks with sunshine. Rayber observed that something disturbed him. Then he realized that the place reminded him of Powderhead.

"Let's sit down," he said, wanting both to rest and to observe the boy's agitation. He sat down on a bench and stretched his legs in front of him. He suffered Bishop to climb into his lap. The child's shoelaces were untied and he tied them, for the moment ignoring the boy who was standing there, his face furiously impatient. When he finished tying the shoes, he continued to hold the child, sprawled and grinning, in his lap. The little boy's white head fitted under his chin. Above it Rayber looked at nothing in particular. Then he closed his eyes and in the isolating darkness, he forgot Tarwater's presence. Without warning his hated love gripped him and held him in a vise. He should have known better than to let the child onto his lap.

His forehead became beady with sweat; he looked as if he might have been nailed to the bench. He knew that if he could once conquer this pain, face it and with a supreme effort of his will refuse to feel it, he would be a free man. He held Bishop rigidly. Although the child started the pain, he also limited it, contained it. He had learned this one terrible afternoon when he had tried to drown him.

He had taken him to the beach, two hundred miles away, intending to effect the accident as quickly as possible and return bereaved. It had been a beautiful calm day in May. The beach, almost empty, had stretched down into the gradual swell of ocean. There was nothing to be seen but an expanse of sea and sky and sand and an occasional figure, stick-like, in the distance. He had taken him out on his shoulders and when he was chest deep in the water, had lifted him off, swung the delighted child high in the air and then plunged him swiftly below the surface on his back and held him there, not looking down at what he was doing but up, at an imperturbably witnessing sky, not quite blue, not quite white.

A fierce surging pressure had begun upward beneath his hands and grimly he had exerted more and more force downward. In a second, he felt he was trying to hold a giant under. Astonished, he let himself look. The face under the water was wrathfully contorted, twisted by some primeval rage to save itself. Automatically he released his pressure. Then when he realized what he had done, he pushed down again angrily with all his force until the struggle ceased under his hands. He stood sweating in the water, his own mouth as slack as the child's had been. The body, caught by an undertow, almost got away from him but he managed to come to himself and snatch it. Then as he looked at it, he had a moment of complete terror in which he envisioned his life without the child. He began to shout frantically. He plowed his way out of the water with the limp body. The beach which he had thought empty before had become peopled with strangers converging on him from all directions. A bald-headed man in red and blue Roman striped shorts began at once to administer artificial respiration. Three wailing women and a photographer appeared. The next day there had been a picture in the paper, showing the rescuer, striped bottom forward, working over the child. Rayber was beside him on his knees, watching with an agonized expression. The caption said, OVERJOYED FATHER SEES SON REVIVED.

The boy's voice broke in on him harshly. "All you got to do is nurse an idiot!"

The schoolteacher opened his eyes. They were bloodshot and vague. He might have been returning to consciousness after a blow on the head.

Tarwater was glaring to the side of him. "Come on if you're coming," he said, "and if you ain't, I'm going on about my bidnis."

Rayber didn't answer.

"So long," Tarwater said.

"And where would your business be?" Rayber asked sourly. "At another tabernacle?"

The boy reddened. He opened his mouth and said nothing.

"I nurse an idiot that you're afraid to look at," Rayber said. "Look him in the eye."

Tarwater shot a glance at the top of Bishop's head and left it there an instant like a finger on a candle flame. "I'd as soon be afraid to look at a dog," he said and turned his back. After a moment, as if he were continuing the same conversation, he muttered, "I'd as soon baptize a dog as him. It would be as much use."

"Who said anything about baptizing anybody?" Rayber said. "Is that one of your fixations? Have you taken that bug up from the old man?"

The boy whirled around and faced him. "I told you I only gone there to spit on it," he said tensely. "I ain't going to tell you again."

Rayber watched him without saying anything. He felt that his own sour words had helped him recover himself.

He pushed Bishop off and stood up. "Let's get going,"
he said. He had no intention of discussing it further, but
as they moved on silently, he thought better of it.

"Listen Frank," he said, "I'll grant that you went to
spit on it. I've never for a second doubted your intelligence.
Everything you've done, your very presence here proves
that you're above your background, that you've broken
through the ceiling the old man set for you. After all,
you escaped from Powderhead. You had the courage to
attend to him the quickest way and then get out of there.
And once out, you came directly to the right place."

The boy reached up and picked a leaf from a tree
branch and bit it. A wry expression spread over his face.
He rolled the leaf into a ball and threw it away. Rayber
continued to speak, his voice detached, as if he had no
particular interest in the matter, and his were merely the
voice of truth, as impersonal as air.

"Say that you went to spit on it," he said, "the point
is this: there's no need to spit on it. It's not worth spitting
on. It's not that important. You've somehow enlarged the
significance of it in your mind. The old man used to enrage
me until I learned better. He wasn't worth my hate and
he's not worth yours. He's only worth our pity." He
wondered if the boy were capable of the steadiness of
pity. "You want to avoid extremes. They are for violent
people and you don't want . . ."—he broke off abruptly
as Bishop let loose his hand and galloped away.

They had come out into the center of the park, a concrete
circle with a fountain in the middle of it. Water rushed
from the mouth of a stone lion's head into a shallow pool
and the little boy was flying toward it, his arms flailing
like a windmill. In a second he was over the side and in.
"Too late, goddammit," Rayber muttered, "he's in." He
glanced at Tarwater.

The boy stood arrested in the middle of a step. His
eyes were on the child in the pool but they burned as
if he beheld some terrible compelling vision. The sun shone
brightly on Bishop's white head and the little boy stood
there with a look of attention. Tarwater began to move
toward him.

He seemed to be drawn toward the child in the water
but to be pulling back, exerting an almost equal pressure
away from what attracted him. Rayber watched, puzzled
and suspicious, moving along with him but somewhat to
the side. As he drew closer to the pool, the skin on the
boy's face appeared to stretch tighter and tighter. Rayber
had the sense that he was moving blindly, that where Bishop

was he saw only a spot of light. He felt that something was being enacted before him and that if he could understand it, he would have the key to the boy's future. His muscles were tensed and he was prepared somehow to act. Suddenly his sense of danger was so great that he cried out. In an instant of illumination he understood. Tarwater was moving toward Bishop to baptize him. Already he had reached the edge of the pool. Rayber sprang and snatched the child out of the water and set him down, howling, on the concrete.

His heart was beating furiously. He felt that he had just saved the boy from committing some enormous indignity. He saw it all now. The old man *had* transferred his fixation to the boy, *had* left him with the notion that he must baptize Bishop or suffer some terrible consequence. Tarwater put his foot down on the marble edge of the pool. He leaned forward, his elbow on his knee, looking over the side at his broken reflection in the water. His lips moved as if he were speaking silently to the face forming in the pool. Rayber said nothing. He realized now the magnitude of the boy's affliction. He knew that there was no way to appeal to him with reason. There was no hope of discussing it sanely with him, for it was a compulsion. He saw no way of curing him except perhaps through some shock, some sudden concrete confrontation with the futility, the ridiculous absurdity of performing the empty rite.

He squatted down and began to take off Bishop's wet shoes. The child had stopped howling and was crying quietly, his face red and hideously distorted. Rayber turned his eyes away.

Tarwater was walking off. He was past the pool, his back strangely bent as if he were being driven away with a whip. He was moving off onto one of the narrow tree-shaded paths.

"Wait!" Rayber shouted. "We can't go to the museum now. We'll have to go home and change Bishop's shoes."

Tarwater could not have failed to hear but he kept on walking and in a second was lost to view.

Goddam backwoods imbecile, Rayber said under his breath. He stood looking at the path where the boy had disappeared. He felt no urge to go after him for he knew that he would be back, that he was held by Bishop. His feeling of oppression was caused now by the certain knowledge that there was no way to get rid of him. He would be with them until he had either accomplished what he came for, or until he was cured. The words the old man had scrawled on the back of the journal rose before him: THE PROPHET

I RAISE UP OUT OF THIS BOY WILL BURN YOUR
EYES CLEAN. The sentence was like a challenge renewed.
I will cure him, he said grimly. I will cure him or know
the reason why.

CHAPTER SEVEN

The Cherokee Lodge was a two-story converted warehouse, the lower part painted white and the upper green. One end sat on land and the other was set on stilts in a glassy little lake across which were dense woods, green and black farther toward the skyline, gray-blue. The long front side of the building, plastered with beer and cigaret signs, faced the highway, which ran about thirty feet away across a dirt road and beyond a narrow stretch of iron weed. Rayber had passed the place before but had never been tempted to stop.

He had selected it because it was only thirty miles from Powderhead and because it was cheap and he arrived there the next day with the two boys in time for them to take a walk and look around before they ate. The ride up had been oppressively silent, the boy sitting as usual on his side of the car like some foreign dignitary who would not admit speaking the language—the filthy hat, the stinking overalls, worn defiantly like a national costume.

Rayber had hit upon his plan in the night. It was to take him back to Powderhead and make him face what he had done. What he hoped was that if seeing and feeling the place again were a real shock, the boy's trauma might suddenly be revealed. His irrational fears and impulses would burst out and his uncle—sympathetic, knowing, uniquely able to understand—would be there to explain them to him. He had not said they were going to Powderhead. So far as the boy knew, this was to be a fishing trip. He thought that an afternoon of relaxation in a boat before the experiment would help ease the tension, his own as well as Tarwater's.

On the drive up, his thoughts had been interrupted once when he saw Bishop's face rise unorganized into the rearview mirror and then disappear as he attempted to crawl over the top of the front seat and climb into Tarwater's lap. The boy had turned and without looking at him had given the panting child a firm push onto the back seat again. One of Rayber's immediate goals was to make him understand that his urge to baptize the child was a kind of *sickness* and that a sign of returning health would be his ability to begin looking Bishop in the eye. Rayber felt that once he could look the child in the eye, he would have confidence in his ability to resist the morbid impulse to baptize him.

When they got out of the car, he watched the boy closely, trying to discover his first reaction to being in the country again. Tarwater stood for a moment, his head lifted sharply as if he detected some familiar odor moving from the pine forest across the lake. His long face, depending from the bulb-shaped hat, made Rayber think of a root jerked suddenly out of the ground and exposed to the light. The boy's eyes narrowed so that the lake must have been reduced to the width of a knife-blade in his sight. He looked at the water with a peculiar undisguised hostility. Rayber even thought that as his eye fell on it, he began to tremble. At least he was certain that his hands clenched. His glare steadied, then with his usual precipitous gait, he set off around the building without looking back.

Bishop climbed out of the car and thrust his face against his father's side. Absently Rayber put his hand on the little boy's ear and rubbed it gingerly, his fingers tingling as if they touched the sensitive scar of some old wound. Then he pushed the child aside, picked up the bag and started toward the screen door of the lodge. As he reached it, Tarwater came quickly around the side of the building with the distinct look to Rayber of being pursued. His feeling for the boy alternated drastically between compassion for his haunted look and fury at the way he was treated by him. Tarwater acted as if to see him at all required a special effort. Rayber opened the screen door and stepped inside, leaving the two boys to come in or not as they pleased.

The interior was dark. To the left he made out a reception desk with a heavy plain-looking woman behind it, leaning on her elbows. He set the bags down and gave her his name. He had the feeling that though her eyes were on him, they were looking behind him. He glanced around. Bishop was a few feet away, gaping at her.

"What's your name, Sugarpie?" she asked.

"His name is Bishop," Rayber said shortly. He was always irked when the child was stared at.

The woman tilted her head sympathetically. "I reckon you're taking him off to give his mother a little rest," she said, her eyes full of curiosity and compassion.

"I have him all the time," he said and added before he could stop himself, "his mother abandoned him."

"No!" she breathed. "Well," she said, "it takes all kinds of women. I couldn't leave a child like that."

You can't even take your eyes off him, he thought irritably and began to fill out the card. "Are the boats for rent?" he asked without looking up.

"Free for the guests," she said, "but anybody gets drowned, that's their lookout. How about him? Can he sit still in a boat?"

"Nothing ever happens to him," he murmured, finishing the card and turning it around to her.

She read it, then she glanced up and stared at Tarwater. He was standing a few feet behind Bishop, looking around him suspiciously, his hands in his pockets and his hat pulled down. She began to scowl. "That boy there—is yours too?" she asked, pointing the pen at him as if this were inconceivable.

Rayber realized that she must think he was someone hired for a guide. "Certainly, he's mine too," he said quickly and in a voice the boy could not fail to hear. He made it a point to impress on him that he was wanted, whether he cared to be wanted or not.

Tarwater lifted his head and returned the woman's stare. Then he took a stride forward and thrust his face at her. "What do you mean—is his?" he demanded.

"Is his," she said, drawing back. "You don't look it is all." Then she frowned as if, continuing to study him, she began to see a likeness.

"And I ain't it," he said. He snatched the card from her and read it. Rayber had written, "George F. Rayber, Frank and Bishop Rayber," and their address. The boy put the card down on the desk and picked up the pen, gripping it so hard that his fingers turned red at the tips. He crossed out the name *Frank* and underneath in an old man's meticulous hand he began to write something else.

Rayber looked at the woman helplessly and lifted his shoulders as if to say, "I have more than one problem," and shrug it off, but the gesture ended in a violent tremor. To his horror he felt the side of his mouth give a series of quick jerks. He had an instant's premonition that if he wished to save himself, he should leave at once, that the trip was doomed.

The woman handed him the key and, looking at him suspiciously, said, "Up the steps yonder and four doors down to the right. We don't have anybody to tote the bags."

He took the key and started up a rickety flight of steps to the left. Halfway up, he paused and said in a voice in which there was a remnant of authority, "Bring up that bag when you come, Frank."

The boy was finishing his essay on the card and gave no indication of hearing.

The woman's curious gaze followed Rayber up the stairs until he disappeared. She observed as his feet passed the level of her head that he had on one brown sock and one gray. His shoes were not run-down but he might have slept in his seersucker suit every night. He was in bad need of a haircut and his eyes had a peculiar look—like something human trapped in a switch box. Has come here to have a nervous breakdown, she said to herself. Then she turned her head. Her eyes rested on the two boys, who had not moved. And who wouldn't? she asked herself.

The afflicted child looked as if he must have dressed himself. He had on a black cowboy hat and a pair of short khaki pants that were too tight even for his narrow hips and a yellow t-shirt that had not been washed any time lately. Both his brown hightop shoes were untied. The upper part of him looked like an old man and the lower part like a child. The other, the mean-looking one, had picked up the desk card again and was reading over what he had written on it. He was so taken up with it that he did not see the little boy reaching out to touch him. The instant the child touched him, the country boy's shoulders leapt. He snatched his touched hand up and jammed it in his pocket. "Leave off!" he said in a high voice. "Git away and quit bothering me!"

"Mind how you talk to one of them there, you boy!" the woman hissed.

He looked at her as if it were the first time she had spoken to him. "Them there what?" he murmured.

"That there kind," she said, looking at him fiercely as if he had profaned the holy.

He looked back at the afflicted child and the woman was startled by the expression on his face. He seemed to see the little boy and nothing else, no air around him, no room, no nothing, as if his gaze had slipped and fallen into the center of the child's eyes and was still falling down and down and down. The little boy turned after a second and skipped off toward the steps and the country boy followed, so directly that he might have been attached to him by a tow-line. The child began to scramble up the steps on his hands and knees, kicking his feet up on each one. Then suddenly he flipped himself around and sat down squarely in the country boy's way and stuck his feet out in front of him, apparently wanting his shoes tied. The

ountry boy stopped still. He hung over him like someone bewitched, his long arms bent uncertainly.

The woman watched fascinated. He ain't going to tie
them, she said, not him.

He leaned over and began to tie them. Frowning furiously,
he tied one and then the other and the child watched, completely absorbed in the operation. When the boy finished
tying them, he straightened himself and said in a querulous
voice, "Now git on and quit bothering me with them laces,"
and the child flipped over on his hands and feet and scrambled
up the stairs, making a great din.

Confused by this kindness, the woman called, "Hey
boy."

She had intended to say, "Whose boy are you?" but she
said nothing, her mouth opening on a vanished sentence.
His eyes as they turned and looked down at her were the
color of the lake just before dark when the last daylight
has faded and the moon has not risen yet, and for an instant
she thought she saw something fleeing across the surface
of them, a lost light that came from nowhere and vanished
into nothing. For some moments they stared at each other
without issue. Finally, convinced she had not seen it,
she muttered, "Whatever devil's work you mean to do,
don't do it here."

He continued to look down at her. "You can't just
say NO," he said. "You got to do NO. You got to show
it. You got to show you mean it by doing it. You got to
show you're not going to do one thing by doing another.
You got to make an end of it. One way or another."

"Don't you do nothing here," she said, wondering what
he would do here.

"I never ast to come here," he said. "I never ast for
that lake to be set down in front of me," and he turned
and moved on up the stairs.

The woman looked in front of her for some time as
if she were seeing her own thoughts before her like unintelligible handwriting on the wall. Then she looked down
at the card on the counter and turned it over. "Francis
Marion Tarwater," he had written. "Powderhead, Tennessee.
NOT HIS SON."

CHAPTER EIGHT

After they had had their lunch, the schoolteacher suggested they get a boat and fish awhile. Tarwater could tell that he was watching him again, his little eyes protected and precise behind his glasses. He had been watching him ever since he came but now he was watching in a different way: he was watching for something that he planned to make happen. The trip was designed to be a trap but the boy had no attention to spare for it. His mind was entirely occupied with saving himself from the larger grander trap that he felt set all about him. Ever since his first night in the city when he had seen once and for all that the schoolteacher was of no significance—nothing but a piece of bait, an insult to his intelligence—his mind had been engaged in a continual struggle with the silence that confronted him, that demanded he baptize the child and begin at once the life the old man had prepared him for.

It was a strange waiting silence. It seemed to lie all around him like an invisible country whose borders he was always on the edge of, always in danger of crossing. From time to time as they had walked in the city, he had looked to the side and seen his own form alongside him in a store window, transparent as a snakeskin. It moved beside him like some violent ghost who had already crossed over and was reproaching him from the other side. If he turned his head the opposite way, there would be the dim-witted boy, hanging onto the schoolteacher's coat, watching him. His mouth hung in a lopsided smile but there was a judging sternness about his forehead. The boy never looked lower than the top of his head except by accident for the silent country appeared to be reflected again in the center of his eyes. It stretched out there, limitless and clear.

Tarwater could have baptized him any one of a hundred times without so much as touching him. Each time the temptation came, he would feel that the silence was about to surround him and he was going to be lost in it forever. He would have fallen but for the wise voice that sustained him—the stranger who had kept him company while he dug his uncle's grave.

Sensations, his friend—no longer a stranger—said. Feelings. What you want is a sign, a real sign, suitable to a prophet. If you are a prophet, it's only right you should be treated like one. When Jonah dallied, he was cast three days in a belly of darkness and vomited up in the place of his mission. That was a sign; it wasn't no sensation.

It takes all my time to set you straight. Look at you, he said—going to that fancy-house of God, sitting there like an ape letting that girl-child bend your ear. What did you expect to see there? What did you expect to hear? The Lord speaks to prophets personally and He's never spoke to you, never lifted a finger, never dropped a gesture. And as for that strangeness in your gut, that comes from you, not the Lord. When you were a child you had worms. As likely as not you have them again.

The first day in the city he had become conscious of the strangeness in his stomach, a peculiar hunger. The city food only weakened him. He and his great-uncle had eaten well. If the old man had done nothing else for him, he had heaped his plate. Never a morning he had not a-wakened to the smell of fatback frying. The schoolteacher paid scarce attention to what he put inside him. For breakfast, he poured a bowl of shavings out of a cardboard box; in the middle of the day he made sandwiches out of lightbread; and at night he took them to a restaurant, a different one every night run by a different color of foreigner so that he would learn, he said, how other nationalities ate. The boy did not care how other nationalities ate. He had always left the restaurants hungry, conscious of an intrusion in his works. Since the breakfast he had finished sitting in the presence of his uncle's corpse, he had not been satisfied by food, and his hunger had become like an insistent silent force inside him, a silence inside akin to the silence outside, as if the grand trap left him barely an inch to move in, barely an inch in which to keep himself inviolate.

His friend was adamant that he refuse to entertain hunger as a sign. He pointed out that the prophets had been fed. Elijah had lain down under a juniper tree to die and had gone to sleep and an angel of the Lord had come and waked him and fed him a hearth-cake, had done it moreover twice and Elijah had risen and gone about his business, lasting on the two hearth-cakes forty days and nights. Prophets did not languish in hunger but were fed from the Lord's bounty and the signs given them were unmistakable. His friend suggested he demand an unmistakable sign, not a pang of hunger or a reflection of himself in a store window, but an unmistakable sign, clear and suitable—water bursting forth from a rock, for instance, fire sweeping down at his command and destroying some site he would point to, such as the tabernacle he had gone to spit on.

His fourth night in the city, after he had returned from listening to the child preach, he had sat up in the welfare-woman's bed and raising his folded hat as if he were threatening the silence, he had demanded an unmistakable sign of the Lord.

Now we'll see what class of prophet you are, his friend said. We'll see what the Lord has in mind for you.

The next day the schoolteacher had taken them into a park where trees were fenced together in a kind of island that cars were not allowed in. They had only but entered it when he felt a hush in his blood and a stillness in the atmosphere as if the air were being purged for the approach of revelation. He would have turned and run but the schoolteacher parked himself on a bench and pretended to go to sleep with the dimwit in his lap. The trees rustled thickly and the clearing rose to his mind's eye. He imagined the blackened spot in the center of it between the two chimneys, and saw rising from the ashes the burnt-out frames of his own and his uncle's bed. He opened his mouth to get air and the schoolteacher woke up and began asking questions.

He prided himself that from the first night he had answered his questions with the cunning of a Negro, giving no information, knowing nothing, and each time he was questioned, raising his uncle's fury until it was observable under his skin in patches of pink and white. A few of his ready answers and the schoolteacher was willing to move on.

They had walked deeper into the park and he began to feel again the approach of mystery. He would have turned and run in the opposite direction but it was all on him in an instant. The path widened and they were faced with an open space in the middle of the park, a concrete circle with a fountain in the center of it. Water rushed out of the mouth of a stone lion's head into a shallow pool below and as soon as the dim-witted boy saw the water, he gave a whoop and galloped off toward it, flapping his arms like something released from a cage.

Tarwater saw exactly where he was heading, knew exactly what he was going to do.

"Too late, goddamit," the schoolteacher muttered, "he's in."

The child stood grinning in the pool, lifting his feet slowly up and down as if he liked the feel of the wet seeping into his shoes. The sun, which had been tacking from cloud to cloud, emerged above the fountain. A blinding brightness fell on the lion's tangled marble head and gilded the stream of water rushing from his mouth. Then the light, falling more gently, rested like a hand on the child's white head. His face might have been a mirror where the sun had stopped to watch its reflection.

Tarwater started forward. He felt a distinct tension in the quiet. The old man might have been lurking near, holding his breath, waiting for the baptism. His friend was silent as if in the felt presence, he dared not raise his voice. At each step the boy exerted a force backward but he continued nevertheless to move toward the pool. He reached the rim of it and lifted his foot to swing it over the side. Just as his shoe touched the water, the schoolteacher bounded forward and snatched the dimwit out. The child split the silence with his bellow.

Slowly Tarwater's lifted foot came down on the edge of the pool and he leaned there, looking into the water where a wavering face seemed trying to form itself. Gradually it became distinct and still, gaunt and cross-shaped. He observed, deep in its eyes, a look of starvation. I wasn't going to baptize him, he said, flinging the silent words at the silent face. I'd drown him first.

Drown him then, the face appeared to say.

Tarwater stepped back, shocked. Scowling, he straightened himself and moved away. The sun had gone in and there were black caves in the tree branches. Bishop was lying on his back, roaring from a red distorted face, and the schoolteacher stood above him, staring at nothing in particular as if it were he who had received a revelation.

Well, that's your sign, his friend said—the sun coming out from under a cloud and falling on the head of a dimwit. Something that could happen fifty times a day without no one being the wiser. And it took that schoolteacher to save you and just in time. Left to yourself you would already have done it and been lost forever. Listen, he said, you have to quit confusing a madness with a mission. You can't spend your life fooling yourself this way. You have to take hold and put temptation behind you. If you baptize once, you'll be doing it the rest of your life. If it's an idiot this time, the next time it's liable to be a nigger. Save yourself while the hour of salvation is at hand.

But the boy was shaken. He scarcely heard the voice as he walked off deeper into the park and down a path he scarcely saw. When he finally took note of his surroundings, he was sitting on a ·bench, looking down at his feet where two pigeons were moving in drunken circles. On the other side of the bench was a man of a generally gray appearance who had been examining a hole in his shoe when Tarwater sat down but who stopped then and devoted himself to a close scrutiny of the boy. Finally he reached over and plucked Tarwater's sleeve. The boy looked up into two pale yellow-rimmed eyes.

"Be like me, young fellow," the stranger said, "don't let no jackasses tell you what to do." He was grinning wisely and his eyes held a malevolent promise of unwanted friendship. His voice sounded familiar but his appearance was as unpleasant as a stain.

The boy got up and left hastily. An interesting coincident, his friend observed, that he should say the same thing as I've been saying. You think there's a trap laid all about you by the Lord. There ain't any trap. There ain't anything except what you've laid for yourself. The Lord is not studying about you, don't know you exist, and wouldn't do a thing about it if He did. You're alone in the world, with only yourself to ask or thank or judge; with only yourself. And me. I'll never desert you.

The first sight that met his eyes when he got out of the car at the Cherokee Lodge was the little lake. It lay there, glass-like, still, reflecting a crown of trees and an infinite overarching sky. It looked so unused that it might only the moment before have been set down by four strapping angels for him to baptize the child in. A weakness working itself up from his knees reached his stomach and came upward and forced a tremor in his jaw. Steady, his friend said, everywhere you go you'll find water. It wasn't invented yesterday. But remember: water is made for more than one thing. Hasn't the time come? Don't you have to do something at last, one thing to prove you ain't going to do another? Hasn't your hour of dallying passed?

They ate their lunch in the dark other-end of the lobby where the woman who ran the place served meals. Tarwater ate voraciously. With an expression of intense concentration, he ate six buns filled with barbecue and drank three cans of beer. He might have been preparing himself for a long journey or for some action that would take all his strength. Rayber observed his sudden appetite for the poor food and decided that he was eating compulsively. He wondered if the beer might loosen his tongue, but in the boat he was as glum as ever. He sat hunched over, his hat pulled down, and scowled at the spot where his line disappeared in the water.

They had managed to get the boat away from the dock before Bishop came out of the lodge. The woman had drawn him to an icecooler and produced a green popsickle which she held up for him while she gazed fascinated into his mysterious face. They were in the middle of the lake before he came clattering down the dock, the woman running behind. She snatched him just in time to keep him from plunging over the edge.

Rayber made a frantic grabbing motion in the boat and cried out. Then he reddened and scowled. "Don't look," he said, "she'll take care of him. We need a break."

The boy gazed darkly where the accident had been prevented. The child was a black spot in the glare of his vision. The woman turned him around and started leading him back to the lodge. "It wouldn't have been no great loss if he had drowned," he observed.

Rayber had an instant's picture of himself, standing in the ocean, holding the child's limp body in his arms. With a kind of convulsive motion, he cleared his head of the image. Then he saw that Tarwater had observed his discomposure; he was looking at him with a distinct attention, a peculiar prescient look as if he were about to penetrate some secret.

"Nothing ever happens to that kind of child," Rayber said. "In a hundred years people may have learned enough to put them to sleep when they're born."

Something appeared to be working on the boy's face, struggling there, some war between agreement and outrage.

Rayber's blood burned beneath his skin. He tried to restrain the urge to confess. He leaned forward; his mouth opened and closed and then in a dry voice he said, "Once I tried to drown him," and grinned horribly at the boy.

Tarwater's lips parted as if only they had heard, but he said nothing.

"It was a failure of nerve," Rayber said. The glare on the water gave him the sensation of glancing at white fire each time he looked up or out where it was reflected on the water. He turned down the brim of his hat all the way around.

"You didn't have the guts," Tarwater said as if he would put it in a more accurate way. "He always told me you couldn't do nothing, couldn't act."

The schoolteacher leaned forward and said between his teeth, "I've resisted him. I've done that. What have you done? Maybe you attended to him the quickest way but it takes more than that to go against his will for good. Are you quite sure," he said, "are you quite sure you've overcome him? I doubt it. I think you're chained to him right now. I think you're not going to be free of him without my help. I think you've got problems that you're not capable of solving yourself."

The boy scowled and was silent.

The glare pierced Rayber's eyeballs fiercely. He did not think he could stand an afternoon of this. He felt recklessly compelled to pursue the subject. "How do you like being in the country again?" he growled. "Remind you of Powderhead?"

"I come to fish," the boy said disagreeably.

Goddam you, his uncle thought, all I'm trying to do is save you from being a freak. He was holding his line unbaited in the blinding water. He felt a madness on him to talk about the old man. "I remember the first time I ever saw him," he said. "I was six or seven. I was out in the yard playing and all of a sudden I felt something between me and the sun. Him. I looked up and there he was, those mad fish-colored eyes looking down at me. Do you know what he said to me—a seven year old child?" He tried to make his voice sound like the old man's. " 'Listen boy,' he said, 'the Lord Jesus Christ sent me to find you. You have to be born again.' " He laughed, glaring at the boy with his furious blistered-looking eyes. "The Lord Jesus Christ had my welfare so at heart that he sent a personal representative. Where was the calamity? The calamity was I believed him. For five or six years. I had nothing else but that. I waited on the Lord Jesus. I thought I'd been born again and that everything was going to be different or was different already because the Lord Jesus had a great interest in me."

Tarwater shifted on the seat. He seemed to listen as if behind a wall.

"It was the eyes that got me," Rayber said. "Children may be attracted to mad eyes. A grown person could have resisted. A child couldn't. Children are cursed with believing."

The boy recognized the sentence. "Some ain't," he said.

The schoolteacher smiled thinly. "And some who think they aren't are," he said, feeling that he was back in control. "It's not as easy as you think to throw it off. Do you know," he said, "that there's a part of your mind that works all the time, that you're not aware of yourself. Things go on in it. All sorts of things you don't know about."

Tarwater looked around him as if he were vainly searching for a way to get out of the boat and walk off.

"I think you're basically very bright," his uncle said. "I think you can understand the things that are said to you."

"I never came for no school lesson," the boy said rudely. "I come to fish. I ain't worried what my underhead is doing. I know what I think when I do it and when I get ready to do it, I don't talk no words. I do it." There was a dull anger in his voice. He was becoming aware of how much he had eaten. The food appeared to be sinking like a leaden column inside him and to be pushed back at the same time by the hunger it had intruded upon.

The schoolteacher watched him a moment and then said, "Well anyway, as far as the baptizing went, the old man could have spared himself. I was already baptized. My mother never overcame her upbringing and she had had it done. But the damage to me of having it done at the age of seven was tremendous. It made a lasting scar."

The boy looked up suddenly as if there had been a tug at his line. "Him back there," he said and jerked his head toward the lodge, "he ain't been baptized?"

"No," Rayber said. He looked at him narrowly. He thought that if he could get the right words in now, he might do some good, might give him a painless lesson. "I may not have the guts to drown him," he said, "but I have the guts to maintain my self-respect and not to perform futile rites over him. I have the guts not to become the prey of superstitions. He is what he is and there's nothing for him to be born into. My guts," he finished, "are in my head."

The boy only stared at him, his eyes filmed with a dull cast of nausea.

"The great dignity of man," his uncle said, "is his ability to say: I am born once and no more. What I can see and do for myself and my fellowman in this life is all of my portion and I'm content with it. It's enough to be a man." There was a light ring in his voice. He watched the boy closely to see if he had struck a chord.

Tarwater turned an expressionless face toward the rim of trees that made a paling around the lake. He appeared to stare into emptiness.

Rayber subsided again but he could stand it only a few minutes. He finished the cigaret and lit another. Then he decided to start off on a new tack and leave the morbid alone for a while. "I'll tell you what I've planned for us to do in a couple of weeks," he said in an almost affable tone. "We're going up for a plane ride. How about that?" He had been considering this, holding it in reserve, thinking it would be the greatest marvel he could produce, something that would surely stir the glum child out of himself.

There was no response. The boy's eyes looked glazed.

"Flying is the greatest engineering achievement of man," Rayber said in an irked voice. "Doesn't it stir your imagination even slightly? If it doesn't I'm afraid there's something wrong with you."

"I done flew," Tarwater said and suppressed a belch. He was entirely occupied with his nausea which he could feel minutely rising.

"How could you have flown?" his uncle asked angrily.

"Him and me give a dollar to go up in one at a fair once," he said. "The houses weren't nothing but matchboxes and the people were invisible—like germs. I wouldn't give you nothing for no airplane. A buzzard can fly."

The schoolteacher gripped both sides of the boat and pushed forward. "He's warped your whole life," he said hoarsely. "You're going to grow up to be a freak if you don't let yourself be helped. You still believe all that crap he taught you. You're eaten up with false guilt. I can read you like a book!" The words were out before he could stop them.

The boy did not even look at him. He leaned over the side of the boat and shuddered. The column, released, formed a sweetly sour circle on the water. A wave of dizziness came over him and then his head cleared. A ravenous emptiness raged in his stomach as if it had reestablished its rightful tenure. He washed his mouth out with a handful of the lake and then wiped his face on his sleeve.

Rayber trembled at his recklessness. He felt certain he had produced this by the word *guilt*. He put his hand on the boy's knee and said, "You'll feel better now."

Tarwater said nothing, glaring with his red-lidded wet eyes at the water as if he were glad he had polluted it.

"It's just as much relief," his uncle said, pressing his advantage, "to get something off your mind as off your stomach. When you tell somebody else your troubles, then they don't bother you so much, they don't get in your blood and make you sick. Somebody else shares the weight. God boy," he said, "you need help. You need to be saved right here and now from the old man and everything he stands for. And I'm the one who can save you." With his hat turned down all around he looked like a fanatical country preacher. His eyes glistened. "I know what your problem is," he said. "I know and I can help you. Something's eating you on the inside and I can tell you what it is."

The boy looked at him fiercely. "Why don't you shut your big mouth?" he said. "Why don't you pull that plug out of your ear and turn yourself off? I come to fish. I never came to have no traffic with you."

His uncle snapped the cigaret out of his fingers and it hit the water with a hiss. "Every day," he said coldly, "you remind me more of the old man. You're just like him. You have his future before you."

The boy put down his line. With rigid deliberate movements he lifted his right foot and pulled off his shoe, then his left foot and pulled off that shoe. Then he jerked the straps of his overalls off his shoulders and pulled them down, over his bottom and off. He had on a pair of long thin old man's drawers. He pulled his hat tight down on his head so that it would not possibly come off, then he threw himself out of the boat and swam away, smashing the glassy lake with his cupped fists as if he would like to make it sting and bleed.

My God! Rayber thought, I touched a nerve that time! He kept his eye on the hat in the receding spasm of water. The empty overalls lay at his feet. He grabbed them and felt in the pockets. He took out two stones, a nickel, a box of wooden matches and three nails. He had brought along the new suit and shirt and laid them out on a chair.

Tarwater reached the dock and climbed onto it, the drawers clinging to him, the hat still ground down on his forehead. He turned just in time to see his uncle thrust the bundled overalls below the surface of the water.

Rayber felt as if he had just run across a mined field. At once he was afraid he had made a mistake. The thin rigid figure on the dock did not move. It seemed no more than a wraith-like column of fragile white-hot rage, materialized for an instant, the makings of some pure unfathomable passion. The boy turned and started rapidly toward the lodge and Rayber decided it would be best to linger on the lake a while.

When he came in, he was startled to see Tarwater lying on the far cot in his new clothes and to see Bishop sitting on the other end of it, watching him as if he were mesmerized by the steel-like glint that came from the boy's eyes and was directed into his own. In the plaid shirt and new blue trousers, he looked like a changeling, half his old self and half his new, already half the boy he would be when he was rehabilitated.

Rayber's spirits rose cautiously. He was holding the shoes with the contents of the overall pockets in them. He set them down on the bed and said, "No hard feelings about the clothes, old man. That was just my round."

There was a strange suppressed excitement about the boy's whole figure, as if he had settled on an inevitable course of action. He did not get up, did not acknowledge the shoes, but he acknowledged his uncle's presence by shifting the glint in his eyes slightly, on him and then away. The schoolteacher might have been just enough present to be ignored. Then he looked back at Bishop, triumphantly, boldly, into the very center of his eyes.

Rayber stood puzzled in the doorway. "Who wants to go for a ride?" he asked.

Bishop jumped off the bed and was at his side in an instant. Tarwater started at the little boy's abrupt disappearance from his field of vision, but he did not get up or turn his face toward the schoolteacher in the door.

"Well, we'll leave Frank to his meditations," Rayber said and swung the child around by the shoulder and left with him, hastily. He wanted to escape before the boy changed his mind.

CHAPTER NINE

The heat was not as intense on the road as it had been on the lake and he drove with a sense of refreshment he had not felt in the five days Tarwater had been with him. Once out of sight of the boy, he felt a pressure had been lifted from the atmosphere. He eliminated the oppressive presence from his thoughts and retained only those aspects of it that could be abstracted, clean, into the future person he envisioned.

The sky was a cloudless even blue and he drove without destination, though he meant before they returned to the lodge to stop and have the car filled for tomorrow's trip to Powderhead. Bishop was hanging out the window, his mouth open, letting the air dry his tongue. Automatically, Rayber reached over and locked the door and pulled him back in by his shirt. The child sat, solemnly taking his hat off his head and putting it on his feet, then taking it off his feet and putting it on his head. After he had done this a while, he climbed over the seat and disappeared into the back of the car.

Rayber continued to think of Tarwater's future, his thoughts rewarding except when every now and then the boy's actual face would lodge in the path of a plan. The sudden intrusion of the face made him think of his wife. He seldom thought of her anymore. She would not divorce him for fear she would be given custody of the child and she was now as far away as she could get, in Japan, in some welfare capacity. He was aware of his good fortune in getting rid of her. It was she who had prevented his going back and getting Tarwater away from the old man. She would have been glad enough to have had him if she had not seen him that day when they went to Powderhead to face the old man down. The baby had crawled into the door behind old Tarwater and had sat there, unblinking, as the old man raised his gun and shot Rayber in the leg and then in the ear. She had seen him; Rayber had not; but she would not forget the face. It was not simply that the child was dirty, thin, and gray; it was that its expression had no more changed when the gun went off than the old man's had. This had affected her deeply.

If there had not been something repellent in its face, he said, her maternal instinct would have made her rush forward and snatch it. She had even had that in mind before they arrived and she would have had the courage to do it in spite of the old man's gun; but the child's look had frozen her. It was the opposite of everything appealing. She could not express her exact revulsion, for her feeling was not logical. It had, she said, the look of an adult, not of a child, and of an adult with immovable insane convictions. Its face was like the face she had seen in some medieval paintings where the martyr's limbs are being sawed off and his expression says he is being deprived of nothing essential. She had had the sense, seeing the child in the door, that if it had known that at that moment all its future advantages were being stolen from it, its expression would not have altered a jot. The face for her had expressed the depth of human perversity, the deadly sin of rejecting defiantly one's own obvious good. He had thought all this was possibly her imagination but he understood now that it was not imagination but fact. She said she could not have lived with such a face; she would have been bound to destroy the arrogant look on it.

He reflected wryly that she had not been able to live with Bishop's face any better though there was no arrogance on it. The little boy had climbed up from the floor of the back seat and was hanging over breathing into his ear. By temperament and training she was ready to handle an exceptional child, but not one as exceptional as Bishop, not one bearing her own family name and the face of "that horrible old man." She had returned once in the last two years and demanded that he put Bishop in an institution because she said he could not adequately care for him—though it was plain from the look of him that he thrived like an air plant. His own behavior on that occasion was still a source of satisfaction to him. He had knocked her not quite halfway across the room.

He had known by that time that his own stability depended on the little boy's presence. He could control his terrifying love as long as it had its focus in Bishop, but if anything happened to the child, he would have to face it in itself. Then the whole world would become his idiot child. He had thought what he would have to do if anything happened to Bishop. He would have with one supreme effort to resist the recognition; with every nerve and muscle and thought, he would have to resist feeling anything at all, thinking anything at all. He would have to anesthetize his life. He shook his head to clear it of these unpleasant thoughts.

After it had cleared, they returned one by one. He felt a sinister pull on his consciousness, the familiar undertow of expectation, as if he were still a child waiting on Christ.

The car apparently of its own volition had turned onto a dirt road which without warning pierced his abstraction with its familiarity. He put on his brakes.

It was a narrow corrugated road sunk between deep red embankments. He looked about him angrily. He had not had the least intention of coming here today. His car was on the crest of a hill and the embankments on either side had the look of forming an entrance to a region he would enter at his peril. The road sloped down a quarter of a mile or so within his sight and then turned to disappear behind an edge of the wood. When he had been on this road the first time, he had ridden it backwards. A Negro with a mule and wagon had met him and his uncle at the junction and they had ridden, their feet dangling from the back of the wagon. He had leaned over most of the way, watching the mule's hoofprints in the dust as they rolled over them.

He decided finally that there would be wisdom in looking at the place today so that there would be no surprises for him when he returned tomorrow with the boy, but for some few moments, he did not move on. The road that lay in front of him he remembered as being four or five miles long. Then there was a stretch through the woods that would have to be walked and then the field to be crossed. He thought with distaste of crossing it twice, today and again tomorrow. He thought with distaste of crossing it at all. Then as if to stop his thinking, he put his foot down hard on the accelerator and took the road defiantly. Bishop jumped up and down, squealing and making unintelligible noises of delight.

The road grew narrower as it approached its end and presently he found himself going over what was no more than a rutted wagon path, his speed reduced to nothing. He stopped the car finally in a little clearing grown up in Johnson grass and blackberry bushes where what was left of the road touched the edge of the wood. Bishop jumped out and made for the blackberry bushes, attracted by the wasps that buzzed over them. Rayber leapt out and grabbed him just before he reached for one. Gingerly he picked the child a blackberry and handed it to him. The little boy studied it and then, with his fallen smile, returned it to him as if they were performing a ceremony. Rayber flung it away and turned to find the trail through the woods.

He took the child by the hand and pulled him along

on what he thought might shortly become a path. The forest rose about him, mysterious and alien. Descending to speak with the shade of my uncle, he thought irritably and wondered if the old man's charred bones would be lying in the ashes. At the thought he almost stopped but did not. Bishop could barely walk for gaping. He lifted his face to stare open-mouthed above him as if he were in some vast overwhelming edifice. His hat fell off and Rayber picked it up and clamped it on his head again and pulled him on. Somewhere below them out of the silence a bird sounded four crystal notes. The child stopped, his breath held.

Rayber knew suddenly that alone with Bishop he could not go to the bottom and cross the field. Tomorrow with the other boy, with his brain engaged, he would be able to make it. He remembered that somewhere along here there was a point where one could look out between two trees and see the clearing below. When he had first walked through the wood with his uncle, they had stopped at that place and his uncle had pointed down to where, far across the field, a sagging unpainted house stood in a bare hard-packed yard. "Yonder it is," he said, "and someday it'll be yours—these woods and that field and that fine house." He remembered that his heart had expanded unbelievably.

Suddenly he realized that the place *was* his. In the stress of having the boy return to him, he had never considered the property. He stopped, astounded by the fact that he owned all of this. His trees stood rising above him, majestic and aloof, as if they belonged to an order that had never budged from its first allegiance in the days of creation. His heart began to beat frenetically. Quickly he reduced the whole wood in probable board feet into a college education for the boy. His spirits lifted. He pulled the child along, intending to find the opening where the house could be seen. A few yards below, a sudden patch of sky indicated the spot. He let Bishop go and strode toward it.

The forked tree was familiar to him or seemed so. He put his hand on one trunk, leaned forward and looked out. His gaze moved quickly and unseeing across the field and stopped abruptly where the house had been. Two chimneys stood there, separated by a black space of rubble.

He stood expressionless, his heart strangely wrenched. If the bones were lying in the ashes he could not see them from this distance, but a vision of the old man, farther away in time, rose before him. He saw him standing on the edge of the yard, one hand lifted in an astounded greeting, while he stood a little way off in the field, his fists clenched, trying to shout, trying to make his adolescent fury come out in clear sensible words. He had only stood there shrilling, "You're crazy, you're crazy, you're a liar, you have a head full of crap, you belong in a nut house!" and then had turned and run, carrying away nothing but the registered change in the old man's expression, the sudden drop into some mysterious misery, which afterwards he had never been able to get out of his mind. He saw it as he stared at the two denuded chimneys.

He felt a pressure on his hand and glanced down, continuing to see the same expression and barely noting that it was Bishop he was looking at now. The child wanted to be lifted up to see. Absently he picked him up and held him in the fork of the tree and let him look out. The dull fence, the empty gray eyes seemed to Rayber to reflect the ravaged scene across the field. The little boy turned his head after a moment and gazed instead at him. A dreaded sense of loss came over him. He knew that he could not remain here an instant longer. He turned with the child and went quickly back through the woods the way he had come.

On the highway again, he drove gripping the wheel, his face tense, his mind turned on the problem of Tarwater as if his own and not only the boy's salvation depended on his solving it. He had ruined his plan by going to Powderhead too soon. He knew he could not go there again, that he would have to find another way. He went over the afternoon's experience in the boat. There, he thought, he had been on the right track. He had simply not gone far enough. He decided that he would put the whole thing verbally before the boy. He would not argue with him but only tell him, tell him in so many plain words that he had a compulsion and what it was. Whether he answered, whether he cooperated, he would have to listen. He could not escape knowing that there was someone who knew exactly what went on inside him and who understood it for the good reason that it was understandable. He would go the whole way this time and tell him everything. The boy should at least know that he had no secrets. Casually while they ate their supper, he would lift the compulsion from his mind, expose it to the light, and let him have a good look at it. What he did about it would be his own affair. All at once this seemed to him extremely simple, the way he should have proceeded in the first place. Only time simplifies, he thought.

He stopped for gas at a pink stucco filling station where pottery and whirligigs were sold. While the car was being filled, he got out and looked for something to take as a peace offering, for he wanted the encounter to be pleasant if possible. His eye roved over a shelf of false hands, imitation buck teeth, boxes of simulated dog dung to put on the rug, wooden plaques with cynical mottos burnt on them. Finally he saw a combination corkscrew-bottleopener that fit in the palm of the hand. He bought it and left.

When they returned to the room, the boy was still lying on the cot, his face set in a deadly calm as if his eyes had not moved since they left. Again Rayber had a vision of the face his wife must have seen and he experienced a moment's revulsion for the boy that made him tremble. Bishop climbed onto the bottom of the cot and Tarwater returned the child's gaze steadily. He seemed unaware that Rayber was in the room.

"I could eat a horse," the schoolteacher said. "Let's go down."

The boy turned his head and regarded him evenly, with no interest but with no hostility. "It's what you'll get," he said, "if you eat here."

Rayber, unamused, pulled out the corkscrew-bottleopener and dropped it negligently on his chest. "That might come in handy sometime," he said and turned and began to wash his hands at the basin.

In the mirror, he saw him pick it up gingerly and look at it. He pushed the corkscrew out of the circle and then meditatively pushed it back. He studied it back and front and held it in the palm of his hand where it fit like a half-dollar. Presently he said in a grudging voice, "I don't have no use for it but I thank you," and put it in his pocket.

He returned his attention to Bishop as if this were its natural place. He lifted himself on one elbow and fixed the child with a narrow look. "Git up, you," he said slowly. He might have been commanding a small animal he was successfully training. His voice was steady but experimental. The hostility in it seemed contained and directed toward some planned goal. The little boy was watching with complete fascination.

"Git up now, like I tol' you to," Tarwater repeated slowly.

The child obediently climbed down off the bed.

Rayber felt a twinge of ridiculous jealousy. He stood by, his brows working irritably as the boy moved out of the door without a word and Bishop followed him. After a moment he slung his towel into the basin and walked after them.

The lodge was shaking with the stamping of four couples dancing at the other end of the lobby where the woman who ran the place had a nickelodeon. The three of them sat down at the red tin table and Rayber turned off his hearing aid until the racket should stop. He sat glaring around him, disgruntled at this intrusion.

The dancers were about Tarwater's age but they might have belonged to a different species entirely. The girls could be distinguished from the boys only by their tight skirts and bare legs; their faces and heads were alike. They danced with a furious stern concentration. Bishop was entranced. He stood up in his chair, watching them, his head hanging forward as if any moment it might drop off. Tarwater, his eyes dark and distant, stared through them. They might have been insects buzzing across the surface of his vision.

When the music whined to a stop, they clambered back to their table and sprawled in their chairs. Rayber turned his hearing aid on and winced as Bishop's bellow blared into his head. The child was jumping up and down in his chair, roaring his disappointment. As soon as the dancers saw him, he stopped making the noise and stood still, devouring them with his gape. An angry silence fell over them. Their look was shocked and affronted as if they had been betrayed by a fault in creation, something that should have been corrected before they were allowed to see it. With pleasure Rayber could have dashed across the room and swung his lifted chair in their faces. They got up and pushed each other out sullenly, packed themselves in a topless automobile and roared off, sending an indignant spray of gravel against the side of the lodge. Rayber let out his breath as if it were sharp and might cut him. Then his eyes fell on Tarwater.

The boy was looking directly at him with an omniscient smile, faint but decided. It was a smile that Rayber had seen on his face before. It seemed to mock him from an ever-deepening inner knowledge that grew in indifference as it came nearer and nearer to a secret truth about him. Without warning its meaning pierced Rayber and he felt such a fury that for the moment all his strength left him. Go, he wanted to shout. Get your damn impudent face out of my sight! Go to hell! Go baptize the whole world!

The woman had been standing for some time at his side, waiting to take their order but she could have been invisible for all the notice he paid her. She began tapping the menu on a glass, then she slid it in front of his face. Without reading it, he said, "Three hamburger plates," and thrust it aside.

When she was gone, he said in a dry voice, "I want to lay some cards on the table." He sought the boy's eyes and steadied himself by the hated glint in them.

Tarwater looked at the table as if waiting for the cards to be laid on it.

"That means I want to talk straight to you," Rayber said, rigidly keeping the exasperation out of his voice. He strove to make his gaze, his tone, as indifferent as his listener's. "I have some things to say to you that you'll have to listen to. What you do about what I have to say is your own business. I have no further interest in telling you what to do. I only intend to put the facts before you." His voice was thin and brittle-sounding. He might have been reading from a paper. "I notice that you've begun to be able to look Bishop in the eye. That's good. It means you're making progress but you needn't think that because you can look him in the eye now, you've saved yourself from what's preying on you. You haven't. The old man still has you in his grip. Don't think he hasn't."

The boy continued to give him the same omniscient look. "It's you the seed fell in," he said. "It ain't a thing you can do about it. It fell on bad ground but it fell in deep. With me," he said proudly, "it fell on rock and the wind carried it away."

The schoolteacher grasped the table as if he were going to push it forward into the boy's chest. "Goddam you!" he said in a breathless harsh voice. "It fell in us both alike. The difference is that I know it's in me and I keep it under control. I weed it out but you're too blind to know it's in you. You don't even know what makes you do the things you do."

The boy looked at him angrily but he said nothing.

At least, Rayber thought, I've shocked that look off his face. He did not say anything for a few moments while he thought how to continue.

The woman returned with the three plates. She set them down slowly, giving herself time for observation. The man's face had a sweaty harassed look and so did the boy's. He threw her an ugly glance. The man began to eat at once as if he wanted to get it over with. The little boy took his bun apart and began to lick the mustard off it. The other boy looked at his as if it were probably bad meat and did not touch it. She left and watched indignantly for a few seconds from the kitchen door. The boy finally picked his hamburger up. He raised it half-way to his mouth and then put it down again. He picked it up and put it down twice without biting into it. Then he pulled his hat down and sat there, his arms folded. She had had enough and closed the door.

The schoolteacher leaned forward across the table, his eyes pin-pointed and very bright. "You can't eat," he said, "because something is eating you. And I intend to tell you what it is."

"Worms," the boy hissed as if his disgust could not be contained an instant longer.

"It takes guts to listen," Rayber said.

Tarwater leaned toward him with a kind of blaring attention. "You ain't got nothing to say to me that I don't have the guts to listen to," he said.

The schoolteacher sat back. "All right," he said, "then listen." He folded his arms and looked at him for an instant before he began. Then he started coldly. "The old man told you to baptize Bishop. You have that order lodged in your head like a boulder blocking your path."

The blood drained from the boy's face but his eyes did not swerve. They looked at Rayber furiously, the glint in them gone.

The schoolteacher spoke slowly, picking his words as if he were looking for the steadiest stones to step on across a rushing stream. "Until you get rid of this compulsion to baptize Bishop, you'll never make any progress toward being a normal person. I said in the boat you were going to be a freak. I shouldn't have said that. I only meant you had the choice. I want you to see the choice. I want you to make the choice and not simply be driven by a compulsion you don't understand. What we understand, we can control," he said. "You have to understand what it is that blocks you. I wonder if you're smart enough to take this in. It's not simple."

The boy's face seemed dry and old as if he had taken it in long ago, and now it was part of him like the current of death in his blood. The schoolteacher was touched by this muteness before the facts. His anger left him. The room was silent. A pink cast had fallen from the windows over the table. Tarwater looked away from his uncle at Bishop. The little boy's hair was pink and lighter than his face. He was sucking his spoon; his eyes were drowned in silence.

"I want to put two solutions before you," Rayber said. "What you do is up to you."

Tarwater looked at him again, with no mockery, no glint in his eye, but with no anticipation either, as if his course were irrevocably set.

"Baptism is only an empty act," the schoolteacher said. "If there's any way to be born again, it's a way that you accomplish yourself, an understanding about yourself that you reach after a long time, perhaps a long effort. It's nothing you get from above by spilling a little water and a few words. What you want to do is meaningless, so the easiest solution would be simply to do it. Right here now, with this glass of water. I would permit it in order to get it out of your mind. As far as I'm concerned, you may baptize him at once." He pushed his own glass of water across the table. His look was patient and ironical.

The boy's glance touched the top of the glass and then bounded off. His hand lying by the side of his plate twitched. He jammed it into his pocket and looked the other way, out the window. His whole aspect seemed shaken as if his integrity had been dangerously challenged.

The schoolteacher pulled back the glass of water. "I knew that would be too cheap for you," he said. "I knew you would refuse to do anything so unworthy of the courage you've already shown." He raised the glass and drank the rest of the water. Then he set it down on the table. He looked tired enough to collapse; his aspect was so weary that he might just have attained the top of a mountain he had been climbing for days.

After an interval he said, "The other way is not so simple. It's the way I've chosen for myself. It's the way you take as a result of being born again the natural way—through your own efforts. Your intelligence." His words had a disconnected sound. "The other way is simply to face it and fight it, to cut down the weed every time you see it appear. Do I have to tell you this? An intelligent boy like you?"

"You don't have to tell me nothing," Tarwater murmured.

"I don't have a compulsion to baptize him," Rayber said. "My own is more complicated, but the principle is the same. The way we have to fight it is the same."

"It ain't the same," Tarwater said. He turned toward his uncle. The glint had reappeared. "I can pull it up by the roots, once and for all. I can do something. I ain't like you. All you can do is think what you would have done if you had done it. Not me. I can do it. I can act." He was looking at his uncle now with a completely fresh contempt. "It's nothing about me like you," he said.

"There are certain laws that determine every man's conduct," the schoolteacher said. "You are no exception." He saw with perfect clarity that the only feeling he had for this boy was hate. He loathed the very sight of him.

"Wait and see," Tarwater said as if it needed only a short time to be proved.

"Experience is a terrible teacher," Rayber said.

The boy shrugged and got up. He walked off, across the room to the screen door where he stood looking out. At once Bishop climbed down off his chair and started after him, putting on his hat as he went. Tarwater stiffened when the child approached but he did not move and Rayber watched as the two of them stood there side by side, looking out the door—the two figures, hatted and somehow ancient, bound together by some necessity of nerve that excluded him. He was startled to see the boy put his hand on Bishop's neck just under his hat, open the door and guide him out of it. It occurred to him that what he meant by "doing something" was to make a slave of the child. Bishop would be at his command like a faithful dog. Instead of avoiding him, he planned to control him, to show who was master.

And I will not permit that, he said. If anyone controlled Bishop, it would be himself. He put his money on the table under the salt-shaker and went out after them.

The sky was a bright pink, casting such a weird light that every color was intensified. Each weed that grew out of the gravel looked like a live green nerve. The world might have been shedding its skin. The two were in front of him halfway down the dock, walking slowly, Tarwater's hand still resting just under Bishop's hat; but it seemed to Rayber that it was Bishop who was doing the leading, that the child had made the capture. He thought with a grim pleasure that sooner or later the boy's confidence in his own judgment would be brought low.

When they arrived at the end of the dock, they stood looking down into the water. Then to Rayber's chagrin, the boy lifted the child like a sack under the arms and lowered him over the edge of the dock into the boat that was tied there.

"I haven't given you permission to take Bishop out in the boat," Rayber said.

Tarwater may have heard or he may not; he did not answer. He sat down on the edge of the dock and for a few moments looked across the water at the opposite bank. Part of a red globe hung almost motionless in the far side of the lake as if it were the other end of the elongated sun cut through the middle by a swath of forest. Pink and salmon-colored clouds floated in the water at different depths. Suddenly Rayber wanted nothing so much as a half hour to himself, without sight of either of them. "But you may take him," he said, "if you'll be careful."

The boy didn't move. He was leaning forward, his thin

shoulders hunched, his hands gripped on the edge of the dock. He seemed poised there waiting to make a momentous move.

He dropped down into the boat with Bishop.

"You'll look after him?" Rayber asked.

Tarwater's face was like a very old mask, colorless and dry. "I'll tend to him," he said.

"Thanks," his uncle said. He experienced a short feeling of warmth for the boy. He strolled back down the dock to the lodge and when he reached the door, he turned and watched the boat move out into view on the lake. He raised his arm and waved but Tarwater showed no sign of seeing him and Bishop's back was turned. The small black-hatted figure sat like a passenger being borne by the surly oarsman across the lake to some mysterious destination.

Back in his room, Rayber lay on the cot trying to feel the release he had felt when he started out in the car in the afternoon. More than anything else, what he experienced in the boy's presence was the feeling of pressure and when it was taken off for a while, he realized how intolerable it was. He lay there thinking with distaste of the moment when the silent mutinous face would appear again in the door. He imagined the rest of the summer spent coping with the boy's cold intractability. He began to consider the possibility of his leaving of his own accord and after a moment he knew that this was actually what he wanted him to do. He no longer felt any challenge to rehabilitate him. All he wanted now was to get rid of him. He thought with horror of being stuck with him for good and began to consider ways that he might hasten his departure. He knew he would never leave as long as Bishop was around. The thought flew through his mind that he might put Bishop in an institution for a few weeks. He was shaken and turned his mind to other things. For a while he dozed and dreamed that he and Bishop were speeding away in the car, escaping safely from a lowering tornado-like cloud. He awoke to find the room growing dim.

He got up and went to the window. The boat with the two of them in it was near the middle of the lake, almost still. They were sitting there facing each other in the isolation of the water, Bishop small and squat, and Tarwater gaunt, lean, bent slightly forward, his whole attention concentrated on the opposite figure. They seemed to be held still in some magnetic field of attraction. The sky was an intense purple as if it were about to explode into darkness.

Rayber left the window and threw himself on the cot again but he was no longer sleepy. He had a peculiar sense of waiting, of marking time. He lay with his eyes closed as if listening to something he could hear only when his hearing aid was off. He had had this sense of waiting, kin in degree but not in kind, when he was a child and expected any moment that the city would blossom into an eternal Powderhead. Now he sensed that he waited for a cataclysm. He waited for all the world to be turned into a burnt spot between two chimneys.

All he would be was an observer. He waited with serenity. Life had never been good enough to him for him to wince at its destruction. He told himself that he was indifferent even to his own dissolution. It seemed to him that this indifference was the most that human dignity could achieve, and for the moment forgetting his lapses, forgetting even his narrow escape of the afternoon, he felt he had achieved it. To feel nothing was peace.

He watched idly as a round red moon rose into the lower corner of his window. It might have been the sun rising on the upsidedown half of the world. He came to a decision. When the boy came back he would say: Bishop and I are returning to town tonight. You may go with us under these conditions: not that you *begin* to cooperate, but that you cooperate, fully and completely, that you change your attitude, that you allow yourself to be tested, that you prepare yourself to enter school in the fall, and that you take that hat off your head right now and throw it out the window into the lake. If you can't meet these requirements, then Bishop and I are leaving by ourselves.

It had taken him five days to reach this state of clarity. He thought of his foolish emotions the night the boy had come, thought of himself sitting by the side of the bed, thinking that at last he had a son with a future. He saw himself again following the boy down back alleys to end finally at a detestable temple, saw the idiot figure of himself standing with his head in the window, listening to the mad child preach. It was unbelievable. Even the plan to take the boy back to Powderhead seemed ridiculous to him now and going to Powderhead this afternoon was the act of an insane person. His indecision, his uncertainty, his eagerness up to now appeared shameful and absurd to him. He felt that he had regained his senses after five days of madness. He could not wait for them to return so that he could deliver his ultimatum.

He closed his eyes and went over the scene in detail,

seeing the sullen face at bay, the haughty eyes forced to look down. His power would lie in the fact that he was indifferent now whether the boy stayed or went, or not indifferent for he positively wanted him to leave. He smiled at the thought that his indifference lacked that one perfection. Presently he dozed again, and again he and Bishop were fleeing in the car, the tornado just behind them.

When he awoke again, the moon travelling toward the middle of the window had lost its color. He sat up startled as if it were a face looking in on him, a pale messenger breathlessly arrived.

He got up and went to the window and leaned out. The sky was a hollow black and an empty road of moonlight crossed the lake. He leaned far out, his eyes narrowed, but he could see nothing. The stillness disturbed him. He turned the hearing aid on and at once his head buzzed with the steady drone of crickets and treefrogs. He searched for the boat in the darkness and could see nothing. He waited expectantly. Then an instant before the cataclysm, he grabbed the metal box of the hearing aid as if he were clawing his heart. The quiet was broken by an unmistakable bellow.

He did not move. He remained absolutely still, wooden, expressionless, as the machine picked up the sounds of some fierce sustained struggle in the distance. The bellow stopped and came again, then it began steadily, swelling. The machine made the sounds seem to come from inside him as if something in him were tearing itself free. He clenched his teeth. The muscles in his face contracted and revealed lines of pain beneath harder than bone. He set his jaw. No cry must escape him. The one thing he knew, the one thing he was certain of was that no cry must escape him.

The bellow rose and fell, then it blared out one last time, rising out of its own momentum as if it were escaping finally, after centuries of waiting, into silence. The beady night noises closed in again.

He remained standing woodenly at the window. He knew what had happened. What had happened was as plain to him as if he had been in the water with the boy and the two of them together had taken the child and held him under until he ceased to struggle.

He stared out over the empty still pond to the dark wood that surrounded it. The boy would be moving off through it to meet his appalling destiny. He knew with an instinct as sure as the dull mechanical beat of his heart that he had baptized the child even as he drowned him, that he was headed for everything the old man had prepared him for, that he moved off now through the black forest toward a violent encounter with his fate.

He stood there trying to remember something else before he moved away. It came to him finally as something so distant and vague in his mind that it might already have happened, a long time ago. It was that tomorrow they would drag the pond for Bishop.

He stood waiting for the raging pain, the intolerable hurt that was his due, to begin, so that he could ignore it, but he continued to feel nothing. He stood light-headed at the window and it was not until he realized there would be no pain that he collapsed.

PART

3

CHAPTER TEN

The headlights revealed the boy at the side of the road, slightly crouched, his head turned expectantly, his eyes for an instant lit red like the eyes of rabbits and deer that streak across the highway at night in the path of speeding cars. His pantslegs were wet up to the knees as if he had been through a swamp. The driver, minute in the glassed cab, brought the looming truck to a halt and left the motor idling while he leaned across the empty seat and opened the door. The boy climbed in.

It was an auto-transit truck, huge and skeletal, carrying four automobiles packed in it like bullets. The driver, a wiry man with a nose sharply twisted down and heavy-lidded eyes, gave the rider a suspicious look and then shifted gears and the truck began to move again, rumbling fiercely. "You got to keep me awake or you don't ride, buddy," he said. "I ain't picking you up to do you a favor." His voice, from some other part of the country, curled at the end of each sentence.

Tarwater opened his mouth as if he expected words to come out of it but none came. He remained, staring at the man, his mouth half-open, his face white.

"I'm not kiddin', kid," the driver said.

The boy kept his elbows gripped into his sides to prevent his frame from shaking. "I only want to go as far as where this road joins 56," he said finally. There were queer ups and downs in his voice as if he were using it for the first time after some momentous failure. He appeared to listen to it himself, to be trying to hear beyond the quaver in it to some solid basis of sound.

"Start talking," the driver said.

The boy wet his lips. After a moment he said in a high voice, entirely out of control, "I never wasted my life talking. I always done something."

"What you done lately?" the man asked. "How come your pantslegs are wet?"

He looked down at his wet pantslegs and kept looking. They seemed to turn his mind entirely from what he had

427

been going to say, to absorb his attention completely.

"Wake up, buddy," the driver said. "I say how come are your pantslegs wet?"

"Because I never took them off when I done it," he said. "I took off my shoes but I never taken off my pants."

"When you done what?"

"I'm going home," he said. "It's a place I get off at on 56 and then down that road a piece I take a dirt road. It's liable to be morning before I get there."

"How come your pantslegs are wet?" the driver persisted.

"I drowned a boy," Tarwater said.

"Just one?" the driver asked.

"Yes." He reached over and caught hold of the sleeve of the man's shirt. His lips worked a few seconds. They stopped and then started again as if the force of a thought were behind them but no words. He shut his mouth, then tried again but no sound came. Then all at once the sentence rushed out and was gone. "I baptized him."

"Huh?" the man said.

"It was an accident. I didn't mean to," he said breathlessly. Then in a calmer voice he said, "The words just come out of themselves but it don't mean nothing. You can't be born again."

"Make sense," the man said.

"I only meant to drown him," the boy said. "You're only born once. They were just some words that run out of my mouth and spilled in the water." He shook his head violently as if to scatter his thoughts. "There's nothing where I'm going but the stall," he began again, "because the house is burnt up but that's the way I want it. I don't want nothing of his. Now it's all mine."

"Of his whose?" the man muttered.

"Of my great-uncle's," the boy said. "I'm going back there. I ain't going to leave it again. I'm in full charge there. No voice will be uplifted. I shouldn't never have left it except I had to prove I wasn't no prophet and I've proved it." He paused and jerked the man's sleeve. "I proved it by drowning him. Even if I did baptize him that was only an accident. Now all I have to do is mind my own bidnis until I die. I don't have to baptize or prophesy."

The man only looked at him, shortly, and then back at the road.

"It's not going to be any destruction or any fire," the boy said. "There are them that can act and them that can't, and them that are hungry and them that ain't. That's all. I can act. And I ain't hungry." The words crowded out as if they were pushing each other forward. Then he was suddenly silent. He seemed to watch the darkness that the headlights pushed in front of them, always at the same distance. Sudden signs would spring up and vanish at the side of the road.

"That don't make sense but make up some more of it," the driver said. "I gotta stay awake. I ain't riding you just for a good time."

"I don't have no more to say," Tarwater said. His voice was thin, as if many more words would destroy it permanently. It seemed to break off after each sound had found its way out. "I'm hungry," he said.

"You just said you weren't hungry," the driver said.

"I ain't hungry for the bread of life," the boy said. "I'm hungry for something to eat here and now. I threw up my dinner and I didn't eat no supper."

The driver began to feel in his pocket. He pulled out half a bent sandwich wrapped in waxed paper. "You can have this," he said. "It don't have but one bite out of it. I didn't like it."

Tarwater took it and held it wrapped in his hand. He didn't open it.

"Okay, eat it!" the driver said in an exasperated voice. "What's the matter with you?"

"When I come to eat, I ain't hungry," Tarwater said. "It's like being empty is a thing in my stomach and it don't allow nothing else to come down in there. If I ate it, I would throw it up."

"Listen," the driver said, "I don't want you puking in here and if you got something catching, you get out right now."

"I'm not sick," the boy said. "I never been sick in my life except sometimes when I over ate myself. When I baptized him it wasn't nothing but words. Back home," he said, "I'll be in charge. I'll have to sleep in the stall until I get to where I can build me back a house. If I hadn't been a big fool I'd have taken him out and burned him up outside. I wouldn't have burned up the house along with him."

"Live and learn," the driver said.

"My other uncle knows everything," the boy said, "but that don't keep him from being a fool. He can't do nothing. All he can do is figure it out. He's got this wired head. There's an electric cord runs into his ear. He can read your mind. He knows you can't be born again. I know everything he knows, only I can do something about it. I did," he added.

"Can't you talk about something else?" the driver asked.
"How many sisters you got at home?"

"I was born in a wreck," the boy said.

He took off his hat and rubbed his head. His hair was
flat and thin, dark across his white forehead. He held
the hat in his lap like a bowl and looked into it. He took
out a box of wooden matches and a white card. "I put
all this here in my hat when I drowned him," he said.
"I was afraid my pockets would get wet." He held up
the card close to his eyes and read it aloud. "T. Fawcett
Meeks. Southern Copper Parts. Mobile, Birmingham, Atlanta." He stuck the card in the inside band of his hat and
put the hat back on his head. He put the box of matches
in his pocket.

The driver's head was beginning to roll. He shook it
and said, "Talk, dammit."

The boy reached into his pocket and pulled out the combination corkscrew-bottleopener the schoolteacher had given
him. "My uncle give me this," he said. "He ain't so bad.
He knows a heap. I speck I'll be able to use this thing
some time or other," and he looked at it lying compact
in the center of his hand. "I speck it'll come in handy,"
he said, "to open something."

"Tell me a joke," the driver said.

The boy didn't look as if he knew any joke. He didn't
look as if he knew what a joke was. "Do you know what
the greatest invention of man is?" he asked finally.

"Naw," the driver said, "what?"

He didn't answer. He was staring ahead again into
the darkness and seemed to have forgotten the question.

"What's the greatest invention of man?" the truck driver
asked irritably.

The boy turned and looked at him without comprehension.
There was a choking sound in his throat and then he said,
"What?"

The driver glared at him. "What's the matter with you?"

"Nothing," the boy said. "I feel hungry but I ain't."

"You belong in the booby hatch," the driver muttered.
"You ride through these states and you see they all belong
in it. I won't see nobody sane again until I get back to
Detroit."

For a few miles they rode in silence. The truck moved
slower and slower. The driver's lids would fall as if they
were weighted with lead and he would shake his head
to open them. Almost at once they would close again.
The truck began to veer. He shook his head once violently
and pulled off the road onto a wide shoulder and leaned

back and began to snore without once looking at Tarwater.

The boy sat quietly on his side of the cab. His eyes were open wide without the least look of sleep in them. They seemed not to be able to close but to be open forever on some sight that would never leave them. Presently they closed but his body did not relax. He sat rigidly upright, a still alert expression on his face as if under the closed lids an inner eye were watching, piercing out the truth in the distortion of his dream.

They were sitting facing each other in a boat suspended on a soft bottomless darkness only a little heavier than the black air around them, but the darkness was no hindrance to his sight. He saw through it as if it were day. He looked through the blackness and saw perfectly the light silent eyes of the child across from him. They had lost their diffuseness and were trained on him, fish-colored and fixed. By his side, standing like a guide in the boat, was his faithful friend, lean, shadow-like, who had counseled him in both country and city.

Make haste, he said. Time is like money and money is like blood and time turns blood to dust.

The boy looked up into his friend's eyes, bent upon him, and was startled to see that in the peculiar darkness, they were violet-colored, very close and intense, and fixed on him with a peculiar look of hunger and attraction. He turned his head away, unsettled by their attention.

No finaler act than this, his friend said. In dealing with the dead you have to act. There's no mere word sufficient to say NO.

Bishop took off his hat and threw it over the side where it floated right-side-up, black on the black surface of the lake. The boy turned his head, following the hat with his eyes, and saw suddenly that the bank loomed behind him, not twenty yards away, silent, like the brow of some leviathan lifted just above the surface of the water. He felt bodiless as if he were nothing but a head full of air, about to tackle all the dead.

Be a man, his friend counseled, be a man. It's only one dimwit you have to drown.

The boy edged the boat toward a dark clump of bushes and tied it. Then he removed his shoes, put the contents of his pockets into his hat and put the hat into one shoe, while all the time the gray eyes were fixed on him as if they were waiting serenely for a struggle already determined. The violet eyes, fixed on him also, waited with a barely concealed impatience.

This is no time to dwaddle, his mentor said. Once it's done, it's done forever.

The water slid out from the bank like a broad black tongue. He climbed out of the boat and stood still, feeling the mud between his toes and the wet clinging around his legs. The sky was dotted with fixed tranquil eyes like the spread tail of some celestial night bird. While he stood there gazing, for the moment lost, the child in the boat stood up, caught him around the neck and climbed onto his back. He clung there like a large crab to a twig and the startled boy felt himself sinking backwards into the water as if the whole bank were pulling him down.

Sitting upright and rigid in the cab of the truck, his muscles began to jerk, his arms flailed, his mouth opened to make way for cries that would not come. His pale face twitched and grimaced. He might have been Jonah clinging wildly to the whale's tongue.

The silence in the truck was corrugated with the snores of the driver, whose head rolled from side to side. The boy's jerking arms almost touched him once or twice as he struggled to extricate himself from a monstrous enclosing darkness. Occasionally a car would pass, illuminating for an instant his contorted face. He grappled with the air as if he had been flung like a fish on the shores of the dead without lungs to breathe there. The night finally began to fade. A plateau of red appeared in the eastern sky just above the treeline and a dun-colored light began to reveal the fields on either side. Suddenly in a high raw voice the defeated boy cried out the words of baptism, shuddered, and opened his eyes. He heard the sibilant oaths of his friend fading away on the darkness.

He sat trembling in the corner of the cab, exhausted, dizzy, holding his arms tight against his sides. The plateau had widened and was broken by the sun which rose through it majestically with a long red wingspread. With his eyes open, his face began to look less alert. Deliberately, forcefully, he closed the inner eye that had witnessed his dream.

In his hand he was clutching the truck driver's sandwich. His fingers had clenched it through. He loosened them and looked at it as if he had no idea what it was; then he put it in his pocket.

After a second he grabbed the driver's shoulder and shook him violently and the man woke up and grabbed the steering wheel convulsively as if the truck were moving at a high rate of speed. Then he perceived that it was not moving at all. He turned and glared at the boy. "What do you think you're doing in here? Where do you think you're going?" he asked in an enraged voice.

Tarwater's face was pale but determined. "I'm going home," he said. "I'm in charge there now."

"Well get out and go then," the driver said. "I don't ride nuts in the day time."

With dignity the boy opened the door and stepped down out of the cab. He stood, scowling but aloof, by the side of the road and waited until the gigantic monster had grated away and disappeared. The highway stretched in front of him, lean and gray, and he began to walk, putting his feet down hard on the ground. His legs and his will were good enough. He set his face toward the clearing. By sundown he would be there, by sundown he would be where he could begin to live his life as he had elected it, and where, for the rest of his days, he would make good his refusal.

CHAPTER ELEVEN

After he had walked about an hour, he took out the truck driver's pierced sandwich which he had stuck, still wrapped, in his pocket. He undid it and let the paper blow behind. The truck driver had bitten off one of the pointed ends. The boy put the unbitten end in his mouth but after a second he took it out again with faint teeth marks in it and put it back in his pocket. His stomach alone rejected it; his face looked violently hungry and disappointed.

The morning had opened up, clear and cloudless and brilliant. He walked on the embankment and did not look over his shoulder as cars came behind him and swiftly passed, but as each one disappeared on the narrowing strip of highway, he felt the distance between himself and his goal grow longer. The ground under him was strange to his feet, as if he were walking on the back of a giant beast which might any moment stretch a muscle and send him rolling into the ditch below. The sky was like a fence of light to keep it in. The glare forced him to lower his lids but on the other side of it, hidden from his daily sight but present to his inner eye that remained rigidly open, there stretched the clear gray borders of the country he had saved himself from crossing into.

He repeated every few yards, to force himself on faster, that he would soon be home, that there was only the rest of the day between him and the clearing. His throat and eyes burned with dryness and his bones felt brittle as if they belonged to a person older than himself and with much experience; and when he considered it—his experience—it was apparent to him that since his great-uncle's death, he had lived the liftetime of a man. It was as no boy that he returned. He returned tried in the fire of his refusal, with all the old man's fancies burnt out of him, with all the old man's madness smothered for good, so that there was never any chance it would break out in him. He had saved himself forever from the fate he had envisioned when, standing in the schoolteacher's hall and looking into the eyes of the dim-witted child, he had seen himself trudging off into the distance in the bleeding stinking mad shadow of Jesus, lost forever to his own inclinations.

The fact that he had actually baptized the child disturbed him only intermittently and each time he thought of it, he reviewed its accidental nature. It was an accident and nothing more. He considered only that the boy was drowned and that he had done it, and that in the order of things, a drowning was a more important act than a few words spilled in the water. He realized that in this small instance the schoolteacher had succeeded where he had failed. The schoolteacher had not baptized him. He recalled his words: "My guts are in my head." My guts are in my head too, the boy thought. Even if by some chance it had not been an accident, what was of no consequence in the first place was of no consequence in the second; and he had succeeded in drowning the child. He had not said NO, he had done it.

The sun, from being only a ball of glare, was becoming distinct like a large pearl, as if sun and moon had fused in a brilliant marriage. The boy's narrowed eyes made a black spot of it. When he was a child he had several times, experimentally, commanded the sun to stand still, and once for as long as he watched it—a few seconds—it had stood still, but when he turned his back, it had moved. Now he would have liked for it to get out of the sky altogether or to be veiled in a cloud. He turned his face enough to rid his vision of it and was aware again of the country which seemed to lie beyond the silence, or in it, stretching off into the distance around him.

Quickly he set his mind again on the clearing. He thought of the burnt spot in the center of it and he imagined with a careful deliberateness how he would pick up any burnt bone that he might find in the ashes of the house and sling it off into the nearest gulley. He envisioned the calm and detached person who would do this, who would clear out the rubble and build back the house. Beyond the glare, he was aware of another figure, a gaunt stranger, the ghost who had been born in the wreck and who had fancied himself destined at that moment to the torture of prophecy. It was apparent to the boy that this person, who paid him no attention, was mad.

As the sun burned brighter, he became more and more thirsty and his hunger and thirst combined in a pain that shot up and down him and across from shoulder to shoulder. He was about to sit down when ahead in a brush-swept space off the side of the road he saw a Negro's shack. A small colored boy stood in the yard, alone except for a

razor-backed shoat. His eyes were already fixed on the
boy coming down the road. As Tarwater came nearer he
saw a cluster of colored children watching him from the
shack door. There was a well to the side under a sugarberry
tree and he quickened his pace.

"I want me some water," he said, approaching the forward
boy. He took the sandwich from his pocket and handed
it to him. The child, who was about the size and shape
of Bishop, put it to his mouth with the same motion that
he took it and never removed his eyes from the boy's face.

"Yonder hit," he said and pointed with the sandwich to
the well.

Tarwater went to it and cranked the bucket up level
with the rim. There was a dipper but he did not use it.
He leaned over and put his face to the water and drank.
He drank until he began to feel dizzy. Then he pulled
off his hat and thrust his head into the water. As it touched
the deeper parts of his face, a shock ran through him,
as if he had never been touched by water before. He
looked down into a gray clear pool, down and down to
where two silent serene eyes were gazing at him. He
tore his head away from the bucket and stumbled backwards
while the blurred shack, then the hog, then the colored
child, his eyes still fixed on him, came into focus. He
slammed his hat down on his wet head and wiped his sleeve
across his face and walked hastily away. The little Negroes
watched him until he was off the place and had disappeared
down the highway.

The vision stuck like a burr in his head and it took him
more than a mile to realize he had not seen it. The water
had strangely not assuaged his thirst. To take his mind
off it, he reached in his pocket and pulled out the schoolteacher's present and began to admire it. It reminded him
that he also had a nickel. The first store or filling station
he came to, he would buy himself a drink and open it
with the opener. The little instrument glittered in the center
of his palm as if it promised to open great things for him.
He began to realize that he had not adequately appreciated
the schoolteacher while he had the opportunity. The lines
of his uncle's face had already become less precise in
his mind and he began to see again the eyes shadowed with
knowledge that he had imagined before he went to the
city. He returned the corkscrew-bottleopener to his pocket
and held it there in his hand as if henceforth it would be
his talisman.

Presently up ahead, he caught sight of the crossroads
where 56 joined the highway he was on. The dirt road

was not ten miles down from this point. There was a patched-together store and filling station on the far side of the crossroad. He hastened on in anticipation of the drink he was going to buy, his thirst growing by the second. Then as he came closer, he saw the large woman who stood in the door of the place. His thirst increased but his enthusiasm fled. She was leaning against the frame, her arms folded, and she filled almost the whole entrance. She was a black-eyed woman with a granite-like face and a tongue persistent to question. He and his great-uncle had traded at this place on occasion and when the woman was there, the old man had liked to linger and discourse, for he found her as pleasant as a shade tree. The boy had always stood by impatiently, kicking up the gravel, his face dark with boredom.

She spotted him across the highway and although she did not move or raise her hand, he could feel her eyes reeling him in. He crossed the highway and was drawn forward, scowling at a neutral space between her chin and shoulder. After he had arrived and stopped, she did not speak but only looked at him and he was obligated to direct a glance upward at her eyes. They were fixed on him with a black penetration. There was all knowledge in her stony face and the fold of her arms indicated a judgment fixed from the foundations of time. Huge wings might have been folded behind her without seeming strange.

"The niggers told me how you done," she said. "It shames the dead."

The boy pulled himself together to speak. He was conscious that no sass would do, that he was called upon by some force outside them both to answer for his freedom and make bold his acts. A tremor went through him. His soul plunged deep within itself to hear the voice of his mentor at its most profound depths. He opened his mouth to overwhelm the woman and to his horror what rushed from his lips, like the shriek of a bat, was an obscenity he had overheard once at a fair. Shocked, he saw the moment lost.

The woman did not move a muscle. Presently she said, "And now you come back. And who is going to hire out a boy who burns down houses?"

Still aghast at his failure, he said in a shaky voice, "I ain't ast nobody to hire me out."

"And shames the dead?"

"The dead are dead and stay that way," he said, gaining a little strength.

"And scorns the Resurrection and the Life?"

His thirst was like a rough hand clenched in his throat. "Sell me a purple drink," he said hoarsely.

The woman did not move.

He turned and went, his look as dark as hers. There were circles under his eyes and his skin seemed to have shrunk on the frame of his bones from dryness. The obscenity echoed sullenly in his head. The boy's mind was too fierce to brook impurities of such a nature. He was intolerant of unspiritual evils and with those of the flesh he had never truckled. He felt his victory sullied by the remark that had come from his mouth. He thought of turning and going back and flinging the right words at her but he had still not found them. He tried to think of what the schoolteacher would have said to her but no words of his uncle's would rise to his mind.

The sun was behind him now and his thirst had reached the point where it could not get worse. The inside of his throat felt as if it were coated with burning sand. He moved on doggedly. No cars were passing. He made up his mind that he would flag the next car that passed. He hungered now for companionship as much as food and water. He wanted to explain to someone what he had failed to explain to the woman and with the right words to wipe out the obscenity that had stained his thought.

He had gone almost two more miles when a car finally passed him and then slowed down and stopped. He had been trudging absently and had not waved it down but when he saw it stop, he began to run forward. By the time he reached it, the driver had leaned over and opened the door. It was a lavender and cream-colored car. The boy scrambled in without looking at the driver and closed the door and they drove on.

Then he turned and looked at the man and an unpleasant sensation that he could not place came over him. The person who had picked him up was a pale, lean, old-looking young man with deep hollows under his cheekbones. He had on a lavender shirt and a thin black suit and a panama hat. His lips were as white as the cigaret that hung limply from one side of his mouth. His eyes were the same color as his shirt and were ringed with heavy black lashes. A lock of yellow hair fell across his forehead from under his pushed-back hat. He was silent and Tarwater was silent. He drove at a leisurely rate and presently he turned in the seat and gave the boy a long personal look. "Live around here?" he asked.

"Not on this road," Tarwater said. His voice was cracked from dryness.

"Going somewheres?"

"To where I live," the boy croaked. "I'm in charge there now."

The man said nothing else for a few minutes. The window by the boy's side was cracked and patched with a piece of adhesive tape and the handle to lower it had been removed. There was a sweet stale odor in the car and there did not seem enough air to breathe freely. Tarwater could see a pale reflection of himself, eyeing him darkly from the window.

"Don't live on this road, huh?" the man said. "Where do your folks live?"

"No folks," Tarwater said. "It's only me. I take care of myself. Nobody tells me what to do."

"Don't huh?" the man said. "I see it's no flies on you."

"No," the boy said, "there's not."

There was something familiar to him in the look of the stranger but he could not place where he had seen him before. The man put his hand in the pocket of his shirt and brought out a silver case. He snapped it open and passed it over to Tarwater. "Smoke?" he said.

The boy had never smoked anything but rabbit tobacco and he did not want a cigaret. He only looked at them.

"Special," the man said, continuing to hold out the case. "You don't get one of this kind every day, but maybe you ain't had much experience smoking."

Tarwater took the cigaret and hung it in the corner of his mouth, exactly as the man's was hung. Out of another pocket, the man produced a silver lighter and flashed the flame over to him. The cigaret didn't light the first time but the second time he pulled in his breath, it lit and his lungs were unpleasantly filled with smoke. The smoke had a peculiar odor.

"Got no folks, huh?" the man said again. "What road do you live on?"

"It ain't even a road to it," the boy said. "I lived with my great-uncle but he's dead, burnt up, and now it's only me." He began to cough violently.

The man reached across the dashboard and opened the glove compartment. Inside, lying on its side, was a flat bottle of whiskey. "Help yourself," he said. "It'll kill that cough."

It was an old-looking stamped bottle without the paper front on it and with a bitten-off cork in the top. "I get that special too," the man said. "If there's flies on you, you can't drink it."

The boy grasped the bottle and began to pull at the cork,

and simultaneously there came into his head all his great-uncle's warnings about poisonous liquor, all his idiot restrictions about riding with strangers. The essence of all the old man's foolishness flooded his mind like a rising tide of irritation. He grasped the bottle the more firmly and pulled at the cork, which was too far in, with his fingers. He put the bottle between his knees and took the schoolteacher's corkscrew-bottleopener out of his pocket.

"Say, that's nifty," the man said.

The boy smiled. He pushed the corkscrew in the cork and pulled it out. Never a thought of the old man's but he would change it now. "This here thing will open anything," he said.

The stranger was driving slowly, watching him.

He lifted the bottle to his lips and took a long swallow. The liquid had a deep barely concealed bitterness that he had not expected and it appeared to be thicker than any whiskey he had ever had before. It burned his throat savagely and his thirst raged anew so that he was obliged to take another and fuller swallow. The second was worse than the first and he perceived that the stranger was watching him with what might be a leer.

"Don't like it, huh?" he said.

The boy felt a little dizzy but he thrust his face forward and said, "It's better than the Bread of Life!" and his eyes glittered.

He sat back and took the cork off the opener and put it back on the bottle and returned the bottle to the compartment. Already his motions seemed to be slowing down. It took him some time to get his hand back in his lap. The stranger said nothing and Tarwater turned his face to the window.

The liquor lay like a hot rock in the pit of his stomach, heating his whole body, and he felt himself pleasantly deprived of responsibility or of the need for any effort to justify his actions. His thoughts were heavy as if they had to struggle up through some dense medium to reach the surface of his mind. He was looking into thick unfenced woods. The car moved almost slow enough for him to count the outside trunks and he began to count them, one, one, one, until they began to merge and flow together. He leaned his head against the glass and his heavy lids closed.

After a few minutes the stranger reached over and pushed his shoulder but he did not stir. The man then began to drive faster. He drove about five miles, speeding, before he espied a turnoff into a dirt road. He took the turn and raced along for a mile or two and then pulled his car off the side of the road and drove down into a secluded declivity near the edge of the woods. He was breathing rapidly and sweating. He got out and ran around the car and opened the other door and Tarwater fell out of it like a loosely-filled sack. The man picked him up and carried him into the woods.

Nothing passed on the dirt road and the sun continued to move with a brilliant blandness on its way. The woods were silent except for an occasional trill or caw. The air itself might have been drugged. Now and then a large silent floating bird would glide into the treetops and after a moment rise again.

In about an hour, the stranger emerged alone and looked furtively about him. He was carrying the boy's hat for a souvenir and also the corkscrew-bottleopener. His delicate skin had acquired a faint pink tint as if he had refreshed himself on blood. He got quickly into his car and sped away.

When Tarwater woke up, the sun was directly overhead, very small and silver, sifting down light that seemed to spend itself before it reached him. He saw first his thin white legs stretching in front of him. He was propped up against a log that lay across a small open space between two very tall trees. His hands were loosely tied with a lavender handkerchief which his friend had thought of as an exchange for the hat. His clothes were neatly piled by his side. Only his shoes were on him. He perceived that his hat was gone.

The boy's mouth twisted open and to the side as if it were going to displace itself permanently. In a second it appeared to be only a gap that would never be a mouth again. His eyes looked small and seedlike as if while he was asleep, they had been lifted out, scorched, and dropped back into his head. His expression seemed to contract until it reached some point beyond rage or pain. Then a loud dry cry tore out of him and his mouth fell back into place.

He began to tear savagely at the lavender handkerchief until he had shredded it off. Then he got into his clothes so quickly that when he finished he had half of them on backwards and did not notice. He stood staring down at the spot where the displaced leaves showed him to have lain. His hand was already in his pocket bringing out the box of wooden matches. He kicked the leaves together and set them on fire. Then he tore off a pine branch and set it on fire and began to fire all the bushes around the spot until the fire was eating greedily at the evil ground, burning every spot the stranger could have touched. When it was a roaring blaze, he turned and ran, still holding the pine torch and lighting bushes as he went.

He barely noticed when he ran out of the woods onto the bare red road. It streaked beneath him like fire hardened and only gradually as his breath choked him did he slow down and begin to take his bearings. The sky, the woods on either side, the ground beneath him, came to a halt and the road assumed direction. It swung down between high red embankments and then mounted a flat field plowed to its edges on either side. Off in the distance a shack, sunk a little on one side, seemed to be afloat on the red folds. Down the hill the wooden bridge lay like the skeleton of some prehistoric beast across the stream bed. It was the road home, ground that had been familiar to him since his infancy but now it looked like strange and alien country.

He stood clenching the blackened burnt-out pine bough. Then after a moment he began to move forward again slowly. He knew that he could not turn back now. He knew that his destiny forced him on to a final revelation. His scorched eyes no longer looked hollow or as if they were meant only to guide him forward. They looked as if, touched with a coal like the lips of the prophet, they would never be used for ordinary sights again.

CHAPTER TWELVE

The broad road began to narrow until it was no more than a rutted rain-washed gulley which disappeared finally into a blackberry thicket. The sun, red and mammoth, was about to touch the treeline. Tarwater paused an instant here. His glance passed over the ripening berries, turned sharply and pierced into the wood which lay dark and dense before him. He drew in his breath and held it a second before he plunged forward, blindly following the faint path that led down through the wood to the clearing. The air was laden with the odor of honeysuckle and the sharper scent of pine but he scarcely recognized what they were. His senses were stunned and his thought too seemed suspended. Somewhere deep in the wood a woodthrush called and as if the sound were a key turned in the boy's heart, his throat began to tighten.

A faint evening breeze had begun to stir. He stepped over a tree fallen across his path and plunged on. A thorn vine caught in his shirt and tore it but he didn't stop. Farther away the woodthrush called again. With the same four formal notes it trilled its grief against the silence. He was heading straight for a gap in the wood where, through a forked birch, the clearing could be seen below, down the long hill and across the field. Always when he and his great-uncle were returning from the road, they would stop there. It had given the old man the greatest satisfaction to look out over the field and in the distance see his house settled between its chimneys, his stall, his lot, his corn. He might have been Moses glimpsing the promised land.

As Tarwater approached the tree, his shoulders were set high and tense. He seemed to be preparing himself to sustain a blow. The tree, forked a few feet from the ground, loomed in his way. He stopped and with a hand on either trunk, he leaned forward through the fork and looked out at an expanse of crimson sky. His gaze, like a bird that flies through fire, faltered and dropped. Where it fell, two chimneys stood like grieving figures guarding the blackened ground between them. His face appeared to shrink as he looked.

He remained motionless except for his hands. They clenched and unclenched. What he saw was what he had expected to see, an empty clearing. The old man's body was no longer there. His dust would not be mingling with the dust of the place, would not be washed by the seeping rains into the field. The wind by now had taken his ashes, dropped them and scattered them and lifted them up again and carried each mote a different way around the curve of the world. The clearing was burned free of all that had ever oppressed him. No cross was there to say that this was ground that the Lord still held. What he looked out upon was the sign of a broken covenant. The place was forsaken and his own. As he looked, his dry lips parted. They seemed to be forced open by a hunger too great to be contained inside him. He stood there open-mouthed, as if he had no further power to move.

He felt a breeze on his neck as light as a breath and he half-turned, sensing that someone stood behind him. A sibilant shifting of air dropped like a sigh into his ear. The boy turned white.

Go down and take it, his friend whispered. It's ours. We've won it. Ever since you first begun to dig the grave, I've stood by you, never left your side, and now we can take it over together, just you and me. You're not ever going to be alone again.

The boy shuddered convulsively. The presence was as pervasive as an odor, a warm sweet body of air encircling him, a violent shadow hanging around his shoulders.

He shook himself free fiercely and grabbed the matches from his pocket and tore off another pine bough. He held the bough under his arm and with a shaking hand struck a match and held it to the needles until he had a burning brand. He plunged this into the lower branches of the forked tree. The flames crackled up, snapping for the drier leaves and rushing into them until an arch of fire blazed upward. He walked backwards from the spot pushing the torch into all the bushes he was moving away from, until he had made a rising wall of fire between him and the grinning presence. He glared through the flames and his spirits rose as he saw that his adversary would soon be consumed in a roaring blaze. He turned and moved on with the burning brand tightly clenched in his fist.

The path twisted downward through reddened tree trunks that gradually grew darker as the sun sank out of sight. From time to time he plunged the torch into a bush or tree and left it blazing behind him. The wood became less dense. Suddenly it opened and he stood at its edge, looking out on the flat cornfield and far across to the two chimneys. Planes of purpling red above the treeline stretched back like stairsteps to reach the dusk. The corn the old man had left planted was up about a foot and moved in wavering lines of green across the field. It had been freshly plowed. The boy stood there, a small rigid, hatless figure, holding the blackened pine bough.

As he looked, his hunger constricted him anew. It appeared to be outside him, surrounding him, almost as if it were visible before him, something he could reach out for and not quite touch. He sensed a strangeness about the place as if there might already be an occupant. Beyond the two chimneys, his eyes moved over the stall, gray and weathered, and crossed the back field and stopped at the far black wall of woods. A deep-filled quiet pervaded everything. The encroaching dusk seemed to come softly in deference to some mystery that resided here. He stood, leaning slightly forward. He appeared to be permanently suspended there, unable to go forward or back. He became conscious of the very breath he drew. Even the air seemed to belong to another.

Then near the stall he saw a Negro mounted on a mule. The mule was not moving; the two might have been made out of rock. He started forward across the field boldly, raising his fist in a gesture that was half-greeting and half-threat, but after a second his hand opened. He waved and began to run. It was Buford. He would go home with him and eat.

Instantly at the thought of food, he stopped and his muscles contracted with nausea. He blanched with the shock of a terrible premonition. He stood there and felt a crater opening inside him, and stretching out before him, surrounding him, he saw the clear gray spaces of that country where he had vowed never to set foot. Mechanically he began to move forward. He came out on the hard ground of the yard a few feet from the fig tree, but his eyes took the far circuit to it, lingering above the stall and moving beyond it to the far treeline and back. He knew that the next sight to meet his eyes would be the half-dug gaping grave, almost at his feet.

The Negro was watching him steadily. He began to move forward on the mule. When the boy finally forced his eyes to move again, he saw the mule's hooves first and then Buford's feet hanging at its sides. Above, the brown crinkled face was looking down at him with a scorn that could penetrate any surface.

The grave, freshly mounded, lay between them. Tarwater

lowered his eyes to it. At its head, a dark rough cross was set starkly in the bare ground. The boy's hands opened stiffly as if he were dropping something he had been clutching all his life. His gaze rested finally on the ground where the wood entered the grave.

Buford said, "It's owing to me he's resting there. I buried him while you were laid out drunk. It's owing to me his corn has been plowed. It's owing to me the sign of his Saviour is over his head."

Nothing seemed alive about the boy but his eyes and they stared downward at the cross as if they followed below the surface of the earth to where its roots encircled all the dead.

The Negro sat watching his strange spent face and grew uneasy. The skin across it tightened as he watched and the eyes, lifting beyond the grave, appeared to see something coming in the distance. Buford turned his head. The darkening field behind him stretched downward toward the woods. When he looked back again, the boy's vision seemed to pierce the very air. The Negro trembled and felt suddenly a pressure on him too great to bear. He sensed it as a burning in the atmosphere. His nostrils twitched. He muttered something and turned the mule around and moved off, across the back field and down to the woods.

The boy remained standing there, his still eyes reflecting the field the Negro had crossed. It seemed to him no longer empty but peopled with a multitude. Everywhere, he saw dim figures seated on the slope and as he gazed he saw that from a single basket the throng was being fed. His eyes searched the crowd for a long time as if he could not find the one he was looking for. Then he saw him. The old man was lowering himself to the ground. When he was down and his bulk had settled, he leaned forward, his face turned toward the basket, impatiently following its progress toward him. The boy too leaned forward, aware at last of the object of his hunger, aware that it was the same as the old man's and that nothing on earth would fill him. His hunger was so great that he could have eaten all the loaves and fishes after they were multiplied.

He stood there, straining forward, but the scene faded in the gathering darkness. Night descended until there was nothing but a thin streak of red between it and the black line of earth but still he stood there. He felt his hunger no longer as a pain but as a tide. He felt it rising in himself through time and darkness, rising through the centuries, and he knew that it rose in a line of men whose lives were chosen to sustain it, who would wander in the world,

strangers from that violent country where the silence is
never broken except to shout the truth. He felt it building
from the blood of Abel to his own, rising and engulfing
him. It seemed in one instant to lift and turn him. He
whirled toward the treeline. There, rising and spreading
in the night, a red-gold tree of fire ascended as if it would
consume the darkness in one tremendous burst of flame.
The boy's breath went out to meet it. He knew that this
was the fire that had encircled Daniel, that had raised Elijah
from the earth, that had spoken to Moses and would in
the instant speak to him. He threw himself to the ground and
with his face against the dirt of the grave, he heard to
command. GO WARN THE CHILDREN OF GOD OF
THE TERRIBLE SPEED OF MERCY. The words were
as silent as seeds opening one at a time in his blood.

When finally he raised himself, the burning bush had
disappeared. A line of fire ate languidly at the treeline
and here and there a thin crest of flame rose farther back
in the woods where a dull red cloud of smoke had gathered.
The boy stooped and picked up a handful of dirt off his
great-uncle's grave and smeared it on his forehead. Then
after a moment, without looking back he moved across
the far field and off the way Buford had gone.

By midnight he had left the road and the burning woods
behind him and had come out on the highway once more.
The moon, riding low above the field beside him, appeared
and disappeared, diamond-bright, between patches of darkness. Intermittently the boy's jagged shadow slanted across
the road ahead of him as if it cleared a rough path toward
his goal. His singed eyes, black in their deep sockets, seemed
already to envision the fate that awaited him but he moved
steadily on, his face set toward the dark city, where the
children of God lay sleeping.

World Literature Anthologies from MENTOR

☐ **CLASSIC SCENES edited and translated by Jonathan Price.** In this single volume are 48 outstanding examples of playwriting genius—all of them enticing invitations to both amateur and professional performers. Each scene is accompanied by commentary that sets the scene in historical perspective, places it within the body of the play, and explores the key aspects involved in bringing the characters and actors vividly alive. (#ME1779—$2.75)

☐ **STORIES OF THE AMERICAN EXPERIENCE edited by Leonard Kriegel and Abraham H. Lass.** Vivid insights into American life by some of our greatest writers, including Hawthorne, Melville, Twain, Harte, Crane, Shaw, Steinbeck, Faulkner, and other outstanding American writers. (#ME1605—$2.25)

☐ **MASTERS OF THE SHORT STORY edited by Abraham Lass and Leonard Kriegel.** Complete with individual biographical and critical forewords, here is a superlative gathering of twenty-seven great stories offering unforgettable insight into the greatness of literature. The great masters included are: Balzac, Pushkin, Poe, Gogol, Flaubert, Borges, Kafka and Camus. (#ME1744—$2.50)

☐ **THE SECRET SHARER AND OTHER GREAT STORIES edited by Abraham H. Lass and Norma L. Tasman.** Brilliant examples of some of the finest writers such as Prosper Merimee, Bernard Malamud, Dorothy Parker, Willa Cather, and Stephen Vincent Benet. (#MJ1801—$1.95)